"A sizzling ... fast-paced and intriguing."
—*Joyfully Reviewed*

"I really adore this series and *Moon Burning* doesn't disappoint . . . Ms. Monroe is an incredible author."
—*TwoLips Reviews*

Moon Craving

"[A] sexy, stay-up-all-night read."   —*RT Book Reviews*

"A book that will grab you right from the beginning."
—*Romance Reviews Today*

"Ms. Monroe captivates the readers with her spine-tingling explosive action and highly intense, sensual love story."
—*Fallen Angel Reviews*

Moon Awakening

"Simply awesome . . . Stunningly sexy and emotionally riveting . . . Easily one of the best paranormals I've ever read!"   —*Joyfully Reviewed*

"A sensual, humorous story with intriguing and entrancing characters . . . Outstanding . . . I'm looking forward to future stories."   —*Fresh Fiction*

continued . . .

PRAISE FOR LUCY MONROE AND HER NOVELS

"[A] wicked and wonderful temptation . . . Give yourself a treat and read this book. Lucy Monroe will capture your heart."   —Susan Wiggs, *New York Times* bestselling author

"Lucy Monroe's romances sizzle!"
  —JoAnn Ross, *New York Times* bestselling author

"If you enjoy Linda Howard, Diana Palmer and Elizabeth Lowell, then I think you'd really love Lucy's work."
  —Lori Foster, *New York Times* bestselling author

"Monroe brings a fresh voice to historical romance."
  —Stef Ann Holm, *USA Today* bestselling author

"Lucy Monroe is an awesome talent."   —*The Best Reviews*

"A fresh new voice in romance."   —Debbie Macomber

"Romance as only Lucy Monroe does it . . . Joy, passion and heartfelt emotions."   —*The Road to Romance*

"A perfect 10!"   —*Romance Reviews Today*

"An intense, compelling read from page one to the very end. With her powerful voice and vision, Lucy packs emotion into every scene . . . [A] sizzling story with tangible sexual tension."   —Jane Porter, bestselling author

"Lucy has written a wonderful full-blooded hero and a beautiful, warm heroine."
  —Maggie Cox, *USA Today* bestselling author

"A charming tale . . . The delightful characters jump off the page!"   —Theresa Scott, bestselling author

Dragon's Moon

A CHILDREN OF THE MOON NOVEL

Lucy Monroe

BERKLEY SENSATION, NEW YORK

THE BERKLEY PUBLISHING GROUP
Published by the Penguin Group
Penguin Group (USA) Inc.
375 Hudson Street, New York, New York 10014, USA

Penguin Group (Canada), 90 Eglinton Avenue East, Suite 700, Toronto, Ontario M4P 2Y3, Canada
(a division of Pearson Penguin Canada Inc.) • Penguin Books Ltd., 80 Strand, London WC2R 0RL,
England • Penguin Group Ireland, 25 St. Stephen's Green, Dublin 2, Ireland (a division of Penguin
Books Ltd.) • Penguin Group (Australia), 250 Camberwell Road, Camberwell, Victoria 3124, Australia
(a division of Pearson Australia Group Pty. Ltd.) • Penguin Books India Pvt. Ltd., 11 Community
Centre, Panchsheel Park, New Delhi—110 017, India • Penguin Group (NZ), 67 Apollo Drive,
Rosedale, Auckland 0632, New Zealand (a division of Pearson New Zealand Ltd.) • Penguin Books
(South Africa) (Pty.) Ltd., 24 Sturdee Avenue, Rosebank, Johannesburg 2196, South Africa

Penguin Books Ltd., Registered Offices: 80 Strand, London WC2R 0RL, England

This is a work of fiction. Names, characters, places, and incidents either are the product of the author's
imagination or are used fictitiously, and any resemblance to actual persons, living or dead, business
establishments, events, or locales is entirely coincidental. The publisher does not have any control over
and does not assume any responsibility for author or third-party websites or their content.

DRAGON'S MOON

A Berkley Sensation Book / published by arrangement with the author

PUBLISHING HISTORY
Berkley Sensation mass-market edition / September 2012

Copyright © 2012 by Lucy Monroe.
Excerpt from *Warrior's Moon* by Lucy Monroe copyright © 2012 by Lucy Monroe.
Excerpt from *Ecstasy Under the Moon* by Lucy Monroe © 2012 by Lucy Monroe.
Cover art by Gregg Gulbronson.
Cover design by George Long.
Interior text design by Laura K. Corless.

ISBN: 978-0-425-24662-7

BERKLEY SENSATION®
Berkley Books are published by The Berkley Publishing Group,
a division of Penguin Group (USA) Inc.,
375 Hudson Street, New York, New York 10014.
BERKLEY SENSATION® is a registered trademark of Penguin Group (USA) Inc.
The "B" design is a trademark of Penguin Group (USA) Inc.

PRINTED IN THE UNITED STATES OF AMERICA

10 9 8 7 6 5 4 3 2 1

ALWAYS LEARNING   PEARSON

For my mom, my greatest fan and supporter while she lived, missed more than I'll ever be able to put into words now that she's gone—and still one of my greatest inspirations to write. I love you, Mom . . . but you knew that and know it still.

THE BEGINNING

Millennia ago God created a race of people so fierce even their women were feared in battle. These people were warlike in every way, refusing to submit to the rule of any but their own . . . no matter how large the forces sent to subdue them. Their enemies said they fought like animals. Their vanquished foe said nothing, for they were dead.

They were considered a primitive and barbaric people because they marred their skin with tattoos of blue ink. The designs were simple at first, a single beast depicted in unadorned outline over their hearts. The leaders were marked with bands around their arms with symbols that told of their strength and prowess in battle. Mates were marked to show their bond.

And still, their enemies were never able to discover the meanings of any of the blue-tinted tattoos.

Some surmised they were symbols of their warlike nature and in that they would be partially right. For the beasts represented a part of themselves these fierce and independent people kept secret at the pain of death. It was a secret they had kept for the centuries of their existence while most migrated across the European landscape to settle in the inhospitable north of Scotland.

Their Roman enemies called them Picts, a name accepted by the other peoples of their land and lands south . . . they called themselves the Chrechte.

Their animallike affinity for fighting and conquest came from a part of their nature their fully human counterparts did not enjoy. For these fierce people were shape-changers.

The bluish tattoos on their skin were markings given as a right of passage when they made their first shift. Some men had control of that change. For others, the full moon controlled their change until they participated in the sacred act of sex. The females of all the races both experienced their first shift into animal form and gained control thereafter with the coming of their first menses.

Some shifted into wolves, others big cats of prey and yet others into the larger birds—the eagle, hawk and raven.

The one thing all Chrechte shared in common was that they did not reproduce as quickly or prolifically as their fully human brothers and sisters. Although they were a fearsome race and their cunning was enhanced by an understanding of nature most humans could not possess, they were not foolhardy and were not ruled by their animal natures.

One warrior could kill a hundred of his foe, but should she or he die before having offspring, the death would lead to an inevitable shrinking of the race. Some Pictish clans and those recognized by other names in other parts of the world had already died out rather than submit to the inferior but multitudinous humans around them.

The Faol of Scotland's Highlands were too smart to face the end of their race rather than blend. These wolf shifters saw the way of the future. In the ninth century AD, Keneth MacAlpin ascended to the Scottish throne. Of Faol Chrechte descent through his mother, nevertheless, his human nature had dominated.

He was not capable of "the change," but that did not stop him from laying claim to the Pictish throne (as it was called then) as well. In order to guarantee his kingship, he betrayed his Chrechte brethren at a dinner, killing all of the remaining royals of their people—and forever entrenched a distrust of humans by their Chrechte counterparts.

Despite this distrust but bitterly aware of the cost of MacAlpin's betrayal, the Faol of the Chrechte realized that they could die out fighting an ever-increasing and encroaching race of humanity, or they could join the Celtic clans.

They joined.

As far as the rest of the world knew, though much existed to attest to their former existence, what had been considered the Pictish people were no more.

Because it was not in their nature to be ruled by any but their own, within two generations the Celtic clans that had assimilated the Chrechte were ruled by shape-changing clan chiefs who shared their natures with wolves. Though most of the fully human among them did not know it, a rare few were trusted with the secrets of their kinsmen. Those that did know were aware that to betray the code of silence meant certain and immediate death.

Stories of other shifter races, the Éan and Paindeal, were told around the campfire, or to the little ones before bed. However, since the wolves had not seen a shifter except their own in generations, they began to believe the other races only a myth.

But myths did not take to the sky on black wings glinting an iridescent blue under the sun. Myths did not live as ghosts in the forest, but breathing air just as any other man or animal. The Éan were no myth; they were ravens with abilities beyond that of merely changing their shape.

And they trusted the Faol of the Chrechte less than the wolves ever trusted humans. But just as the Faol before them, the time had come for the Éan to learn to deal with their mistrust and join the human clans.

Their future as a race depended on it.

Prologue

Today I have seen the Dragon.

—Confucius

Donegal Holding, Highlands of Scotland
1142 AD, Reign of Dabid mac Mail Choluim, King of Scots

"*I* had another dream about the wolves' sacred stone."
Ciara had waited until their mother had eaten her porridge
and returned to her tiny bedroom to once again stare at the
wall as if it held the very meaning of life to share this bit of
information with her brother.

His head snapped up and his hands stilled in their
sharpening of his broadsword. Wolf's eyes the same deep
green as her own focused on Ciara, silently demanding she
continue.

It used to be a game. Or at least she'd been convinced it
was. Before. Before Da's death and Mum's decline.

Now, Ciara knew that for whatever reason, her brother
believed her dreams the salvation of their people.

Galen said the old stories were true, that the wolves
once had a magic stone used in the coming of age ceremony to make them stronger. To even turn some into

conriocht . . . werewolves—not merely a person who could shift into a wolf, if that gift were not amazing enough for her people. No, the old stories claimed that some would shift into *conriocht*, half man–half wolf and larger than either. Giants that could not be bested in battle, even by other wolves.

Certainly not by the Éan.

She didn't know if she believed it. And if she did, if she wanted to help such a thing come about. But Ciara loved her brother and spending the day searching for the stone with clues from her dream was yet a joy.

Despite how Galen had changed these last two years.

"The *Faolchú Chridhe*." He whispered the ancient name given to the stone by their people in stories older than the wolves' history with the clans in a voice laced with awe.

The wolf's heart . . . how could they have lost it as a people, if indeed it did exist?

"What did you dream?" he demanded, his emerald eyes glowing with the shine of a zealot.

Fear she did not understand skittered down her spine, making her hands shake as she put away their morning dishes. For one thing she never doubted was that her brother loved her.

"It was like the others," Ciara forced from between suddenly dry lips, her throat tight with that inexplicable fear. "I saw a stone that could have been an emerald, but for the fact it was as big as a laird's fist." Surely no emerald of that size existed anywhere in the world. "'Twas on a dark stone altar in a cavern that glowed with a pale green light like I've never seen before."

"The glowing, that's new."

It wasn't, but she'd thought it too fanciful to mention before. Galen's recent press for more and more information led her to admit to it now though.

"Where was the cavern?" He asked it every time, as if by doing so would make her know.

It never did. Though she tried to tell him all she could remember that might help. "I felt as if I was deep in the earth."

"You felt?" he asked with doubt that bothered her, though she never said so.

"Yes."

"Could you see the entrance to the cavern?"

"No, I felt as if it was behind me, but I could not turn away from the *Faolchú Chridhe* in my dream."

"So no proof you were deep in the earth?"

"No," she had to admit.

"'Tis more likely in the hills. Birds would not bury our stone deep in the earth. 'Tis not in their nature."

Galen's belief the Éan had stolen the *Faolchú Chridhe* had been birthed two winters past, after Da's death and her brother started spending more time with Wirp. Their da had never had a good word to say about the other Chrechte the old stories claimed had once existed, either.

But Wirp was worse; he'd acted as if the Faol were better than everyone and male wolves the most superior of all. The old man had made her *that* uncomfortable. No one was happier than Ciara that Wirp had fallen afoul of their new laird, Barr. Though she was careful not to let her brother know it.

"It felt like deep in the earth," she repeated stubbornly.

"I told you under the ground is not the Éan's playground."

"And if it was not the bird shifters that stole the wolves' stone?"

"It was."

"You are so certain, but all you have are old men's stories to prove it."

"And your dreams."

"My dreams only say the *Faolchú Chridhe* exists, not that anyone stole it from us. Besides, they could be no more than night fancies."

"Nay. They are prophecy and we must pay heed."

Then why not heed that the cavern was underground? She did not ask because she did not want to argue with her brother. He might decide not to go looking for the stone. She saw little enough of him as it was now; she would not give up this day.

* * *

Galen did want to search for the stone, but he insisted on taking another warrior with them, saying three sets of wolf senses were better than two.

Ciara did not agree. She did not like this warrior any better than she had liked Wirp. Worse, she worried her brother would give her to Luag in marriage.

Her menses had started early. Though she was but twelve summers. He would wait at least two more before pressing her to wed, but then she was done for. The fear that thought caused was fully realized, making her sick to her stomach, even as she tried to hide her revulsion.

It would do no good. Luag was with them now and would not be going anywhere until they exhausted themselves searching or by some miracle found the *Faolchú Chridhe* this day.

They had been searching for hours and were deep in the forest when Luag lifted his head and sniffed the air. "I smell raven."

Ciara could not understand the disgust so evident in his voice. She knew their clan's healer was both raven and wolf, though Ciara had never told anyone. She rarely revealed what her dreams told her, except to her brother. And she never told him dreams that had anything to do with the Éan.

"Let's go hunting," Luag said with a smile that was more snarl than anything.

Galen shook his head. "We have things of more import to do here."

"It's all part of the same goal," Luag argued.

"I'll not hunt when we have Ciara with us."

Was her brother saying he would hunt the raven if she were not with him? Ciara could not let herself believe his unreasoning prejudices went that deep. And how did they plan to hunt a bird? Would they make wings out of tree branches and fly then? They hadn't brought bows with them and their wolf forms would hardly be helpful.

She shook her head. Sometimes warriors made no sense

to her. Everyone knew that a wolf's prey was grounded animals, not birds of the air.

"Is she so weak then?" Luag asked with disdain.

Normally Ciara would have balked at being called weak, but she welcomed any opportunity to be seen as deficient in this wolf's eyes.

"My sister is not weak, but she *is* too young."

"She's seen twelve summers."

"A girl still."

"On the cusp of womanhood."

For a terrifying moment, Ciara thought they were perhaps arguing about more than whether the wolves should hunt with her present. And the argument nauseated her. She'd heard rumors that English nobility gave their children in marriage that young, but it didn't happen in the Highlands.

Not even if she'd been a laird's daughter. And she was not. Galen wouldn't give her into marriage for at least a couple of years and if he followed the usual traditions, she'd be older than that still.

'Twas not as if she had a great dowry already accumulated. She'd barely started embroidery on the linens for her own home.

"No." Galen's tone said he would not be moved despite the years of seniority the other warrior had on him. No matter what the topic of the argument, he was not giving in.

Relief shuddered through her and Ciara took a breath into lungs burning for oxygen.

Luag did not look pleased. "She can stay here then."

"It is not safe."

"We are on our own hunting grounds."

Which was not strictly true; they were at least two hours north of their pack's territory. Galen's look said as much to the other wolf.

"She can stay in the cave," Luag offered as if making a great concession.

Ciara expected Galen to argue once again, but he nodded instead and her heart clenched. "Fine."

She opened *her* mouth to argue, but one look from Galen and she knew it was useless. Betrayal burning in her breast, she turned without a single acknowledgment to either of them and went back into the cave they had just been exploring. There had been no secret passages they could find, but they had spent a goodly amount of time looking. So she knew it was not inhabited by other predators . . . or prey.

Galen followed her. "Stay here until we return. We are *not* in our own hunting grounds."

She gave her brother a look of disdain rather than words. She knew that as well as he did. It was his *friend* who made the stupid claim otherwise, not her.

Galen threw Luag a glare showing he appreciated that truth, and then looked back at Ciara. "I do not want you harmed."

"I will be fine."

"Aye. I know."

A year ago, she might have made the claim, but Galen would not have believed it. Then her menses had come and her first shift. Now Galen had more faith in her ability to protect herself.

Ciara loved her wolf and liked nothing better than to go hunting with her brother, but she saw no point in hunting birds in their wolf form. Besides, she had absolutely no desire to hunt with Luag. She didn't trust him not to try to mate with her in the fur.

Which was not to say that she would not follow the male wolves when they left. She was ever curious and since Da's death Galen had become so overprotective, it was like to smother her worse than an Englishman's feather-stuffed pillow.

Ciara quickly removed her plaid and then the chemise she wore under it, allowing the shift to take her as soon as she was unencumbered by clothing.

Taking pains to mask her own scent, she lifted her wolf's snout and sniffed the air. Guided by the ever-helpful wind, she took off at a lope after the other wolves, who at least showed the practicality of hunting flying prey in their human skin. Though what they expected to do without bow and arrow, she did not know.

She trailed them for a short quarter of an hour before she heard the sound of Luag's voice lifted in cruel laughter.

Why would they laugh at their prey? Chrechte did not do that. All life was precious, even that which they had to take in order to eat and survive.

Ciara peeked through the leaves concealing her, blinking at what she saw. Her brother and Galen faced two young boys who wore skin loincloths rather than plaids.

Surely this was not who they hunted. Luag said he smelled ravens. Birds. Not bird shifters. That was too wicked to contemplate. *Chrechte did not hunt their own.*

They just didn't.

But the scent of raven was strong on the wind and there were no birds evident to her keen wolf's eyes.

A band of pain constricted around her heart as she fought the proof of her senses. Her brother could be no party to what her eyes insisted they saw.

Chrechte children as prey.

"Where is your protector?" Luag taunted loudly, his voice filled with ugly gloating. "Has he turned coward and run away?"

"Our prince fears no one," the oldest boy boldly proclaimed.

But the younger looked terrified.

And Ciara knew that look. She'd worn it before herself, when she had gotten into trouble by following her curiosity rather than the rules for safety laid down by parents and clan.

"They've no protector with them," Galen said, proving he was as astute at reading these young ones as he had always been at knowing Ciara.

"Is this true? Did you two abominations sneak away from your protectors?"

"We wanted to hunt," the littlest one claimed in a trembling voice.

She expected her brother to offer to escort the boys home, hoped for it. That would be the brother she knew and loved.

Instead, Luag laughed again, that lacing of cruelty more pronounced. "All the easier to rid the world of two more useless birds."

No. He did not mean that.

He could not.

Despite the evidence of her wolf's senses, she refused to believe these boys were Luag and Galen's prey.

But Ciara's horror only grew as her brother's voice carried on the now still air. "We are Chrechte warriors, we don't kill children."

Implying if these had been adult raven shifters, he would have killed without remorse? Definitely proving that he'd known they hunted shifters, not simply birds. Please, please . . . *please, no.* Her brother was not evil.

"These devil's spawn aren't children."

Primal instincts roared up inside Ciara. She had never experienced the like before, but the desire to rip Luag's throat out made her wolf's body tense in preparation to spring.

Children were to be protected. Always. That they were Chrechte only made their protection that much more imperative. Their race did not reproduce easily. Her parents had been considered blessed beyond measure to have succored two children of the Faol past infancy.

"We're not spawn," the older boy said defiantly, even as his small body shook with fear.

Luag drew his fist back and Ciara's haunches bunched a split second before leaping.

One hit from a warrior's fist could kill a child.

But before she could jump from her hiding place, a mighty roar sounded from the sky. So loud and filled with anger, it froze even Luag—who now stared above them with shock and denial.

Looking up, Ciara understood his reaction. She could no more believe her eyes than her dreams of the strangely glowing cavern. Yet, this was no nighttime fancy. A great red dragon flew against the clear blue sky, his scarlet scales so dark they looked near black, his furious roars shaking the treetops.

The boys looked unafraid though and Ciara knew this . . . this mythical creature of old was their ultimate protector. Perhaps even the prince the older boy had spoken of.

The dragon's head turned toward her brother and Luag, amber eyes fixed balefully on the men who had threatened the young shifters. Luag threw his dirk, not at the dragon but at the smallest boy. No doubt hoping to distract the dragon so Luag could run. The coward.

The knife missed the child's body but cut his arm as it flew past. The boy fell backward, crying out as blood welled from the cut.

The dragon roared again and then opening his great mouth even wider, orange flames shot out, devouring everything in their path.

Unable to move in her shock, Ciara stood by while her brother died with a scream that would haunt her nightmares. Luag was already running, but it was to no avail. The dragon had command of the skies and flew after the tormenter of children. Another blast of flame and Luag's screams were even more terrible than her brother's had been; he and the trees he'd tried to hide amidst turned into naught but ash.

'Twas a miracle the entire forest did not catch, but the dragon cast his flame with care.

The dragon turned and flew back, landing near the boys who clambered onto his back with more speed than sense. They were gone moments later, the sky clear as if no mythical creature had ever been.

All that remained were the ashes of her brother, Luag and some trees. And her own heart. She had stood by while Galen died a terrible death. She had done nothing for him, or for the boys.

Not that the little ones had needed her help, but she should never have stood by while they were threatened to begin with. The knowledge that she could have died with her brother no boon against the pain.

Luag's ashes she left for the wild animals to piss on, but Ciara scooped her brother's ashes into the skin she'd retrieved from her things in the cave. Tears mixed with bits of bone and ash as she gathered the precious remains, leaving the grit of her brother's life behind on her bare hands.

She would spread his ashes in the wind from the top of *Ben Bristecrann* just as they had done their father's.

With no time for grieving, she walked through what was left of the day and the night that followed to reach the hill. It had gotten its name from the tree split by lightning that still grew by some miracle on its summit. Her da had claimed the place was blessed.

Since his ashes mixed with its soil, she thought it was sacred anyhow. Ciara spoke the words of Chrechte passing in a broken voice as the wind picked up what remained of her brother and took it to join their father.

It was late morning of the next day before she reached their cottage and could inform her mother of Galen's death.

Ciara told no one of the dragon. Only that Luag had led her brother into danger and she had come upon both of them dead in the forest. She told her clan she'd prepared and lit her own funeral pyres and they'd not doubted her.

She was her da's daughter after all and he'd been known as one of the most stubborn men in the Highlands. Luag had no family to complain of her actions or question whether she had spread his ashes as she had her brothers.

Ciara did not volunteer the truth, for the heart still burning with anger and pain in her chest said he deserved his final resting place.

Mum showed no reaction to the news, seemingly oblivious to what Ciara's words meant when told of their loss.

Ciara realized her miscalculation when she found her mum dead the next morning, the bed soaked with her life's blood and cuts too deep in her wrists for even the Faol to survive.

Chapter 1

He is king who fears nothing; he is king who desires
nothing!

—Lucius Annaeus Seneca

Land of the Éan, Highlands of Scotland
1149 AD

"You are certain this is the right path you take?"

At his grandmother's voice, Prince Eirik Taran Gealach
Gra turned from his contemplation of the forest below. One
day soon, this view would be naught but a memory for him.
He refused to grieve the consequences of a choice he had
made for the good of the Éan though.

He was their prince. It was his duty.

Bowing his head, he greeted the raven shifter whose hair
was still more black than silver despite her many years.
"Anya-Gra."

Grandmother she might be, but she was still the spiritual leader of the Éan and the oldest member of the Triumvirate.

"I cannot help but think you give up too much for the
sake of our people." Troubled brown eyes in a face lined
with concern met his.

Now was not the time to question the decision he had made and the three members of the Triumvirate (including his grandmother) had approved. They had known this day was coming since he had refused the ceremony that would declare him king of his people, sovereign over their lands.

To accept the role would have prevented the Éan from joining the clans honorably before Eirik's death. At the time, his grandmother had counseled against jeopardizing the future of their people that way, though she had insisted he take his father's name as was custom.

Anya-Gra herself had declared that the good of their people demanded sacrifice. Eirik had agreed and he had made that sacrifice, becoming the first Prince Eirik not to be named king. Now she balked at him making another forfeit they both knew to be necessary.

"You agreed the Éan need to join the clans to survive; when it was first spoken of, it was your idea."

"Aye, but at the cost of your leadership of our people?" She shook her head.

"I do not cede leadership of the Éan; I only give up the daily running of a clan. It is the only way. I will not kill a clan chief just so that I might play political leader."

"Why not? You are a dragon." Eirik's younger cousin asked as he joined them on the platform outside what had been home to the Éan royalty for more than two centuries.

A home among the trees, reachable only through flight; none of the humans that lived among them had ever seen inside its walls. And in less than the passage of two full moons, he would no longer see it, either.

"Fidaich, who would you have me kill in battle for his position?" Eirik demanded of his favorite kin. "Those who have fought beside our people these past seven years, protecting us and helping us to find a way out of this secret life in the forest? The Sinclair? Buchanan? The Donegal maybe? I would have to kill my own brother by marriage to take that clan's leadership, not to mention one of our own."

For Crispin, the laird-in-training under Barr, would surely challenge Eirik should he do the unthinkable and kill the acting laird and man married to Eirik's only sister,

Sabrine. Hell, Sabrine would probably kill Eirik before Crispin ever got the chance to put forth a challenge.

That thought, at least, came close to bringing a smile to Eirik's face.

Fidaich shrugged, showing a bloodthirsty side not often seen among the ravens. "There are other clans in the Highlands."

"None that will guarantee our people's safety by the word of their chief and pack leader." He had both with the Sinclair.

And those of the Éan joining the Balmoral and Donegal clans had the same.

"With a dragon as our prince, we need no other leader's assurances." Fidaich drew himself up, trying to look older than his thirteen years.

One day, the boy would be a great warrior, but there was still too much of the child who had nearly died at the hands of a sadistic wolf now. Fidaich had more reason than most not to trust the wolves, or care that one might have to die for Eirik to take place as a clan laird.

Which did not mean Eirik shared his young cousin's attitudes. He'd killed the wolves that threatened Fidaich and Canaul in a moment of horror that would forever burn in Eirik's memories.

"I cannot be everywhere and well you know this. If we do not have the loyalty of a clan, we only trade one hunting ground where raven are the prey for another."

"In the old days—"

"What you know of the old days is from the stories told to entertain children. They were not so filled with glory and victory as the storytellers would have you believe," Anya-Gra gently chided the boy.

Fidaich pouted, a clear reminder he was yet to become a man. "Those stories are our history."

"Aye." Grandmother's eyes filled with sadness. "Part of it. The rest of our history is not shared so often."

But it was shared and Fidaich was well told on the unhappy lessons of the Chrechte's past.

"The old ways nearly decimated all the peoples of the

Chrechte." Eirik laid a hand on his cousin's shoulder. "Is that what you want?"

Fidaich deflated like a pig's bladder with a small leak. "No."

"Nor, I am sure, does he wish to see the loss of our people's identity, either." Anya-Gra spoke mildly, but the rebuke was there.

How could she think Eirik, last true prince of their people, would allow such a thing? "We do not."

The Éan were an ancient race that by their very nature would always stand apart from the human clans and the Faol that currently lived among them. While Eirik would not be clan leader, he was still their people's prince.

His new duties removed him from the politics of running a clan but left him with responsibilities easily as far reaching, if not more so, than the ones he currently carried.

When his grandmother made no word of reply, Eirik reminded her, "Both you and I are on the new Chrechte council."

Each of the Highland packs living among the clans had members on the council. A shifter from each group of the Éan joining the different clans had been appointed a spot on the council as well. Anya-Gra, as spiritual leader, held her position independently of which clan she chose to make her home.

Right now that clan was the Donegal, so she could be close to Eirik's sister, Sabrine. Not to mention Sabrine's son, Anya-Gra's only great-grandchild thus far.

Both the Faol and the Éan were to be represented in the council and given the opportunity to contribute to interpreting and enforcing the ancient laws governing the Chrechte.

Eirik could not be certain this would prevent the past from repeating itself, but he had faith. If he did not, he would not have agreed to the terms put forth for the Éan joining the clans.

He was their prince and would protect his people with his life and when necessary with the dragon that lived inside him.

Eirik reminded his grandmother, "It has been agreed that in matters of the Éan, I have final say . . . even for those among the other clans."

It was not a perfect solution, and relied on the integrity and cooperation of the Faol lairds, but Eirik would trust Barr, Talorc or Lachlan with his life. Trusting them with the lives of his people was that much harder, but he would do it.

For the good of the Éan and their long-term survival.

"If the council is so good, why are there no members from the Lowland clans?" Fidaich demanded.

Anya-Gra chuckled. "Oh, child . . . we are Chrechte. Even the raven are too contentious to be fully united."

It was true. Some of the Éan had refused their prince and Triumvirate's recommendation to merge with the Highland clans. A handful of ravens, a couple of eagles and a few of the humans who had made their home among the Éan had elected to remain in the forest. They would continue to live as the Éan had for the past two hundred years, hunted like prey and forced to hide their very existence.

"You should stay here and lead the Éan that do not want to join the clans," Fidaich said, showing his thoughts were in a similar place to Eirik's, if not drawing the same conclusions.

"Nay. If they will not follow me to the clans, they will not follow my lead in the forest any longer, either." By choosing to stay, those ravens had in effect rejected him as their chief before he ever gave over leadership to a clan laird.

Fidaich frowned. "But *you* gave them the option, even when the Triumvirate said you shouldn't."

Eirik gave Anya-Gra a look of censure. Fidaich should not know of the Triumvirate's discussion and he could only have heard about this particular one from a single source.

"The Triumvirate is not always right." The two members besides his grandmother had wanted Eirik to use his dragon to subdue the Faol and take over leadership of all the Chrechte as in days of old. He was no MacAlpin and told them so. "As for the Éan who wish to remain in the forest: if they trusted my lead, they would not have chosen to stay."

Shaking her head, Anya-Gra sighed. "'Tis not that simple, grandson. And well you know it. Some do not want the more civilized life among humans."

"They risk being hunted to death if they stay." And well she knew *that*.

Though the smaller group had a better chance of living undetected by the Faol still intent on eradicating Eirik's kind.

His grandmother's eyes took on the glazed look that said she saw things others could not. "For some, the freedom to live as they have always lived is worth that peril."

"I thought you supported the move to the clans." Her dislike of his willingness to forfeit ruling status in his adopted clan notwithstanding.

"I do." Her expression shifted to an old sadness. "But I understand our people who cannot make the change. There are still Faol who live in the caves of the forest, you know."

He had heard that rumor, but never gave it credence. "We do not see them."

"They do not hunt us like some of the misguided wolves among the clans. Besides, they have claimed for their territories mountainous lands a fair distance from our own forests."

He did not ask how she knew of these wild Faol packs then. His grandmother knew much it should be impossible for her to know. For instance, she had always maintained it was only a small segment of the Faol that hunted the Éan in these modern clansmen times. The rest of the Éan had believed it was all wolves. She had been proven right.

Fidaich harrumphed. "Maybe I should stay with the Éan here."

Eirik's dragon rumbled and it came out of his chest in a growl that would rival any wolf. "You do not trust me, either?"

He did not bother reminding his young cousin that both Fidaich's parents were set on the move to the Sinclair holding. Nor did Eirik mention that Fidaich's best friend and conspirator in the trouble the boys managed to find so easily was also coming. None of that mattered.

They were cousins, but Eirik was prince. Either his Éan brethren had faith in his decisions . . . or they did not.

Including his family.

Fidaich flinched. "Of course I trust you."

"Then, you will come with me to the Sinclairs."

"At least you would not have us live among the clan that tried to kill me."

Ah, the dramatic bent of a boy on the cusp of manhood. "'Twas not the entire clan." Just two wolves with sadistic hearts and no Chrechte honor.

Chrechte did not kill children. Enemy or not.

That day in the forest was the first time Eirik's dragon had killed. The two boys had gone missing and he'd joined the search party, finding them with his keener dragon senses fastest.

And just in time as well. His dragon hearing had picked up the warrior's threat to Fidaich and Canaul, and the sincerity behind it. Without doubt, the older wolf had meant to kill the children. Eirik had reacted with revulsion and fury. Without thought or hesitation, his dragon had incinerated two other Chrechte until naught was left but ash.

Their screams haunted him as no ghost could ever hope to. He had protected the boys and the secret of the Éan's prince and dragon, but the cost was not one Eirik would ever forget.

He had not killed in battle; he had annihilated his foe with a power they could not hope to match or defend against.

Ħer legs dangling over the stone edge, Ciara waited atop the lower bailey tower. One of two in the lower half of the wall surrounding the Sinclair fortress, it was the perfect vantage point for her first glimpse of the newcomers that would join her adopted clan. She was not supposed to be here, but it was a favored spot for her to find both privacy and peace.

Most of the clan had gathered in the lower bailey both yesterday and today for the same purpose, but Ciara did not like the crush of so many around her.

There was no crowd now. The humans and other Chrechte had gone home, disappointed once again when night fell with no sign of the newcomers. But Ciara waited as the moon rose, unable to return to the keep—her need to see these new clanspeople too strong to deny.

As a member of the Faol, she had been told those coming were Chrechte; she strongly suspected they were Éan.

Her dreams were not all nightmares and she had seen the birds in the sky shifting back to human form and donning the plaid of the Sinclair.

Were these Chrechte refugees like her, looking for a new life among the Sinclair?

Ciara hadn't actually been looking toward anything when she came to live with Laird Talorc and his lady, Abigail. Numb with grief after her mother's death so close on top of her dear brother Galen's grisly demise, Ciara had simply done as she was told.

Laird Barr had informed her she needed a new life without so many memories around her and Ciara had accepted his instruction in action, if not in her heart. She'd come to live among his former clan, the Sinclairs, without a single argument.

What had there been to argue? Ciara had no family any longer, no loved ones to hold her among the Donegal.

She had spent the past seven years doing her best to serve her new clan, though her old one would not recognize her. Gone was the stubborn girl who loved her family and people with every passionate fiber of her heart.

Ciara did her best to feel as little as possible; she had no desire to love with a devotion that could so easily destroy her again.

Laird Barr's hope that she might forget painful memories more easily away from all that was familiar had proven fruitless, but she did not blame his plan.

The memories were burned into Ciara's mind with a dragon's flame; it was impossible for her to ever forget or feel completely safe again. That fateful day in the forest and what followed lived inside her in a maelstrom of grief, awe, confusion, disbelief and sometimes utter terror.

Not that she ever let these feelings come fully to the surface, but Ciara often woke in the night to her brother's final scream, only to realize it had been her own. She dreamed of blood-soaked walls and a waxen-faced woman searching their cottage for a son and husband that would never again be there.

Ciara was grateful for the stone walls that kept her nightmares private, but she was even more thankful that far from forcing Ciara to marry when she came of age, Laird Talorc and his second, Niall, frightened off any prospective suitors. Chrechte and human alike.

Laird Talorc and Abigail treated Ciara like a cherished member of the family, to be protected and watched over. She knew they thought she was broken.

Too broken to be forced to mate.

She did and said nothing to dissuade them of that belief.

She wanted no true family to lose again; she had no desire to ever marry or have children that could be taken from her by that undefeatable enemy, death. She hoped she never met her mate, or that he was already committed to another.

Helping to care for Abigail and Talorc's twins, now in their fourth summer, was difficult enough. The boys did their best to worm their way into Ciara's heart. It took all her stubborn resolve not to let herself love them.

And deep inside, in a place she refused to acknowledge, she feared she already did . . . even more than she feared the dragon that had killed her brother.

Shaking off her thoughts, she peered through the moon-lit night, seeking out her first glimpse of the Éan soon to join their clan. She wasn't supposed to know about the Éan at all. No one but a select few were. And Ciara, better than most, understood why.

However, it was not her fault she knew many things she should not. Even without the eavesdropping. Her dreams and visions had grown more frequent since she had seen the scarlet dragon breathing fire from the sky.

And of late, the *Faolchú Chridhe* called to her even more insistently than her dead brother's screams and mother's spilled blood. Ciara rarely slept, and when she did sleep it was to dream, each dream growing more fraught with urgency than the last. She could not eat because that urgency followed her into wakefulness, making her stomach tight and filling her with dread she did not understand.

Ciara did not know what to do.

Perhaps it was time to tell another soul about the existence of the wolves' stone. Would that knowledge be safer in Laird Talorc's hands than it had been in Galen's? Pain sliced through Ciara at the probability it would.

Galen had wanted the power of the stone to destroy the Éan. Laird Talorc would want it to help them.

In her silent, stealthy wanderings around the keep, Ciara had heard enough to know this to be true. She knew Talorc was aware of her presence. He was a wolf with a wolf's senses, but he never scolded her. Maybe he knew she had no one to tell the secrets she overheard.

The faint sounds of multiple horses had Ciara looking up and dismissing all thought of secrets and the *Faolchú Chridhe* for now. A group of perhaps twenty people riding on horseback came into view. She watched intently as they rode closer and closer to the fortress without being challenged.

It had to be the Éan.

They got close enough that with her wolf's eyesight she could tell that some wore plaids, while others wore clothing made of tanned hides and fur.

The huge warrior that led them wore what looked like a kilt made of leather, wide cuffs at his wrist of the same and a strap around his bicep that held a wicked-looking knife. He wore his long sword in another scabbard on his back, the hilt sticking up over his left shoulder. The leather strap holding it in place bisected his otherwise naked chest—a chest devoid of hair but rippling with muscle.

A medallion of some kind glinted in the moonlight, hanging from a leather cord around his neck. He wore no boots, but sandals that wrapped around and laced at his ankles. They almost looked like what the Roman soldiers of ancient times had worn. She'd seen drawings carved into cave walls in her search with her brother for the *Faolchú Chridhe*.

Was this warrior Éan? He was bigger than those he rode with, at least a head taller than any of the other men. Giant, she would guess he stood even taller than the laird's second-in-command, Niall, and easily as broad.

Ciara had not thought Éan warriors large like that. Certainly they were not in her dreams. The Éan were strong, but in her dreams they were smaller in build to the Faol.

Her brother always claimed they were the smallest of the Chrechte peoples, too. Galen had said it sneeringly, but being so much smaller than him herself, Ciara had wondered why he found the difference so worthy of disgust.

This man was not undersized in any way and he had the regal bearing of a king. How would he tolerate Talorc's leadership?

Would the huge warrior challenge her laird, the man who considered himself her father?

Anxiety spiked through her as the new Chrechte moved closer. Mere feet from the drawbridge that was still down on Laird Talorc's order, the lead warrior's features became distinct.

And all the air in Ciara's lungs escaped in one long exhale.

This man who meant to become a Sinclair was breathtaking, though his expression was as fierce as the glint in his amber eyes. Eyes that glowed with Chrechte power, even in the moonlight. A jawbone that looked hewn from rock was set in stern lines, his neck and shoulders held in arrogant rigidity that warned danger for any who crossed him.

Atavistic fear pressed against her solar plexus, making it hard to draw breath.

The warrior lifted his head, a gaze even keener than her own honing in on Ciara with unerring accuracy. He should not be able to see her tucked up against the wall as she was, but she knew he did. He did not look away, either. Nor could she.

Never before had she felt such a connection with another. Her wolf whispered a word she refused to hear, her mind whirling with thoughts she was determined never to have.

Unable to break gazes with the warrior and yet unwilling to remain as she was, Ciara surged to her feet. The nights without sleep, the days she had eaten less than enough to sustain a sparrow much less a wolf caught up with her in that one confusing moment. Swaying on her feet, she tilted forward.

She jerked back, but overcompensated and one foot slipped out from beneath her.

Suddenly, unbelievably, despite her wolf's grace, she pitched forward. She tumbled into the night air, her hands scrabbling for purchase on the stone, one finger connecting. She tried to make it two, to get a better grip, but she could feel her fingertips giving way even as she did so.

She refused to let the joints unbend, but she could feel blood welling around cuts in her fingers from the stone. The wetness proved her undoing. No amount of will could force her fingers to hold as the wet blood made them slip and she fell.

Her wolf howled as she tried to shift, hoping against all to live.

But it was not the hard ground that broke her fall. Sharp talons curled around her body, warm scales that felt like living chain mail pressed against her face and suddenly she was not falling, but flying upward. In the arms of a dragon.

That was the last her tormented mind could take. Ciara welcomed the black oblivion as it came.

Chapter 2

The dragon wing of night o'erspreads the earth.

—SHAKESPEARE

The woman's body went limp in his arms and Eirik knew she had fainted.

Fury fueled by an inexplicable worry and having to shift into his dragon where other Sinclairs might be watching filled him as Eirik flew back toward his people.

At least it was night, but the moon was nearly full and a keen-eyed Sinclair could not help but notice a dragon flying in the sky over their holding.

What had the bloody-minded female been thinking to climb onto the tower, instead of staying safe inside it?

What was she doing out at all this late at night? He could smell her wolf, so he knew she was Chrechte. Did she think that made her safe from dangers that lurked in darkness?

Despite his anger, he was careful when he laid her on the grass to regain her senses. He was dressed and strapping his sword back on when her eyes fluttered.

Eyes the color of emerald looked up at him in confusion. "You are dragon."

He did not deny it.

"You are." She tried to rise, but fell back weakly. "You are *the dragon.*"

"And you are clumsy for a Faol."

She shook her head, but he did not think it was in denial. Dark shadows marred the perfect pale skin below eyes in an oval-shaped face, so lovely it almost hurt to look at her. Her collarbones were outlined by that same pale skin, as if she had not been eating enough. And her hands trembled.

Was Talorc not taking care of his people?

Eirik could not believe it of the arrogant but honorable Chrechte laird.

The trembling could simply be from fear though. He could smell it on her, a sour stench that did not coincide with her beauty or Chrechte spirit.

"My . . . I . . ."

"What were you doing on top of the tower?"

"Waiting for you."

He gave her a look that doubted her words. Was she addled then? He could sense the heat of her blush before her alabaster skin turned pink.

"I mean for all of you. I wanted to see the new Chrechte that would join our clan."

"You are a Sinclair." Of course she was. She wore their plaid, though her dress was a little different.

Her skirt was the pleated tartan of the Sinclair, but she wore a black bodice laced over her white blouse, a tartan shawl pinned to her shoulders.

It was far too many layers for a wolf to wear for easy shifting. Did the Sinclair not teach his Chrechte the importance of speed when doing so? It could make the difference between life and death.

Had Eirik not been able to shift near instantly only moments before, that death would have been hers.

"I was a Donegal."

So, she had married into the clan. Why that knowledge should make his dragon feel like casting fire Eirik did not know.

"And now you are a foolish Sinclair who does not know

better than to keep your vigil of curiosity on the top of a tower. You are no bird to save yourself with a shift."

She frowned, clearly affronted by his plain speaking. Too bad. Someone should have spoken to her of such before.

"Your husband has failed in his duty to protect you." And Eirik would tell the idiot just that when he met him.

"I have no husband."

"Then how did you come to be a Sinclair when you were a Donegal?" Only his younger cousin would dare to interrupt Eirik's discourse with the Sinclair wolf.

Ciara turned her head so she could see Fidaich. "I came to live with the Sinclairs after your prince killed my brother and mother."

Low exclamations and gasps sounded from the others, indicating they had heard the woman's accusation.

Fidaich grabbed her arm and shook her. "You take that back. My cousin is no murderer like the Faol."

Eirik's dragon growled.

"Not all wolves are killers," the boy's mother reprimanded, apparently oblivious to the dragon's precarious temper.

But both the Sinclair woman and Fidaich ignored Eirik's aunt to glare at one another.

"Release her," Eirik ordered in a voice none had ever been foolish enough to ignore.

Fidaich did so but stared up at Eirik with frustration. "She cannot be allowed to make such false claims against you."

"They are not false." The woman's voice was laced with absolute certainty, but worse—with pain.

Eirik did not like it.

Fidaich did not, either. "They are."

"Not."

Eirik rolled his eyes. *"Fidaich."*

Just one word, but his cousin subsided. Eirik met the now accusing gaze of the woman. Her fear had not diminished, but now it was laced with anger and hurt.

"Explain."

"You killed my brother with your fire and my mother

took her own life because of it. Therefore, you murdered them both."

His dragon had only ever killed two men in that way. One had been this woman's brother. But how had she known?

"'Twas not murder, he was protecting me and Canaul," Fidaich growled, clearly unable to keep well out of it.

The woman started. "You were one of the boys Luag meant to harm?"

"Your brother was this Luag?" Eirik asked before Fidaich could answer.

The utter revulsion that came over the woman's features denied Eirik's words before she said a vehement, "Nay."

"The other one?"

"His name was Galen. He was a good brother."

"But not a good Chrechte."

Shame dropped her eyes from his and made his dragon want to sneeze with its acrid scent. "He was deceived by those he thought were friends."

"He would have allowed his friend to murder a child."

"So, you killed him."

"I did not know he was any less a threat than the man with a fist raised to my cousin."

"He was."

"I could not risk it." Not that he'd even considered the matter.

"You burned them to ash."

"Aye."

"I left Luag's remains in the forest for the animals." She said it as if admitting something no one else knew.

As far as Eirik was concerned, she'd done exactly right. "'Twas no less than the would-be killer of children deserved."

She nodded and he helped her to her feet, unable to let her sit so defenselessly in the grass any longer. It just didn't feel right. "You saw me."

"Yes." She pulled away from him as soon as she was standing.

"How?"

She swayed a little but seemed to stay standing by sheer will alone. "Does it matter?"

"It does if you were in a position to protect the boys and did not choose to do so." He knew not all Faol were bad, but to think this woman lacked honor in that way made something in Eirik's gut twist sickly.

"I was going to intervene, but you got there too quickly."

"Barely quickly enough to stop Luag from killing my cousin with a single blow."

"I was set to attack him as a wolf."

"You hesitated too long. If I did not see you, you could not have reached Fidaich in time." Eirik made no effort to soften the censure in his tone.

This woman accused him of killing not only her brother but her mother as well by his actions in protecting Fidaich and Canaul. He would give no quarter on the circumstance of her brother's death. Chrechte did not harm children.

And none should stand by while one tried to.

"The only one who killed that day was you."

"Would you have rather I left my cousin to the nonexistent mercies of your Luag?"

"He was not mine."

But Eirik was not listening, nor did he care how much revulsion she showed at every mention of Luag's name. He had heard enough from this female wolf who accused him of murder when she had stood by while Éan children were threatened.

He regained his mount and nudged his horse into movement. The Sinclair wolf could walk. The bridge into the fortress was close enough.

Nevertheless, Eirik was not surprised to hear Lais offer the woman a ride on one of the extra horses. As healer to their people, the eagle shifter was the only one with the authority to do so without Eirik's say-so.

Lais must have seen how weak the woman was, the way she swayed on her feet, and chosen to show more pity than the woman's brother had had for two Éan children caught playing in the forest.

The quiet words of acceptance and gratitude reached Eirik's ears before he kneed his horse into a gallop.

$\mathcal{I}$gnoring the looks of censure he received from the others, Lais helped Ciara onto the back of Eirik's extra mount. It was the only horse well trained enough that he had no worries about it dumping the obviously shaky woman on the ground.

"I am Lais. I don't know if you remember me, but I was once a Donegal as well, Ciara."

"You know my name." Ciara searched his features until her green gaze glimmered with recognition. "You are here with the Éan? But you were a friend of Rowland's. Of Wirp's."

"I was never their friend." Though he'd been misled into believing himself so at one time.

She pondered that for a moment and then nodded ever so slightly. "Like my brother, you were deceived."

"Yes." Which was why, of all the Éan, he was probably the only one who would understand Ciara's defense of a man who had stood by while Chrechte children were threatened.

He was also one of the few Chrechte, maybe the only other one besides himself, who knew the toll that day in the forest had taken on Eirik's soul. And how much Ciara's accusations would have bothered the prince.

"Do you remember my brother?" Ciara asked softly.

"I did not know him well. He spent most of his time with Luag, some with Wirp."

"Yes."

"He would have mated you to Luag." And a damn shame it would have been. Luag had been a sadistic, honorless man who did not deserve the wolf that shared his soul.

"You can't know that." But Ciara's tone said she knew the truth of it, just as Lais did. The scent of grief and sadness coming off of her told their own story.

Wishing he had not reminded her of her brother's other failings, Lais said, "You never told anyone of the dragon."

"No."

"How did you explain your brother and Luag's disappearance?"

"I told everyone Luag had led Galen into harm's way and caused both their deaths. It was the truth and the Chrechte of our clan could scent it. I masked the deceit in my scent when I told them I had built my own pyres and burned them as is right and true."

"You can do that?"

"Yes."

"That's unheard of."

"Others in my family had similar talents."

He did not doubt it, but he could not help being glad her brother was dead. A wolf who hated the Éan but had the ability to mask a lie? He could have wreaked havoc in a way even Rowland could not have competed with.

"Your prince did kill my brother."

"But he did not murder him."

She did not answer, but her lack of argument said it all.

"How did you know he is our prince?"

"How could he be anything else?" Ciara asked in a tone that said she doubted his intelligence but he should not doubt hers.

Lais laughed. "You're an arrogant little thing, aren't you?"

"I don't mean to be."

"With eyes as green as yours, I always suspected you and your mother were descendant of the Faol royalty."

"MacAlpin killed all the royals of our line."

"Only those counted by matriarchy."

"It does not matter; the Sinclair recognizes Scotland's king. To be royalty among the Faol can have no meaning."

After seeing what the royal family of the Éan did for their people, Lais wasn't sure he agreed. Besides, Scotland's king had less sway in the Highlands than with the Lowland clans. "Laird Sinclair only submits to King David when he wants to."

"He is a Highland laird and Chrechte as well." Ciara gave Lais an almost-there smile. "How could it be any other way?"

He chuckled. "It could not."

"And your prince? Does he intend to submit to Laird Talorc?" There was very real worry tingeing her tone now.

"As clan leader, yes."

"As pack leader?"

"Only wolves belong to packs. Birds are flocks and ours knows no clan boundaries."

"That won't be easy."

"Eirik is aware." Anya-Gra had not let the prince forget it, voicing her concerns right up until the Éan left the forest, each of three groups taking a different direction.

"Why don't you call him prince?"

"Because I am his friend."

Ciara recoiled.

Lais sighed. "Eirik is no murderer."

"That is your opinion."

"It is yours as well, when you are thinking clearly."

"Thank you for telling me my innermost thoughts."

"I understand wanting to believe those you hold dear are good people . . . and having to accept when you realize they were not."

"My brother *was* a good person. He was deceived."

"Do you enjoy your life among the Sinclairs?" he asked, refusing to continue such an argument.

She might well be right. He knew what it was to be deceived. Would her brother have shifted his thinking if exposed to the truth? There was no answer to that quandary in the violence of the past.

"Laird Talorc and Abigail have been very kind to me."

"You live with the laird?" Lais asked with surprise and humor he made no attempt to mask.

Eirik had agreed to make his home in the keep until the Éan were settled amidst the clan.

"I have a room next to their children."

That was an interesting way of putting it. She could have said that she was part of the family, or treated like family, but she avoided doing so.

It probably made Lais a bad friend, but he could not help looking forward to the times to come with Eirik and Ciara under the same roof.

There was something there. Lais had never seen Eirik shift so fast and not once into a dragon in front of his people.

Eirik kept the dragon private and Lais thought he was probably the only Éan who understood why.

Everyone else speculated it had something to do with the power or pride of the dragon, but Lais knew Eirik feared his dragon as much as he embraced it. To burn another Chrechte to ash was not an easy event to carry on one's conscience.

"Eirik killed your brother in protection of the young of our race, but he saved your life this night. Will you let that go unremarked in your bitterness?"

Ciara jerked so hard she almost fell off her horse but shook her head. "No. I would tell him of my appreciation." A moment of silence passed. "I am not bitter."

"Good." He thought about what he had to say next. "You can show your genuine appreciation and continue to maintain the secret of Eirik's dragon."

"Laird Talorc does not know he is a dragon?" Ciara asked, anxiety coloring her voice and making her heart quicken.

"Aye, he does, but others do not. It is a closely guarded secret."

"Because of Faol like Wirp and Luag."

"Aye."

"Perhaps news of such a being would frighten them off."

"Or make Eirik the greatest target to them all."

"I will not betray his secret."

"Thank you."

She was silent as they entered the lower bailey, the only clan there to meet them the night guard who spoke in low tones with Eirik before sending a young soldier running toward the keep.

Eirik's people had all dismounted and gathered their belongings by the time the Sinclair made it down the hill from the keep. His hair stuck up as if he'd been drawn from his bed and he wore only a sword and his kilt.

Nevertheless, he was smiling. "I'm glad you and your people have finally made it." Like the friend that he was, the Sinclair reached out and pulled Eirik in a warrior's embrace.

Eirik returned it before stepping back. "I did not mean to pull you from your bed."

"It happens." The Sinclair gave the shrug Eirik knew could irritate the man's wife, Abigail, no end.

"We were going to camp outside the wall." Eirik let some censure bleed into his voice. "I saw the drawbridge was down, so changed my plan."

The smile the Sinclair gave was smug. "I had a feeling you would be here tonight."

"The security of your people is more important than a little inconvenience."

Instead of taking umbrage at Eirik's clear censure, Talorc merely let his grin grow wider. "You are all my people now, too. Abigail insisted you would feel more *welcome* if the drawbridge was down."

"You allow your lady to dictate in matters of clan security?" Eirik asked with no little shock.

"You know Abigail." But there was something in the Sinclair's voice and then he looked over Eirik's shoulder.

Eirik turned his head to see a group of warriors entering the lower bailey as the sound of the drawbridge being lifted could be heard.

"You had a guard on watch outside the walls."

"Of course."

Eirik almost smiled. "It seems your life is filled with headstrong women, but you know how to handle them for the most part."

"Women?" Talorc asked with a puzzled frown that went dark as he seemed to comprehend all that Eirik had said. *"For the most part?"*

Eirik indicated the woman Lais had been referring to as Ciara. The prince had heard her tell Lais she lived in the keep. He had not missed his second's amusement at that fact, either.

The Sinclair bellowed, "What in the hell is Ciara doing down here in the middle of the night?"

The woman in question jumped and then bit her lip before giving a small wave to her laird. The Sinclair did not look amused, nor did he look particularly surprised.

Eirik doubted the other man would take the rest of his ward's exploits with the same equanimity. "A better question might be: what was she doing on top of the west tower?"

Clearly able to hear them, though she stood several feet away, Ciara glared at Eirik as if he had betrayed her most bosom-held secret. He let his own disapproval show in the look he returned her.

If she had expected him to keep her dangerous actions from her laird, she was not only deluded about her brother—the woman was a fool.

The Sinclair's eyes began to glow with the wolf's light and the scent of his fury was so strong, Eirik wasn't sure the pack alpha would not shift right there. His own dragon roared for a chance to come out.

"Ciara was *on top*?" Talorc asked with deadly quiet.

"Until she fell."

Talorc did not ask Eirik to repeat himself. He did not question how Ciara came to be in the lower bailey now, in one piece. He simply turned toward the tower and bellowed a man's name.

Seconds later a guard came running up, breathless and pale with fear. "Yes, laird?"

"My daughter was on top of your tower."

"C-Ciara, laird?"

"Do I have another one I do not know about?"

"N-no, of course not, Alpha. It's just that, I didn't . . . she didn't . . . how did she . . ." Clearly overcome by too many questions and no answers his laird was going to accept, the guard's voice trailed off. "How did she get off, sir?" the hapless guard was foolish enough to make as his one complete sentence.

"She fell."

Grief mixed with fear and the guard dropped to his knees. "I'm so sorry, Alpha." He offered his neck for whatever the other wolf meant to do.

"She lives." The Sinclair shook his head, his fury still strong, but a resignation about it.

Eirik lifted one brow in question.

The laird sighed and it was not a happy sound. "She is far too adept at masking her scent."

"She's sneaky."

"Aye." Talorc sounded proud, despite his anger.

"How does she live?" the guard asked with a fair amount of trepidation.

Talorc turned his anger back on the still-kneeling guard. "Our new clansman saved her." His tone and manner implied it should not have been necessary.

The guard seemed oblivious in his shock. The look of awe and respect he gave Eirik surprised him, but not as much as the gratitude wafting off the young wolf's skin. He bowed his head to Eirik. "Thank you."

"You have a personal interest in the laird's daughter?"

The guard's eyes widened in fear as he slid a sideways glance toward his laird and then the huge blond man who had silently joined them just as Eirik had told the Sinclair of his adopted daughter's exploits. Niall, Talorc's second, glared at the guard with death in his eyes.

The young wolf vehemently shook his head. "Nay, 'tis just that she is favored by many in our clan."

Niall nodded as did the Sinclair, but Eirik noted both men gave the guard matching looks of warning.

Chapter 3

Dreaming of a tomorrow, which tomorrow, will be as
distant then as 'tis today.

—LOPE DE VEGA

The Sinclair dismissed his guard with instructions to
do better in future or risk losing his ability to procreate.

The wolf's clear acceptance of the threat as truth and fear
because of it left a sour stench in the air after he was gone.

Talorc grasped forearms with Eirik. "Thank you for
saving my daughter."

"She is clan now."

"Aye."

The object of their discussion chose that moment to
come up to them. Ciara looked up at the man who called
himself her father. "Laird Talorc, I am sorry for the trouble
I caused."

Eirik was shocked to note the Sinclair mask his fury
and his demeanor turn gentle. "It is all right, Ciara. I know
you did not mean to cause grief."

"I didn't. I thought I would return to the keep and no
one would be the wiser."

This was supposed to placate her laird? Her belief she
could get away with it and thus cause no worry to others?

"I saw you," Eirik corrected her. "Others could have as well."

"No, they could not," she disagreed in a soft but firm voice, her tone far too certain.

"You cannot know that."

She just shrugged, the movement so like her adopted father that the corner of Eirik's mouth curved in an almost smile. But then, the truth hit him. She could only be so certain in one circumstance.

"You've been up there before. Many times. And never been caught."

She glared at him, this time her expression leaving no doubt she had not expected that truth to be revealed. The anxious glance she slid toward Talorc said as much as well.

The laird frowned, some of his fury leaking through to scent the air around them as his demeanor lost a bit of its patient calm. "Is this true?"

Ciara bit her lip, clearly deciding whether or not to tell the truth. How interesting that she even considering lying to her pack alpha, much less laird. Did she think she could get away with it? Could she mask more than her scent?

Finally, she nodded. "It's peaceful. Quiet."

"Ciara." The exasperation in Talorc's voice was laced with weariness. "I'm going to have to tell Abigail. She will wring her hands with worry. She will cry."

The laird made it sound like such an eventuality was the worst possible outcome.

From Ciara's expression, she agreed with that assessment. "No, please. You cannot tell her. She already worries too much."

"She loves you."

Ciara shook her head. And like before, Eirik got the distinct impression she wasn't arguing her laird's words, but trying to negate their impact.

"Please, laird."

"Promise me you will not do it again and I won't tell her. I'll know the problem is no longer there for her to worry about."

Eirik wondered how Talorc intended to keep anyone

else from telling his wife and then realized, he probably had no intention of doing so. In fact, he was probably counting on someone letting the information slip.

"I promise."

"What do you promise?" Eirik asked, when Talorc did not press for clarification.

Again, Ciara glared at him.

He simply stared back, waiting for her answer.

The Sinclair gave Eirik a look of respect and then turned one of expectation on Ciara.

She frowned, but then said, "Not to climb up on top of the west tower again."

Talorc smiled and nodded, looking pleased.

Eirik simply shook his head. It was clear that while Talorc was a smart man when dealing with his strong-headed females, he had not lived his life with a sister like Sabrine.

Eirik commanded, "Promise you won't go on top of the other towers, either."

"Who are you to dictate to me?" Ciara demanded, her voice husky with anger.

It went straight to his groin and he was so damn surprised, he nearly answered. He was no virgin, but never before had a female affected him so strongly that she could elicit arousal on the sound of her voice alone.

And to be excited by this woman who had called him murderer? 'Twas completely unacceptable.

And yet he'd barely bitten back the words proclaiming himself prince of his people and worthy of demanding anything he wanted of her, when Talorc spoke. "I'm sure you meant your promise to include all the towers, Ciara, but it will do us both good to hear you say so. For Abigail's sake, of course."

Ciara turned her glare on her adopted father and his eyes flared briefly in surprise, and then a smile came over his features that Eirik could not understand the reason for.

"Of course," Ciara grumbled. "I promise not to climb up on *any of the towers*."

Niall chuckled and when Ciara turned her frown on him, it turned into a full guffaw. "I think I'm going to like having Eirik in our clan," the laird's second-in-command said.

Ciara did not look like she agreed. Not one little bit, but then that was no surprise. Was it?

She blamed him for not only her treacherous brother's death, but that of her mother as well.

*C*iara moved her goblet of ale a bit to the left and then back to its original place beside her bowl. A gentle feminine hand rested on her arm and Ciara stilled, looking up.

Abigail frowned thoughtfully, her light brown eyes darkened by worry. "Are you all right?"

"Of course." Though Ciara wasn't. She hadn't been since the dragon showed up to join their clan.

Not only did he cause excitations in her body that she was unused to experiencing, but she was worried about his future plans as a member of the clan.

He and Laird Talorc seemed to be great friends, but Ciara could not banish her fears Eirik would try to wrest power over the clan from her laird. He was a dragon after all, much more powerful than a wolf—even one of Laird Talorc's superiority.

In the sennight since his people had joined the clan, Eirik seemed to play an increasingly important role in the running of things. And Laird Talorc, in his arrogance, showed not the least sign of worry at this event.

Even Guaire consulted Eirik before going to his laird when assigning duties and crofter's huts to the Éan and the humans that had come with them. Ciara had asked Niall about it, but he'd just given one of his rare smiles and told her not to worry herself, that all was as it should be. Niall claimed that his mate's loyalty would always be first and foremost to the Sinclair.

Which Ciara believed, but it wouldn't matter if Laird Talorc died in a challenge with a dragon, would it? So Ciara worried. Though she didn't want to. She didn't want to care.

"You are fidgeting," Abigail said in that soft voice that seemed to only carry one tone.

Ciara made sure Abigail could see her speak to read her lips when she said, "I am not very hungry."

"You are never hungry, but you must eat." The stern expression on Abigail's kind face brooked no argument.

Ciara didn't give one. She'd avoided as many mealtimes as possible since the dragon had moved into the keep and begun sharing their table. This latemeal she'd been thwarted though. Talorc himself had found her in the great hall earlier and told her not to eat with the children as she often pretended to.

He wanted her presence at the table at latemeal. After seven years living with his family as one of them, Ciara could hardly refuse.

"I'm not eating for two," she said to Abigail, letting the other woman know that Ciara was aware of her joyous secret.

Pure happiness suffused Abigail's features. "I am with child? I had hoped, but it was too soon to be sure."

"You mean Talorc does not know?"

Abigail shook her head. "He didn't know with the boys, either. Niall figured it out first. I thought he and his twin, Barr, were the only wolves with such a strong sense of smell."

"There is very little change in your body's scent yet."

"Then how?"

Ciara weighed continuing to hide her secrets against the need to tell someone about the *Faolchú Chridhe*. Perhaps she could start with this small revelation and build toward the visions that stole her rest and demanded her action. "I had a dream."

Abigail assessed Ciara for a long, silent moment and then asked, "Do you dream of things that come to pass?"

"Sometimes." She'd dreamed of her mother's death long before it happened, so long that she'd made herself forget until she walked into the bedroom that stank with spilled blood. "The dreams are different, special and I wake up knowing they are real."

Abigail's eyes burned with curiosity. "What did you dream about me?"

"I saw you in the chair by the great fireplace. You suckled a babe in your arms while the boys played a game with their sticks Niall whittled for them on the bearskin near the hearth."

Far from looking like she doubted Ciara's words, Abigail's expression was naught but excited hopefulness. "Was the babe a boy or girl?"

"Girl."

Abigail reached out and hugged her so tight, Ciara squeaked. "Thank you, daughter. Thank you."

Abigail released her and Ciara could not help it. She laughed. To be believed was gift enough, but to have her knowledge received with such joy was fantastic.

The conversations around them stopped, quietness descending like a blanket over the head table.

Confused, Ciara looked around her, finally meeting Guaire's eyes and asking a question with her own. Had Talorc said something important and she missed it?

Guaire was smiling and he shook his head in silent answer to her unasked question. "You laughed," he mouthed to her.

Frowning in confusion, she looked at Laird Talorc, but he was busy kissing his mate. Ciara's gaze shifted beyond the happy couple only to snag on the fierce amber gaze of the dragon. Unlike the rest of the room, his attention had not shifted to the laird and his lady.

It was fixed firmly on Ciara. He said nothing, but his eyes burned with a message that found an answer deep inside her. Desire, hot and bright, burned through her body.

And she had no idea what to do about it.

"What did you tell her?" Niall asked.

Forcing herself to look away from Eirik, Ciara shook her head. It was not her secret to share, though she was sure once they stopped kissing, Laird Talorc would do so.

Niall's face showed a sudden comprehension. "Our lady is carrying again."

Ciara nodded just slightly.

"How did you know?" Eirik asked, his voice drawing her gaze back to him and his eyes trapping it once again.

"By scent," Niall answered for her.

But the dragon shook his head. "No. You just realized the truth. If Ciara shared this Chrechte gift of yours, you would have known by now."

Ciara almost laughed again, the assumption that her new clan would have learned all her secrets by now morbidly funny to her. Eirik knew more of her secrets because he'd shared in one of them.

"She spends more time with our lady," Guaire argued on Niall's behalf.

But Eirik's expression said he did not accept the argument. "It is something more."

Ciara refused to answer the implied question. "If you did not know the news, why did everyone go silent?" she asked instead.

"You laughed," Guaire repeated.

"So?"

"You never laugh."

"Not unless you are entertaining the children and then it is rare enough," Niall added.

Heat suffused Ciara's cheeks. "I laugh."

But she didn't. She knew it. Laughter came from joy and joy came from allowing herself to feel.

"My wife carrying is reason enough to laugh," Laird Talorc said, deep satisfaction lacing his voice.

"Indeed it is," Eirik acknowledged with an unreadable look at Ciara, before turning to bang their laird on the back in congratulations.

Within moments the simple latemeal had turned into a celebration. One of the soldiers pulled out a flute and began playing. Another joined in with a bladder pipe and another with a drum. Noisy laughter filled the hall as some jumped up from their tables to engage in a spontaneous dance.

Eirik and three of his Éan joined the other soldiers and began dancing a warrior's entertainment unlike anything she had ever seen before. It was a dance, but a mock fight as well, dirks sharpened to such an edge they could have split a baby's hair were thrust and tossed and caught with such assurance, Ciara could not help clapping along with the rest of the clan.

The sound of the Éan soldiers' hardened leather soles stomping on the wooden floor blended with the music, the synchronized movements of their feet adding to the amazing intricacy of the warrior's dance.

Ciara had never seen the like and was sure none of the other Sinclairs had, either.

Abigail's toneless laughter joined the others and Ciara smiled, an unfamiliar feeling settling in her belly.

She was happy.

Unable to remember the last time she had felt this carefree, terror filled her. Like love, happiness came at a cost and in her life that cost had always been pain.

Terrified at the realization of how close she had allowed herself to grow to the Sinclairs, Ciara jumped to her feet, intent on escape. Those around her misunderstood and thought she meant to join the dancing, the men moving into the formation of a jig.

Ciara looked wildly around her, but upon seeing the terrible joy on the faces of her adopted family knew she could not leave. She let herself be pulled onto the floor and danced for the first time since her mother's death.

It was another hour before she was able to slip out of the great hall unnoticed by the other revelers. Sneaking outside the stone building, Ciara hurried to Abigail's garden.

She stopped in front of the patch of rosemary that she and the laird's wife had planted not long after Ciara arrived at the Sinclair holding. Abigail had told her it was for remembrance, so that Ciara's memories of her mother could be associated with a fragrant herb rather than blood and death.

Ciara had been too polite to tell the gentle woman who used to be English that she was mad if she thought it would work, but over the years . . . this patch of rosemary *had* helped.

"We had no gardens like this in the forest. It was not safe to do so."

Ciara jumped and spun around at the sound of Eirik's voice. "I did not hear you arrive."

Moonlight glistened off long black hair that shimmered with crimson when the sun shone while his amber eyes glowed with that look that made her feel weak at the knees. Other ravens' hair glinted blue; it must be his dragon that made Eirik's different. Ciara thought it was beautiful, not that she would ever tell the prince any such thing.

"All Éan are trained to travel in the forest like a wraith with no scent or sound." That he, as their prince, would be better at it than anyone else went without saying, though his tone implied she should realize this truth.

"Because the Faol hunted your people." She hated that knowledge, but not nearly so much as the proof that pointed to her brother being one of those misguided wolves.

"Only some of the wolves wanted us dead," he said as if reading her mind. "Those few are enough to be a risk for all my people though."

"The pack alphas have been working on cutting this malignancy from their clans."

"Aye, though how you are aware of this begs question."

"I live in the keep. I hear things."

"The Sinclair must trust you despite your brother's past."

"He does not know it."

"You have never even told him the truth of what you saw in the forest?"

"Lais said Laird Talorc already knows of your dragon."

"He does. His former second-in-command witnessed my first transformation."

"How?"

"He was married to my sister and attended my coming-of-age ceremony."

That was not the full story, she was sure, but Ciara did not expect Eirik to share confidences with her. She was sister to one who had proven himself enemy.

"Did you know you were a dragon?" Were there more among the Éan?

Perhaps, as misguided as her brother and his friends were, they had reason to be worried about the Éan's power. Though such worries still would not justify hunting other Chrechte and killing them like animals in the forest.

"Until I shifted into a dragon for the first time seven years ago, the Éan believed the dragon to be myth."

"When you killed my br . . . when you saved your cousin?" she amended, a sick feeling sending chills over her and then she shook her head. No, he'd said he discovered his dragon at his coming-of-age ceremony.

Eirik looked oddly at her.

"Never mind. My mind is muddled. I am tired." So very tired, but sleep eluded her night after night.

He turned away, looking toward the near-full moon that pulled her toward the change. "That *was* the first time I killed as a dragon."

"You didn't know what your fire would do." She did not know how she was so certain, but she was.

"I had an idea." His tone mocked her.

"Yes, but you had not yet learned to control it," she guessed.

"I cast fire only when I want to," he said, affronted.

Warriors. They could be so sensitive. "No doubt, but you had to learn how to cast less and more depending on what was needed in defense of your people."

He turned back to face her again, a strange expression in his dragon's eyes. "You think the fire is so easily manipulated, that a mere man might only cast a little if he wants to?"

"No, but a man who is a dragon also? Yes." Chrechte had to learn to control other gifts, why not fire?

"You know nothing."

"Or you do not know as much as you think you do." He might be prince of his people, but he was only eight years older than her nineteen years. She'd heard Niall saying so to Guaire.

"I am the dragon. I know."

"You controlled your fire enough not to set the forest ablaze," she pointed out.

He didn't reply and she wondered if he'd even been aware of exerting such precise control at the time.

"I may be merely a wolf, but I had to learn to mask my scent, to control my urge to shift, to hunt and to stifle my desire to kill when the wolf rules my form. It took a lot of practice to catch prey and not kill it." And she was beginning to suspect that no matter how well trained a warrior and raven, Eirik's dragon was still wild.

"Why would you practice such a thing?"

"Because a wolf must know the power of her jaw and fangs if she is to be safe around cubs." Perhaps the ravens did not understand this, not being birds of prey, but surely the eagles among them had to train for such control.

"The children of the Éan are safe with me."

"You don't cast fire around them, but what if you did? Could you stop them from being hurt?"

"I didn't hurt Fidaich or Canaul that day, did I?"

"No. The only one that hurt a child that day was Luag." How she hated to say the foul man's name, even if he was dead.

"If your brother had given you to him in marriage, this Luag would have hurt you, too."

By the sacred stone. And they accused women of gossiping. Warriors were worse than grandmothers for sharing everyone's business. "You've been speaking to Lais."

"He remembers you and your brother. He said Galen changed after your father died, though he thought your father might have shared Rowland and Wirp's beliefs."

"He did."

Memories of her father were not comforting ones in light of her brother's death and how it came to pass.

And Galen *had* meant to give her to Luag. She'd known it as a frightened girl and she could not erase that knowledge now, no matter how much she might wish to. She reminded herself that her adopted family seemed content for her to remain unwed, never pressing her to take a mate. Still a film of sweat broke out between her breasts and down her back as old fears assailed her.

Refusing to give in to them, Ciara moved toward the rosebushes, Abigail's favorite part of the garden. Ciara inhaled deeply of their fragrance to calm herself, to remind herself the past was just that. Done and over.

"I am sorry."

There was no deceit in Eirik's scent. The only thing

was, she didn't know what the dragon regretted . . . her brother's change or his death.

"Me, too," Ciara said, meaning both.

Eirik moved closer, his big body coming between her and the rosebushes. "You left the party early."

"So did you." Ciara found herself not only unable to back away but fighting a near-uncontrollable urge to step closer.

"I followed you."

"Why?" But she knew.

His spicy Chrechte scent and arousal eclipsed even the strong aroma of the roses.

His eyes burned with a desire unlike anything that had ever been directed at her. "You know why."

"No."

"Yes." His big hands cupped her face. "There is something about you, Ciara of the Sinclairs. Something I cannot deny."

"I am nothing special." Just a shell of a femwolf, her heart as good as dead inside her.

"I do not agree."

"Even though I did not protect your cousin and his friend?"

"You meant to."

"But you said . . ."

"You were barely more than a child yourself. It was seven years ago, but sometimes I forget that."

"I do as well."

"Let me help you forget all of it, for a little while."

She had never believed anyone could help her, but this Chrechte dragon?

He could make her forget how to shift into a wolf.

"Yes."

Chapter 4

Teach not thy lip such scorn, for it was made for kissing, lady, not for such contempt.

—SHAKESPEARE

Eirik smiled, his white teeth glinting in the moonlight.

That smile made Ciara's thighs clench in a way she did not understand, her belly feel hollow. She lifted her hands to press against his as they held her face.

Just that small touch went through her with the power of a lightning bolt. And finally she understood how the broken tree could continue to live after its brush with lightning. It craved that touch again, so it had to go on.

His thumbs brushed her cheeks. "You are beautiful."

"Thank you," she whispered, not knowing what else to say.

"You are going to taste so good."

"I am?" He was going to taste her? Is that how kissing between men and women worked?

Remembering some of the kisses she'd witnessed between the laird and Abigail, Ciara thought maybe it was.

"Aye," he said in a tone that made her inside swirl with molten lava as he lowered his head, and then his mouth covered hers.

Lips gentle but masterful tasted of mead and something else that could only be her dragon. More potent than *usquebagh*, whiskey only the warriors were supposed to drink, the kiss inundated Ciara's every sense.

She could only taste Eirik. No other scent reached her sensitive nose. His drowned out even the pungent aromas of the garden. The air around her was filled with his warmth, despite the chill of night. Her skin craved more contact than the kiss and yet that was enough to make her more lightheaded than her lack of sleep or eating could do. She could only hear his harsh breaths, his strong dragon's heartbeat that had increased in tempo with every second of the kiss.

Wanting more of the nectar of his lips, Ciara's wolf whined for her to open her mouth. Her instincts driving her, she did and the dragon took immediate advantage. Sliding his tongue inside, he gave her what she craved while challenging her to do the same.

She was helpless to deny him, tasting, being tasted, kissing so deeply the intimacy of it overwhelmed her.

Never had she been so physically connected to another person. His arousal pushed at her, demanding acknowledgment her body was helpless to deny.

Her nipples hardened almost painfully, her own scent revealing changes in her no human man would detect. But Eirik's growl against her lips told her that he knew . . . and liked it.

Moving his hands from her face to her hips, he pulled her flush to him so she felt the rigidity that proved his own need. He wanted her. She wanted him. It was incredible, this desire between them.

He was amazing. So big . . . so strong. Even stronger than a wolf. That should have frightened her; she'd seen what the dragon could do, but all she felt was riotous desire. Her hands slid down his smooth but rigidly muscled chest.

He'd worn a shirt to latemeal, but discarded it when he and the other warriors were dancing. His skin was so hot, but she found she craved that heat. She explored each dip and ripple of muscle, her hands unable to stay still once they started.

He devoured her mouth, the predator in him demanding a submission her lips were only too happy to give.

The kiss went on and on until she felt as if she would fall if he did not hold her up. The pleasure was beyond anything she had known. Never in all her life had she felt so close to her wolf, so intimately connected with another and so very alive.

It was the last thought that had her tearing from his arms and gasping for air to calm the heat of her body.

No. She could not do this. She could not risk these feelings.

"What is wrong?" He looked around, his body tense for confrontation. "There is no one near. I would know."

If only it were that simple. She would much rather fear another rather than herself. "I cannot do this."

"This?"

"You know."

"It was just a kiss."

"That . . ." She swung her hand wildly as if pointing to what they had just done. *"That was not just anything."*

"I'm glad you think so." Sounding far too satisfied, he came toward her.

But this time she showed her intelligence and backed up. When he did not stop, she put her hand up, warding him off. "No. Please."

"What is the matter, Ciara?"

"I do not want a mate."

"I wasn't offering to claim you."

That stopped her short. "Sex constitutes a claiming."

"We weren't having sex, we were kissing." And his scent told her he wanted to continue doing so. "Besides, the Éan do not recognize that stricture."

"Talorc is laird of this clan."

"He is not lord over my people though."

Ciara felt like she was drowning, her fear at what his words implied was so great. "Do you plan to murder Talorc as you did my brother?"

She could not believe she had phrased her concern that way. It had not been her intention to make such an accusation again. Not after her talk with Lais. Certainly, Eirik was not happy about it. All arousal in the air disappeared as fury so great it was more than a scent, she could actually taste it on the air, replaced it.

Eirik's scowl condemned her in a way no one had ever done, not even him when he accused her of not protecting the Éan children. But he did not answer her question.

"Please." Ciara tugged at her pleats, the heart that was supposed to be stone feeling ripped open in her chest. "He is the right laird for this clan. You cannot take that from him. You cannot take him from us."

"Talorc is my friend." Eirik's voice dripped with disgust.

"Friends have killed friends before."

"I only answer because of your very obvious fear, but know this, I will not tolerate you seeding doubts among the clan along these lines." The ice in his tone chilled her.

But not enough that she would not press for answers. "So, tell me you don't want to be clan leader."

"I do not."

After several seconds of silence, she realized he wasn't going to add anything to that simple statement. But truthfully, he did not need to. His sincerity was as apparent as his desire had been earlier.

"Thank you," she whispered.

"Make no mistake, woman, my loyalty is to Talorc, not the little femwolf he calls daughter but has not the decency to even call him by name. I do not need *your* thanks."

With that he left.

She'd meant to push him away. She could admit that to herself. Her worry had been real, but the way she'd phrased it had been inflammatory and the dragon had caught fire and burned her.

'Twas for the best. Truly.

Only, why was there pain when she was working so hard to save herself from it?

A minute later she was joined by another of the Éan and she knew that despite Eirik's disgust of her, he had been unwilling to leave a woman alone and unprotected outside at night.

Ciara sighed. "Hello, Lais."

"Eirik sent me to stay with you until you returned to the keep."

Just as she'd thought, but why did the knowledge make her heart, that stupid organ that was supposed to be hardened to stone, twinge? "I've spent many an evening out here by myself."

"Does your laird know that?"

Probably not, so she forbore answering.

A shadow in the sky had Ciara turning her head. The dragon flew away from the keep, his dark scales barely discernable in the darkness. Her hand lifted involuntarily in a silent entreaty she was powerless to prevent.

"He is amazing, is he not?" Lais asked.

Amazing? Yes. Awesome. Incredible. And very, very frightening, but she was no longer sure that was merely because the huge creature could cast fire and end a man's life in the span of a heartbeat.

"He is very angry with me."

Lais snorted. "Oh, aye."

"It's probably for the best." She hadn't meant to say that aloud.

What was the matter with her? In a sennight, she had lost the control she'd fought so hard for these past seven years. She did not want these desperate feelings Eirik elicited in her. She would prefer not to feel at all, because emotions of that depth were dangerous . . . very, very dangerous.

They frightened her as even his enraged beast could not do.

"You think so?" Lais asked with apparent interest.

She shrugged.

"You remind me of the laird when you do that."

"We are not related by blood."

"I know."

But he called her daughter and she was too selfish and frightened to name him father. Eirik's parting shot had pierced the armor around her heart and Ciara wanted to scream at him because of it. She gave as much as she could;

she really did, but she would not risk ever feeling the kind of pain that had so nearly destroyed her seven years ago.

Barr had suggested she leave her clan for a reason. Ciara had stopped eating the day she found her mother's dead body. She'd stopped sleeping, too . . . and barely spoke.

Abigail and Laird Talorc had coaxed Ciara back into life, such as it was. She owed them so much, but she could not give them unfettered love. She had none left inside her dead heart.

Ciara did not wish to think what it would mean to her sanity if her heart was not as dead as she had believed.

These thoughts got her nowhere. Instead of focusing on her own shortcomings or the unequal relationship she had with her adopted family, Ciara needed to turn her attention onto something else.

"So, the dragon prince is your friend." Right. Discussing Eirik was such a great improvement over thinking about him.

Did she have no control at all over what came out of her mouth?

"He accepted me when others questioned my motives, helped to heal me when I thought naught could so."

"With the Éan's sacred stone?" Had her brother been right? Did the Éan still have possession of their sacred stone?

Lais jerked as if startled. "What do you know of the *Clach Gealach Gra*?"

So it was called the moon's heart stone. As fitting as the wolves naming theirs the wolf's heart. And his words had certainly not been a denial of its existence.

"I know only that each of the Chrechte peoples once had them." She looked up into the sky, searching for a glimpse of her dragon. The dragon. Not *hers*. Never could Eirik be hers. "The old stories say that the stones can be used to connect with God and his creation in the coming-of-age ceremony to bring gifts beyond the great one bestowed in our ability to share nature with an animal."

"I had thought all Faol ignorant of the sacred stones."

Which meant Barr and Laird Talorc had never heard the

old stories telling of the wolves' sacred stone, or if they had, the stories had been dismissed as legend. Much as those of the Éan once were.

"What else do the ancient stories of the Faol say?" Lais asked, his curiosity almost urgent.

"That when a member of the family of the stone—the royal family—touches it, the sacred stone can do other miraculous things like healing."

"I thought what happened to me a miracle."

"I'm sure it was, but not a miracle that could not happen for another of the Chrechte given the right circumstances." At least that was what Galen had told her.

"The wolves have no such stone."

"You are so sure of this."

"The Faol would not have given up such a treasure if they had it."

"Our ancient coming-of-age ceremonies were violent, filled with a sexual aspect the modern clansmen would not find so easy to stomach, I think. Perhaps we gave up the stone when we gave up our ceremonies."

"Perhaps. Or mayhap MacAlpin stole the stone like he stole the throne of Scotland from his relatives."

It was as plausible a supposition as any Galen had put forth, Ciara supposed. "Some Faol believe it was stolen by the Éan and that they hid it but have forgotten over the centuries where."

"Faol like Wirp and Luag, you mean."

Feeling chastised though Lais had not actually said anything against her, Ciara nodded. "Aye, men like that."

"More like there never was a sacred stone for the wolves. What need would such powerful shifters have for extra gifts?"

The *Faolchú Chridhe* existed, but she wasn't going to tell Lais so. Then she would have to explain how she knew and she was not ready yet to share that secret. When she did, she was determined to do so with the man who called her daughter.

'Twould only be right.

* * *

Eirik spun and kicked out, connecting solidly with the Sinclair's thigh.

The Chrechte laird stumbled but did not go down. "You'll teach that move to our soldiers."

"Naturally."

They spent each morning in mock combat with one another before training the Sinclair soldiers (human, Faol and Éan) together. Eirik had discovered the predator's approach to fighting different than that of the raven. Both were effective, but together were devastating to their foe.

As even the most elite soldiers realized when they faced either their laird or the Éan prince in mock battle.

"Ciara has changed since you arrived." The Sinclair's fist connected with Eirik's left shoulder.

Eirik went with it, lifting his right arm to block the next blow, but his movements were near as disjointed as his thoughts. He did his best to hide the temporary effect the laird's words had on him with a practiced sequence of moves that ended with Eirik's arm around the laird's throat. "Having new members is bound to shake the clan up a little."

"Aye." Talorc broke Eirik's hold with a sneaky move of his own. "But new blood, new ways, they can be good for our people."

They fought in silence broken only by the sound of flesh hitting flesh for several minutes before finally breaking apart and facing one another in preparation for the next bout.

"Wouldn't you agree?" the Sinclair asked.

And Eirik had to think quickly to remember the laird's last words. "Yes."

"Ciara's change is particularly welcome." Talorc gave Eirik a look he could not quite read.

"Good." But Eirik did not think the laird would be as happy with the events of the night before.

The kiss that should not have happened, the sexual desire

that had flared hotter than dragon's fire between Eirik and Ciara.

The two warriors moved closer, circling each other. Eirik was watching for any opportunity as he knew Talorc was as well.

Finally, the Sinclair swept his foot out with a wolf's speed to try to trip Eirik. "When Ciara came to live with us, she barely ate, spoke only occasionally and never, ever smiled."

Eirik was no wolf though. He was not even purely raven. He was dragon. Jumping over the swiftly moving foot, he used the momentum to gain a short distance from the other warrior. Enough space to land a solid kick.

He kicked out with his right leg, while leaping forward to land an openhanded blow against Talorc's head. "She seems fine now."

The Sinclair avoided the kick and moved so that the blow was glancing, while bringing his own arm up toward Eirik's chin. "She has nightmares and barely sleeps. She's stopped eating again."

The blow landed, knocking Eirik's head back as the older man's words sunk in. "And you claim she is doing better since my arrival?"

"Yes. The dreams and lack of sleeping started before you came; Abigail and I feared Ciara would become a ghost among us again, but she has not." The laird stopped fighting in order to meet Eirik's eyes. "Since her family's deaths, Ciara has held her emotions so close, there are times she seems not to feel anything at all."

"And yet you treat her as your daughter."

"The first day she came into my keep and I looked in her eyes I saw pain unlike anything I had seen before. She hid it after that, but I never forgot it was there. She does not have to call me father for me to know I am hers. One day, she will realize this as well."

Eirik felt regret for his words the night before, but the woman he knew was not lacking emotion at all. She was filled with anger. Toward him.

Perhaps it was time to tell Talorc the truth of Ciara's brother's death.

Ciara had lost her peaceful sanctuary on top of the towers, so she sought her next favorite place of solace—the forest. And solace she did need. She'd done her best to stay out of Eirik's way, but her emotions were in more turmoil than they'd ever been. Busy seeing his people settled in, he seemed just as intent on avoiding her.

That did not stop him from giving her looks that made her thighs clench, her toes curl and her heart pound uncomfortably in her chest whenever he did see her though. He alternated between those heated looks and scowls that let her know he was still angry with her for questioning his intentions toward Laird Talorc.

Knowing the dragon was so disgusted with her did no good at tamping down her own feelings, either. Ciara had never been as aware of her own femininity. Her wolf wanted out to howl, to hunt . . . to mate.

Thankfully, Eirik was not another wolf to recognize the signs, or take advantage of them. It was all she could do to keep her reactions hidden from her adopted family.

It did not help that Ciara was still wavering in her decision to tell Laird Talorc of her dreams.

She berated herself for her indecision. She knew she could trust her laird, but to give the dreams to him was to let go of the last bit of her life she had shared with her brother.

With her mind in such turmoil, Ciara had no choice but to let the beast take over some nights. Unbeknownst to anyone else, she had taken to running in the forest after the others living in the keep were safely asleep.

Ciara had learned that in her wolf form, she could jump from her window to the castle wall, though it did not look possible. Then she would jump the nine feet from the top of the wall to the grass below. While the towers were more than three times that high, the castle wall was tall enough to keep marauders out, but not a determined femwolf in.

She was sleeping no better and disturbing dreams were

plaguing her more than ever before. Worse than the night-mares of her brother's or mother's deaths, were the heated dreams replaying the kiss between her and Eirik.

Some did not end with her pulling away, either.

Those scared her the most.

The only sleep she got was in her wolf form, snuggled up at the base of her favorite tree. It was old, so tall she could not see the top if she looked straight up from the base. So big around, a whole family could live inside its trunk if it were hollow.

A tree that had grown since the beginning of time, or at least since the beginning of the Chrechte in the Highlands— she felt a connection to God and the Chrechte that had lived before her here. It was a special place. Perhaps even a sacred one.

So, she should not have been surprised to find someone else had found sanctuary at its base. A human woman curled against the bark, her body shivering in the cool summer night.

Moved by pity and concern, Ciara padded over in her wolf form and nudged the human female.

The woman flinched and whimpered, but did not scream. She sat up, looking wildly around before letting her gaze settle fully on Ciara.

Pale hair hung down around a face pinched with worry and blue eyes filled with tears. "Please tell me you're the one. The dreams led me here, but if you're not the one, you're probably going to eat me. I don't want to be eaten. I don't think that would be much of an improvement over my father's fists."

Ciara was so shocked by the implication that a Highland man beat his daughter, she barked.

The other woman started, but seemed to try to force herself to relax. She put a trembling hand out as if to shake Ciara's hand, or maybe let the wolf scent her. "My name is Mairi. Please tell me you are a shifter and not a wild wolf."

Ciara's wolf took over, sniffing Mairi's hand. She smelled of herbs, dried blood and fragile human skin, but nothing to give concern.

"My father is a wolf," Mairi continued to prattle. "His first mate was a non-shifting Chrechte like me. My mother. *Please be the wolf I dreamed about.* Father took a Chrechte for his second wife. He and my brother don't think much of me, and neither does his new wife for that matter. I don't have a wolf. They call me weak. Defective. Useless."

The human woman's voice broke on the last words and Ciara had to suppress the urge to growl. The anger growing inside her was not directed at Mairi and Ciara would not have the other woman frightened because of it.

Mairi clearly knew about their people and her scent said her story was true. But Ciara knew from her own experience, deceit could be masked.

Still she nudged the woman to stand. Mairi did, wincing as she gained her feet and Ciara's determination to stay in her wolf's skin faltered.

The scent of dried blood was strong, but so was that of desperation and fear. This human needed help.

Chapter 5

> If you ignore the dragon, it will eat you. If you try to
> confront the dragon, it will overpower you. If you ride
> the dragon, you will take advantage of its might and
> power.
>
> —CHINESE PROVERB

Ciara turned and trotted around the tree so she could
shift. When she came back, Mairi was leaning against the
tree, her face set in misery.

But it transformed with anticipation when she saw Ciara.
"You *are* the one. You're the princess of our people who can
gift me with the ability to be a wolf, with strength to protect
myself."

"I don't know what you mean." She had never heard of
such a thing. Not even in the ancient stories. "Besides, I'm
not a princess. I'm an orphan."

"Oh, no, my dreams do not lie. They led me here, to you.
Only a princess of our people would dare roam the woods
alone at night, unafraid of what might be lurking in the
shadows."

"You are alone."

"But I'm scared spitless." Mairi nodded as if to rein-
force the claim, though her scent did that well enough, fear
and fatigue coming off her in waves. "If I had any choice, I
would not be out here; you can be assured of that."

"You need help. You will find sanctuary with my clan."

"If your clan takes me in, my father will consider it an act of war. He will insist on my return."

"This same father whose fists have driven you into the forest alone and unprotected?"

Shame tinted Mairi's cheeks. "Yes."

"Your father's dishonor is not yours."

"If I could shift—"

"He would find another reason to hurt you. Men like him always do." She thought of Luag and what kind of man he would be now if he had lived. Her reflection sent a shiver of old dread down her spine.

Ciara would help Mairi, whatever it took.

But the talkative yet frightened woman was shaking her head as if reading Ciara's thoughts. "I . . . it wouldn't be right . . . I can't put your clan at risk."

"Our laird will not fear the wrath of a man who takes his anger out on his own daughter."

"He says I am stupid, that it's my fault," Mairi admitted as if telling a horrible secret about herself, not her abominable father. "My father says I make him too angry to hold back his fists."

"He can't be much of a Chrechte if he cannot control himself any better than that. And you cannot be so stupid if you made it all the way to this part of the Sinclair lands without being discovered before now." They were only an hour's walk from the keep, much too close for any but a truly clever woman to have traveled without detection.

Mairi shook her head, wincing as she did so. "I think perhaps your father was a very special man."

"Yes, he is."

"You said you were an orphan."

"The Sinclair and his lady adopted me when the last of my family was lost to me."

"He won't want to make an enemy of my father." Mairi's voice was heavy with defeat. "Father is a laird and very powerful."

Ciara would have none of it. "You do not know Talorc of the Sinclairs. There is no laird in the Highlands that he fears."

Laird Talorc respected the Balmoral and his old second-in-command Barr, currently acting laird of the Donegals, but he feared no man, wolf or even dragon. It went without saying that no English baron or Lowland Scotland laird would intimidate him, either.

"I have heard of the Sinclair. 'Tis why I came to his holding and not another." Mairi's expression showed awe and a desperate hope Ciara understood too well. "Many fear him and his brother by marriage, the Balmoral."

"And rightly they should."

"You do not fear him though?" Mairi asked warily.

"No. He does not prey on those weaker than him."

"That is good." Though Mairi still didn't sound entirely convinced and Ciara could not blame her. To be hurt by the one who was supposed to protect you had to have destroyed her trust in all who would have authority over her.

She whispered, "I wish I did not fear my father. My brother is not afraid of him."

"Your father has broken the ancient laws of our people. Chrechte do not beat their children." Though clearly some did. It made Ciara's stomach knot with tension.

Mairi frowned. "I have heard my father say that the old laws don't matter any longer, that the Faol have to make a new way."

Laird Talorc and the secret council Ciara was not supposed to know existed would want to hear that. A pack leader who dismissed their oldest tenets to live by was a danger to them all, Faol and Éan alike.

Grief now mixed with pain and fear in Mairi's scent and Ciara felt empathy for her. She knew the pain of accepting that the one you looked up to most in the world lacked what all Chrechte deemed of greatest importance—honor.

"Your father is part of the secret group determined to eradicate the Éan, isn't he?" Ciara was guessing, but it just made sense.

A Chrechte so twisted he would hurt his only daughter was a man who would entertain unreasonable prejudices as well. And that *new way for the Faol* business just sounded too much like something Luag would have said to Galen.

"How did you know?"

"I didn't, but I suspected." She reached out and touched the other woman in comfort. "I have known others of like mind."

"They want to kill all the Éan and say that the Faol cannot thrive until they are the only Chrechte left. My father hunts often, but once a month, he and others go hunting and it is not for game to feed the clan."

Memories made Ciara clench her jaw so words would not come out.

"He wants the *Faolchú Chridhe*," Mairi whispered.

"No," Ciara practically shouted. "The sacred stone would not be safe in his foul hands."

"You are right." Mairi's expression turned even more miserable. "He wants its power to overthrow Scotland's king."

"How does he know of the sacred stone's existence?"

Mairi's eyes glistened with tears. "My mother had the sight. She told him everything she saw, including her dreams of the *Faolchú Chridhe* and the power that can be drawn through it."

Mairi's voice softened when she mentioned her dam, but it was evident that she did not approve her mother's choice to share such sacred things with a man like her father.

"She was deceived by her loyalty to her husband," Ciara comforted the other woman.

Mairi nodded. "But he had no loyalty to her."

"I am sorry." The words felt inadequate, but Ciara had no others.

"He wanted more children, a son, but my mother miscarried with her two pregnancies after me. The last one when I was six summers. She drowned in the loch she did our washing in two months later."

Was Mairi saying her father had killed her mother?

"He knew." Mairi said it like she'd had too much drink and Ciara realized the woman's condition was worsening.

"What did he know?" she asked as she tried to ease the human woman to the ground.

But Mairi fought Ciara's efforts, remaining standing against the tree. "He knew that to have more children, he had to bed another and he could not do that while my mother lived. She was his true mate."

Ciara's stomach roiled at the implications. For a Chrechte to kill his mate was anathema to even the worst among their people. "You realized this so young?"

"No, but later, I knew and I hated him for it, even before he learned of my deficiency, that I am not wolf."

Ciara had no words of comfort for something so evil.

"I have it, too, the sight, but I never told him." Mairi sounded pleased by her deception.

And well she should be.

Ciara asked, "Not even to stop the beatings though?"

"No. It would not have been worth it. I would not help him in any of his plans."

"You are strong of mind and spirit." Ciara's voice was warm with approval and she hoped the other woman heard it.

"For a human, you mean."

"For anyone. I told my brother about my dreams and he would have misused the *Faolchú Chridhe* for his own gain." And that was Ciara's own shame to bear.

It was Mairi's turn to extend comfort and she did. "It was not wrong of you, to trust the one you loved."

Ciara wished she could believe that. "His ignorance cost him his life." It was the first time she'd admitted it aloud.

"I'm glad you can finally acknowledge that."

Both women jumped at the sound of Eirik's deep masculine voice, but Ciara felt more than shock. A lot more.

Even the gravity of her talk with Mairi could not diminish Ciara's instant reaction to the prince's presence.

Ciara spun to face him. He stood as naked as she in the moonlight, both having left their clothes behind to shift into their animal forms apparently. She could not help letting her gaze slide down his body where it snagged on the quite impressive protuberance from between his legs.

He was physically prepared to mate and against all logic and her will, her body throbbed in response.

"As flattering as your interest is, *faolán*, now is not the time to pursue it."

He called her *little wolf*? Arrogant warrior! She might

be smaller than he, but she was no babe in arms. However, her wolf preened at the endearment, snapping for a chance to come forth and scent the dragon.

Ciara gritted her teeth and fought her feral nature with all her considerable will. "Do not mistake curiosity for interest."

Even if her own wolf wanted to do so.

He laughed, his head thrown back, his body showing no signs of losing its own *interest*. "You are a spitfire, but I am no fool. Say what you like, your body tells the truth."

Why did she find it so difficult to mask her scent around this man? What had become ingrained habit for her flew the way of the sparrow seeking warmer climes for the winter when he came near. Her body betrayed her in ways it never did with others, not since she'd taken to hiding her thoughts and emotions so long ago behind a façade of unperturbed calm.

It was the only way to allay Abigail's potent concern and Laird Talorc's rough brand of compassion.

"What are you doing here?" Ciara demanded, ignoring Eirik's claim and hoping he would let the matter drop.

"You run at night, alone in the woods." The censure in his tone would have done their laird proud. "It is not safe."

"So, you've been watching over me?" Why would the dragon do such a thing?

She did not need a protector, nor did she need to know he saw himself as such. Her wolf and feminine instincts both found that possibility far too appealing.

"Aye."

"I don't believe you." His appearance tonight had to be happenstance. "I would have noticed."

It was not as if a dragon flying overhead in the sky could be so easily overlooked.

He rolled his eyes as if reading her thoughts. "A raven is not so easy to detect."

Oh, of course. Her mind was too muddled with lack of sleep and meeting up with injured women in the forest.

Still, the raven watching her rather than the dragon did

not explain everything. "Why not expose my behavior if you disapproved of it so much?"

"Who is this?" he asked, indicating Mairi and ignoring Ciara's query altogether.

For some reason, Ciara found herself moving between the two to block Mairi's view of the Éan shifter in all his naked glory. "A human woman seeking sanctuary."

Mairi made a sound that could be taken for disagreement.

"You do not want sanctuary from the Sinclair?" Eirik asked, sounding nonplussed.

Ciara would have hugged Mairi for confusing the bossy dragon except to do so would probably cause pain for the other woman.

"I do not wish to cause war between the two clans, but there are facts I must make your laird aware of. When the Sinclair realizes the likely consequences of taking me in, I'm sure he won't offer sanctuary. But perhaps I could see my hurts tended to?"

"I told you, Laird Talorc will not fear your father." And Ciara wasn't letting Mairi go back to the evil Chrechte, not ever.

That settled in her own mind at least, she turned on Eirik. "You should leave."

"You need my help if you hope to get the human woman into the keep this night to have her injuries tended to."

Ciara opened her mouth to deny it, but then snapped it shut. She could go to the gatehouse and call for the bridge to be let down. Only if she did that, everyone would know she'd been outside the walls at night against the laird's orders. The night guards would be punished for her actions.

Laird Talorc would look a fool to the clan because others would see the situation as Ciara successfully defying him . . . once again, when that had not been her intention at all. She never would have left the keep if she'd thought there was even a remote chance she would be caught outside the walls.

It was just that her dreams drove her beyond endurance.

Regardless, Ciara could not ignore Mairi's plight. The other woman was in far too fragile a state to risk waiting for morning to sneak back inside the keep.

"How are you going to help us?" Even as Ciara asked the question, she realized the answer and was shaking her head in absolute denial. "No. No. No. We are not two small children to ride the back of your dragon."

Had wolves been meant to fly, God would have given them wings. Yes, he would.

She remembered her reaction when the dragon had snatched her right out of the air and from certain death. She'd fainted.

"Do you have a better idea?"

She was trying to think of one when Mairi crumpled to the ground. Ciara dropped to her knees beside the injured woman, grateful when she felt the rise and fall of Mairi's chest against her hand. But the other woman's breathing was shallow and the mottling of bruises around her neck and face hinted she could be injured far worse where her plaid covered her.

What kind of man did this to his daughter?

Ciara brushed Mairi's pale hair back from her face. "We have to get her back to the keep. Now."

"Yes."

There was no help for it, but that didn't mean Ciara had to like it. Wolves ran. They jumped, even great distances. But they did not fly.

She, however, was about to. Again. She could only hope this time that she kept her wits about her.

Ciara turned her head toward Eirik. "Shift into your dragon. I'll lift her onto your back and then climb on behind her to keep her from falling."

Was she really going to ride the dragon that had cast fire and killed her brother?

Looking down at the unconscious woman beside her, Ciara could only find one answer inside her heart.

Yes.

Eirik shifted right there, with a flash of crimson light and a low dragon's growl. At least as fast as any wolf shifter

Ciara had ever seen, and quicker than most, the transformation from man to dragon was over in seconds.

Eirik's beast was magnificent and *huge*. Much bigger close-up than he had seemed in the sky (and he'd been plenty imposing then), the red dragon stood half again as tall as a laird's warhorse and easily twice as long. His wings spread out with a whoosh of air that sent Ciara's hair flying around her face as he stood on his back legs.

And, if it were possible, he looked even more massive like this.

Familiar amber eyes surveyed Ciara and the unconscious Mairi. Were dragons as cognizant of their human counterparts as wolves?

There was no reason to believe otherwise, but the sense of feral strength coming from Eirik the dragon was immense. And still, Ciara felt no fear. Far from it.

She *should* be terrified; she knew what destruction this beast could do, but all she felt was awe and this ridiculous inescapable enchantment to be in his presence.

'Twas not right. Mythical creature of magic or not, this beast had killed her brother, even if it had not been murder.

However, her wolf refused to see Eirik as enemy. She wanted to roll on her back and show belly, but not out of mere recognition of the more powerful predator. Oh, no. That would be too simple and easy to ignore. Her wolf craved the dragon's touch, it wanted to be nuzzled, scented and *accepted*.

That was *never* going to happen.

Ciara fought her wolf's urges even as she considered the problem at hand. "How am I going to get Mairi onto your back?"

He moved, his body shockingly agile for so great a beast, and simply picked Mairi up in his forearms.

As much as Ciara knew the other woman needed his help, the sight of Mairi in Eirik's arms made Ciara's wolf howl inside her. The wolf insisted this was not right. Another woman should not be held so carefully against Eirik's massive crimson-scaled chest.

Ciara ignored her Faol instincts and took a step back. "I'll shift into my wolf and run back to the keep then."

Eirik shook his great head and gave a growl that couldn't be taken as anything but a very adamant negative. If she was still in doubt, the way his tail whipped out, wrapped around her waist and tugged her toward him was enough to make his thoughts on the subject known.

She pushed at the living rope surrounding her to no avail. "We don't have time to argue. I don't know how injured Mairi is. We've got to get her to Abigail."

Ciara had to fight both the urge to simply caress his tail and learn the feel of the dragon's scales close-up, and the overwhelming sense of safety this odd embrace gave her.

Eirik nodded, his determined amber gaze telling her he agreed, but that they were going to do things his way.

Stubborn dragon prince.

"I know you think I need you watching over me, but I am perfectly safe in the forest."

He growled and shook his head, his tail tightening its hold on her. His warmth surrounded her like a shield and she wanted to relax, rest here where she felt safe enough to sleep, when she *never* felt that safe anymore.

Could the dragon protect her dreams? 'Twas a whimsical if very tempting thought. And she dismissed it.

"You are bossy, you know that, right?"

A dragon's shrug moved its wings and once again a soft wind caressed her face. Ciara found it so ridiculously endearing, an unwilling smile curved her lips when really, she wanted to frown. "Arrogant beast."

The chuff that came from his mouth could be naught but laughter.

"How am *I* to get on your back then? I am not a bird. I cannot fly." And the thought of scrambling up his huge body as the boys had done that day so long ago in the forest was not in the least appealing.

Eirik shook his head and chuffed again. And then, without warning, she found herself being lifted off the ground.

An embarrassing squeak came out of her mouth before she clamped it shut. And the tip of his tail caressed her back as if to soothe her. Darn it if she did not indeed feel soothed.

Annoying dragon know-it-all.

He set her standing on his massive thigh, his legs bent to make a step of sorts. And she found herself doing exactly what she'd sworn not to, climbing up his back like a child in a tree. He positioned his wings so she could use one to hold onto as she moved up his back.

His scales were warm and not exactly slick, but they were smooth. Still, with his tail against her back and his wings nearly closed around her, she was in no danger of slipping. When she settled against his neck, she draped her legs on either side, resting them against where his wings joined his shoulders. She curled her arms around his neck, her fingers locked but careful not to choke him.

It was as secure a spot as she could hope for in order to ride the mythical beast.

Ciara felt the muscles under her thighs bunch and knew Eirik was getting ready to leap into the sky.

'Twas just like riding a horse. She nodded to herself. Yes. That was it.

So, she was a great deal farther from the ground than when she rode even the biggest horse in the stable. It did not matter. It would not be so bad.

Eirik took a couple of running steps and then leapt upward.

"A horse. Just like a horse," she muttered over and over to herself.

But horses did not fly, no more than wolves.

And Eirik was still rising in the sky with Mairi in his arms and Ciara on his back, his great wings creating a powerful draft below them. Ciara peeked around his neck to look down. Her grip on the dragon's neck tightened. They flew well above the tops of the trees . . . trees so tall she could barely see their tops from the ground.

But the terror that had sparked in her at the thought of flight did not show itself now that she was high in the sky on a dragon's back. Exhilarated rather, the sense of enchantment returned.

She was flying and it was magnificent! She wanted to shout her glee, but worried she might draw attention to them and then decided they were too far from the ground for her voice to carry to anyone below.

She threw her head back and laughed. Thoroughly captivated, she laughed as she had not since she was a small child. The dragon's head came up and he bugled, a sound that was like bubbled happiness exploding around her.

"It is magical," she shouted, hoping he could hear her through the rushing wind around them. "Wonderful!"

She'd ever believed there could be no greater gift than the ability to share her life with the wolf that shared her soul. But to fly? To see the world from above, to feel the cold wind on her face and the amazing body of a dragon below her? This was a gift beyond measure.

She hugged the dragon's neck and whispered, not sure she wanted him to hear, but certain the words had to be said. "Thank you for this. Thank you."

Chapter 6

He is the best man who, when making his plans, fears
and reflects on everything that can happen to him, but
in the moment of action is bold.

—HERODOTUS

Eirik landed in the area behind the keep that the
Sinclair used to train his elite soldiers. He had waited to
approach until the wall and tower guards were looking
elsewhere and would have waited for a cloud to cover the
moon as well, but the human woman in his arms was too
wounded for such a delay.

Even so, he had been tempted to stay in the air longer just
to experience the joy pouring off Ciara in delicious waves.

She had not wanted to fly but had loved it once they
were in the air. A fearless Chrechte if he had ever met one.

'Twas why he had not been willing to tell Talorc about
Ciara sneaking from the fortress at night. Eirik was too
impressed by her sneakiness and courage.

By happenstance, he had been there the first time she'd
made the jump from her window to the wall. She could not
have known it would work. *He had not believed it would*
and had shifted to his dragon with no hope of catching her
this time before she landed gracefully on the wall walk.
The leap should have not been possible, even for a wolf.

But she'd made it and he had to respect that.

Besides, his raven had enjoyed watching over her as Ciara ran through the forest, a sense of possessive protectiveness usually reserved for family filling him as he flew above her.

Ciara had not liked finding out she'd been watched over, however. Independent *faolán*.

If he were not in his dragon form, he would be smiling as he gently laid the human woman, Mairi, onto the ground. Dragons did not smile though and any attempt to do so would be more frightening than reassuring.

He was unsurprised when Lais stepped out of the shadows. Eirik had called to the healer through the mental link he shared with all the Éan before he ever took flight. As a direct descendant of the first keeper of the *Clach Gealach Gra*, Eirik could communicate with his people at will. He could also hear them when they needed him to, but had been trained to block the attempts as well.

"She has not regained her senses?" Lais asked, already examining Mairi's bruises and scowling over them.

"No," Ciara answered, probably assuming Lais had been talking to her. She squirmed in her perch on Eirik's neck. "I need to get down."

Having her naked body astride him, even in his dragon form, had been a challenge to Eirik's self-control. He could smell her scent, taste her on the air around them and the feel of her thighs against his neck only made him think of what they would feel like wrapped around his body when he was a man.

The desire to shift right now, while she was still astride his beast burned inside him. He forced himself to ignore it; this was not the time to give in to his carnal lusts.

He flicked his tail up to give her something to hold on to as she climbed down while folding his wings back to create a protective shield for her—both so she would not fall and to hide her nakedness from Lais. Were he to look up from his patient, which he showed no signs of doing.

Fortunately for Eirik's temper, she dismounted from the opposite side to where Lais knelt by Mairi. For whatever reason, Eirik's dragon was ready to cast fire at the thought of Lais witnessing Ciara's nudity.

They were Chrechte, damn it. Not the tamed humans among the clans. Eirik was in no way influenced by civilized conventions, but if Lais were to lay eyes on Ciara in all her nude beauty, Eirik was not entirely sure he would be able to control the instincts of the beast.

Lais nodded his head toward a pile of cloth on the ground. "I brought covering for Ciara as you asked."

Eirik hadn't asked, he'd ordered. Nevertheless, he said, *Thank you,* through the mental link before calling forth his human form.

As soon as he had completed the shift, he grabbed light fabric he knew to be one of his shirts and tossed it to Ciara. "Cover yourself."

"Bossy dragon." But her beautiful green eyes still glowed with the happiness she'd experienced in flight and her mouth curved in a sweet smile he wanted to kiss.

She pulled the shirt on quickly. The hem hung down past her knees and in the moonlight it did an adequate job of preserving her feminine modesty. But if he looked closely, he could see her nipples, still hard from the cold air, poking against the thin material.

He was looking closely. Very, very closely. So intently in fact, that he could just make out the juncture of her thighs behind the fall of fabric.

He wanted nothing more in that moment than to rip the damn thing back off again and have his way with the little wolf that hid her caring heart behind a mask of indifference.

Looking at her standing there in his shirt, he had to smile. Compared to him, she was a wee thing, but it was easy to forget that with her fierce spirit.

A spirit the Sinclair insisted that she had kept locked deep inside herself until Eirik's arrival. Eirik thought it was fury at her brother's killer coming to live among her clan that had brought her emotions to the surface.

But unlike Ciara, Talorc had not blamed Eirik for Galen's death, or the subsequent suicide of Ciara's mother. The laird maintained that the feelings Ciara was finally exhibiting did not run along the lines of hatred.

Unwilling to argue the matter, Eirik had left the deluded laird to his illusions.

"And you?" Ciara demanded.

Eirik's brows drew together in confusion. "What?"

"Mairi could wake up any moment."

"Aye, 'twould be a good thing."

"Not while you are still naked," Ciara gritted out.

And Eirik smiled. It pleased him more than it should that the femwolf was apparently afflicted by a strain of un-Chrechte-like modesty on his behalf as well.

She'd made it clear that she was no more interested in finding a mate right now than he was. And though she had finally acknowledged that her brother's death was of Galen's own making, it did not follow that she would ever consider aligning her life with his killer.

If Eirik *were* looking for a mate, which he was not. He had too much to do for his people right now to spend time trying to placate or woo a woman. He could not even be sure a woman existed that he could share his life with, much less one that he could call true mate. He had two natures besides his human one to appease when choosing his lifelong bed partner.

The raven and dragon were often at odds inside him when it came to choosing a course of action. What were the chances they would agree on his mate?

"What has you scowling?" Ciara asked in a teasing tone. "You were smiling just a moment ago."

"Is a near-dead human woman found on Sinclair land not reason enough to frown?" he asked as he donned his kilt.

It was made of the hide from the first boar he had brought down on his own. His aunt had tanned the leather before fashioning a hunter's kilt from it, since his mother had not been alive to do so and his sister had been too busy protecting their people as a full-fledged guardian warrior.

As prince of his people, he had never worn a plaid, not even the weave of muted forest tones the Éan had taken to be their own colors.

He had not decided if joining the Sinclairs would change that fact.

Ciara bit her lip, the happy glow fading from her features, her gaze quickly averting to look at the woman lying in the grass. "We should get her inside. I need to wake Abigail."

"Abigail's healing herbs are a wonder to be sure, but they cannot compare to a Chrechte's gift."

"Lais is a healer?" Ciara's voice had dropped low in wonder. "I thought only the sacred stones could be used to heal."

Eirik grabbed her shoulders and spun her to face him squarely. "What do you know of the *Clach Gealach Gra*?"

She rolled her eyes, not in the least impressed by his angry demand. Which, considering the fear she had shown toward him thus far, was some kind of miracle. "Lais asked me the same thing."

Eirik tossed a look of censure toward his people's healer that went unnoticed. "Did he?"

Lais had paid Eirik no heed, but Ciara nodded. "You act like only the Éan have ever heard the stories of the ancient Chrechte and their ways."

"The Faol tell stories of the *Clach Gealach Gra*?" None of the wolves the Éan had taken into their confidence had mentioned this.

Ciara looked at him as if wondering at his sanity. "The world does not begin and end with the Éan, Master Dragon. There are other Chrechte in the world and they have their own pasts, though there is no doubt that at one time they intertwined."

"Do not say that aloud."

"That the Chrechte share a common history so long ago none of us can be sure of the truth and the myth in our ancient stories?"

"Do not mention my other form," he said through gritted teeth.

She rolled her eyes. Again. "You really think you are going to keep your secret from the clan with the way you go flying off in your dragon form when you get into a snit?"

"I do not have snits." And he had never taken his dragon form when there was risk of being seen except around her.

She was bad for his secrets and too much a challenge to his self-control.

"Of course not, Your Royal Highness. A *prince* would never admit to something so mundane." Ciara said the word *prince* like another might say *dung*.

But he refused to be drawn. "Do not attempt to change the subject. I asked what you knew of our sacred stone."

"Very little."

"Do not lie."

"I am not." Her eyes threw green daggers at him.

"She can mask her deceit," Lais inserted and then went back to full concentration on his patient.

The daggered look turned onto the once-again-oblivious healer.

Eirik said, "That is not possible."

"Just as it is impossible to turn into a dragon," Ciara said with pure sarcasm. "I'll make a note of that."

"The Sinclair said you were quiet. Biddable."

With an expression of affront, she demanded, "Are you saying I am not?"

"Aye."

She crossed her arms, no doubt having no idea how it impacted the fit of his shirt on her. The action put her lovely breasts into relief, making her dusky nipples press against the thin linen. The hem had drawn up as well, exposing more of her enticing legs.

All of it topped by an expression that tempted him to tame her. "You? Are arrogant."

"And you have yet to admit how you came to know about our sacred stone."

"My brother."

Just mention of the man filled Eirik with fury. "He told you of our stone? Had he plans to steal it?"

"Of course not. He told me the stories of the sacred stones, how they could bestow gifts during the coming-of-age ceremony and be used to heal those of Chrechte decent."

"Like me." The words were spoken in a weak feminine

voice and had both Eirik and Ciara spinning to face Mairi and Lais.

"You are Chrechte?" Eirik asked with disbelief.

The woman had no scent of animal at all.

"My father is."

"But you have no beast."

"She can give me one." Mairi pointed to Ciara. "She is keeper of the *Faolchú Chridhe*."

"The wolves have a sacred stone?" He glared at Ciara.

He would not believe it. What stories had she told this broken human? If it were true, Talorc would have revealed such to Eirik. If not the Sinclair, then Barr. Eirik's brother by marriage would not have kept something so important from him.

Ciara did not meet his eyes, something secretive in her demeanor. "It was lost before we joined the clans."

"But she can find it," Mairi claimed.

The slight wince was barely there on Ciara's face, but he saw it. Had she made the claim to Mairi and not expected to be held accountable for it, or did Ciara not want the Éan to know of her hopes to find the *Faolchú Chridhe*? Did Ciara share her brother's view of the Éan?

"Is this true?" Eirik demanded, wanting more answers than he would ask for. "Never mind. You can mask any lie you tell me. I will ask Talorc."

He turned toward the keep, determined to do just that.

"Wait." Ciara's voice was too urgent to deny.

He stopped, not turning back toward her.

"I have not told him yet." He could hear her moving toward him and then feel her hand on his arm. "Please, let me tell him."

He spun to face the femwolf, knocking her hand away from him with his quick movement. "You have not bothered to tell your laird?"

She shook her head. "I haven't told anyone since Galen. I was afraid to, afraid it would spark the same madness in them."

"You blame your sacred stone for your brother's idiocy?"

"No, I blame his desire to use its power, but I couldn't be sure . . ."

Her lack of trust in Talorc staggered Eirik. "The man believes himself your father," he bit out.

"He is, in all the ways that count, but Galen was my brother, my protector. And still, finding the *Faolchú Chridhe* was more important to him than anything else." Her voice was husky with an old grief, but her eyes glittered with fresh fear.

"Talorc is nothing like your brother."

"I know."

"And still you have not told him of the wolves' sacred stone?"

"I planned to."

"When?"

"Soon."

"Why wait?" He wanted her to admit it, her mistrust of her own father and laird.

"It has great power, temptation for even the most honorable Chrechte. It can call forth the *conriocht*, not just the wolf."

A werewolf? They were myth.

Eirik almost laughed at his own arrogance. He shared nature with a dragon and he doubted the existence of the *conriocht*? A creature that was said to tower over other men and had the snout, fangs and claws of a wolf and the strength of ten men, the *conriocht* would be invincible to all but a dragon.

Though it could not fly.

"So, you would deny this power to your laird, to your fellow Faol."

"Perhaps it was denied us for a reason. The *Faolchú Chridhe* disappeared and while my brother claimed it was stolen by the Éan, I am not so sure. Perhaps the leaders of our people saw the misuse of its power and hid it to stop such a thing from happening again."

"'Tis all conjecture."

She nodded. "It doesn't matter. It wants to be found now and will give me no rest until it is."

"Your dreams."

"What do you know of my dreams?"

"Only that they keep you awake at night. You look as if you sleep less than a mother with twin babes and a new litter of pups to care for at once."

Her shoulders drooped. "I am tired. So very tired."

"Tonight you will sleep. Tomorrow, we speak to the Sinclair."

Her mouth twisted as if she found something darkly funny, but she nodded. "Tomorrow."

Eirik turned back to Lais and Mairi. "Is she well enough to be carried inside yet?"

"She is, though barely. She had many injuries . . . broken bones, bleeding inside, severe bruising in many places. I have healed what I could, but she needs more tending and sleep. I need rest before I can continue." It was obvious Lais did not like admitting the last.

Eirik respected him all the more for doing so and nodded. "I will carry her into the keep."

"No," both his healer and that keeper of secrets, Ciara, said together.

He ignored Ciara to give Lais a questioning look.

"I have enough strength to carry her."

Eirik took in the protective stance Lais had over the human, the way he held his body between her and the other two Chrechte. Even more telling was the fierce light in Lais's brown gaze. The usually even-tempered man looked ready to throw down in battle over the right to transport the broken woman into the keep.

Eirik took a deliberate step backward. *Think long and hard before you take a human woman as a mate,* he said through their mental link. "Take her to Ciara's room," he said aloud.

Mairi would need watching and Ciara, for all her secrets, was the only logical choice. Talorc would not tolerate an unattached male sleeping in the same room as the female, human, or not. So, healer, or no—Lais was out.

That left Ciara.

Who, unsurprisingly, did not argue Eirik's order to have

Mairi carried to her room. For all her attempts to show herself otherwise, she had a caring nature she could not hide.

She followed them into the keep, the still quality of her silence bothering Eirik, though it should not.

She wanted none of him and he wanted nothing of such a deceitful Chrechte. Her reasons for not telling the Sinclair about the *Faolchú Chridhe* would imply Ciara did not share Galen's view of the Éan, but that was only if Eirik accepted as truth those claims.

Her ability to mask her deceit and the secrets she kept meant that he could not accept anything she said so easily.

When they got to her bedchamber, Ciara quickly drew a traditional plaid in the Sinclair colors of blue and black around her. She made pleats with nimble fingers before wrapping the end over his shirt in a diagonal across her chest. She pulled a blanket of the same fabric back on the bed for Lais to lay Mairi down and then stepped back, allowing the healer room to care for his patient.

"I will awaken the laird and tell him of the night's happenings," she said in a subdued voice before quickly leaving the room.

Chapter 7

The greatest good you can do for another is not just to
share your riches but to reveal to him his own.

—Benjamin Disraeli

Ciara retreated to a corner in her own room as it
filled with people.

Laird Talorc and Abigail had both come to meet the
woman Ciara had found in the woods—the laird to assess
the worth of Mairi's plea for sanctuary and Abigail to
assess the condition of her health. Eirik was still there as
well as Lais, who hovered protectively over Mairi.

Ciara could only be grateful that Niall as second-in-
command and Guaire as seneschal had not been called in
as well. Though she had no doubts as to their presence
on the morrow when she revealed her long-held secrets to
Laird Talorc.

"I do not think she would have survived the night if
Ciara had not found her," Lais was telling Abigail as the
gentle woman, who could not hear but read lips, mixed some
herbs in a cup before pouring hot water Ciara had brought
up from the kitchens over them.

"We will have to give thanks for my daughter's disobedience and reckless behavior then." The look Abigail cast Ciara left no question the issue was far from settled, however.

Mairi, on the other hand, met Ciara's eyes with an expression of such gratitude it hurt to see.

Ciara dropped her gaze, uncomfortable with the thanks in the other woman's eyes and heartily wishing Abigail did not have to be disappointed in her again. Ciara had never been the daughter the older woman deserved and she only hoped the girl babe Abigail now carried would make up for Ciara's deficit.

She had not meant to hurt her adopted parents, but the looks in their eyes when she told them how she'd come upon Mairi had reflected pained disappointment. How many times had she seen that look?

First from her father of birth when he spoke of a Chrechte's need for sons, then in her mother's eyes when it was Ciara who would come to comfort her rather than the husband she cried out for in the night. The look of disappointment in Galen's face when they searched for, and did not find, the *Faolchú Chridhe* had grown with each failed attempt.

Then Ciara had come to live with Laird Talorc and Abigail and soon seen that her inability to love them as they deserved as parents caused them grief as well. At least her ability to help with the twins had made up somewhat for her other shortcomings. Until lately.

Once again, she was not what her family needed her to be and did not know how to change that fact without opening herself to far too much pain.

Once Mairi had drunk some of the tea Abigail had prepared, Laird Talorc approached the woman in the bed. "You wear the MacLeod colors."

The words sounded like an accusation and Ciara was not surprised when Mairi flinched. "It is my father's clan."

Ciara felt she should have recognized the predominately yellow plaid. Only, being neither friend nor declared enemy, the MacLeod clan's was not a tartan she had ever seen before.

"You deny your father's family?" Laird Talorc asked, censure still heavy in his voice.

And Ciara did not understand it. Surely he did not blame the young woman from wanting to escape the abuse her body gave evidence to? He had said many times in her hearing that the ancient laws still had value and one of them stated that to prey on those weaker was not the Chrechte way.

"I meant he is laird," Mairi clarified. "But as to him being my family, his clan being mine? I see no benefit to wearing colors that do not protect me."

Ciara admired Mairi's spirit after all she had been through and nodded her head to show her understanding, catching Mairi's gaze as she did so.

Mairi sent her a weak smile of thanks and Talorc turned to glare at Ciara. "You have something to say, daughter?"

Ciara swallowed the lump trying to form in her throat and nodded.

She did not understand her laird's attitude but feared his anger was not directed toward Mairi at all. He was furious with Ciara for being outside the fortress walls and allowing that resentment to spill forth in his dealings with the wounded woman.

Talorc crossed his arms, his stance combative. "Yes?"

"He beat her near to death."

Laird Talorc's expression shifted, twisting into a scowl, his fury rising at her words, rather than abating as she'd intended. But this time, Ciara was positive the object of her laird's fury was not in the room at all.

'Twas the MacLeod he despised so fully.

Still, that did not mean he would give Mairi sanctuary. Though Ciara could not imagine Laird Talorc doing anything else. He would never send the defenseless woman back to the MacLeod to be beaten again.

"When I came here, I had little to offer the clan," she reminded her laird.

He shrugged. "You were grieving."

"I was unresponsive. Angry. Unwilling to be part of the family that had taken me in," she admitted with shame, despairing of ever being able to make up for her lack. "Abigail cried more than once over me."

"Oh, Ciara," Abigail said, proving she had been following the conversation . . . one way or another.

"You never raised your hand to me, though you must have found me very frustrating . . . must still find me a great trial." She whispered the last as she dropped her head, not wanting to see the truth of her words in her father's eyes.

"I have never had the desire to hurt you," Laird Talorc, the only father who had ever wanted *her*, said with quiet vehemence. "And an honorable man does not hurt a child."

"Or someone too weak to protect herself," Ciara said with a glance toward Mairi, who though no longer a child, was in no way strong enough to stand against a Chrechte male.

Talorc made a sound of disgust. "The MacLeod is no honorable Faol. He preys on the weak."

"So, his daughter, who was beaten near to death, she has reason to seek sanctuary with another clan." Ciara raised her head so she could once again meet his eyes.

He was looking at her with a hope she did not understand in this context. "Perhaps."

The word shocked her as she fully expected him to offer Mairi the protection of the Sinclair. "Please."

"Do you entreat me as your laird?" he asked with an expression she hoped she was finally reading aright.

"No, I entreat you as my father, a better father than the MacLeod could ever hope to be." Talorc had earned the title and the praise.

And her love as a daughter, no matter how much it might terrify her to give it. It had always been there, she realized and pretending it wasn't would not make it hurt any less if she lost her second family as she had her first.

Abigail made a sound that Ciara just knew meant she was crying. When Ciara looked at her, the older woman's eyes were indeed spilling tears, but her smile was brighter than the full moon shining through the window.

Ciara felt unwelcome moisture in her own eyes and she turned her head to hide her weakness.

Her father reached out and gently turned it back with a hold on her chin. "It is all right."

She blinked away the moisture. "Is it?"

She had finally admitted she had a family to lose again. It did not feel all right. It felt petrifying.

"Aye, daughter. It is." He gave her a stern look. "Do not think this will get you out of a firm lecture from your mother for sneaking out to run alone at night."

Ciara almost laughed, but the amusement bubbled up to end on an aborted hiccup of sound. "I will not."

"I will give Mairi of the MacLeod sanctuary."

"Wait," the bruised woman said from the bed.

Talorc turned toward her. "You came onto my lands broken from another Chrechte's fists. You sought sanctuary."

"But I would not have you extend it without fully considering the consequences."

"Your father will consider it an act of war." Talorc's tone said it did not matter.

"Yes." Mairi looked away. "He does not value me, but he does value his pride. To have another clan take me in would prick it."

"And for that, he would go to war," Abigail said with clear disgust.

Talorc smiled indulgently at his wife. Eirik caught Ciara's gaze and asked with his eyes if Abigail were truly that naïve. Ciara gave a slight nod of her head. She believed most people good and petty tyrants like the MacLeod the exception rather than the rule.

If she had not been so optimistic, she never would have taken a chance on Talorc of the Sinclairs though and so none of them would ever complain.

The dragon shook his head, the warrior braids at his left temple swinging gently.

"The MacLeod is no ally of the Sinclairs." Talorc's tone implied nor would the man ever be.

"But you are not at war with him," Mairi said, wincing when she tried to move.

Lais jumped forward and laid a hand on her shoulder.

"I could not heal you completely. You must be careful with yourself."

She blushed and nodded, wonder glowing in her blue gaze.

Lais smiled at her, tucking the blankets more firmly around her. "Good girl."

"I am not a girl," Mairi claimed quietly.

Lais's smile heated and Ciara felt she should look away, it was so intimate. "I know," he said, his own tone low and approving.

Eirik smirked. Abigail smiled mistily and Ciara wondered if she'd just seen what she thought she had . . . the birth of a mating.

Her father shook his head, smacking the Éan healer on his shoulder. "I'll preside over the mating so your prince can stand beside you."

Mairi's eyes widened, her mouth opening and closing, but no sound issuing forth.

Lais's smile shifted to a glare he directed first at his friend and then his laird, but he didn't deny the teasing words.

"I don't understand," Mairi finally managed to say in a voice laced with both confusion and trepidation.

"The issue of your sanctuary has been settled," Talorc replied.

"Welcome to our clan," Abigail said in her soft voice.

Mairi gave a soft sob, tears spilling down her cheeks. "Thank you."

Talorc frowned. "'Tis not a thing to cry over."

Mairi swiped at her cheeks. "No, of course not."

"We will leave you to rest." Talorc turned to go, his hand on Abigail's waist to guide her with him.

The tension draining from her features, Mairi's exhaustion became obvious. "Again, my sincerest thanks," she said softly toward the laird's retreating back.

Ciara's father just raised his hand in acknowledgment, guiding Abigail out of the room.

Lais fussed over Mairi a bit more and then turned to Ciara. "You will watch over her?"

"Yes, of course." Ciara's voice came out choked, her throat tight for some reason.

"You will come and get me if she shows any distress."

Ciara nodded, but Mairi frowned.

"I made it all the way from my father's lands to here. I will make it through one night inside the warmth of a keep, sleeping on an actual bed," Mairi said with clear exasperation.

Lais didn't look the least repentant and Mairi just sighed. "I do appreciate you healing me and . . . and . . . well, caring for me."

"It is my pleasure." With that he leaned down and did the unthinkable, placing a tender kiss on the human woman's temple.

The human women among the clans did not allow such liberties, but then nothing about this night was usual, was it? And far from looking offended, Mairi appeared quite happy about Lais's gesture of affection.

Lais left with another glance over his shoulder when he reached the door, but Eirik shoved the other man through. He turned his head toward Ciara. "We will talk with the Sinclair in the morning."

"Yes."

"You will sleep tonight."

Did he really think he could just will it so? She didn't bother to argue though. Ciara merely shrugged, not agreeing, not denying.

He came to her then, his stride purposeful, and then laid his hands on either side of her face. "No dreams tonight."

"Maybe the *Faolchú Chridhe* will listen to you and leave me to rest."

"It will," he said with such confidence, she almost believed him.

"I do not know if I can trust you, Ciara of the Sinclairs, but I will have you rested. You will collapse and be of no use to anyone if you do not."

His words should offend, but they didn't. Why should he trust her? She was nothing to him. "I will do my best."

"See that you do." He withdrew his hands from her and

she felt their loss but managed to stifle her wolf's whimper. "Good night."

"Good night." Hers was whispered as he strode rapidly from the room.

Ciara made a pallet on the floor beside her narrow bed.

Mairi's eyes fluttered. "What are you doing? You cannot sleep on the floor."

"I have furs. I will be fine."

"But . . ."

"The bed is too narrow to share without me worrying I will jostle you in the night." Especially with her nightmares.

"Your sleep is not restful."

"Nay."

"Mine has not been these past six months, either. At first I thought it was because my father planned to give me to one of his soldiers in marriage. The man is unkind and not at all hygienic, but I came to realize that it was the dreams filling me with a sense of dread that will not leave even upon waking."

"The *Faolchú Chridhe* is at risk. It needs to be found." For good or for ill.

"Before it falls into the wrong hands."

Ciara could not think of worse ones than those that had beaten Mairi so mercilessly. "We will discuss it with my father on the morrow."

"Perhaps later in the morning," Mairi said sleepily.

Ciara smiled, snuffed the wall sconce and drew the skin over her window, throwing the room into darkness. "Sleep as late as you can; Abigail says it is good for healing."

Though sleep had never healed Ciara's heart. Perhaps because it was such an elusive thing in her life.

She felt her way to her makeshift bed and crawled into it.

A few moments passed in silence and Ciara thought Mairi had drifted off again, but she was wrong.

"Ciara?"

"Yes?"

"Will you help me find my wolf?"

"I don't know if it is possible."

"It is." Mairi's voice was quiet, but it rang with conviction.

"I am not a princess."

"My dreams said otherwise."

Dreams. She would have grown to hate them, but sometimes her dreams were happy and 'twas the only time she felt true joy.

"Your dreams could be wrong."

"They aren't."

"You're very sure."

"My mother taught me the difference between a seer's dreams and an ordinary one. I *am* sure."

"If I can, I will do it." Ciara could promise no more and considering all that Mairi had risked to come to them, she could do no less.

Eirik waited with the Sinclair and his second-in-command in the great hall for Lais to accompany Ciara and Mairi down the stairs.

Niall had not been happy to find out that Mairi had made it so deep into Sinclair lands without detection and was still complaining to Talorc about it. "How did a wee woman get past our guards and our clansmen?"

"Perhaps she had divine help," Abigail said from behind Eirik.

The twins were with her, running for their father and the big warrior sitting next to him. Niall's scowl turned to an instant smile and he took one boy up on his knee to examine some treasure the child had brought in with him.

The other twin was asking his father if he could see the man's dirk and Abigail was giving Talorc a look that promised serious retribution if the man said yes.

The sound of people on the stairs had Eirik tearing his gaze from the domestic scene to watch their descent. Mairi moved gingerly, leaning heavily on Lais's arm, but looking better than the night before.

Ciara, on the other hand, wore a haunted expression, dark bruises marring the skin below her eyes. Eirik's dragon growled at the sight. She had not slept.

Tonight she would, if he had to wrap her in his arms and guard her dreams with his own. As prince of his people, Eirik could speak to any Éan in his mind, but as dragon gifted by the *Clach Gealach Gra*, he could soothe the minds of others.

He had started to do just that the night before with Ciara but had thought better of revealing his ability. Now, he knew the next opportunity he had, he would use it.

Lais reached the bottom of the stairs with Mairi, looking like a man who had found his mate and did not know what to do about it.

The twins ran to Ciara and threw arms around her in exuberant hugs. "We missed you," Drost confided. "Mama said you were tired."

"She said you was sleeping," Brian added.

Eirik frowned. "You do not look like you slept."

"You should have come play with us," Drost said.

Ciara shook her head but smiled. "I should have."

Mairi sent a worried glance, riddled with guilt toward Ciara. "I should not have taken your bed."

"Yes, you should have. My dreams disturbed me, not my pallet on the floor."

"You got to sleep on the floor?" Drost asked with an askance look at his mother. "We never get to."

"I want to sleep on the floor," Brian announced before climbing back into Niall's lap and crossing his arms just like Talorc when he wanted to make a point.

"Your mother prefers you sleep in a bed." Talorc's tone said that no matter how he might want to indulge his sons, they would have to get their mother's approval first.

"Well, if you really want to sleep on the floor, then I'll make you a pallet on the floor of our bedchamber tonight," Abigail offered with a sweet smile directed at her husband.

The Sinclair's frown was immediate. "Why *our* floor?"

"Because it will be an adventure."

And he wouldn't be so quick to lay blame for the boys sleeping in a bed on their mother if them sleeping on the floor meant Talorc would have to spend it *sleeping* as well. Abigail was a clever and a sneaky woman.

Eirik liked her.

Ciara smiled on the scene, a wistful expression in her eyes Eirik did not understand.

Unsure what drove him to do it, Eirik rose and went to her. He took her arm and led her to the chair he'd been sitting in by the large fireplace. "Sit, *faolán*."

"Why'd he call Ciara little wolf, Niall?" Drost asked the big warrior. "She's not little; she's bigger'n me."

Niall looked up at Eirik, his expression a challenge. "I don't know. Eirik, why don't you tell us why you called our laird's daughter by the endearment?"

Ciara was so exhausted, Eirik could tell she wasn't really listening to what was being said around her. Hell, she hadn't even balked at taking his chair. In his experience, she was not the biddable wolf Talorc claimed.

"What's an endearment?" Brian asked.

"Like when your father calls you cub, or his little man," Abigail answered when no one else did.

Talorc and Niall were too busy glaring at Eirik.

"Oh." Drost swung his legs, kicking Niall, but the man didn't so much as blink. "But she's not a cub."

"No, she is not."

"Well?" Talorc prompted, his hostile gaze fixed firmly on Eirik. "Is there a reason *you* discovered my daughter in the forest last night?"

"I've been following her, watching her from the air when she runs at night."

"Last night was not an isolated incident?" the Sinclair demanded, his attention on Ciara now.

She didn't answer.

"Ciara?"

She looked up, her eyes bloodshot, her face pale. "Yes?"

"You need to go back to bed." Talorc's tone was firm, but caring, whatever he had meant to say gone in the face of his adopted daughter's clear exhaustion.

"I do?" She looked around her, no doubt noticing the looks of concern being directed her way. "But I just got up."

"Abigail, can you make her a tea to help her sleep?" the Sinclair asked his wife.

"I've tried . . . they don't seem to work."

"I can help her sleep."

That had Niall and Talorc's hostile regard back on him, only ratcheted up a notch.

"No." Talorc's tone left no room for argument.

"I can calm her mind and my dragon can protect her dreams."

"Do you have to be in the room to do this?" Talorc demanded, clearly understanding the distinction Eirik had been making.

"Once I calm her mind, she will sleep, but I cannot protect her dreams without touching her."

"So, she would only waken again, like she does with my teas," Abigail said worriedly.

Eirik nodded.

The Sinclair opened his mouth to speak, but what he would have said was lost as Ciara pitched forward. She would have landed against the hard floor, but both Eirik and Abigail grabbed her.

Ciara sat up, shaking her head. "I don't know what's wrong with me."

"Not enough sleep," Talorc said. "For too many nights."

Abigail sighed. "Not enough food."

"Too many dreams," Mairi added.

And everyone stared at her.

"I have them, too, but I can't tell you about it until Ciara is rested enough to join in the conversation. I won't betray her secrets by revealing my own."

"You may hold her in our bed," Talorc said, his words grudging. "The door will remain open and we will be checking on you."

Eirik should have been offended, but it took all he could do to stifle his urge to laugh.

No matter how appealing he found the pretty little wolf,

he preferred his bed partners to be conscious. Besides, she needed rest, not sexual exertions.

"We will sleep in the forest, because I need to be in my dragon form to protect her dreams. I do not believe Abigail would appreciate me breaking the bed she finally convinced you to build for her. You can send a chaperone, but it must be one of the Éan or the few trusted Faol that already know of my other form."

The laird agreed, sending Niall and Guaire to accompany Eirik and Ciara into the forest.

She was so out of her head with lack of sleep that Ciara did not even ask where they were going or why she'd been put on a horse with the giant blond warrior.

Eirik's dragon roared at this but settled some as he reminded himself the other Chrechte was happily mated . . . to Guaire. His dragon was still unhappy and Eirik only hoped the ride went quickly, or the beast would have its way and he would end up snatching Ciara right off of Niall's horse.

Chapter 8

Healing is a matter of time, but it is sometimes also a matter of opportunity.

—HIPPOCRATES

Lais lifted Mairi into his arms, ignoring her squeak of surprise and turned to face his laird. "I will do another session of healing on her."

Talorc nodded. "Abigail will accompany you."

"If you wish, but my power to heal is stronger when there are no distractions."

"I believe your patient will be distraction enough," Talorc said wryly.

Mairi gasped at this and squirmed, but Lais carefully kept her close. "Exactly," he agreed with his laird. "Adding further distractions to the mix will hamper my ability to heal my patient, but I will bow to your will."

The laird shook his head. "You are almost as arrogant as your prince."

"I believe that is the pot calling the kettle," Abigail said with a small laugh.

Since Lais agreed, he did his best to hide his amusement. He liked his head just where it was. Attached to his shoulders.

"You will not take advantage of her innocence," the Faol declared. "She is under my protection."

Lais did not blame the laird for doubting his honor. After what Lais had done to his own people, he did not expect the trust of other Chrechte.

'Twas why Eirik's friendship was so important to Lais. The prince had never once questioned Lais's motives or actions.

But the insult to his integrity still wounded. "She is my patient. She is safe under my care."

"Of course she is safe with you," Abigail soothed and then glared at Talorc. "My husband did not mean to imply otherwise."

The laird didn't look in the least repentant. "He wants her."

Abigail blushed and gave Mairi a pitying look.

Mairi made a high-pitched sound of protest, but she didn't try to get out of his arms again. Her wounds must be paining her. And that was all that mattered right now.

"I will treat her as if she were another ward of the Sinclair," Lais said.

"Good." The wolf alpha's eyes promised retribution if Lais did not do as he'd promised. "Because for now, that is exactly what she is."

"But I . . . my father . . . he won't . . ." Mairi's sweet feminine voice rambled out in confusion.

Talorc ignored her, his face softening near miraculously as he looked at his wife. "'Tis time to take the boys digging in your herb garden, I think."

"The last time you did that, they dug up my thyme and our dinners suffered," Abigail said with asperity, but an amused twinkle in her eye.

"Then you had best come supervise us."

"I suppose I had better at that." The Sinclair's lady's lips twitched with humor.

"By your leave," Lais said to the laird, indicating the stairs with his chin.

Talorc's attention came back to Lais and Mairi. "Do what you can for her. She is no warrior to suffer such pain."

Lais should not have been surprised that the Sinclair laird had noticed Mairi's discomfort, or that the wolf cared about it, but part of him was. And it shamed Lais to realize he had his own judgments based on past experience to overcome.

"I will."

Talorc nodded and then led his family from the great hall.

Lais carried Mairi up to his bedchamber.

He'd been taken aback when the laird had offered him a room in the keep beside Eirik's. But Talorc had said that with Lais's Chrechte gift of healing, he would be an invaluable member of the clan and best kept close to the laird's family.

Healing Mairi in Lais's nest would help him focus and draw on the strength of his Chrechte gift. His weapons nearby, the furs Lais had brought with him from his home in the forest were arranged in a way that made his eagle feel comfortable and safe, despite them being on the floor.

He kept a bowl of fragrant herbs used for healing in the high window, the scent soothing and a reminder at the same time. Anya-Gra had taught him that while his ability to heal others was a great gift, he did not have to use it alone. One of her daughters had spent the last seven years training Lais in the use of herbs, tinctures and other treatments in healing ailments for both Chrechte and human.

The only furniture in the room, a long narrow table against the wall opposite the bed, held jars, pots and pouches filled with his tools as a healer from this training. In the center rested a small wooden box. Decorated with a carved dragon on the top, it had a raven, an eagle and a hawk decorating three sides and nothing on the back. Inside, rested the small amber stone Anya-Gra had given Lais the day after he had gone to live among the Éan.

A memento to the fact he'd been given a second chance, the dark yellow crystal helped him remember that day of healing in the cavern seven years past. Anya-Gra had also worked with Lais in using it to focus and enhance his healing gift.

Kicking the door shut, he bumped the bar with his

shoulder so it fell in place, ensuring no one could barge in and interrupt them. To break his focus at a crucial moment in her healing could have very detrimental effects on Mairi's recovery.

"This isn't Ciara's room," the sweet blonde said as he laid her on his furs, her blue gaze filled with confusion.

He settled a smaller, rolled-up fur under her head. "It is mine."

"But 'tis not seemly." She tried to get up but barely lifted her head before settling back with a pained expression. "I cannot be in the room of an unmarried soldier."

Though he trained with the warriors, he was not one of them. "I am healer, not a soldier."

He poured water from the ewer kept in his room into the large wooden bowl he used for all manner of things. It had been carved thin and polished to a high finish by one of the skilled woodworkers among the humans that had made their lives with the Éan in the forest.

"Pffft." Her mouth pursed adorably and the urge to kiss her was almost stronger than his will. "That is hardly an important distinction."

It was to Lais. He would never again attempt to hurt another Chrechte unless in defense of others. "You heard the laird. Your virtue is safe."

She blushed so brightly, it nearly hid the remaining bruises on her face. "That is not what I meant. I never thought . . . You wouldn't want . . . I'm ugly with bruises . . . You . . ."

The diminutive human woman was charming and much too desirable when she got flustered. Lais found himself smiling despite having to fight an internal battle of lust. "You are safe in my company."

"I never doubted it, but that is not the point."

"What is the point then, little one?" Her trust in him was an even stronger aphrodisiac than her beauty.

He needed to draw a breath not infused so strongly with her scent. He stood and went to his table, gathering herbs and cloths for treating her.

"My name is Mairi."

"Is *that* the point?" He could not stop himself teasing as he placed the things he'd gathered beside the bowl of water.

"Of course not."

In better control of his desires, Lais arranged her more carefully on the furs so there was no undue pressure on any of the areas that would be giving her the most pain. He had to fight from turning each touch into a caress and was proud of himself when he managed it.

Her breathing turned shallow and she closed her eyes, two spots of color burning high on her cheeks.

"Did I hurt you?" He had tried not to.

"No."

"What ails you then?" But his eager senses told him before she opened her mouth.

Mairi had been excited by his touch.

She fisted her hands in the skirt of her plaid. "You are very close." Her voice was laced with accusation.

"I can hardly heal you from across the room."

"I did not expect you could." Her eyes snapped open, their blue depths reflecting a message he did his best to ignore. "I just . . . you *are* close and it feels strange."

"Aye." Pretending ignorance to her might spare her feelings, but it would not change the truth between them.

"For you, too?" she asked in surprise.

He shrugged, no intention of answering that question or what it implied. If she could not see the way his kilt was starting to tent from his arousal, he certainly wasn't going to point it out. He had never been attracted to a patient before, but the night prior had been the first time that healing someone had made him ache with the need for sex.

He would be ashamed of his reaction, only he knew his eagle wanted to claim this human as their mate.

Lais's reaction to Mairi was inevitable.

"Why do I feel so drawn to you?" Her features were pale with pain, but a confused desire burned in her sky gaze.

"You are my patient."

"It is more than that. With my father's view on how to deal with his frustrations at my lack, you can believe I have spent much time with the MacLeod healer. I was never so drawn to her. I was grateful to her, but never felt the odd sensations I do with you."

He laughed, Mairi's naïveté sweetly amusing.

"You are amused because you do not think I realize this is a man-woman thing," Mairi said quietly. "But I don't feel drawn to the others this way, either."

"Others?" he asked, knowing he would regret doing so.

"Your prince, the laird, that big blond warrior who looks ready to kill at a moment's notice."

He'd never heard Niall described as such, but close enough to it that Lais smiled. "He is a great warrior, but would not harm you."

"If you say so."

"I do."

"You are one that likes the last word," she accused.

The pain never quite leaving her face reminded him he might need his amber stone for this healing session.

He got up and retrieved it from the box. "You are one that likes to talk a lot."

"It is true." She didn't sound too happy about Lais's observation though. "My father finds it most annoying."

"I do not." He knelt beside her again, laying the amber stone near her head, his fingers touching her golden hair.

'Twas all he could do not to bury his fingers in the silken strands. But everything about her intoxicated him with more potency than well-aged whiskey. Her scent, so feminine and so right, teased at his nostrils and he could not help taking a deep breath to feed his eagle's need.

It was a mistake and he realized that immediately, but not soon enough to prevent the shudder of his body as his craving for the MacLeod woman grew.

Were she not yet so painfully wounded, he would not be able to subdue his need for her. Of that he was certain.

Perhaps the Sinclair had been right to question Lais's control, if not his honor.

"I'm glad," she said softly. "I do not wish to give you a disgust of me."

"'Tis not possible. You have shown great determination and courage, I can do naught but admire you." And want her with a hunger he doubted even Eirik's dragon could match.

She said nothing as Lais bathed her feet with herb-infused water that would keep away infection from the few scratches that remained. They had been torn and battered the night before and he'd started his healing there, unaware far more serious wounds awaited his Chrechte touch.

"So, why am I so drawn to you and not the others?"

"I told you, I am your healer. You feel my power working inside you. It draws you to me." 'Twas a good excuse if wholly spurious.

"So, you are not drawn to me?"

"You are daring in your speech for an innocent maid."

"Only with you. I hid from the man my father chose to wed me as much as possible and only spoke to him when I could not avoid it."

For a woman who liked to talk as much as his Mairi, that said much about her feelings for the man her father had chosen for her. Lais's eagle had his own opinion of said warrior and a bloodthirsty way of dealing with him in mind.

"You are spoken for?" he asked her in a tone made hard by his dislike of the possibility.

"Am I truly the Sinclair's ward?"

The Sinclair had given her sanctuary, but today, he had given her more . . . he had given her a place in his family. "He said it. It is so."

"Then . . . no."

"Explain."

"My father promised my hand without my consent."

"'Tis not uncommon, particularly for a laird's daughter." Though a man whose habits led to his daughter spending time with their clan's healer was not one who would choose carefully for her prospective mate.

"But if I am no longer under his authority, then his promise on my behalf is no longer binding. Since I never agreed to it, I am not bound by my own words, either." She shivered. "And it is a good thing, too. The man has too many of my father's traits."

"He would have beaten you?" Lais asked, fury toward this unknown clansman growing inside him. "Is he Chrechte?"

The Macleod clan had an illness that needed Niall's skills rather than Lais's to heal.

"Yes, though he is not a very strong wolf."

"Even a weak wolf is much stronger than most humans."

"Yes." She turned her head away. "He *did* beat me. Not all of these bruises are from my father's fists."

Eirik had told Lais through the royal Éan mind link last night that Mairi had been beaten by her father and was in need of healing, but to hear it from her own lips was worse than a kick to Lais's gut.

"Why?" Not that the why mattered because naught could ever justify such cruel cowardice, but Lais felt the need to understand as much about this human woman as possible.

Even if he would never claim her for mate, she would always be important to him. He had been given a new life among his brethren, but he knew he did not deserve it. He would never ask a wife to take on a warrior with such a compromised past.

No matter how much his eagle craved the touch of this woman. She was a patient and she could never be anything else.

Nevertheless, Lais would do his best to protect her from this point forward. Understanding how she came to be here was a necessary step toward doing that.

"I ran away the night before I was supposed to wed Ualraig." Mairi's eyes pleaded for understanding. "I could not bear the thought of marriage to a man so like my father. Ualraig was only willing to take me as his wife because he was sure I was not his true mate and he could still share his seed with a femwolf, given the opportunity."

"How do you know this?"

"He told me."

Lais cursed. No wonder she avoided conversing with the bastard. "They found you."

"They are Chrechte. Of course they did, but I'd gotten almost to the northern border of our land." She sounded proud of that fact and she should.

To have eluded her Chrechte hunters that long was indeed an accomplishment.

"How did you get away the second time?" And manage to make it all the way to Sinclair land on this occasion as well.

"They left me for dead." She took a deep breath and let it out, her distress still all too apparent to his senses. "I woke to so much pain and realized if I did not go, I would die exactly as they intended. I knew of an old warrior who lived on the border of our land, ostensibly to protect it, but really my father did not like him."

"He helped you?"

"After a fashion. I stole his horse."

"You did not have a horse when Ciara found you."

"No. I sent him back the way we came. He was a smart horse, he's no doubt home by now."

That explained her ability to make it so far, but not how she had done so undetected.

"So, your father believes you are dead?"

"I do not think so, not by now."

"What do you mean?"

"They would have gone back for my body, after the wild animals got to it."

The MacLeod laird's evil was even worse than Lais had first thought. Even a laird could not admit to killing his own daughter. So, he had taken measures to make sure he was not accused of doing so.

"They meant to make it look like wild animals had gotten you when you ran away," Lais said with disgust, his stomach rolling at the thought. "You were still alive when they left you. A Chrechte would have known."

"Yes."

And still the two vicious bastards had left her so hurt she would not have been able to protect herself from a piglet, much less a wild boar. "Evil."

"Yes."

"But you were not so fragile as they thought and you were clever enough to make your way here." He let the admiration he felt sound in his voice.

She deserved it.

"I was already very close. I think my father hoped to blame my death on another clan, so he left me where he and his soldier found me near the border of MacLeod land."

"You outwitted him."

"I did, but if Ciara had not found me last night, I do not think I would have survived to the morning."

Lais knew she wouldn't have. "But you did."

"Yes and in the end, that is all that matters."

No, her father's perfidy and cruelty had to be addressed, but not now and not by her.

He began to remove Mairi's plaid.

She grabbed at the fabric, tugging it close to her. "What are you doing?"

"I need to see what I can of your injuries."

He had no choice but to use his inner sight for her internal injuries and bones. Though it used much more of his power and exhausted him in the process. He could not waste his energy trying to *see* through her plaid for her modesty's sake.

"But I can't be unclothed in your presence." She swallowed, looking and smelling very nervous all of a sudden. "It would not be right."

"I am a healer," he said with exasperation.

"Are you saying you've seen scores of women without their clothing so you could heal them?" she demanded, sounding riled at the thought.

He did not bother to dignify that ridiculousness with an answer. He simply tugged at the plaid she grasped so tightly.

Refusing to let go, she shook her head.

"Our Chrechte gifts do not come without cost," he told her.

"What does that have to do with you undressing me?"

"You could undress yourself, but your ribs are still too tender to allow you to lift your arms easily."

"You are going off topic again."

He would have smiled at her testiness, but this was not an argument he could give in on. "I only have so much strength to heal with my Chrechte gift before I will need sleep and time before attempting to heal you further."

"So?"

"So, if I waste my power to protect your modesty, I will not be able to effect a change on your more serious wounds."

"What do you mean waste your power?"

"I have to see your wound to heal it. Doing so with my eyes allows me to focus my energies on the healing rather than the seeing."

"But last night—"

"I made the mistake of protecting your modesty and used my energy to *see* your wounds without taking off your clothing." After he had already wasted too much working on the superficial wounds on her feet and face that had been obvious even in the moonlight.

"But you helped so much."

"And have a lot more to do to make you well. I am not even certain I saw all your internal injuries last night." By the time he'd realized how very damaged she really was, Lais had half exhausted himself trying to see her bruises under the clothes.

"You can see through my clothes?" she asked in shock.

"Nay. 'Tis not like that. Part of my gift is the ability to sense or *see* the injury, but if I use my strength to do that, then I have less available to heal what I find with my mind's eye," he tried explaining again.

'Twas not as if he could see the creamy curves of her skin, but the injuries called to his inner sight and he *understood* what they were and what needed to happen to heal them.

"You are not just going to remove my dress, are you?"

"Nay."

"You want to take off all of my clothes?" she asked in a small voice.

"They beat you all over."

"Yes."

He let her draw her own conclusions.

After a few moments of silence, she finally nodded, looking away. "Very well."

"I do not do this to embarrass you, little one."

"I believe you." But she still kept her gaze averted.

His eagle wanted to comfort her. "Perhaps I should bring Abigail in after all."

After all she had been through, Mairi deserved every consideration he could give to her.

That got Mairi looking at him, the panic in her face a kick to his gut. "No. Please. I would rather no one else witnessed my nudity."

"But she is our lady, a healer as well."

"And she will see my shame."

"Your shame?" Being nude before him caused her to feel shame?

Tears filled Mairi's eyes. "The cuts, the bruises—the evidence my father and the man who was to take me to wed thought so little of me, they beat me with no care if I lived or died."

"Oh, sweet one, the injuries to your person are their shame, not yours." He brushed his hand over her shoulder, the need to comfort greater than any other craving in that moment.

The moisture in her eyes overfilled and slid down her temples. "It does not feel like it."

"Mairi, you are beautiful, kind and sweet. You deserve to be protected, not hurt." And he would protect her.

"I ran away. I embarrassed my father; I should have kept his promise on my behalf."

"No." Lais cupped her face, forcing her wet eyes to meet his. "You cannot honor the promises of a man who has no honor."

"He said I was an unnatural daughter, that I was no use to him. He hates me."

"He is an evil bastard that I would gladly eviscerate with my eagle's claws."

Her drowning eyes widened.

And he could not stand it any longer. She was his, though he could never fully claim her. But he could let her see that she was valuable.

He lowered his mouth and kissed her softly; he would not hurt her. "My eagle wants to mate with you. You are not useless."

He pulled back and she looked up at him sadly. "You don't want to mate me though, do you?"

"I cannot."

She nodded. "I understand." Though clearly she did not.

Lais took hold of her belt, intent on removing it. "Let me show you your value. Let me heal you."

"All right."

Chapter 9

Subdue your passion or it will subdue you.

—HORACE

Eirik lifted Ciara down from Niall's hold and carried her into the cave, leaving the care of the horses to the warrior and his seneschal mate.

Her eyes were hazy and barely open, so he did not set her on her feet lest she fall right over.

"Why have you done this to yourself?" he asked her.

Some of her spirit ignited in her green gaze at that. "I do nothing to myself. I did not ask for these dreams that prevent my sleep, for visions that besiege me until my mind can no longer even think."

"You fight them."

"Of course."

"Why?"

"They only bring pain."

"Because you fight them."

"The last time I gave in to them, I lost a brother." The sadness that filled the space between them squeezed at his own heart.

"You cannot—"

"Please, you said you can help me sleep. You can make the constant edge of worry leave me. Do it. *Please*."

It would take a heart of stone to ignore the femwolf's pleas. She was desperate for rest of both her spirit and her body. He could give that to her.

"Hush. I will help."

"Thank you."

Niall came in then, carrying a pile of furs.

"Place them over there, in the center of the cave," Eirik instructed the big, scarred warrior.

The cavern was large enough for Eirik to release his dragon in comfort and would provide space for the other warriors to rest in relative comfort as well. Not that their comfort was a priority for him, but Eirik was used to considering the needs of his people. This Faol and human had become his people upon his joining the Sinclair clan.

Niall laid out the furs. "You can really help her sleep?"

"I would not claim so if it were not true."

The warrior grunted. "I will help Guaire settle the horses."

Eirik nodded, his focus on laying the already dozing Ciara down among the furs.

She opened her eyes and met his gaze as he leaned over her. "My sleep does not go deep enough. I always wake."

"You will not this night."

"You promise?" she asked with a pain-filled hope.

"I do."

He laid his hands on both sides of her head and concentrated on letting calming thoughts flow between them. She closed her eyes again, but remained tense.

She'd gone so long without real sleep, her beleaguered body had forgotten how to rest. He began to croon with the sounds of his dragon and a small smile lifted the corners of her mouth.

The temptation to press their lips together was too great to resist and he pressed a gentle kiss on her. She sighed against his lips, her body going lax.

And just like that, she'd fallen asleep.

Eirik wasted no time shifting into his dragon form, pulling the small human into his arms while his tail came around to wrap over her legs. He ignored the sounds of Niall and Guaire preparing their own campsite behind his back.

His dragon knew them to be friend, not foe, so it was not bothered by the men's choice of camp spot. His raven had settled into sleep with the woman he considered his mate, already seeking out her dreams.

Eirik had not told the Sinclair that his gift was twofold and both the raven and dragon could influence Ciara's dreams. It was not necessary to share that information and he had not been sure it would be relevant regardless. In the past, his raven had only been able to enter the dreams of his family.

But as his dragon slipped into sleep as well, his power going out to shield Ciara from the *Faolchú Chridhe* that would call to her, his raven sought out Ciara's thoughts in sleep.

They were in a cottage, the bedchamber they entered not much larger than the bed a woman with gray hair slept upon. But she was not asleep. She was dead, the stench of dried and congealed blood too strong to mean anything else.

Eirik could feel Ciara's distress, the deep wound to her heart as she realized her mother had taken her own life.

This was not where Ciara's mind needed to go. Eirik's raven dug deeper into the dreamscape, seeking images of the woman on the bed in happier times. He found them, pulling them to the forefront, taking the dreaming Ciara to an afternoon learning to sew, her mother's hands guiding hers with gentle touches.

Suddenly the dream Ciara looked up and met Eirik's eyes. She knew he was there. She smiled and said, "Thank you."

The cottage fell away and they were now in Ciara's bedchamber. She was in her bed, wearing nothing but her sleeveless shift to sleep in.

Once again she looked at him, this time her eyes not so grateful as wary. "I don't want to have another dream about you."

"Do you dream about me?" he asked, thinking that probably he shouldn't.

"Yes. Dreams that make me ache."

Another night he might give in to the temptation to share such a dream, but right now, this woman needed true rest.

"You will not ache, but will rest." He crossed the room to her bed and knelt beside it. "Relax, *faolán*. I will let nothing harm you here and no dream will bedevil you, either."

"Can I trust you?"

"Aye."

"You killed my brother."

"Aye."

"Another Éan might have later, if he'd kept hunting them."

God willing. Yes. Though this, Eirik's dream self did not say aloud.

Ciara sighed. "I loved him. So much. He told me he was glad I was a little sister, even when father was sad I was not a son."

"He had some wisdom then."

She smiled, her eyes closing slowly. "Yes, some wisdom. And a warm heart . . . when we were younger."

Peace stole over her countenance and then she was asleep. Truly asleep.

Knowing it could do no harm and would probably help, Eirik's dream self climbed onto her narrow bed beside her and took Ciara into his arms. She sighed, turned over and nuzzled into him as if seeking shelter in his arms.

Clearly she found it, because she did not waken again.

Lais was careful as he removed first Mairi's plaid and then the blouse and shift beneath it.

She whimpered when he had to lift her arm to remove the blouse, but bit her lip and kept the sound inside as he gently tugged her shift up her body and off. She was a tiny thing, but her curves were generous. He had to swallow back a moan as first the golden curls between her thighs came into sight and then the pretty pink tips of her breasts.

They tightened in the air, but his libido could not compete with his horror at the sight of so much damage done to her fragile body. The fist-sized bruises marring her beautiful pale skin made bile rise in his throat even as fury rose to match it.

The MacLeod would pay.

This . . . this horrific evidence of abuse was *after* their healing session the night before.

She turned her head away. "I know they are ugly."

"Aye."

She flinched.

"But you? Mairi, lass, you are beautiful."

She gasped and met his gaze. He let the heat he felt at the sight of her nudity, despite all, fill his.

"You find me attractive, even though you do not want me for a mate?"

"'Tis not a matter of want, it is what I can and cannot have. I cannot have you."

"Why?"

"Perhaps one day I will tell you." But not this day, not when he needed her open to him and his touch to effect her recovery.

"Do you have to lay your hands on me to heal me?"

"You know I do."

"I am afraid."

"Of being healed?" That made no sense.

"Of how I will respond to your touch." She looked away again, her body tensing. "I do not know if I can control my reactions."

Her artless desire and honesty about it would be his undoing.

"I have enough self-control for both of us," he claimed with confidence he did not feel.

Not with the way his sex was trying to rise under his plaid. The pleated tartan hid more than the leather hunter's kilt common among the Éan, but it couldn't hide a full erection.

And he was afraid that was exactly where he was headed.

Innocently unaware of his body's desire, Mairi looked at him with absolute trust. "Thank you."

He nodded and then laid one hand over a particularly

nasty bruise on her arm. He'd thought the bone might be broken the night before and had sent healing energy to it, but the injury still looked bad. He took up his amber crystal and pressed it very lightly against the center of the purple bruise.

He released his Chrechte spirit into her, the skin below his growing warm and he could see the wound without even focusing on his inner eye now. There was a crack in the bone and he concentrated on mending it.

She whimpered.

He looked up from the wound to her face. "It hurts?"

No one had ever complained of such before. Patients had remarked on the heat and even a tingling sensation, but never complained of pain.

She shook her head, an expression of desperation in her eyes. And then he smelled it. Her arousal. She was reacting to the spirit of his eagle even as Lais attended to her wounds.

"It is all right," he promised.

"Is it?"

"Aye."

"But I want things I should not. You are helping me and my mind is taking me to a different place a virtuous woman would not go."

"Nay, you have little choice," he assured her. "You are reacting to my eagle."

She breathed out a small laugh, though it clearly pained her. "I'm fairly certain it is not your bird that I want to touch me in unmentionable places."

Unable to stifle the desire to touch, he brushed the back of his fingers down her cheek. "You are truly unique, Mairi." Her humor in what had to be a very uncomfortable situation made him like her all the more. "Remember, my spirit is entering your body through my Chrechte gift." And his eagle wanted her for a mate. "You are merely responding to it."

"Do all your patients react thusly? That cannot be comfortable for you."

"No."

"No, they do not, or no, it is not comfortable?"

"They do not."

"Have any?" she pressed.

"No."

"So, this attraction is unique." She gave a small nod, though he could tell she was careful not to strain muscles that did not want to stretch.

"Yes."

"And you feel it, too."

He refused to answer, moving his hand to another injury and concentrating on healing that one, too.

"You don't have to tell me. I can see for myself." She flicked her gaze to where his kilt revealed the extent of his lack of mastery over his own desires.

"Ignore it."

She laughed, the sound not humorous so much as absolutely disbelieving. "That is your answer to protecting my virtue, ignoring these feelings?"

"Aye. We have no choice." Not if she wanted to leave his room still untouched.

He finished mending the bone in her arm and knew the time had come to focus on her ribs. They had to be giving her a great deal of discomfort, mottled with discoloration the way they were.

He laid the amber stone between her breasts and then both hands on her, one on either side of her rib cage.

A small puff of air escaped her lips. "Oh."

Two of the bones beneath his hands were broken almost all the way through and one had a hairline crack. It was a miracle she had not broken them completely and punctured a lung on her journey to the Sinclair holding.

He let the Chrechte power flow through him into her, not stopping even when he felt the exhaustion building inside him.

Something else was building as well and it was making his cock leak a steady stream of pre-come.

When he finished, he did not immediately remove his hands. He could not. The need to move them up a few inches and cup her perfectly rounded breasts was too strong. He feared if he moved his hands at all, that was where they would go.

"I can breathe without pain," she said in wonder. "Thank you."

"You are welcome."

"There are no healers like you among my father's pack."

"Without the *Faolchú Chridhe*, how can the Faol call upon their gifts?" he asked, though it was obvious they did not need it to confer the ability to procreate their Chrechte heritage.

Or there would be no wolf shifters left in the Highlands, and though their numbers were far smaller than the humans, they were ten times greater than the Éan.

Mairi took a deep breath for the first time without a wince of pain. "It must be found."

"You believe it will give you a wolf." 'Twas a nigh impossible claim to even consider.

Her expression said she did not find it so. Passionate belief and hope glimmered in her blue gaze. "I do."

"How can the *Faolchú Chridhe* give this to you?" Though perhaps, he of all Chrechte, should believe in the chance.

Had he not been given a second chance at his Chrechte gifts by the *Clach Gealach Gra* and its keepers? Still, for a human to be given a wolf, even one with Chrechte blood, seemed too fantastic a possibility for belief.

"With Ciara's help. She can draw the power of the Chrechte through the stone."

"Why?"

"What do you mean? She is keeper of the stone."

"You mistake my meaning. Why do you want this?" And then he answered his own question. "You still seek the approval of a man who beat you unto death?"

"*No,*" Mairi said with deep vehemence. "But if I had a wolf and he tried to beat me again, I could rip his throat out."

She was small. She was fragile. She was human. But Lais thought if she had been Faol, she would have done just that.

"You are a fierce little thing."

"For a human."

"For a Chrechte."

She smiled. "Thank you."

"The wolves' sacred stone must be found, if for no other reason than to stop Ciara's dreams," he agreed. "A body can live only so long on such little bites of sleep."

"She has fought her calling." Mairi sounded confused by that fact.

"Aye."

"I wonder why."

He did not know and right now, could not work up an interest in the answer. He was far too focused on the beautiful woman before him. Bruises still marred her lovely skin, but the more serious ones were showing the effects of his healing.

He could not repair everything, so he left the wounds that had no risk of permanent damage to heal on their own. There was one last wound that needed his touch. A large boot sized mark on her left hip.

His examination the night before had revealed another damaged bone beneath it. It had to be healed, or she risked a true break from something as simple as tripping over a rock in her path.

But he could not yet trust his hands to move from where they rested on her ribs.

He was not the only one affected, either. The pulse in Mairi's neck fluttered, her breathing so shallow her chest barely rose and fell, her mouth opened as if tasting their desire on the air like he was.

"No." He meant it to sound firm, to let her know he would protect her virtue with his will. Instead it came out almost a plea.

He was a healer, damn it, trained as a warrior. He could command his base urges. *He would control them.*

"Lais . . ."

He groaned at the innocent need in her voice. "No," he said again.

"I feel so strange." She touched her own nipple and then jerked her hand away with a moan. "What is happening to me?"

But they both knew, no matter how pure she was.

"You must ignore your desire," he said from a jaw clenched with the need to say something else entirely.

"Why?"

"You know why." She was a human woman, her virtue an important commodity in the negotiation for her marriage. And so he reminded her.

"I am not interested in marriage."

"Because of that fool your father promised you to? Ualraig is a coward infected with cruelty. He is no indication of what a Chrechte man might be in marriage."

"So you say."

"Do you think Talorc would ever beat Abigail?" he asked Mairi, to make her stop and think.

To show her irrevocably how wrong it was to believe her father and Ualraig true examples of how an honorable man would treat those dependent on him.

"I do not think so, but I do not know," she said, shocking Lais with her doubt. "I have been here but a day."

"And what have you heard of the Sinclair before that?" Highlanders kept to themselves, but gossip traveled with the winds it seemed at times.

"His reputation in battle is ruthless, but there are no rumors that he hurts those closest to him. Only a man may hide his ugliest sins."

"If you think so little of our laird, why did you come to the Sinclair holding?" Lais surprised himself at how defensively he reacted to Mairi's words.

He had only joined this clan weeks ago, but the Sinclair was a Chrechte with no smirch to his honor.

"I *don't* think badly of him. I am merely pointing out that trust does not come so quickly."

"You trust me."

"I do."

"Why?" But he knew.

They were mates, though he would not claim her.

"I do not know." Her brows drew together in a troubled frown. "I only know that from the first moment I woke to see your face last night, I have felt safe in your company."

"I am a healer."

She rolled her eyes, letting him know what she thought of his answer. "That is your answer for everything."

He shrugged and it made his hands slide across her soft skin. She caught her breath, though it was clear he had not hurt her. He had to bite back a moan at the feel of the feminine silk below his fingertips.

"I want you to touch me," she said in a tone filled with sweet feminine need.

To ignore it cost him dearly. *"No."*

"Yes."

"Mairi," he warned.

"You can caress me with pleasure without compromising my virtue. It is done by many courting couples."

"What do you know of this type of touching?" he demanded.

"I have heard things."

He narrowed his eyes at her. "You have not allowed another to touch you thus?"

"Of course not." The scent of her arousal mixed with that of anger. "What kind of woman do you think I am?"

A sweetly innocent one. "I promised to protect you from both myself and your desires."

An honorable Chrechte did not break his promises.

"I trust you to do so, but your vow did not include not touching me at all."

"It did."

"No, it did not. If so, you could not have healed me. Your promise was to protect my virtue."

"And I will."

"Yes, you will. You will not take my maidenhead." She grasped his wrists and tugged.

He was Chrechte and she was a human female; her strength nothing compared to his. And yet his hands moved where she guided them, up the scant inches that left her breasts no longer naked.

Because they were covered with his hands, the nipples pebbled against his palms. Carefully arching into his touch, she licked her lips, her eyes going unfocused. Her fingers tightened around his wrists, but she made no move to guide him into a more titillating touch.

"I like that," she said breathlessly, the blue depths of her eyes shining with a happiness he could all too easily find necessary to his own. "Having your hands there. Am I compromised now?"

Her naïveté touched him in a place he thought none could reach. He smiled, shaking his head. "Not yet."

She moved his hands again, just a little, so his palms abraded her sweet buds. She moaned. "That tingles all through me. Surely, now I am compromised."

"No," he growled out. "Not yet."

"But it feels so good."

"Aye, it does."

She went still, meeting his gaze with determined blue orbs. "Then we can give one another pleasure without you breaking your promise."

"You are sneaky," he said with admiration and no little shock.

"It would be a tragedy if I learned nothing of value in the years of my childhood."

He agreed, though with less humor than she seemed to feel about it.

"I have still to heal your leg. It is at risk."

"You will share yourself with me, after?" She was demanding an entirely different sort of promise now.

Chapter 10

"Among all the kinds of serpents, there is none comparable to the Dragon."

—Edward Topsell

"I will share what I can," Lais vowed.

"Then you may heal me."

"Saucy wench."

Mairi grinned. "I find you bring out things in me I have never been certain of letting others see before."

"You are safe now."

"Yes."

"You can trust the Sinclair."

"You are here. I am safe."

Her words made him question his certainty he could not have a mate, but then she did not know his past. If she did, Mairi would not give her trust to Lais so easily.

He slipped his hands from the soft pillows of her breasts, unable to stop himself brushing her nipples as he did so.

She gasped, arching again, higher than before and then frowning and crying out.

"What is it?"

"Nothing. I am fine."

"Do not lie to me."

"My back . . ."

So, they had more to do than he had thought. He said nothing as he laid both his hands on the huge bruise on her outer thigh. He could feel the near break in the bone below, the depth of damage in the muscle and tissues around it.

He wanted to kill the man who had done this to her, Lais's eagle screaming inside him for revenge.

Her small hand pressed against his cheek. "It is all right, Lais. Already, it feels better."

"Healing you is easier than it has ever been." And 'twas a good thing, or he would never have had the strength to do all he had to this point.

"I wonder why," she said, her tone implying they both knew the answer and daring him to say it out loud.

"Better to wonder if I will have the strength to heal your back after this." Though he would. He had no choice.

He spoke a Chrechte blessing over her as he continued to concentrate on healing her leg. He felt a surge of power go through him and he dropped his head in thanks to God.

"It is time to turn you over." He withdrew his hands.

She raised her hand toward him. "Help me?"

"Always." He grabbed her hand and gently pulled while helping her to roll forward with another hold on her hip.

Once she was on her side, facing away from him, he looked down and swore in voluble Chrechte at what he saw. It amazed him that she had lain on her back both the night before and today without complaint. It was covered in bruises.

"Is it very ugly?"

"Nothing about you is ugly, Mairi, but those bastards must have taken turns pummeling your back."

"I rolled into a ball, to protect myself." She let out a hic-cupping breath and he knew she was crying at the memory. "They hit and kicked my back over and over."

"Oh, sweet lass, I am sorry."

"You did not do it. You never would."

She had such faith in him and it was not warranted, not by the man he had once been. No, he would never have beaten a child or a woman, but his crimes were just as bad. "I have to touch you, to learn where you need most healing."

"Yes."

"I am sorry," he said again.

She put her hand over his on her hip, her silent request undeniable. He turned his hand over and laced their fingers together. Then he took the amber crystal with his other hand and touched her as lightly as he could with the smoothest side. She did not flinch away, though it had to hurt.

He went over her back without pausing to heal, simply looking for any cracks in bone. Thankfully, there were none. He healed the worst of her bruises, but she would still have pain on the morrow. He had had to leave too much undone.

When he finished, he was shaking with exhaustion and still his arousal plagued him.

"Are you done?" she asked in a lethargic voice.

"For now."

"Can I turn back over?"

"You would be more comfortable on your side."

"I want to see you."

He nodded, though she could not see him. Withdrawing his hand from hers, he stood. "Do not move."

"All right, Lais."

Questioning his own sanity, he undressed and then stepped over her to join her in the furs.

Her eyes were heavy lidded, though evidence of her continued desire was a delicious fragrance to his eagle's senses. He pulled furs over them before taking her hand in his under the covering. "We will sleep and then I will work on not compromising you."

"You promise?"

"Aye."

"Good," she said sleepily. "An honorable Chrechte keeps his promises."

He smiled at her repeating his own thoughts and allowed himself to drift into sleep as well.

* * *

Ciara woke in the arms of a dragon.

The last thing she remembered was Eirik's hands on her face, his eyes glowing with amber light as they looked into hers . . . a kiss so soft it could have been a butterfly's wings, and then a sense of peace stealing over her in soft waves. After that . . . nothing.

No disturbing dreams, no sense of dread, no fear.

Feeling better than she had in months and more alert than she had in weeks, she blinked in the darkness. She experienced no worry though, to be in the dark with a dragon, and she wondered what magic Eirik had worked on her mind.

Her head was pillowed on one of his great arms, his other curved protectively over her body. Dangerous claws rested without threat under one of her hands. There was a soft fur beneath her, protecting her from the hard ground and another over her, cocooning her with the dragon's warmth.

She could smell both Niall and Guaire near, but could not make out their shapes in the darkness.

Eirik's scent surrounded her, making her wolf giddy. And for just a moment, Ciara would let herself enjoy the sensation of peace and safety she found in the dragon's presence.

A rustle of movement from behind her dragon alerted her to where Niall and Guaire were. And that they too were awake.

"Where are we?" she asked into the darkness. "Why are we here?"

"You're awake." Niall's voice was laced with satisfaction.

She could smell the sweet spice of relief in the air as well, though whether it came from him or Guaire, she could not tell.

Flint striking stone sounded and then a torch burned, bringing light into the cavern. The walls were smooth but for some images carved into them. She would have to get closer with the torch to make out what they were though.

Ciara scooted into a sitting position but still could not see over Eirik's large dragon form.

"You slept an entire day and a night," Guaire said, coming around the dragon's head, Niall beside him.

The big warrior tilted his head as if listening for something and then said, "By my reckoning, it is just past dawn."

"I . . . thank you."

"Dinna thank me. It was your dragon there that kept you sleeping so peacefully. He shifted once, to take care of a bodily need, and you started tossing and turning within seconds. He hasn't moved from your side since." The grudging approval in Niall's voice made her smile.

He smiled back, the scar on his cheek pulling his face oddly, but she didn't mind. Niall was as good a man as her adopted father.

And then, without warning, the dragon shrank around her and with a flash of crimson light was being cuddled by a man. A very naked man.

Guaire's eyes widened in shock that quickly changed to appreciation as he took in Eirik's naked form. "Nice."

Niall growled, his eyes glittering in a way that indicated his wolf was far too close to the surface. Ciara felt her own wolf scratching to get out and without even realizing what she was doing, she'd covered Eirik with the fur she'd slept under.

Guaire grinned at both of them. "Is anyone hungry to break their fast?"

Ciara's stomach rumbled and she realized in surprise that she was indeed hungry.

Eirik still had one arm around her, but he used his other hand to tilt her face up so she was looking at him. "You will eat."

"Yes." Did he think she didn't want to eat? He could not be more wrong.

It was not her fault that her stomach was in such tight knots lately that she could not bear to put food in it.

"You are a troublemaker," she heard Niall tell Guaire.

She pulled her head from Eirik's grasp and turned to

see the other men, only to bite her lip so she didn't giggle. But Niall had pulled Guaire into a heated kiss and Ciara couldn't help thinking that had probably been the seneschal's plan all along. The human knew how to keep his Chrechte warrior dancing to the tune only Guaire could play.

She grinned and turned back to Eirik. "It may be a bit before we can break our fast."

"How long have they been mates?" the Éan prince asked.

"Since before I came to live with the Sinclairs."

"They act as if the mating is new."

"They are in love."

"They are lucky Talorc approved the mating. Among the Éan, those with same-sex mates, or human mates, are expected to produce offspring with another Éan before the mating bond can be consummated."

"That's terrible."

Eirik shrugged as if it really didn't matter. "Perhaps it will no longer be necessary, now that we are not dying off one by one as we are hunted to death in the forest."

"Our laird would never require something like that." Ciara had absolute faith in Talorc's commitment to the most sacred of the Chrechte laws—that a true mating was inviolate. "It would circumvent the true mating bond and love that comes with it."

"Love is only paramount in Heaven. Here, among mortals, other considerations must be taken into account. Waiting to take one's true mate in the ways of our people is a small price to pay for the continuance of our very existence."

"It is a good thing for us Talorc does not agree with you," Niall said as he released his mate, who immediately began setting out food provisions on a small square of the Sinclair plaid. "I would have had to defy my laird; I would not bed a femwolf just to make cubs."

"The Faol have never been at risk for extinction. You have never been forced to make the kinds of choices our leaders had to make for us. There was a time, right after the Éan first escaped to the northern forests that less than two dozen of our people remained and some were past the age of producing offspring."

Ciara sucked in a shocked breath. She'd no idea the Éan had come so close to disappearing forever. Part of her admired Eirik because she knew he would have made the difficult choices she spoke about. Part of her despaired as she realized he put no importance on love.

"In theory, I can understand what you are saying, but it would have broken my heart if Niall had taken a wife," Guaire said. "It near broke my heart the years I waited for him to claim me, as it was."

Ciara scrambled to her feet, and only then realized she wore a shift and nothing else. She threw a glare over her shoulder at Eirik, knowing exactly whose fault that had to be.

She reached out and patted Guaire's arm. "Niall loves you too much to have ever taken someone else to mate."

They might have to keep the truth of their relationship hidden from most of the clan, though she thought that by now many had guessed, but they should never doubt one another's love. It was too pure and bright between them.

Guaire smiled at her and then turned a besotted expression on the big warrior. "I know."

"Love can coincide with duty. 'Tis not always mutually exclusive." Eirik's voice was muffled as he bent to retrieve his kilt and put it on.

"Duty should not dismiss love," Ciara maintained.

Niall grunted his agreement, but Guaire just looked thoughtful.

"What are you thinking, love?" Niall asked him.

"Had our laird's father been more appreciative of his duty and less focused on his obsessive love for the English-woman, he might yet be alive and many in our clan besides him."

"There is that," Niall agreed.

Eirik just handed Ciara an apple. "Eat."

Clearly he was not worried if others agreed with his reasoning, or not.

She ate the apple, an oatcake and some roasted rabbit

Guaire had prepared the night before while she slept. It was wonderful. After she'd drunk from the water skein, she took her clothes away from the light cast by the torch and dressed in the shadows.

"Why are we in a cave?" she asked Eirik, not sure if the search for the *Faolchú Chridhe* had already begun.

"You needed to sleep." Eirik said it like that should answer her question.

It didn't. "So? I don't understand how that ended up with you, myself and two of my father's most trusted warriors in a cavern."

"Eirik claimed his dragon could guard your dreams," Niall replied.

She would have scoffed, but the blond warrior's earlier words made more sense now. Hope and pragmatism warred in her heart. If the dragon could guard her dreams, she could sleep. Only, she did not believe her father would allow her to spend her nights in a cave in the forest.

Ciara finished dressing and then went to stand before Eirik, who was tightening the strap holding his sword's scabbard in place. "Thank you."

"You were of no use in a discussion when you could not keep your eyes open well enough to even retain your seat in the chair."

She remembered almost falling over and feeling like maybe it didn't matter. "I was so tired."

"Aye."

"I feel much better now."

"I am glad." He didn't seem happy. He just seemed . . . like Eirik, prince of the Éan, untouchable.

"I'm sorry I was such a bother."

"It was no bother. My dragon likes you." But the man couldn't care less.

Ciara got the message loud and clear, even if it was disheartening and confusing. She and her wolf were one in the same, though she could distinguish between the feelings and thoughts most related to the wolf rather than her humanity.

Even so, it was her wolf that craved the presence of the

Éan and made no attempt to deny it. Logic told her there could be no future in the feelings the other Chrechte elicited in her. Her human mind fought Eirik's effect on her, but it was hard.

It seemed as if Eirik had no such conflict of spirit. His dragon might like her, but the man could barely stand her.

"Well, please tell your dragon thank you."

Eirik's amber gaze narrowed, but he didn't reply.

Ciara rode behind Niall on his great warhorse for the return to the keep. They were a few yards from the cave entrance when Eirik maneuvered his horse alongside them.

Niall said something she didn't catch because she was too busy trying not to scream as Eirik grabbed her right off the back of the other warrior's horse.

She landed on the dragon shifter's lap, his arm like a steel band around her.

"What do you think you are doing?" she demanded.

"You will ride with me."

"If your dragon objects to her riding with Niall, she can ride my horse while I double up with him," Guaire offered from behind them.

Eirik didn't bother to answer, he just nudged his horse into a gallop.

"That was rude," she chided, but the wind swallowed her words.

She doubted he would answer even if he heard her. The Éan prince might not have designs on Talorc's position as laird, but he was arrogant enough for any royal Chrechte.

He didn't need clan chief status to believe he had the right to dictate the circumstances of others. And after her first truly deep and long-lasting sleep in months, she wasn't going to complain too loudly at Eirik's high-handed methods.

If he was not the kind of man he was, Eirik would never have convinced her father to let her sleep in the dragon's arms in a cavern in the forest.

Of this she was certain.

Apparently, it was not just Eirik's dragon that made her feel safe and secure, either. She found she enjoyed riding with him nearly as much as she had riding his dragon through the sky.

Accepting her feelings as unstoppable and her plight as inevitable, when faced with the arrogance of a prince who was also a dragon, she relaxed against him. She trusted him not to let her fall and simply enjoyed the smells and sounds of the forest as they galloped toward the keep.

Eirik felt Ciara relax against him and his dragon rumbled in approval while his raven urged him to rub his head against hers. He gritted his teeth in frustration but settled her more securely in his embrace.

He did not need these urges, but damned if he was going to sit by while she rode a horse with her body pressed up against another man.

Mated Chrechte or not.

Lais woke with a warm bundle snuggled in close against him. He'd been careful not to put his arms around Mairi before sleep and had not moved from the spot in the furs he'd first lain down on. However, she'd cuddled right up to him and seemed content to be there, despite the fact that his hand rested against her back. She was using his other arm for a pillow.

He found himself smiling and excited as hell, his sex hard between them.

The urge to claim her was strong, but remembering her still-healing injuries quelled it—even better than telling himself his honor hung on his ability to control that need.

Her breathing changed then and he knew she'd woken, too.

She tipped her head back and met his eyes, but made no move to leave his arms. "Have we slept very long?"

He looked out the window high in his wall, trying to determine the angle of the sun and then gave a one-armed shrug. He did not want to jostle her. "Not overlong, though we've missed the midday meal."

Then he blinked, thought again and realized he'd had

the sun's shadows backward in his mind. 'Twas dawn he saw out that window, not dusk.

Talorc had let them sleep the whole day and night. For it would have to be some incredible piece of luck for no one to have checked on them in all this time. Lais was not a great believer in the commodity. So, the Sinclair had to know Mairi had spent her night in Lais's bedchamber and yet, no angry laird had beaten the door down with his fist.

"Lais?" she asked softly, her face still soft from sleep.

"Aye?"

"Is it after?"

"It is, though it is morning and not evening as I first thought upon waking."

"I think I knew that . . . I feel too refreshed and healed to have slept only a couple of hours."

"Do you now?"

"Oh, yes, quite well enough, I think."

"Are you the healer now?"

"Perhaps I am meant to heal your heart."

If only that were true. Still, his lips were curved in a smile when he kissed her for the first time. She tasted familiar and yet altogether different from any woman he had ever kissed.

Mairi did not know to part her lips for him, but he did not mind. Their closed-mouth kisses were hotter than any kiss he'd shared before with a woman and went straight to his groin.

He cupped her breast, squeezing lightly and she made a sweet little sound of need. But then a tentative fingertip glided along his sex and he made his own desperate sound of want.

He teased along the seam of her lips, encouraging her to open for him. It took her a few seconds and a couple of moans, but finally, she did.

He let his tongue explore her mouth, while his hand explored her perfect body . . . very gently. She loved having her nipples touched, but gave a surprisingly strong groan of delight when he caressed the nape of her neck.

He very carefully pressed her back so he could reach

her breasts with his mouth and she let him. Making no sound of complaint, though she still had to be tender.

He would not allow her to be hurt further though, so he held her still when she tried to squirm. "Do not move."

"But it feels too big to stay still."

"I will not hurt you."

"I know."

"If you move, I will stop touching you."

She stilled immediately and that excited him in a way he had not expected. She had a confused look of pleasure on her lovely face as well. "Lais?"

"Yes, little one?"

"Why does it make me feel needy inside to be motionless like this for you?"

"I do not know; perhaps you like to trust me."

"Perhaps I do."

And mayhap he liked her trust, more than he would have ever known and far more than 'twas safe for either of them.

He reached down and cupped both her breasts, rubbing his thumbs over her sensitive nipples. "These are just the right size for me."

He could see her desire to move in the way her body tensed, but she remained still. "Maybe I was made for you."

The look in her eyes when she said it was not one of humor, but of deep longing and obvious doubt. If he had thought that doubt was for his worthiness, he would have denied it, but he knew it was for herself.

He could not stand to see such a look in her eyes. "Mayhap you were. I only know I am a very lucky man to be touching you like this right now."

Her smile was like the sun coming from behind the clouds.

He leaned down and took one of her berry-ripe buds into his mouth, laving it with his tongue, gently tugging it with his teeth and suckling until she whimpered, the scent of her sex calling to him with increasing urgency.

He followed the enticing aroma, moving until his face was between her thighs.

"What are you doing?" she asked, her voice tinged with shock but a lot more desire.

"Saving your virtue," he said just before his first delicate lick along her most intimate flesh.

She tried to jerk her hips, but he was ready for her, his hands holding her legs apart and still.

"Lais," she whined.

And he liked that sound, so like a wolf's whine but she was human.

"Remember, sweet one, do not move, or I stop."

"I can't help it."

"You can."

He caught the gush of wetness his words elicited in her with his tongue. Entranced by her flavor, he alternated between lapping at her entrance and tonguing the swollen, wet passage he craved sinking his sex into, until a steady litany of pleas fell from her lips.

She wanted him, but she needed release. She did not yet know what that was though, so she begged with incoherent words for something she could not name.

To know he had this of her, this innocence. That he had the ability to introduce her to the ultimate pleasure for the very first time caused his cock to pulse with needs of its own.

He shifted his head so he could swirl his stiffened tongue around her pleasure spot and he heard her turn her head into the bedding as she screamed into the furs.

It did not take long from that moment to bring her to completion, but he did not stop in his ministrations to her and she broke. Writhing against him until a second climax overtook her and she screamed his name, the sound muffled by the furs she had stuffed into her mouth.

He reared up on his knees between her thighs and touched himself, his stroke harsh and quick. When he erupted with his own orgasm, it took every bit of his self-control to keep his seed on his hand and not bathe her in it, marking Mairi as his.

Chapter 11

I am not one who was born in the custody of wisdom; I am one who is fond of olden times and intense in quest of the sacred knowing of the ancients.

—GUSTAVE COURBET

The ride back to the Sinclair fortress took less than an hour, every moment both pleasure and torture for Eirik.

By the time they were all assembled in the great hall again, this time without the twins and with Guaire, Eirik was in a piss-poor mood.

Nevertheless, he stood beside Ciara's chair, his hand resting on the high back, his expression daring anyone to make something of his choice of where to stand.

Talorc gave him an amused smirk but said nothing. Abigail's smile was much more innocent, though the look of worry she gave her adopted daughter did not sit well with Eirik's dragon.

There was no safer place for Ciara than with him and all assembled should realize that.

Talorc leaned against the mantel of the empty fireplace, his stance deceptively relaxed. "You are in a better frame of mind to discuss whatever it was that had you worried yesterday?" he asked Ciara.

She nodded. "I'm feeling much more myself."

The Sinclair inclined his head in a silent gesture of thanks toward Eirik. "That is very good to hear. Your mother and I have been concerned."

"I am sorry."

"There is nothing to apologize for. You are our daughter. It is our job to worry."

Just as it was Eirik's job to be concerned for his people and now this clan he belonged to. That concern meant he needed answers about the *Faolchú Chridhe*.

He had a hard time accepting that Ciara had said nothing to Talorc before this. Eirik's dragon trusted her, but he was not sure this time his beast's instincts were right.

Despite the protectiveness he felt toward her and the intimacy of sharing her dreams the night before, Eirik was not certain he could trust her with the Éan's safety like he trusted her adopted father.

Ciara nodded, her green eyes glittering with worry. "I've been having dreams."

"I am aware." The laird frowned. "If I could stop the nightmares, I would."

"They're not all nightmares." She flicked an unreadable glance toward Eirik.

Though he could guess what she was thinking. Her visions of the *Faolchú Chridhe* were naught to do with him, but her dream self had as good as told him that her dreams were sometimes about Eirik.

He got the impression she blamed him for the dreams, though they were hardly his fault. Still, that look had not been one of censure. He'd received plenty of those from her and knew intimately their expression.

He frowned in thought and caught a glimmer of fear in her green gaze before she adroitly masked it. Her Chrechte talents were well developed, but he could still smell traces of her apprehension. It did not appear anyone else did, however.

'Twas odd, that, and why the fear?

Because she was not an Éan and had learned somewhere along the way to fear her Chrechte strengths as much as she relied on them. She did not want him to know about the nature of her dreams about him, which meant they were no doubt of a nature to interest him.

She would learn she could hide little from him, and nothing he set his mind to learn.

"She has the sight," Mairi interjected softly, innocently unaware of the sub currents between Eirik and Ciara.

The Sinclair stared at his daughter, the clan chief clearly nonplussed. "Like when you dreamed about Abigail with the bairn?"

Abigail reached out and touched Ciara's shoulder. "I thought that was the result of your Chrechte senses becoming aware of something and making it known through your dreams. Are you certain that is not the case?"

"Yes." Ciara's hands twisted together in her lap. "It is not the first time. And they aren't all happy like that one."

"Have you seen something that concerns us?" Talorc sounded more curious than convinced.

Were the Faol of the Chrechte so far removed from the ancient ways that they did not know about the seers among them?

Perhaps the Éan joining the clans would save more than their race.

When Ciara bit a lip obviously already swollen from such abuse, Eirik wanted to pull her into his arms and promise all would be well. "I believe so, yes."

"Tell me about the dreams," Talorc instructed far more gently than was the irascible laird's wont.

She flicked a glance up to Eirik and then over to Abigail, before settling her attention back on the laird, her discomfort with the topic obvious. "I've had them since I was a small girl."

The laird nodded encouragingly.

"I saw members of my old clan in their Chrechte forms, but not always the ones they showed to the rest of Donegal pack."

"What do you mean?"

Ciara turned a concerned gaze on Eirik.

Certain he knew what she worried about revealing, he nodded. "He knows already."

The shoulder under his hand relaxed infinitesimally. "In my dreams, I saw Circin and his sister as ravens, flying in the sky."

Talorc's shock could not have been greater. "How?" He shook his head. "You must have seen them when awake at some point."

"No. I knew Lais was an eagle, though he denied it to the whole clan."

"Not even Wirp knew," Lais said in a voice soft with awe.

"You are not convinced," Ciara accused her adopted father.

The Sinclair winced. "I want to be, but 'tis so fantastic."

Ciara drooped, but then squared her shoulders and looked directly at the laird. "There is a secret you hold, one that your father died for."

"Others in our pack know as much," Talorc said almost apologetically.

"But they cannot tell you the details of that secret. I can."

She lifted her right hand and examined it as if her delicate fingers might hold the answers of the universe. "Were my hand that of a saint, I would not have made the many mistakes I have, I think."

Color drained from the Sinclair's face. "How did you . . ."

"She's told you how and now you need to stop your doubting," Abigail said with such an expression of angry exasperation, Eirik didn't like his friend's chances of finding joy in his marital bed that night.

"Aye. I am sorry for doubting you, Ciara."

"I have never lied to you, but you know I have hidden much. It makes you distrustful, I understand."

Talorc looked pained and Abigail on the verge of tears.

"Enough of this," Niall said in his gruff voice. "We all believe you, Ciara."

She nodded, but her gaze was far away. "I dreamed of my father's death, and then my mothers. Hers years before it happened, and 'twas so bloody I dismissed the dream as nightmare. I wasn't prepared." Her voice had turned hollow. "I still see her in dreams."

"Oh, Ciara." Abigail looked like she wanted to hug the younger woman, but she must have seen what Eirik did.

Ciara was barely holding her emotions in check and it didn't take a Chrechte's senses to discern that.

Ciara began to speak again, her tone void of the emotion swirling in her emerald eyes. "I began dreaming of the *Faol-chú Chridhe* when I was barely out of leading strings. I did not know what it was at first, but then I told Galen about my dreams. I thought he would make fun of me."

"He didn't," Eirik interjected with certainty.

She looked up at him briefly and shook her head. "He believed my dreams were prophetic, that I would lead him to the wolves' sacred stone. At first, he made it a game, taking me into the forest to search. Those were such happy days, but then our da died and Galen changed."

"It was no game for him." And never had been, of that Eirik was certain. Particularly in light of the fact that if his sister was the keeper of the stone as her new friend Mairi claimed, Galen would have had the bloodline to call on the power of the stone as well.

"Or the friends who shared his hatred of the Éan." His voice came out harsher than he meant it to be, but the thought of one such as her brother having the power of a Chrechte's sacred stone was chilling.

"No. It was no game for them. That's what we were doing that awful day, when Luag smelled ravens and decided to go hunting instead of searching for a myth. Galen had started bringing his friend along on our searches, but neither of them listened to me about where to look. They were so convinced they knew the right of things."

"And yet they were completely deceived," Lais said.

Ciara took a deep breath and let it out. "Yes."

"Luag did not believe in your dreams." Eirik was certain the Donegal wolf would never have gone hunting the Éan children if he had. The *Faolchú Chridhe* would have been far too important a find.

"Not like Galen did, no." She bit her lip again and Eirik's dragon rumbled in his chest. "He wanted to believe he could have the power of the stone."

"If he was your brother, he would have been able to call it forth," Mairi said with utter conviction.

Ciara did not reply, but Eirik nodded his agreement. The Sinclair did not appear happy at that possibility.

Guaire asked, "You never found signs of the stone?"

He'd been silent thus far, but Eirik could see the seneschal taking things in and weighing their import. Eirik had noticed the human doing so before, when working with Eirik and the laird to settle the Éan among the clan.

When he made an observation, it was always on target and of benefit. Talorc was lucky to have such a seneschal.

"No," Ciara answered. "No sign at all."

But still she believed the *Faolchú Chridhe* was out there to be found. Her connection to it had to be very strong.

"And you are still dreaming about it?" Guaire asked.

"Yes."

Guaire nodded. "Clearly, you must heed these dreams."

Niall nodded his agreement. The Sinclair scowled and Eirik knew it bothered him that his daughter had been plagued by something he could not fix, regardless of his strength and position.

"If for no other reason than that until you do, you will continue to lose sleep," Abigail said with a look of motherly concern to Ciara.

Eirik moved his hand from her shoulder to the nape of Ciara's neck, giving a squeeze to let her know she was not alone. He did not question the impulse. For now he would follow the instincts of his beast.

"The dreams have grown urgent. The stone calls to me now, even when I am awake." She looked up at Eirik, her green gaze haunted, before turning her attention to her adopted father. "I cannot sleep. I cannot eat. The *Faolchú Chridhe* must be found."

"Aye." There was a wealth of determination and the confidence of a clan chief in that single word.

Ciara released a soft sigh of relief. No matter that the secrets she kept might imply otherwise, she trusted the Sinclair. Wholly and completely.

She would learn she could trust Eirik just as deeply. His

dragon demanded it and his raven insisted it should already be that way.

"Before my father and his cronies find it," Mairi added, fear wafting off of her in a sour wave.

The laird turned on her. "Your father knows of the *Faolchú Chridhe*?"

Mairi jumped, but she settled and her fear dissipated in the air around them when Lais put his arm across her shoulder and tugged her into his side.

Her face pinked with embarrassment though and despite the obvious comfort it gave her, she tried to push Lais away. He didn't budge.

She frowned up at him, confusion clear in her blue gaze. Lais merely smiled and Eirik found his own lips curving in amusement. It would not be an easy mating, but it would be a good one.

Mairi then gave a good imitation of someone unaware that a warrior twice her size stood so close. "Many of the Faol know old stories about the *Faolchú Chridhe*. Chrechte history is taught to the young in some packs with far more diligence than it sounds like it is among the Sinclairs."

The pack alpha could have taken offense at what was clearly the accusation of a shortcoming, but he merely nodded. "You are right. My grandfather wanted our pack to integrate more fully into the clan and decreed the ancient stories were no more than myth and there was little benefit in sharing them."

Ciara gasped in shock.

Talorc's mouth twisted in an understanding grimace. "It is surprising considering how important he thought that the ancient Chrechte laws are to all of us."

"Perhaps it is time to change things in our pack," Abigail said.

The Sinclair gave his wife an approving look and nodded. "Perhaps it is."

"But the MacLeod has more recent information than old stories, does he not?" Guaire asked Mairi, his tone musing.

"He does. My mother had the sight as well," Mairi said,

sounding apologetic, though Eirik could not understand why. "She dreamed of the stone when she was pregnant with me. I think because my father is distantly related to the family of the *Faolchú Chridhe*."

"You said last night that Ciara was the keeper of the stone," Eirik said.

"She is. Unlike my father, she is of direct descent from the original keepers of the stone. She is the princess of the Faol. If we lived in the days of our ancestors, she would be our queen." Mairi looked at Ciara, her blue gaze shining with esteem and hope.

Ciara shook her head, a sound of protest coming from her, her distress clear. Shock was in the air around them, and worry.

Eirik ignored it all to drop to his haunches in front of the reluctant princess. He willed her to meet his gaze and she did so, her head coming up just enough that her emerald eyes locked with his.

"To be a keeper of the stone is a great responsibility, but it is also a blessing."

She tried to shake her head, but his hold on her face stopped her. "I don't want to be a princess."

"Would you deny your children their rightful place among the Faol because yours was denied you?"

"No. Of course not. I'm not going to have any children!" she wailed.

His dragon rumbled in denial of that statement, but Eirik did his best to ignore it. "There is nothing to fear in this."

"There is everything to fear."

"I will help you."

"You hate me."

"I don't."

"But—"

"Trust me."

"You are truly a prince . . . I am just a—"

"There is no just. The stone has called to you, claimed you. You can do naught but answer that call." He had known this since he was a small boy. To be born into the royal family of a Chrechte people dictated much about a man's life from birth.

He would help Ciara learn to deal with this truth.

"I am also a seer and I have dreamed of the power for good she wields with the stone." Mairi's voice rang with conviction.

"Ciara is a direct descendant of the original keepers of the stone, of Faol royalty?" the Sinclair asked as if still trying to take in the truth.

There was no doubt in Mairi's set expression. "Yes."

"I can't be," Ciara said, but her voice lacked any conviction. Her eyes beseeched Eirik. "Wouldn't my parents have told me, my brother at the very least?"

Eirik foolishly wished in that moment he could lie. "As you said, he had plans to wield the power of the stone on his own behalf."

"But we were family."

"And he saw the goodness in you, the inability to hate another race of our people simply because they were different in their beast nature." And finally, Eirik knew that to be true.

He still did not trust this woman entirely. She hid too many secrets, but he did not doubt that she had never intended the Éan harm.

"He wanted to create *conriocht*," she admitted in a whisper.

Lais gasped. Mairi moaned with worry, but Talorc and Eirik met one another's gaze with purpose. The *Faolchú Chridhe* would be found and brought to safety before it could fall into the hands of Chrechte that would misuse its power to destroy other shifters.

"All will be well," he promised her, willing her to believe him.

Finally, she nodded, worrying her lower lip.

He groaned and before Eirik could give into an almost overwhelming need to kiss the Faol princess, he surged to his feet and moved back to his stance at her side.

"There is an elder among the Balmoral that knows

all the ancient stories of the Faol," the Sinclair said in a
tone that showed more than anything how much he regretted
there was no such elder among his own clan. "We need to
speak to him."

"I will go to Balmoral Island," Eirik announced, not
even considering the laird might prefer to send a Faol for
this mission.

But Talorc nodded his approval. "You will lead this
quest."

"What? Why?" Ciara asked, clearly uncomfortable with
her adopted father's edict.

What did she think? That Eirik as an Éan would do
something sinister with the wolves' sacred stone? Little did
she know, but the sacred stones of the Chrechte could not
be destroyed and the *Faolchú Chridhe* would continue to
call to Ciara until it was found and used by her.

The Sinclair looked like he would not answer his daughter's challenge, but Abigail smacked him on the shoulder
and Talorc's expression changed.

Whatever the laird's wife had said to him over the mindspeak of mates, he looked properly chastised. "As prince of
the Éan, Eirik's knowledge of the *Clach Gealach Gra* and
ability to defeat any who would try to take possession of
the *Faolchú Chridhe* make him the best warrior for this
mission."

"I am sorry I questioned your decision, laird."

"I do not expect the same unquestioning acceptance of
my orders from family as I do my soldiers," the clan chief
said, as if reciting something he had heard many times
before.

Eirik had to stifle an urge to smile, confident he knew
exactly where the laird had heard those words from. Abigail's smile of approval confirmed his guess.

Talorc turned to Eirik. "You will take Ciara with you.
As she is the keeper of the stone, Abigail believes it will
continue to draw her to itself." The Sinclair's jaw hardened,
his head giving a short jerk as if in answer to a silent question. "And your dragon will continue to protect her dreams
so that she does not become ill."

Eirik noted he was not the only one biting back amusement at his laird's obvious discomfort at having given permission for such. But once again, the man's wife looked quite pleased and he for one, had no desire to draw her wrath.

She was a wily one, he knew.

Ciara opened her mouth to speak, but whatever she meant to say, whether protest or acquiescence, was drowned out by Mairi's plea. "Please let me go, too. I have had many dreams of this stone . . . I don't know why, but I feel I am supposed to come on this journey as well."

Lais frowned down at her. "You need more time to heal."

"Is it that you feel that you should be there, or you crave the wolf your dreams have told you the stone will give to you?" Eirik asked, remembering what the human woman had claimed the night she was found.

Mairi showed no signs of embarrassment at his question. "If you had been beaten as often as I have for nothing more than the fact I have no wolf, you would not be so dismissive about the power of the *Faolchú Chridhe* to heal *all* Chrechte. It is my right as much as any other to be gifted that healing."

"Of course it is," Abigail inserted.

And no one gainsaid her. She was human, but she was lady of the clan and an acknowledged member of the pack despite her lack of wolf.

Mairi nodded her thanks and then frowned at Eirik. "But that is *not* why I believe I am supposed to be there. Once the stone is found, many will be touched by its power. My turn will come, later or sooner, but it will come. I must be allowed to accompany you on this quest because such is in my dreams. If God gives you a vision, do you cut out the bits that are not convenient or logical and expect the vision to come to pass?"

Eirik shook his head at the warm approval in Lais's eyes for Mairi's words. The man had it bad, but it was no excuse for condoning the human woman's disrespectful tone.

Ciara's glare directed at Eirik was even more unwelcome,

however, and he arched one brow in question. What had he done?

"Answer her," Ciara demanded.

Eirik opened his mouth to lambast both women for their disrespect and then repeated Mairi's words in his head and decided she had some reason for her acerbic tone. "I have never had a vision. I would not know."

"I have," Mairi said. "More importantly, my mother taught me the importance of paying attention to every tiny aspect to these special dreams. If she had, she would still be alive."

"If my brother had listened to me about all the points of my dream, I believe we would have found the *Faolchú Chridhe* by now." Ciara frowned up at Eirik as if it were his fault.

As far as he was concerned, that particular failing was for the best. "It is good that he did not then."

Ciara flinched at his words and damned if he did not have to fight the desire to comfort her, but the slight incline of her head acknowledged their truth.

"We will fly to Balmoral Island tonight."

Chapter 12

> All truths are easy to understand once they are discovered; the point is to discover them.
>
> —GALILEO GALILEI

"You intend Ciara to ride on your dragon?" the Sinclair asked.

"Aye. Ciara has proven herself an adept rider." And Eirik's dragon wanted her to ride again, craved it like the beast had shown desire for nothing else.

Lais scowled, his blond brows beetled. "You would have my . . . Mairi ride your dragon as well?"

"You could take her across on a boat," Eirik offered, expecting Lais to refuse.

An eagle preferred to fly.

Besides, the ride to where the Sinclairs kept their boats for the crossing combined with the crossing itself would take several hours longer than direct flight. Even if the eagle was considerably slower than a dragon in the sky.

But Lais nodded rapidly. "'Tis a sound idea, that."

It was a daft idea, but since Eirik was the one to recommend it, even expecting it to be dismissed, he refused to withdraw his words now.

"I will accompany Lais and Mairi in the boat." Ciara sounded far too pleased at that option.

Eirik and her adopted father both said, "No," at the same time.

Surprised that the vehemence in the laird's tone matched his own, Eirik let the other man explain it to his daughter.

"But why not?" Ciara asked just as Eirik had expected her to.

"From the moment you leave this keep and until you return to it with the *Faolchú Chridhe*, you will not leave the dragon shifter's side."

Ah, the man wanted Ciara protected at all costs. 'Twas understandable. Not only was she the laird's daughter but she was princess of the Faol. The *Faolchú Chridhe* would be of limited use to their people without one of her blood to bring forth its full power.

"It is a matter of your safety," Abigail said to her daughter. "Please do as your father asks."

Ciara's eyes filled and she nodded without another word. Her love for her adopted family at least was not in question.

No one commented on the Sinclair's muttering that, "'Twas not a request."

There was little Ciara needed for her journey to the Balmoral holding.

Laird Lachlan, her adopted uncle, would provide for all their needs on his island, but where their journey would take them after that, she did not know. Best to be prepared.

She attached a purse made of the Sinclair tartan and lined with leather to the chain she wore around her hips. Inside was a small knife, used mostly for paring vegetables but useful in other circumstances as well. She'd also packed a handkerchief, a packet of herbs to make a tea both good for calming and to pour over a small wound for cleansing, and her last memento of her brother, his ring.

Under the sleeve of her blouse, Ciara wore the arm

circlet of bronze her father had given her mother on their wedding day. She only took it off to shift. The etched image of two wolves rubbing noses and surrounded by intricate lines had always given her comfort. She needed every boost to her courage she could manage for what was to come ahead. Of that she was certain.

She'd fought the call of the *Faolchú Chridhe* for so long, giving in to it made her mouth dry with fear.

The fear shamed her and she would not give in to it.

Ciara added the short and very sharp dirk with the jeweled handle passed down by her great-great-grandmother. She settled the thin leather around her hips so it rested under her chain and the dirk was almost hidden by the small purse attached to it.

Then she opened the low trunk Abigail and Talorc had given Ciara when she first came to live with them. They'd told her to keep her treasures in it, and she had. Those she'd brought with her and the few she'd accumulated since.

She pushed aside the first Sinclair plaid she'd ever been given, just a shawl really. Abigail had explained that Ciara could wear it over her shoulders while still wearing the Donegal's colors as her skirt. It had given her the opportunity to show her loyalty to the Sinclair while taking her time to give up her old clan . . . the last link to her dead family.

Giving her that shawl was the first of many compassions Abigail had shown Ciara.

Underneath the shawl was a carefully folded plaid of the Donegal colors. Ciara had last worn it six months after coming to the Sinclairs. Abigail had presented her with a skirt in the Sinclair colors, a new, smaller shawl that barely covered her shoulders and pins of bronze stamped with the Sinclair crest to hold it to a new blouse so white, Abigail had to have taken great pains to bleach the fabric.

The laird's lady had also included a bodice of finely spun black wool and explained the clothing a fashionable mix of her homeland and the Highland colors. It was too many layers for a shifter to wear expediently, not to mention too English, but Ciara had found herself unable to tell the human woman such.

She'd merely spoken her thanks and come down the next morning wearing a similar outfit to the one she'd worn every day since. Abigail had made herself a matching tartan and bodice, showing the world they were family, if not by blood.

Ciara pulled out the Donegal plaid and laid it on her bed, then unfolded it to reveal the sword within. With emeralds the same deep green of those on her dirk and the size of her thumb decorating the hilt, it was easily more than half as tall as she was.

It had been her brother's, and their father's before that, and their grandfather's before that. She did not know how long it had been in their family, but the heavy bronze shone with years of care.

The raised images of a *conriocht*, a dragon and a griffin surrounded the grip. The *conriocht* was in the center, with a smaller emerald than the ones on the hilt above the beast's head. The dragon clutched an amber stone in his claws and the griffin had a deep blue sapphire under a forepaw.

The sword was heavy and solid, a fitting sword for a king, she'd always thought.

Ciara's knees turned to water and she sank to the floor beside the bed.

A sword fit for a king.

But surely if he was descendant of the original Faol kings, Ciara's father would have been laird. He had not been a leader, though. He'd been loyal to the laird before Rowland and transferred that loyalty to the laird that did so much to hurt the Donegal clan.

Her father had been long dead by the time Barr had taken over as acting laird of the Donegal clan at the order of Scotland's king.

And Galen had already been firmly under Wirp and Luag's influence.

Barr had rescued their clan from the leadership of an evil but powerful Chrechte, but not in time to save her brother. Barr had done his best to save Ciara though, and she would always be grateful.

She ran her hand over the *conriocht* on the sword. When

had the last true *conriocht* walked the earth? Had it been one of her ancestors? Had he been a good man, or corrupted by his lust for power like Rowland? How long ago had the wolves lost their sacred stone?

And how? Apparently, the Éan still had *their* stone, so how could the wolves have lost something so precious?

Had it been taken by the Éan, like her brother claimed? Or the other people of the Chrechte, the Paindeal . . . those that shared their nature with the big cats of prey.

The elders always said the stories of the Paindeal were myth, but then the Faol that did not hunt them had believed the Éan a myth these many generations.

Ciara grasped the sword, her hand butt up against the hilt. Oddly, the metal felt hot against her skin, though her bedchamber was still cool from the night's drop in temperature. It would not warm until later in the day when the sun moved to this side of the keep.

The sword should be cool as well.

Only its handle grew even warmer against Ciara's palm. And it could have been a trick of the light, though she was not sure how . . . but the emeralds on the hilt seemed to *glow*.

Ciara closed her eyes against this indication of Chrechte magic and a childhood in which she'd been kept in the dark about the truth of her ancestors.

Not only had her father wished she were a son, but he had hidden her family's history from her. Certainty that he had shared it all with Galen only made the ache in her heart hurt worse.

Because for all that Galen loved her, he had kept these secrets from her as well. He had not thought she was important enough to know the truth of her lineage.

Silent tears trickled down her cheeks as Ciara wished for the connection to her past they'd seen fit to hide from her.

Suddenly, she was no longer sitting on the floor of her bedchamber, but standing deep in a cave lit by several torches sticking out from the smooth stone walls. An old woman wearing nothing but a leather loincloth crouched on the ground in the center of the cave.

Her wrinkled body was marked with crude tattoos similar, but more simplified, to the ones the Chrechte marked themselves with to indicate their first shift, matings and positions of leadership. The plain outline of a wolf was tattooed over her heart. Though she was a woman, her arm was marked with a band like that of a pack alpha. Only hers did not have a wolf on it, but the symbol for the Creator, God.

Was she the spiritual leader then? A *kelle*, like the old stories told about, women who were both priestesses and warriors? Her muscles were defined, despite her obvious age, and she crouched with an agility-wrapped tension that spoke of someone prepared to leap into action at any moment.

A wicked-looking dirk dangled from a leather strap between her legs. And the air escaped Ciara's chest as she realized the *kelle* wore a bronze cuff on her arm free of tattoos. It was identical to the one Ciara wore, but without the intricate swirls that must have been added later.

When the old woman raised her head, Ciara saw the thin bronze circlet she wore in her long gray hair. Graced with an emerald that dangled in the middle of the *kelle's* forehead, it clearly marked her as Faol royalty of some kind.

She straightened and Ciara could see a leather-wrapped bundle held tight to her chest. Eyes the same color as Ciara's surveyed the cave, as if trying to see into the very shadows and looking through Ciara as if she were not there at all.

Each move, every line of the *kelle's* body spoke of determination and urgency. She turned toward the back of the cave and revealed a short sword, similar to the one Ciara treasured, strapped to her back. There was no sign of her age in the way she walked with strength and purpose, her head held high.

The *kelle* disappeared in the shadows, and as quickly as Ciara had found herself in the cave, she found herself back on the floor of her bedchamber.

Her eyes were open though she did not remember lifting her lids, and she stared at the wall opposite.

Her mind's eye could still see the *kelle* though and Ciara shuddered at the certainty she had just witnessed not only a moment in the life of one of her ancestors, but the loss of the *Faolchú Chridhe* as well.

Her hand was still on the sword, but the metal no longer felt unnaturally hot. She released it quickly though, as if it could yet burn her. Looking at her palm, she saw no redness to indicate the heat the sword handle had generated.

She wondered where the sword the *kelle* had worn had gone? To another distant relative perhaps, another family within the Faol that might actually tell their daughters the truth of their past?

"What are you doing?" Eirik's voice came from the doorway.

Feeling like she was underwater, Ciara turned her head to see him. Dressed much as he'd been the first time she'd spied him from atop the tower, the dragon shifter filled her doorway, a scowl settled firmly on his chiseled features.

"I was . . ." Trying to understand her past, looking for proof of Mairi's claim Ciara was something more than she thought.

Eirik's gaze moved beyond her to the weapon lying exposed on her bed and his glare turned sulfuric. "You have a sword from one of the ancient Chrechte kings. Where did you get it?"

The accusation and mistrust in Eirik's tone hurt in a way Ciara refused to acknowledge.

"I did not steal it, and my brother didn't, either." She would rather be standing for this conversation, but after the vision she did not trust the strength of her legs.

"You are the one who claims to still follow the ways of the ancient Chrechte. Then you must believe in the visions . . . that I am descendant of a Chrechte king. Why shouldn't I have his sword?" Only they both knew why not. Because she'd had no idea until Mairi came that Ciara's past led back to the original rulers of her race.

"I did not say you stole it," he gritted out with clear reluctance.

She forced herself to rise, only swaying a little as she gained her feet.

Eirik was there before she could blink, holding her arm,

his scowl gone, to be replaced by concern. "What is the matter?"

Waking dreams left her even more weakened than those that disturbed her sleep, but that was her own burden to bear and she certainly would not confide it to him. "Nothing. I am fine."

"You are pale."

"I need more sun."

He frowned, obviously not liking the flippancy of her answer.

"I had a vision," she said, to get his attention off her temporary weakness.

If he had looked concerned before, now he appeared downright worried. "While you were awake?"

The man didn't seem able to decide if he despised her or cared about her and she wasn't risking believing in the one when the other might be lurking around a convenient rock.

"It is not the first time," she said as casually as she could, like these waking visions did not terrify her.

"You did not mention this when we all spoke earlier."

"I did not think it mattered." And she had not wanted to worry her parents further. They had seemed distressed enough by the dreams and the call of the sacred stone.

"You need to speak to my grandmother."

"Why?"

"She is Anya-Gra, spiritual leader of our people."

"A *kelle*?"

"No, a *celi di*. She is no warrior; though she has been trained to protect herself, she would not lift her hand to another. 'Tis not in her nature."

"I thought only men could be *celi di*." Servants of God, not quite priests, but respected as servants of the church all the same. Though not technically under its authority, Highland priests performed religious ceremonies and guided their people's spiritual welfare.

"Among the human clans, this has become the case, but make no mistake, the Chrechte have followed female *celi di* and *kelle* since the beginning of time. Just as they have followed men with such callings."

"I knew that . . . the old stories."

"But the Faol no longer practice such spirituality."

She could not deny his words. "Abigail told me that her friend the abbess said Scripture states there is no distinction between man and woman in faith. Men make the distinctions."

"As we do in so many other things."

"So, your grandmother is a *celi di*?"

"She is and she can help you learn to live with and control your gift."

"The visions can be controlled?"

"I do not know, but my grandmother has never been as ill from them as you were when I arrived here."

"She is not part of the group of Éan that joined the Sinclairs."

"No."

"Where is she then? Did she stay in the forest?"

"How did you know some of the Éan chose to stay?"

"I wasn't sure, but I remembered the stories of the Faol that did the same, when we joined the clans."

"My grandmother claims there are still such Faol in the forest."

"If she is a seer, she would know."

"Aye."

"*Is* she still in the forest?"

"No. She went to the Donegal clan, to live near my sister, the first of our generation to give birth."

"Your sister is Barr's wife, is she not?"

"She is, but few know of the connection."

Ciara shrugged. What should she say? She knew things she should not and not all of them from visions.

"What does the Donegal priest think of your grandmother, I wonder?"

"I do not know, but he is not like many priests. He trained one of the Donegals to be *celi di* and does not assign penances out of cruelty."

"He is indeed a man of God then."

"Most likely."

Silence stretched between them, but he did not release her and she made no move to distance herself from him.

She bit her lip, as she was wont to do when agitated.

"It is hard."

"What?" Could that really be his voice, so soft and understanding?

She looked up at him, losing herself in his amber gaze against all good thinking. "To know things others do not, things you should not know."

"Is it?" He brushed the back of his hand down her cheek.

"Yes."

"Surely it is not all bad."

"Perhaps not." Ciara leaned into Eirik's touch, unable to do anything else.

"It got me Galen's attention when he had pulled away from his family, spending most of his time with his friends instead. It also cost him his life."

"Your brother did not die because you were trying to help him find the *Faolchú Chridhe*. He died because he followed Luag in hunting innocent Éan children."

"Galen didn't want to hurt them," she felt compelled to point out again.

Some of the hardness seeped back into Eirik's expression. "But he did nothing to stop Luag."

"No." She dropped her head, not wanting to see the look of censure on Eirik's features.

Her brother had committed a heinous act in even hunting another Chrechte, the fact he had not wanted to hurt the children did not exonerate him.

"I am sorry you lost your brother."

The words of condolence were so unexpected, she fell mute in shock.

"But not that you killed him," she finally said.

"I cannot be; to feel regret would be to place his life above the children he allowed to be threatened."

"Yes."

"You agree?" He tugged her face back up so their eyes had no choice but to meet.

"I am not a fool."

He nodded, his understanding glowing in the amber of his eyes. "Just a woman with knowledge she does not know what to do with."

Tears threatened at this further understanding and she blinked to keep the moisture back. "Yes."

"Anya-Gra will help you."

"So, I am not the descendant of a king, but a spiritual leader?" she asked, thinking of the old woman she had seen in her dream.

"Probably both. The royal family of the Éan have ruled our people for millennia and each spiritual leader we have had has also come from my line."

"Do you think it was the same with the wolves, before MacAlpin?"

"Aye. I am certain of it."

"But our royal lineage is now spread out like birdseed tossed from a high window among the clans."

"But only you possess the king's sword."

"I have a dirk with the same stones, and the arm cuff of one of my ancestors who was *kelle*, but I do not have her sword."

"As you said, your line has been spread out among the clans, but for you to have all three items, your lineage must be as pure as Mairi claims."

"They never told me."

"Your parents?"

"Or my brother. They all hid it from me, like I didn't matter."

"Mayhap they did not want to burden you with knowledge too heavy to bear."

Her aching heart was touched by Eirik's attempt to console her, but she knew the truth and she shook her head.

Finally finding the strength of will, she pulled away from him to go to the bed and look down at the sword. She was afraid to touch it again and maybe have another vision.

"So, it truly was the weapon of a monarch? I always thought it looked like it should be." Yet even after her vision, she had a hard time believing it.

"Aye. I have one just like it." Eirik drew his sword over his shoulder and swung it down to land against his other hand between them.

It was bronze as well, the edges of the blade sharpened to a much finer bevel than the one she kept in her trunk.

"May I see the handle?" she asked.

He repositioned the weapon so that it laid across his hands, fully open to her inspection.

After examining his sword closely, she stepped away from both it and the weapon lying on her bed. "They are not just alike."

"Are they not?" he asked, as if indulging her.

"No. On your handle, the dragon is the center figure. On mine, the *conriocht* is central."

They both went silent, contemplating what this slight difference could mean.

"Such would imply there is a sword out there somewhere that has a griffin as its center," he said in a tone she had never before heard from the dragon shifter . . . awe.

"A myth . . ."

The look Eirik gave her was wry. "Like the Éan and the true *conriocht*."

"But where are the cat shifters then, the Paindeal?"

Eirik looked thoughtful. "Some of the most ancient stories told of a bridge of land that used to connect Scotland to the land of the Norse. The Chrechte had supposedly traveled over these bridges of land before they fell into the sea and the only way to the land of the Vikings was by water because even an eagle cannot fly that far."

She thought maybe a dragon might be able to, though she did not say it. "You think the Paindeal are still in those lands?"

"Perhaps. Mayhap we will answer that question after we find the wolves' sacred stone."

Deciding the time for secrets was past, there was too much at stake, Ciara said, "I think I saw the woman that hid the *Faolchú Chridhe*."

"In your vision."

"Yes. She was in a cave. It was lit with torches, there

were drawings carved into the wall, but I could not make them out in the meager light." And her attention had been fixed on the woman.

Ciara only remembered the drawings as an impression on the peripheral of her sight.

"Was it the cavern of your other dreams?"

"No, but maybe it's part of the cave system that leads to it."

"So, you think the stone was hidden in a cave?"

"Yes, a cavern, deep in the ground. It glows with a strange green light." Would Eirik believe her any more fully than Galen, or would he too question the certainty she woke from her dreams with?

"I do not spend much time in caves when my dragon is not busy protecting the dreams of seers who are tormented by their gift. Are there known caverns like this?"

"There may be. We should ask our lair . . . um, my father. If he does not know, someone among the Balmoral may."

"It is a sound plan."

For no reason she could discern, she blushed with pleasure under his approval. Eirik's view of her did not matter. *She could not allow it to matter.*

Chapter 13

Nothing weighs on us so heavily as a secret.
—JEAN DE LA FONTAINE

"We need to speak to the Sinclair immediately." Eirik
sheathed his sword. "We have changed our plans for travel
to Balmoral Island as well."

"We are going to join Lais and Mairi on the boat crossing?" Ciara asked hopefully.

Eirik shook his head. "You and I will ride with them
until we are far enough away from the keep and crofter's
huts not to risk having my dragon seen. Then I will shift
and take you to the island. Fidaich and Canaul will stay
with the horses while we are on the island."

"They are only boys."

"Old enough to guard horses."

"What if Mairi's father has sent soldiers to search for
her? The boys would be no match for a full-grown Chrechte warrior. Besides, we are searching for the *Faolchú
Chridhe*, surely Faol soldiers should accompany us."

"You do not trust me to protect you without warriors of
the Faol to help?"

She should say no, remind him that he had already

proven himself to show no pity toward wolves, but she couldn't. No matter what she *should* feel toward the prince of the Éan, Ciara could not shake the certainty that her life was safe with him. And she could hardly claim a dragon was not up to the task of protecting her regardless.

"You are far too busy helping your people settle into the clan to take on this quest," she said, trying another tack and hoping to avoid the question of trust altogether.

She also wished she'd thought of this argument earlier during their discussion with everyone. It might have swayed her father, but then again . . . probably not.

No more than she expected it to sway the Éan prince. If he had already decided his people could be trusted under her father's leadership, Eirik was not going to balk at leaving them to do his own assigned duty for the clan.

"The plans for the search coincide with my need to check on the well-being of the rest of the Éan among the Balmoral and Donegal clans."

"There are more Éan?" she asked. When he'd mentioned his grandmother had gone to live with the Donegals, Ciara had thought she was the only one.

"There are."

"How many?"

"Two groups about the same size as the one I brought to the Sinclair holding."

"A size of tribe that it would be difficult to hide in the forest any longer."

Eirik's eyes narrowed as if surprised at her insight, but he nodded. "If we had not joined the clans, it would have become increasingly easy for our enemies to find us."

"And kill each one they did find," she said with a sick feeling in her stomach.

"Aye."

"I am sorry."

"You are not of the Faol that would kill us."

"No, but it is wrong and makes me feel ashamed of my own heritage."

"It should not. There are too many good Faol to paint

you all with the brush of evil Rowland and those of his ilk would wield."

"My father was loyal to Rowland. He and my mother argued about it. She thought Rowland responsible for the death of our laird before him, though they were accounted friends."

"Your mother was wise."

"Until her mind went after my father's death." True mates, her mother had not been able to withstand the loneliness once he was gone.

"Is that why she took her own life?"

"She was not in her right mind, but I did not think she would do that. I did not even think she was aware enough to want to, but the loss of my brother was one weight too heavy for her to bear."

"She still had you."

"Neither of my parents accorded me much value since I was not a son."

"That is not the way of the Chrechte."

"No, but it was their way." Ciara shook her head. "Still, there was no doubt something I could have done to alleviate my mother's grief. I was too lost in my own thoughts to even notice the direction hers had gone."

"And were there signs? Looking back?"

"I still cannot find them, no matter how I try to remember, but they must have been there."

"No. You said yourself, she was lost to herself at the death of her mate. She would not have made her plans known for she probably did not even realize them herself."

"I . . ."

"It was not your fault."

"You don't think so?"

"I know it and so do you, if you will listen to the voice deep inside you."

"You're pretty arrogant, you know this?"

"So you have said."

"I think it bears repeating."

He shrugged and she found herself smiling, though she

was not sure why. "So, the Éan have only joined two other clans?"

"I trust the Balmoral and Donegal with the safety of my people, but no others."

Again such arrogance, it was breathtaking, but Eirik's sense of duty shone every bit as brightly. "You see it as your job to ensure the safety of your people."

"Aye."

"Your cousin was certain of his protector, that day in the forest. When I saw your dragon for the first time, I knew exactly who he had been referring to." And she had been awestruck.

"To protect and guide the Éan is my greatest honor and responsibility."

She had no difficulty believing him.

"You gave up your role as sovereign to see to the safety and longevity of your race." The selflessness and fore-thought of the act was so overwhelming, she could barely take it in.

"I only followed the Faol to the clans."

When she should have been able to expect that arro-gance again, she was met with humility. The man was a conundrum of a certainty.

"But we came to the clans because of MacAlpin's betrayal," she reminded him. Far from a great personal and voluntary sacrifice like Eirik's own.

"Perhaps that heinous act was the event that made your leaders realize the futility of a way of life so separated from the humans, but they would have come to see what needed to be done eventually regardless."

"You give them a great deal of credit."

"I know what it is to have the burden of your people's safety on your shoulders."

Somehow they had moved closer together, so their bodies almost touched. She wanted to close the distance, wanted to feel his lips on hers again, but that way lay madness.

She took a deliberate step back. "So, you spread that burden among the clans without really relinquishing it at all. I think it takes a true servant to his people, to renounce his position as king in order to allow those he calls his to swear allegiance to clan chiefs."

"I never accepted the mantle of monarch."

What? But that made no sense. She didn't know as much about the ancient ways as he did, but Ciara was certain kings were born among the Chrechte, not chosen. "Why not?"

He looked down at her sword still lying on the bed, a strange expression in his amber eyes. "Because I knew this day would come and if I had taken the oaths of a king, I could not have honorably instructed my people to give their allegiance to another leader."

"You are the kind of leader my father says a man should be. It is why he despises MacLeod so." Even before Mairi had come to the Sinclair lands, rumors of the other laird's selfish behaviors had abounded.

"Why do you think I joined this clan?" Eirik asked wryly.

"I'm glad you did." As soon as the words left her mouth she wished them unsaid. "I mean, for your people's sake and for my father. A pack alpha and clan laird can never have too many trusted warriors."

With a predatory expression, Eirik moved closer to her and she backed up until the stone wall prevented further retreat.

He came so close, the salty musk of his skin overwhelmed her senses. "I think you are glad I am here for more than just your father's sake."

She did not have it in her to lie, but no more was she willing to feed his ego with the truth. Pressing her lips together in firm refusal to speak, she looked up at him.

Undeterred by her silence, Eirik smiled that rare smile she'd learned to watch for and lowered his head. "I too am glad to have joined this clan."

The kiss was like before, and yet different. Eirik explored her lips with his own, his tongue teasing along the entrance to her mouth. But he did not touch her otherwise.

Both of his fists rested on either side of her head on the wall and his lower body was a breath from her own. She could feel his heat all through her but nowhere but their lips did they actually connect.

Her hands pressed against the cold stone behind her, aching with the need to feel smooth skin over hard muscle.

Before she could give in to it, he broke the kiss and stepped back. "We need to speak to your father again before we leave."

Continuing to lean against the wall, Ciara could do nothing but nod.

"I will kiss you again."

Ciara started to nod again but realized what she was doing and shook her head quickly instead.

Eirik's smile was purely feral. "Gather what you need; we will leave after speaking to the Sinclair."

How did Eirik do this to her? Her brains had turned to mush, but she wasn't about to let him see that. She turned and did her best to wrap the sword again in the Donegal plaid.

"When you had your vision, were you touching it?" Eirik asked, pointing to the not-nearly-so-neatly wrapped bundle as the one she'd taken from the trunk.

"How did you know?"

"I did not, that is why I asked."

"Oh, well . . . I was. Touching it, I mean." She sounded like a simpleton and it was all his fault.

"Mayhap we should bring it with us on this quest to find the *Faolchú Chridhe* then."

"It is too big for me to wear."

His lips quirked as if he thought her observation amusing. "It is a man's sword. I will wear it with my own."

"Two swords?" She'd seen other warriors with such, but only one long sword and one short one. She'd never seen a warrior carry two long swords before.

"It would be too heavy," she protested without thinking.

Eirik laughed, his head thrown back, the sound booming in the small bedchamber. "I am a dragon shifter. I could carry an arsenal on my back and still fight with ease."

No doubt that was true, and she would have thought of it, were her mind not still muddled from his kiss. Regardless, she hesitated to bring her brother's sword.

"I will not keep it, if that is what worries you. Nor will I lose it. I know the value of our heritage."

"I know." She frowned at Eirik, not understanding why he would even think she would be afraid of such a thing. "You might be irritating beyond measure and too arrogant for any one man, but you are no thief and are certainly not likely to misplace a Chrechte king's sword."

He was a bloody selfless prince of his people, not even a mere man.

Eirik's lips quirked in a wry smile. "I'm not sure if that is praise or condemnation."

"Like you need praise to add to your overweening confidence."

"Do you not know? It is only overweening if it is not justified. Mine is."

"No doubt." He sounded just like her father.

"If not fear of losing it, then why hesitate to bring the sword?"

There was nothing for it but to tell him the truth. "I don't want to touch it again."

If she could avoid another waking vision, so much the better.

"You may have no choice."

"If we have it with us, that is certainly true."

"You are no coward."

"I'm not." Though sometimes she wanted to be.

"We bring the sword."

She sighed but relented. "Oh, very well."

He picked it up and donned the scabbard so the sword's handle rested opposite his own on the other side of his back. "You can finish gathering your things later. We need to find the Sinclair."

He talked as if she would need some measure of time to do so, but she did not. Making quick work of folding her old Donegal plaid, she put it in the trunk. Then, she grabbed the blanket from her bed before she folded it with a single fur into a bundle she tied with a leather strap. "This is all I need."

"You are certain?" he asked with a surprised frown.

"Yes."

"I expected you to bring more . . . fripperies."

"Why?"

"You are a woman."

"Éan women find fripperies necessary, do they?" She could not see it.

The women of his people she'd seen so far among her clan were quite minimalistic in their dress and appearance. Over time, that might change, but for now they still lived much as she was sure they had in the forest.

"No." He packed a world of the absurdity at such a thought in that single word.

The Sinclair women were not much more focused on their appearance than the Éan that had come to live among them though. "Then why believe I would take a trunk full to travel?"

Not that she thought he would ever stand for that kind of an unwieldy burden on their quest.

Eirik gave a significant look to Ciara's dress and understanding dawned.

"It is like the cross between a clanswoman and an English woman's dress. I know. And with too many layers for an easy shift into my wolf form, but Abigail does not despise her homeland like we do. She has no notion of dressing to make a shift easy and quick."

Eirik frowned. "The laird has not told her that it would be better for you to dress as the other clanswomen?"

"He does not wish to hurt her feelings and no more do I."

"Hurt feelings cannot always be avoided."

"I know." She lived in a keep filled with Chrechte warriors, after all. They were not well acquainted with subtlety or tact, though they tried with their lady. "Abigail has been too kind to me for me to dismiss her feelings though. She is a gentle soul."

"She must be strong to make the laird such a good mate though."

"She is. Gentle does not equal weak."

"But you protect her feelings at the expense of your own comfort."

"It's what family does." And even when Ciara had not wanted to acknowledge she had a family, she'd understood that.

Eirik shook his head, but he didn't argue any further about the unsuitability of Ciara's style of dress for a Chrechte.

They found her father in the twins' room, watching the little boys napping. There was an expression of such love on his features, Ciara's own heart ached with it. Talorc of the Sinclairs, powerful Chrechte alpha and clan chieftain, insisted on putting his sons down for their nap with a story and soothing touch himself more days than not.

His soldiers didn't seem to find their training or duties any less rigorous for their laird's short afternoon respites.

He turned as soon as Ciara stepped into the room. She indicated the corridor with her head and he nodded, but she did not follow him out of the room immediately.

First, she took a moment to place barely there kisses of farewell on her adopted brothers' foreheads. She did not know how long this quest would keep her from the holding and she would miss them. She'd spent near as much time with them since their birth as Abigail and Talorc. How Ciara had deceived herself into believing she had no family to lose, she was not entirely sure.

The needs of the heart made many things possible.

She smiled mistily down at the boys and prayed for their safety while she was gone. Such sweet lads, but both prone to trouble if not watched more closely than a wounded boar. Brian slept sprawled, his cherubic face showing no sign of his mischievous nature when awake. Drost snuggled into the covers, his favorite wooden knife tucked against him like a doll.

One day he would wield a sword like his father and probably be every bit as hard and uncompromising as the laird as well. These boys would be strong, but their strength would always be tempered by honor and compassion. Just as Talorc's was, no matter how he might deny the latter.

Her heart full, she crept quietly from the room and

followed her father and Eirik down the stairs. They found Abigail and Guaire going over the records of the keep's stores at the main table in the great hall.

Abigail looked up with a smile for all of them, but her eyes were on Ciara when she said, "I am glad you came to say good-bye before leaving."

"I would have regardless," Ciara promised. "But we have a question for, um . . . father."

Abigail's smile became brighter and the laird's pleasure could be felt in the air around them. So simple a thing, to use the words that had resided in her heart so long.

She wanted to apologize, but both laird and lady's expression revealed an understanding Ciara would never take for granted.

Abigail made sure they were all seated at the table with watered wine before Talorc asked, "What is your question?"

"I should have asked it this morning, but I am unaccustomed to speaking of my secrets." It was not quite an admission of regret, but close enough. She hoped.

"You will learn it is safe to share them with your family," Abigail said softly. "I did."

The laird smiled at her, a silent message passing between them. "What is your question, daughter?" he asked Ciara.

He'd called her daughter many times, but for today was the first time Ciara had allowed herself to accept the title fully. The word now caused a sweet pain inside her. "I possess a sword that Eirik believes belonged to one of the original Chrechte kings," she said instead of asking about the luminous caves, surprising herself.

And apparently the others at the table as Abigail gasped, Talorc cursed, Guaire said, "Now, that's a treasure to protect," and Talorc growled, swearing a second time. Guaire did not look worried and Ciara was pretty sure the human mate to her father's second-in-command had nothing to worry about.

"Niall . . ." her father snarled.

"Has said nothing he ought not to," Guaire said with the acerbity the seneschal had become known for. He might be almost half the size of his mate, but the man was no pushover. "But I live here. I see things. I know what he does not say, when he does his best to hide things from me. You might recall I was well aware of the import of your and his Chrechte nature long before he would ever have admitted it to me."

Her father gave Eirik a significant look and the Éan prince just rolled his eyes. "Think you that the Éan have no secrets we carry generation to generation? Whatever treasure you protect with your covert words and actions, it is safe from my curiosity. Guaire is right in saying that the fact your daughter had a sword of a Chrechte king in the trunk at the end of her bed is a secret worth knowing."

"Because it means she really is a descendant of the original Faol kings?"

"That and the sword itself has power to help her see visions of the sacred stone."

"Really?" Abigail asked, her soft brown eyes glowing with interest.

Ciara nodded but kicked Eirik's ankle under the table. He hadn't needed to share that bit of information.

The look he gave her was bland, but his tone was firm. "No more secrets, remember, *faolán*?"

Her father's chuckle stopped the words of protest from fully forming and she simply nodded.

"I take it that is the second sword you wear," Talorc observed.

"It is." Eirik went to draw the Faol sword. "Do you want to see it?"

Her father's nod, his eyes filled with a deep desire she never would have expected sent a sharp stab of guilt through Ciara. She should have told him about the sword long before this. She'd known it was special, even if she had not known its true illustrious heritage.

Eirik drew the sword and laid it on the table, the emeralds in the hilt not glowing like they had in her bedroom, but looking magical all the same.

Her adopted father reached out slowly, his blue gaze dark with reverence. "'Tis truly of the ancient Chrechte. Look at the *conriocht* on the handle."

"Pick it up. Try the warrior's dance with it," Eirik said in a voice Ciara found compelling, though she found the suggestion odd.

Her father saw nothing wrong with it though, because he did exactly as Eirik suggested. Wielding the sword through the pattern of movement she had seen many times before, he yet managed to make the dance something more than it had ever been.

And Ciara realized the stones in the hilt were glowing now.

Talorc stopped and held the sword like it had been made for him. "The handle is hot."

"I was taught that none but those of my line could wield the sword given me upon my father's death," Eirik said. "That it would accept only a Chrechte of righteous heart as its master."

"It's a sword, not a horse," Ciara's adopted father said with some disbelief.

Chapter 14

Learning carries within itself certain dangers because
out of necessity one has to learn from one's enemies.
—LEON TROTSKY

"Aye, but it is connected to your *Faolchú Chridhe*
through the stones in the hilt," Eirik claimed. "Our tradi-
tion says that the original sacred stone was cut into the
large stone used in our ceremonies, and a series of smaller
ones."

"I have never heard of such," her father replied.

Eirik shrugged, clearly unsurprised. "Originally these
stones were held by different members of the family that
had been entrusted with the protection and use of the *Clach
Gealach Gra* on behalf of our people. Later, some of the
smaller stones were lost while others were used in jewelry
to decorate weapons that became as important as blood-
lines in claiming the title of spiritual leader or king."

"You believe it was the same among the Faol?" Ciara
asked, thinking it sounded right.

Eirik looked down at her. "Aye."

"So, he is feeling the heat in the handle because he is
also of the bloodline."

"Aye." Eirik touched her temple as if imparting a truth

directly to her. "Fate sent you to this home for a reason when you lost the last of the family of your birth."

"I have always believed that." Abigail reached out to take Ciara's hand and squeezed. "You were meant to be my daughter."

The lump in Ciara's throat prevented her from replying.

"You are saying any other warrior could not wield this sword just as easily?" her father demanded of Eirik, clearly uncomfortable with the overt emotion swirling around them.

"Exactly."

"I do not believe it."

"Call another warrior inside."

Guaire jumped up. "I'll find Niall and ask him to send a soldier to the great hall."

Talorc inclined his head in acknowledgment and the seneschal left the great hall. Her father laid the sword on the table. "Was that your question, Ciara?"

"What?"

"Whether I could wield the sword, or not?"

"Oh . . . uh . . . no. I did not realize Eirik thought you could, or that some could not. The sword has nothing to do with my question."

"Directly," Eirik interjected.

And she nodded in agreement. She could not deny the connection between it and the *Faolchú Chridhe*, not after her waking vision.

When her father just gave her a look of question, she swallowed and prepared to share more of the secrets she'd kept held so close for so long.

"Is this about your dreams?" Abigail asked, clearly trying to help Ciara get the words out.

Ciara swallowed again and then forced the words from her tight throat. "In my dreams, I see the *Faolchú Chridhe* in a vast cavern that glows with a strange green light. It's not torches, but almost as if the walls themselves put off the light. Do you know of caves or a cavern such as this?"

Saying it out loud made it sound even more fanciful than when she thought about it.

Before her father had a chance to answer, Guaire came in with Everett, one of the Chrechte soldiers.

Abigail smiled in welcome, but Talorc wasted no time in indicating the sword on the table. "Use that to demonstrate the beginning sword movements taught to all warriors."

Everett did not ask why but simply obeyed his laird. However, it was quickly obvious he did not like the sword he was using. His movements lacked grace and the sword looked more like a heavy boulder in his hand the way it moved than a weapon of such impressive craftsmanship.

Nevertheless, Everett finished his demonstration before setting the sword back on the table with a frown.

"It is beautiful, but the weight is all wrong. I'd probably end up cutting my own arm off if I tried to use this sword in battle. Was it a gift sent north by our lady's family?" he asked in confusion.

"Nay. You may leave, Everett."

Everett shrugged and did so, showing no reluctance to get back to his training.

Eirik crossed his arms and looked at Ciara's father. "Do you still doubt the unique nature of that weapon?"

"Everett is a competent warrior." Her father's confusion was even more pronounced than his soldier's had been. "He has moved up the ranks and now trains the younger soldiers."

"But he cannot wield the sword of the *Faolchú Chridhe*." Eirik evinced no surprise at that turn of events.

"You really think my father is like me, a descendant of the keepers of the stone," Ciara said with some awe.

"I do. You yourself said that those that remained with that blood in their veins, no matter how diluted, were scattered among the Highland clans."

"But some must have more connection to the stone than others," Guaire observed while it was clear Abigail and Talorc were sharing a silent conversation between mates through their mindspeak.

"Aye. They do. You heard the Sinclair say the handle grew heated in his palm?"

"Yes."

"That is a sign the sword accepts him. It is not enough to carry the blood of original keeper of the stone; it must also call to you."

No one present who knew Everett and Talorc could doubt Eirik's words, because the warrior and his laird were distant cousins. "Then we should leave it with my father."

"Not until we have found the *Faolchú Chridhe*." Eirik's voice said he would not be moved.

He put action to words and slid the sword back into its scabbard.

"But—"

"I agree," her father said over her objections. "The sword is yours, Ciara, and must remain with you."

She looked beseechingly at her mother.

But though Abigail gave her a look of understanding, she said, "Your father is right. Please listen to him."

There was no point in arguing further, so Ciara simply gave a silent gesture of agreement. She didn't have to be happy about it, but she wasn't going to pout like a child, either.

Much.

"What do you think of this oddly lit cavern?" Eirik asked their laird, closing the subject of the sword with finality.

"It is not so uncommon in caves, particularly those with some source of water, to glow as Ciara describes. I can think of none that open into a large cavern like you describe though." Talorc wrinkled his brow. "You should begin your search with those caves our people have always considered sacred. Mayhap there are passages we are not aware of that lead to this cavern."

"I do not know why I am certain, but there is no question in my mind that the cavern is deep in the earth," Ciara said. "It would not be so far a stretch to think there are passages we have forgotten that were once used by our ancestors."

Her father nodded, not questioning her belief the cavern was deep in the ground. Unlike her brother, the Sinclair laird was clearly not stuck on the idea that the Éan had stolen the *Faolchú Chridhe*.

"Not all such caves are on friendly lands," Guaire said and then pursed his lips at the look his laird cast him. "Niall does not keep secrets from me, but one."

Her father jerked his head in acknowledgment.

Further discussion revealed that there were four sets of caves that Talorc knew about which the Faol of the Chrechte had considered sacred for many generations. Two were on Sinclair and Donegal lands, one was located in the MacLeod's holding and one was in the unclaimed forest to the north.

"Mayhap the Balmoral will know of others," Talorc suggested. "I dinna think they come across the water to perform their sacred rites, so they must have someplace consecrated on the island."

"We'll start the search there then, after we talk to his elders," Eirik said, though he didn't sound as if he expected to find the *Faolchú Chridhe* on Balmoral Island.

Her father frowned. "If Ciara's family of birth came from land near the Donegal holding, mayhap you should start there."

"I don't know if they did," Ciara said. She knew far too little about her first family's history, she'd come to realize. "After all, Eirik—prince of the Éan—ended up here, though his family used to live in the wild forests of the north, but closest to my former clan's lands."

"And the *Clach Gealach Gra* is here on Sinclair land, in the caves that have been considered sacred by our people for longer than any can remember."

Perhaps *that* was where they should start their search, Ciara mused to herself. Only, those caves were still used so frequently for Chrechte sacred rites, what chance was there that a forgotten hidden cavern existed that had not been discovered in all these generations?

"It used to be Donegal land," Abigail reminded them all. "Circin was certainly upset about that strip of land being ceded to the Sinclairs by Scotland's king as part of my dowry."

Talorc nodded, looking rather pleased by the memory.

"But before that, it was claimed by the Sinclair and more importantly, the pack that hunted on Sinclair lands before joining the clan."

"Your pack?" Guaire asked.

Ciara's father nodded. "Aye. My ancestors were the original Chrechte of this area, though the pack split when joining the clans and some went to the Donegal while others came to the Sinclair."

"Which simply proves that those particular caves are on a piece of land that has been in dispute for generations," Eirik said.

Talorc sighed and nodded. "We will continue with the original plan."

"I know you do not want Ciara away from your holding any longer than absolutely necessary, but I will keep her safe," Eirik promised.

"See that you do."

The ride through the forest was quiet, the only sound from their party the carefully placed footfalls of the well-trained warhorses under the four travelers. An eagle and two ravens flew above them in the sky.

Eirik had surprised Ciara; taking heed of her worry for the young Éan, Fidaich and Canaul, he had assigned a seasoned warrior to join them in watching over the horses. She was even more surprised to discover both boys could shift.

"You said your coming-of-age ceremony was only seven years ago," she said quietly, bringing up the topic that had been worrying at her mind as they rode.

"Aye."

"But Fidaich and Canaul can shift already."

"The ability to shift comes early for the Éan; some can take their bird form when they are small children, though most wait until that time when bodies change from child to adult."

"And these two?"

"Fidaich started shifting this year, which was no surprise, but Canaul began shifting soon after. He is a year younger."

"Having his best friend shift without him must have been too much for his raven."

"Aye." There was a hint of a smile at the edges of Eirik's lips. "I was the same with my cousin who was two years older than me."

"I imagine everyone attributed your early shifting to you being the prince and of royal blood."

Eirik shrugged, but Ciara was sure she was right. "Still, I do not understand the coming-of-age ceremony if you already shift."

"It is different. It is when we are gifted with special talents and our ability to pass the raven on to the next generation relies on our connection to the *Clach Gealach Gra* during our coming-of-age ceremony."

Horror filled her at the thought of the Éan losing their stone as the Faol had misplaced theirs. "You are serious?" She had to know.

"Aye."

"But the wolves give birth to wolves without the *Faol-chú Chridhe*."

"It is a good thing, or there would be no Faol walking the earth today."

"Do you think one of the other races of the Chrechte stole our stone in hopes of just that eventuality?" Her vision today didn't intimate such, but still she wondered.

"I do not know, but does the why of it matter now? Centuries have passed. Any who had plans for the loss of the stone are gone."

It was a freeing thought, that the enmities of the past had no place in the present. "If the coming-of-age ceremony is not linked to the Éan's first change, how do you know when it is time for it?"

"It can be performed any time after the first change and before an Éan has seen twenty summers. However, if it is performed too early or late, the special talents conferred by the stone are weak."

"Who determines the time has come?"

"The stone. It calls to Anya-Gra, the parents and sometimes the Éan himself."

"It called to you."

"Yes, but it had been taken and was not in the Sacred Caves."

"I didn't know."

"You were not meant to. My sister returned it in time for my final blessing."

"You would not have your dragon if she had not." The prospect was untenable.

"Lais would not be able to heal, either."

"Do you think the *Faolchú Chridhe* will confer special talents like that as well?"

"Yes."

"But it's not the same." They'd already established that from the fact the Faol could reproduce without any coming-of-age ceremony. Stone or no stone.

"Each race has its differences. For instance, all Éan have control of their change from the first time their bird takes them."

"Truly?" Among the Faol, most males could not control their change, so it was dictated by the full moon, until they participated in the sacred act of sex. White wolves and their descendants were the exception.

"Aye."

"I wonder if it is like that for the Paindeal."

"If they continue to walk the earth at all."

"I'm sure they do."

He frowned, his attention all around them as he sought out potential threats. "You cannot be sure."

"Yes, I can."

"Because of the dreams," he said with sudden understanding.

"Yes."

"You have dreamed of the Paindeal as well? You did not say."

"Only when I was very young and I have always thought they were just dreams." Until today when so many things had become clearer and more confusing as the case may be. "Nothing prophetic. It wasn't a secret I knew I was keeping."

"You have spent too many years hiding the truth of yourself."

But she hadn't been hiding. "I didn't *know* about myself."

"You do not take my meaning. You have hidden your ability to connect to the *Faolchú Chridhe*."

"There were many times I thought it all in my head."

"Aye. You deserved to know the truth, but it was never given to you."

"I am so angry with my family," she admitted. "But they're dead and I feel dishonorable being so mad at them. Only, I can't make the feelings go away." Too many feelings refused to be stifled inside her now.

"They hurt you deeply with their dishonesty and the pain is fresh because you have just discovered their treachery."

"You are right," she whispered. She did not want to harbor anger toward those she had loved and who were irrevocably gone, but the pain inside her would not go away.

"Their deceptions harmed your people as well."

"Only Galen knew of the *Faolchú Chridhe*."

"But if your mother and father had told you the truth of your lineage, you would have known how important finding the sacred stone was for all of the Faol."

"Do you think it called to my father?"

"Nay."

"I don't, either." And for some reason, that truth made her sad, but her father had not been wise in his loyalties.

A caw sounded from above. Ciara looked up in time to see one raven chasing another through the sky. It reminded her of when cubs played and she smiled. Though she doubted Eirik, or the eagle shifter, for that matter, were going to be so tolerant.

The two ravens flew back into formation with the eagle, though she saw no signs of the eagle physically reining them in.

"They're young still," she said to Eirik.

"They are feeling the freedom of belonging to the clan rather than living in hiding in the forest."

"That's a good thing, right?"

"When it does not put them, or those they are assigned to guard, at risk."

"They will learn. After all, Fidaich is related to you."

"Canaul is the son of one of our fiercest warriors."

"The eagle flying with them," she guessed.

"Aye. Canaul's mother was a raven; he took after her in the shift."

"Was?"

"She disappeared in the forest."

One of the victims of the wolves who believed all Éan had to die. "I am sorry."

Eirik shrugged. "You have nothing to apologize for."

"I hate it."

"What?"

"That your people were hunted by mine."

"It is not over, but Barr and your father have fought hard to clear their clans of those who would continue."

"Not the Balmoral?"

"There were none among his pack that belonged to this secret society of wolves."

"I'm surprised there were any among the Sinclair."

"So was your father."

"He banished them?"

"The ones he did not kill; they were caught hunting Éan."

"And you? Have you killed wolves besides Luag and Galen?"

"I am protector of my people."

It was an answer . . . of sorts.

Another caw sounded from above. Ciara made a point of not looking up this time though. She hoped the young ravens' antics would be less annoying to their prince if she pretended to ignore them.

The rumble very much like a wolf's growl that sounded from Eirik's chest said her hope was in vain.

"You know, if you were willing to travel by boat, rather

than as a dragon, we could take our horses with us on the crossing." The boats that made this possible required a minimum of two rowers, and not one of them a still healing and fragile human woman. "And we would not need a guard, Éan, or otherwise, for our horses."

"Birds fly over water. We do not ride boats."

Right. Arrogant dragon. "Lais is riding in a boat."

"He would trust Mairi's crossing to no other."

"Is she really his mate?" Ciara asked in a whisper, though she doubted the others could have heard her regardless.

Lais and Mairi lagged behind because the healer insisted the other woman's horse maintain a slower pace. He was coddling her like she was as broken as she'd been before his sessions healing her. Though it was clear she was much better and well able to ride a horse without trouble.

It was amusing and really, a little sweet. Though Ciara was sure Lais would not thank her for saying so.

Eirik looked up at the sky and then at Ciara, his expression giving nothing away. "Only time will tell."

"But he's so protective of her."

"He is a healer."

"Never mind." Eirik clearly had no intention of giving her a direct answer.

Even though it was perfectly obvious from the way he'd spoken the night Ciara had found Mairi that Eirik believed the MacLeod's daughter and Lais to be mates.

"Why ask if you do not want an answer?"

"If I wanted doublespeak, I would go to the English, thank you."

Instead of taking offense, Eirik laughed. Loud and full of real mirth, it was such an arresting sound that Ciara felt a strange tightening in her chest. She wanted to hear more.

Unfortunately, the sound cut off almost immediately. "Quiet," he ordered.

She didn't ask why but did her best to discern his reason for caution. She could hear nothing in the forest that seemed out of place, but she noted the eagle high in the sky was flying far to the left of them rather than directly above. And the two younger ravens were far to the right.

Suddenly, Lais and Mairi had caught up and Eirik had taken lead while Lais dropped to the back, with Ciara and Mairi's horses between them. The two men drew their swords at the same time, both their attention fixed to the left, though Ciara still could discern no untoward sound.

If she didn't know better, she would think the two warriors were communicating with mindspeak. But only some family and true mates could mindspeak. Though, perhaps among the Éan, this was another difference from the Faol.

Mairi did not make a sound, but it was clear she was aware something was amiss. Ciara's wolf's hearing could tell the other woman's heart rate had increased and fear scented the air around them.

Eirik's head came up and he sniffed at the air, a frown showing on his strong features. He'd noted Mairi's scent of fear and wasn't happy about it.

The danger must be closer than Ciara realized for the dragon to be worried in this way.

She let her horse move next to Mairi's until they were close enough for her to reach out to the other woman. Ciara took Mairi's hand and leaned so she could speak directly into the human woman's ear. "You must control your fear. If wolves from your father's pack hunt us, they will smell it."

The scent of fear spiked, but Mairi made a clear attempt to calm herself. Taking deep breaths, she even closed her eyes as if she trusted Ciara to make sure her horse stayed its course.

"Good. Remember, we have five Chrechte warriors with us and one is a dragon." Calling the two raven youths warriors was stretching it a bit, but Mairi needed the assurances. "Naught will happen to you. I promise."

Mairi squeezed her hand, her fear fading a bit. And Ciara had an idea. She'd never tried anything like this before, but there was nothing to lose by it.

They were taught that human children of Chrechte parents shared none of their gifts because they did not share the ability to shift. Ciara had not always been convinced of this.

If MacAlpin had not had Chrechte cunning, would he

have been able to betray and kill the others of his line the way he had done?

"Concentrate on the scents of the forest around you," she instructed Mairi. "Can you do that for me?"

Mairi nodded with a tiny jerk of her head.

"Good. Can you smell the trees?"

"Yes," Mairi barely whispered on a puff of air.

"Now, smell the earth, the dead leaves, the boar who traveled here earlier today, the fern and heather. Let their sun-warmed fragrance fill your senses."

The scent of Mairi's fear began to dissipate.

"Good. Keep concentrating on the fern and heather." Two scents found throughout the forest, they would mask Mairi's own without causing any who hunted them to stop and consider.

Mairi continued to breathe deeply, her eyes closed, but her scent was almost completely gone now.

"Now think about that smell surrounding you. Imagine your very skin giving off the perfume of heather, the leafy smell of a fern."

It worked; Mairi's scent was masked completely by the scents of the forest around them.

Chapter 15

No doubt but there is none other beast comparable to
the mighty dragon in awesome power and majesty, and
few so worthy of the diligent studies of wise men.

—GILDAS MAGNUS, *ARS DRACONIS*

Ciara did not know if the other woman had been able
to do this because she had the gift of sight, more of her
father's Chrechte blood than she'd ever realized, or simply
because any child of a Chrechte could do it.

And it did not matter. All that was of any importance in
that moment was that Mairi's scent would not give them
away to their enemy.

"Open your eyes now, Mairi."

The other woman did, their blue depths glazed with her
effort to concentrate on masking her scent.

Eirik's head snapped around and he stared at Ciara with
shocked question, though he remained silent as a good
warrior should.

Ciara smiled, her pride in Mairi's accomplishment
warm inside her. She tilted her head toward Mairi to let
Eirik know the human had done it, not Ciara. Not that she
could have, but perhaps among the Éan such would have
been possible.

Eirik narrowed his eyes in acknowledgment but turned around to focus on where he led them.

Ciara leaned sideways to speak in Mairi's ear again. "It is very important you keep your focus on these scents. You are too new at this to maintain the mask on your scent without full concentration."

Mairi nodded, this time firmly.

Eirik's horse veered to the right and Ciara followed him, nudging Mairi's leg to make sure she did the same. The path narrowed through the trees and Ciara was forced to ride ahead of Mairi, rather than beside her, but the other woman did not slip in her concentration for even a second.

They rode in complete silence for two hours before Eirik put his fist in the air to call them to a halt.

He looked back at them over his shoulder. "We are in no danger of being discovered by the MacLeod soldiers spied from the sky."

So, the eagle and ravens *had* been on guard duty. No wonder Eirik had been so frustrated with them. More to the point, the Éan had been able to communicate the danger to Eirik.

"You are sure?" Mairi asked in a strained voice, interrupting Ciara's thoughts.

No sooner had Eirik said, "Aye," than Mairi's entire body sagged and her scent became discernable once again amidst the fragrances of the forest. While it was no longer spiced with fear, there was an undeniable element of relief in it.

She slumped sideways and Ciara caught her before the other woman fell off her horse. Lais was there in a heartbeat, pulling Mairi right onto the blond warrior's lap atop his horse.

"Masking her scent was hard on her." The healer's concern was apparent, but so was his pride in Mairi's accomplishment. "She did it though, and no wolf to share her soul, either."

"That she did," Eirik agreed.

Ciara shook her head at the way the men talked about

Mairi, instead of to her. She reached out and patted Mairi's leg. "You did as well as any wolf."

Mairi gave her a tired grin. "Really?"

"Most certainly. Better than I the first time I tried to mask my scent." She did not mention she'd been a child at the time.

Her father had not believed in waiting for the first change to begin training his children in the ways of the Chrechte. Since both her parents had been Faol and their parents before them, there was no question that Ciara or Galen would share their soul with a wolf.

"We have another two hours' ride to the water." Eirik looked at Mairi. "Do you need to rest?"

She shook her head and Lais said, "She will ride with me."

Mairi did not argue.

Ciara noted Eirik did not ask *her* if she needed a break and that made her smile. He did not think Ciara weak, despite the toll her dreams had taken on her.

She looked up, taking in the position of the sun. Then she considered what she could see of landmarks around her. Eirik had guided them away from the threat, but with a minimal loss in time to reach the Sinclair boats for crossing the water to Balmoral Island.

It was impressive, though she'd no plans to tell him so. The man had enough confidence in his own abilities without adding her confidence in him to the mix.

He maneuvered his horse so they faced one another, but were side by side. "You did well, teaching Mairi to mask her scent."

"She made all the effort."

"No." He brushed the back of his knuckles along Ciara's cheek, making her want to lean into this touch. "You do not realize it, but as her princess you were able to reach out to the Chrechte within her in a way no one else could have."

But in a way he understood.

"Is this true?" she could not help asking.

"It is. Among the Éan, those of my family are charged with training the human offspring of our Chrechte brethren. Not all have equal abilities, but it takes one of the family of the Gra Gealach to draw whatever Chrechte gifts they do have forth."

"That is amazing."

"It is. My aunt was charged with it when we lived in the forest. Now that we are spread among the clans, others will have to share the burden."

"Your aunt came to the Sinclairs?"

"One of them. Fidaich's mother."

"Oh." Ciara still had a difficult time seeing herself as some kind of princess, but she thought her father should be made aware of this practice among the Éan. Perhaps the Faol could emulate it.

"Thank you," Eirik said when the silence had been stretched between them.

Ciara had been lost in thought, but apparently, he was not finished with their conversation.

"Why?"

"I did not want to engage the enemy. Your safety and that of the human seer are of utmost importance."

"Because of the *Faolchú Chridhe*." Why did part of her wish there was a more personal component to Eirik's concern?

"We must find it before the MacLeod."

"Of course." Ciara should not be disappointed by his answer. She really should not, but her foolish heart ached all the same. "We will."

"Aye, we will."

"You are so certain?"

Her words had been spoken more out of hope, but Eirik had sounded like he had seen the future and knew what would come to be. Perhaps as prince of his people, he had.

Though if he saw visions, would he not have told her? "Do you have what Mairi calls the sight as well?"

"Nay, but there is no doubt the *Faolchú Chridhe* calls to you in a way it does no other."

"How do you know?" Though she herself was certain he spoke the truth, that knowledge an immovable boulder inside her heart.

"'Twould have been found by now otherwise. You have spent seven years denying its call."

"I was afraid of what it could do."

"Because you saw only the selfish lust for power your brother exhibited. You did not understand the gift the sacred stone is and should be to all the Faol."

"No, I did not." She swallowed and then admitted, "I did not let myself see the selfishness driving my brother, either. I needed to believe he wanted the best for the Faol as well."

"He was young and deceived. He might yet have come around to understand the power was not meant for a few, but for all."

"Thank you for saying that."

Eirik shrugged and Ciara had to suppress a smile. He was much like her adopted father in some ways.

"We will wait to take to the sky until we see Lais and Mairi safely launched on the water," Eirik said, clearly done with the other subject.

"All right."

"You are being very agreeable."

She shrugged. It was not her way to disagree for the sake of argument; if he thought otherwise, she could not help that.

When they arrived at the water, the eagle shifter was there to greet them. He bowed his head toward Eirik and grasped Lais's arm in a warrior's greeting.

"Where are Fidaich and Canaul?" Ciara asked Eirik.

"I sent them back to the Sinclair so they could tell him about the MacLeod soldiers on his land."

"What will he do?" Mairi asked worriedly, seemingly oblivious to the implication behind Eirik's claim to have sent the ravens away when they had never come out of the sky.

"He will send Niall and a group of Chrechte soldiers with him to confront the interlopers," Ciara replied when it became apparent none of the warriors intended to do so.

Her father would not take a rival clan's trespass on their

lands lightly. Niall would be on a mission to teach the foolish soldiers a lesson as well as bring them to heel.

Lais added, "Those who survive the encounter will be taken to the Sinclair."

Ciara wanted to kick him for his *helpfulness*. Mairi had gone gray. She might not want to return to her father's clan, but that did not mean Mairi had no concern for her former clansmen. She understood, as Ciara did, that the soldiers may only be guilty of following their laird's orders.

"Will he ransom them back to my father?" Mairi asked with a tremble in her voice. "I do not think he will pay, even for a Chrechte warrior."

Though it was not an unheard-of practice between rival clans to demand payment for the return of those caught in battle (and to kill those the laird refused to pay for, or sell them into slavery), Ciara knew it was not something her father would do. Not unless there was a circumstance in which Talorc *wanted* to return a clan soldier. Then he might demand ransom.

"If he finds them worthy, my father will give them the opportunity to pledge allegiance to him as clan chief and pack alpha."

"Truly?" Mairi asked with hope.

"My father is a Chrechte of great honor."

Eirik grunted. "He is at that."

"What will Laird Sinclair do if the soldiers won't pledge him their loyalty?" Mairi asked, sounding as if she really did not want the answer.

"He will probably give them over to Niall to beat some honor into them." Life in the Highlands was not so civilized as their king would like to believe.

Ignorant of his long-distance Chrechte heritage, King David had been heavily influenced by his years in England. Still, he was considered a good leader by most of his people. Although, while his Highland lairds were as loyal to him as they would be any king, they did not share his fascination with the English way of life.

Mairi flinched, her eyes filled with horror. "That is barbaric."

"A man beating his daughter almost to death is *barbaric*," Eirik said with disgusted conviction. "An honorable wolf teaching another how to live in the true Chrechte way is *necessary*."

"Do not worry yourself," Lais said with a pat on Mairi's shoulder. "Depending on how committed to your father's orders they are, the soldiers may not survive their first encounter with Niall at all."

Ciara had to stifle an amused snicker at the eagle's attempt at comforting Mairi. For a healer, he was awfully bloodthirsty.

Taking pity on the other woman, Ciara said, "Niall is a great warrior. He does not have to kill an enemy to win a fight."

Mairi's smile of relief had barely formed when Lais said, "But he's not a warrior to balk at killing, either. He knows when it is better to end a life than prolong it. Even when that life is Chrechte."

By the look Lais gave her, Ciara knew the words were as much for her sake as they were for Mairi. More so, if he had a brain in his head.

Warriors!

He wanted her to understand and accept Eirik's actions seven years ago in the forest, she comprehended that. But did he comprehend the impact his words had on the human woman standing before him, looking so frightened and tired?

Ciara did not think so.

Besides, as unexpected as she might find her own feelings, Ciara found that she had already come to terms with Eirik's actions. The dragon was protector of his people. Whether Galen had to die was not a point for discussion any longer. The fact was, he did die and not as innocently as she had once tried to make herself believe, either.

"I take your meaning, but I do not think your patient finds your words as comforting as you might have expected." Ciara indicated the pale features of the human woman who looked about ready to faint.

Lais let out a Chrechte curse and Ciara had to turn her

head to hide her smile this time. She felt badly for Mairi, but could not help being amused by Lais's realization of the effect of his words.

Maybe he would think twice before meddling between Ciara and Eirik in future. It was not as if there was something between them that needed meddling, either. Mind-melting kisses aside, Eirik could have no permanent place in her life.

He was not looking for a mate, he had said so. And she did not want one. No mate to lose. No mate that would mean children she would love with everything left of her long-shattered heart.

He would help her find the *Faolchú Chridhe* and that would be that.

'Twas too bad that she'd always been better at deceiving others than her herself. Because she could not make herself believe those words, not even a little bit.

The flight to Balmoral Island was even more magical than the first time Ciara had ridden Eirik's dragon. To be able to see the earth below in all its glorious color and the bright blue of the sky was astounding.

The feel of the wind on her face combined with the bright sunlight was unlike anything she had ever experienced.

The truth was, flying on the back of the dragon could become all too quickly something she craved.

They flew even higher than they had the first time, no doubt Eirik not wanting his dragon to be but a dot in the sky to any who might see him from below.

It was cold, but Ciara was fully dressed for this ride and Eirik had insisted she unfold her fur and blanket to wear like a double cloak. She'd scoffed, intending to shrug them off when they were in the air. Only she'd quickly discovered how very cold the summer air could be when the dragon flew so much faster than any horse she'd ever ridden. And the higher they went, the less the sun warmed her.

She snuggled in her fur-lined plaid against the dragon's neck and laughed with the sheer joy of living in that moment.

194 · Lucy Monroe

She could not remember the last time she had felt such happiness and she did not care, or hope for it to last. For this minute in time, she was truly delighted to be alive.

There was no worry about the *Faolchú Chridhe*, no concern about how easily Ciara lost herself in Eirik's kisses, no secrets to hide or reveal as the case may be, simply Ciara and the dragon in the wide-open sky.

Eirik threw his head back and roared, a sound that went right through his massive dragon's body and vibrated Ciara's as well. And she laughed, loving the sensation of sharing in his delight. Then, he cast fire, huge flames that filled her vision. It was the most incredible adventure of Ciara's life.

In that instant, she felt more connected to him than she had to anyone else . . . ever. She did not question how this could be, she simply enjoyed it for the temporary pleasure that it was.

It took no time at all to fly to the island. However, they did not land on the beach Ciara was used to from the yearly trips to Balmoral Island she had made with her adopted family. Instead, Eirik brought Ciara to a deserted stretch of beach around the curve of the island.

A guard of two men came out from the forest, their eyes big, their mouths dropped open in shock. With hair the color of the red sunset and looking vaguely familiar, the one on the left was a couple of inches taller and a bit broader than the one on the right. Neither could be discounted in a fight, though, she was sure.

The Éan were consistently smaller in stature than the Faol, Eirik being the exception, but her father said they were fierce warriors and he accorded them the same respect he did the wolves among his clan soldiers.

Thankfully, neither man lifted a weapon in threat. She did not want any of her adopted uncle's warriors hurt because they thought to go against a dragon who happened to be their ally. Though the fact they had come out of the forest at all was odd, now that she thought about it.

Chrechte warriors were fierce, but to challenge a dragon?

Only, they did not look like they meant to challenge Eirik, did they?

And surely Eirik's dragon senses would have alerted him to their presence before he landed.

Mulling over these inconsistencies and coming up with nothing to explain them, Ciara climbed off Eirik's back with help from his tail just as she'd done the first time. As soon as she stood on the ground, she dropped both her makeshift cloak and the bundle of Eirik's things she had held in her lap for the flight.

Her hand rested against the handle of her dirk. Something strange was going on here, but she sensed no danger.

A flash of crimson light almost lost in the brightness of the sun heralded Eirik's shift back into his human form. Neither of the men drawing nearer showed any surprise at this. In fact, the shorter one smiled in what had to be welcome.

Ciara cut a quick look to Eirik, but she saw no recognition in his features for the guards. Which was not to say he did not know them, his face was simply void of any expression at all.

Hers might not reflect the joy they'd both experienced in the air, but it no doubt showed her confusion.

As the men came closer, recognition dawned. These were Chrechte warriors she'd often seen in the company of her adopted uncle, the Balmoral. She believed the taller one's name to be Gart and his companion's was Artair.

Even so, why had Eirik landed here and revealed his dragon to them?

"Prince Eirik," Gart said with a bow.

For a wolf to bow, he must hold another in great esteem. Ciara slid a sidelong glance at Eirik and wondered what he had done to gain such respect. Besides shift into a dragon.

She almost laughed at her own naïveté.

"It is Eirik only, now."

"In the company of humans, perhaps," the Balmoral warrior conceded.

Eirik merely inclined his head.

The smaller warrior, Artair, grinned. "Your dragon is amazing, Prince Eirik."

"Aye, each time I take to the sky in that form, I know it."

The two men nodded, their expressions full of awe.

"Lais and a human woman formerly of the MacLeod clan will be arriving by boat in a couple of hours."

"They are welcome."

Eirik inclined his head. "Your laird does not expect us."

"Nay," Gart confirmed.

And the more they conversed, the angrier Ciara became. These men clearly knew about Eirik, that he was prince of the Éan and his dragon was no surprise to them, either. Though seeing it for the first time had clearly been so.

None of this matched with the secrecy still surrounding the Éan among her clan, nor Eirik's declared intent to keep his dragon and position as prince under wraps particularly.

She grabbed his arm and tugged him a few steps away from the guards.

"You trust the Balmoral more than the Sinclair?" she demanded in a furious whisper as the import of the situation became plain.

"They are Faol, they can hear your whispering."

"I know that." She glared. "You said you did not want the Faol to know of your dragon form."

"Niall and Guaire know of my dragon, as do a handful of your father's most trusted soldiers."

"So, what are you saying, the Balmoral and a select few of his Chrechte know as well?" she asked sarcastically.

But Eirik nodded. "Exactly. Your uncle knows of my dragon as do the four soldiers who share this beach's watch."

"Anyone else?" she demanded, though she knew it was not her business to do so.

Eirik raised one sardonic brow, but he answered. "His lady, your mother's sister, the Balmoral's second and Drustan's mate, your father's sister."

"Why the Chrechte who are assigned to this beach?"

"In case of a situation just like this one. Should the Sinclair need to get word to the Balmoral quickly, I am their best hope."

There was no denying that truth. "I think even more than they realize." Eirik raised his brows in question, but she shook her head. "We can discuss it later. For now, we had best begin our trek to the castle."

The only way to the castle was a narrow switchback path up the side of the cliff overlooking the ocean. She wasn't looking forward to the walk. She might be Chrechte, but the long horse ride from the keep to the beach was tiring. Her ride on the dragon had drained the last of her reserves, though for a very different reason.

It had been so wonderfully pleasurable, she'd exhausted herself with joy.

"We will wait for night. Lais will have arrived with the boat by then. I will fly you and Mairi to the keep. Lais will allow her the short ride on my dragon to preserve her strength. Besides, he will fly beside me."

Right. *They would have to wait and see if Mairi was really Lais's mate*, Ciara thought with a heavy dose of sarcasm. She almost snorted her disbelief but kept the unlady-like sound inside her.

Warriors and their games of the mind. As if women were so easily fooled.

"I thought you wanted to get to the keep sooner. That is why we didn't just fly the whole way at night, is it not?"

"The MacLeod soldiers in the forest waylaid our original plans, if you will remember."

"I suppose."

He laid what she thought was a very proprietary hand on her neck. "I am not certain we should go to the keep tonight and not wait for the morning now as well."

Chapter 16

In critical moments even the very powerful have need of the weakest.

—AESOP

"What?" She should step away, but she did not. "Why?"

"I can sleep here in my dragon form more easily and guard your dreams this night." He frowned. "You look almost as exhausted as you did before your sleep last night. I do not like it."

She gave in to the urge to lean into his touch. "I don't, either, but it will take more than one good rest to recover from months of hardly any sleep at all."

She didn't have to be a healer to know that, though Abigail had warned her of this very thing as they said goodbye back at the keep.

Remembering the potent sleep Ciara had experienced with his dragon before, she didn't even consider protesting. Surely speaking to the Balmoral would be just as good in the morning.

"I am surprised to hear you admit as much."

"Why? I am no arrogant warrior, certain I am impervious

to weakness." She was all too aware of how vulnerable she was to the dreams and visions.

She had lived with it for most of her life after all. He could not know just how great the gift of his dragon's protection of her dreams was.

His chuckle warmed her through. "You are an impertinent lass, I think."

"Forthright, mayhap."

"Bossy."

"Bold."

A throat clearing reminded her that they were far from alone.

Blushing, she stepped away from Eirik's touch and turned to face the Balmoral guards. "I apologize. We did not mean to ignore you."

Eirik made a sound suspiciously like a snort, but when she looked at him with a frown, he looked as innocent as a babe.

She shook her head. "Do not think to bamboozle me with your appearance of blamelessness."

He shrugged, but the smile tickling at the corner of his mouth pleased her.

"If we might offer some refreshment?" Artair asked, his expression indicating that he had been listening with avid interest to Ciara and Eirik's conversation.

The poorly suppressed mirth on Gart's face implied he'd been likewise engaged.

Nosy wolves. Her mother often said there were no secrets among the Faol, but her father always disagreed. Talorc said that a clever enough woman could always keep secrets and Abigail always blushed.

"Thank you for the offer; a cup of watered wine would be most appreciated." She gave the Balmoral soldier her best smile.

Honestly, she wouldn't mind a small repast as well, but she would not ask for what they might not easily provide.

Eirik growled beside her and the bigger warrior, Gart, scowled first at her and then his companion, but he turned to lead the way back toward the forest.

* * *

£ais pulled against the oars, making a direct line for Balmoral Island. Mairi had been quiet since they got on the boat and Eirik had leapt into the sky with Ciara on the dragon's back.

Lais was so proud of Mairi's ability to mask her scent, but it was clear the effort had cost her. He was content to let her rest in the stern of the boat, settled as comfortably as he could make her with furs, a skin of watered wine and some food.

She nibbled in silence on some cheese, looking at him, then the water, then the sky where Ciara and Eirik were but a dot and then back at Lais.

He could see a question in her eyes, but fearing he knew what it was, he did not prompt her to ask it.

She offered him the cheese. "Would you like some?"

"Nay." He was hungry, but he would not have her feed him.

She needed her rest and the act would be too intimate, it would give more than his body sustenance. It would give nourishment to his eagle's desires for her as a mate as well.

She sighed and wrapped the cheese in cloth before putting it in the satchel Lais had brought with him on this journey. She adjusted the Sinclair plaid their laird had gifted her with before they left the keep, smoothing her hands along the pleats, clearly pleased to be wearing different colors than the MacLeod.

She settled again, but this time maintained a steady regard on him. "Is it because I am not a wolf?"

He should have known that his Mairi would need no prompting. But that was not the question he expected, though he supposed it could be considered a form of it.

"Nay. While humans are more fragile than shifting Chrechte, you have proven yourself to be strong of mind and spirit."

"You are attracted to me." She sounded very confident, but then she had reason to be on that particular front. "It is not just your eagle that wants me."

"No."

"Then why?"

He could have lied and said that he simply did not want a mate, but while there was a place for deceit, this was not it.

"I do not deserve a mate." There. He had said it.

"How can you say so? You are an amazing man."

"Because I healed you."

"No, because I can trust you not to hurt me."

"I am not the only man who can give you pleasure."

"You are the only one I want to do so."

He should not be so fiercely happy to hear such a vow, but he was. "You are young. That will change."

"It won't. I may not shift into a wolf, but I am Chrechte and there is no other for a Chrechte once they have mated." Her chin set at a mulish angle and she let him see her glare.

"We have not mated."

"Close enough."

"No." He'd been damn careful to make sure it was not close enough.

"Tell me why."

"I was a member of the Donegal clan, before I went to live with the Éan."

"You mean when you came to the Sinclairs?"

"No, that is more recent." He considered stopping there. He had not spilled his people's secrets yet, but he knew he could trust them with her. And he owed her his secrets, if he could give her nothing else.

"The Éan lived in the forest, as a separate tribe. We were hunted by a secret society of the Faol."

"The Fearghall. My father and his cronies belong. He thinks any shifter that isn't a wolf doesn't deserve to live."

Lais should feel no shock at her words, but his breath froze in his chest nonetheless. "Your father belongs to this society . . . the Fearghall?"

A misnomer if ever there was one as it meant superior in valor and from what Lais knew of these Faol, they had not true valor to them. He had never heard the society named before though, since he had not been in the inner circle. He wondered if Galen had ever let it slip to Ciara.

"Yes. Some of the Fearghall believe only the ravens should die because they are not birds of prey, but others, like my father, believe all who shift into an animal different than his have no right to life."

"He's an idiot." But a dangerous one.

She nodded sadly. "He is."

"I, too, was an idiot." The time had come for the full truth of his past.

"How?"

"There were members of the Donegal pack that believed like your father. They hated the Éan simply because we are different."

"I am sorry."

"I am the one who should be sorry. I believed Rowland's lies, that the ravens killed my parents."

"But your parents must have been of the Éan for you to be an eagle."

"One was, the other human. Rowland was convinced I was human as well. *He* killed my parents, but convinced me ravens had done it and fed my hatred of the ravens."

"You never told him you were an eagle."

"No."

"Because you knew that you could not trust him." She sounded so sure and once again her trust in Lais touched him deeply.

"I think so, now, yes. Then, I was just ashamed of being weak, being what I thought was the last of my race."

"There are other eagles?"

"Not many, but yes, there are some. I had my coming-of-age without the *Clach Gealach Gra*."

"What does that mean?"

"It meant that if I had my way and had destroyed it, I would not be a healer." He looked away from her, over the water, its gray surface telling him nothing new. "I do not know if I can give my mate children, if I can pass on my eagle."

"I don't understand."

"Anya-Gra said I was healed by the sacred stone, but I don't know if she meant my heart or my body."

"Who is Anya-Gra?"

"The spiritual leader among the Éan."

"If the stone gave you the power of healing, surely it healed anything else."

"I thought so at first, too, but now that I am charged with healing others, I know better than most that power comes with a cost and that healing is rarely complete with Chrechte power alone."

"Oh."

"I don't deserve to be healed completely," he admitted.

"Now *you* are being an idiot."

"It's true. I would have killed my laird's lady."

"The Donegal laird?"

"Aye."

"She's raven?"

"She is."

"But you did not kill her."

"I tried."

"How?"

"With an arrow."

"So, you are a poor shot."

"No. I was one of the best in our clan."

"Then you must not have tried very hard."

'Twas what Barr had said at the time, but Lais would never forget his guilt. "In time, you will find a mate worthy of you and you will forget this crush you have on me."

Mairi's eyes narrowed. "Will I, then?"

He nodded, but she was no longer looking at him. Her brows were drawn together in thought and he was fairly certain it did not bode well for him.

The Balmoral soldiers had a small hut cleverly disguised by outer bracken, so one had to be almost upon it before seeing it was not merely part of the forest.

Inside, it was clean if small. Two bedrolls were tied and stacked neatly against the far wall. Matching benches that could seat two in a pinch were on either side of the fire pit in the center of the hut.

The pit smoldered in the fashion of a fire that had been recently banked. Gart poked at it and blew on it until a small blaze caught the fresh wood Artair laid across it. They worked in a unison that told of longtime friendship and training together.

"We'll heat stew for our supper," Artair said with a smile for Ciara.

Gart harrumphed and grabbed the stew pot from a shelf on the nearest wall. He hung it by its handle from the tri-legged iron stand over the fire. The big soldier grabbed wooden cups from the same shelf and Artair poured wine from a skin into them before adding water from a bucket.

He served Eirik first. She thought it was because the Éan was a prince, but Eirik took a sip of the watered wine before handing the cup to Ciara.

He'd been testing it for her safety. "If you trust them with your secret, surely you can trust them to serve us a drink."

He ignored her and took his own cup from the Chrechte soldier.

She frowned, but took a sip of her drink, suddenly realizing how very thirsty she was. She should have drunk more water on the journey here, but she had been preoccupied with her thoughts and conversation with Eirik.

Artair indicated one of the benches with his hand. "Please, sit."

She took his offer with alacrity, only to nearly jump out of her skin when Eirik joined her on the small bench. He pressed against her side from hip to shoulder. She tried to bump him with her hip, but he didn't move.

He could be a gentleman and choose to sit on the floor, but perhaps those kinds of manners were not taught among the Éan. Him sitting so close was indecent though.

And she did not care that she had ridden his dragon not a half an hour past. 'Twas not the same. No, it was not. And she would tell him so. Later.

The two warriors shared the other bench, instead of one of them taking the floor, too. She supposed it made sense, but she did not like the way her body heated in inappropriate places at his closeness.

The Balmoral soldiers started to pepper Eirik with questions of what it was like to be a dragon.

"Do you see with colors?" Artair asked.

It was a fair question. Wolves did not.

Eirik nodded. "My vision is very good as well."

"Better than your raven?" Artair asked.

"Much."

Both soldiers went silent to give that truth the respect it deserved.

Then Gart asked, "Does your dragon pull you to shift like your raven?"

"Aye. He's an impatient beast," Eirik replied.

Ciara didn't even pretend not to be interested in the discussion and the stew was bubbling in the pot before she knew it. The delicious aroma from the rabbit stew made her stomach growl embarrassingly.

Artair smiled at her with understanding. "Time to eat, I think."

"Aye," Eirik agreed with a concerned look for her.

"I am fine."

"You do not eat enough."

Oh, for goodness' sake. Did he really need to share her shortcomings with the Balmoral soldiers? "I'm going to eat now."

Gart grabbed shallow wooden bowls that would double for plates and Artair ladled a rich broth filled with vegetables and meat into each. Again, Eirik tasted her stew before she was allowed to eat.

"Are you going to do this from now on?" she asked him with exasperation.

"Aye."

"It's ridiculous. I'm a wolf. I would smell if my food or drink was off."

"I am a dragon, my senses are stronger."

"You are being arrogant again."

"I am protecting you."

"From friendly soldiers?"

"From the possibility they let their food spoil."

"Well, they didn't."

"Nay." He nodded to Artair and Gart. "'Tis tasty."

"Thank you," Gart replied.

Artair shrugged. "He does most of the cooking when we are on watch. I'm better at catching our meal than preparing it."

"Our Artair is a fine hunter," Gart said with some pride. "He'll make a good husband to a lucky clanswoman."

Artair smacked his friend on the back of the head and a bite of stew went flying, but Gart saved the rest of his food with his quick reflexes.

Their conversation continued over the meal but moved to the Éan settling into the Balmoral clan. Apparently, since none of the secret society of the Faol who wanted to kill all the Éan had been found among the Balmoral, the laird had decreed his people would be told the full truth of their new clan members.

To Ciara's surprise, Eirik had agreed. She wondered again if he trusted the Balmoral more than her father, but realized it was not her father the dragon mistrusted. It was the rest of the clan. And since there *had* been members of the secret Faol society among them, only time would prove his people safe with the Sinclairs.

"Our laird assigned two of your warriors to share this guard and others the task of a flying watch over the island," Artair said to Eirik when asked.

Eirik tensed. "Not all are soldiers."

Ciara wanted to soothe him, though she could not understand the urge. He was hardly a child needing comfort, but he was a man who took the well-being of his people very much to heart.

"Oh, no," Artair was quick to reply. "Some have been assigned crofter's huts. Three have gone to work in the castle, in one capacity or another."

"That is as the Balmoral said it would be."

"Our laird can be trusted," Gart said on a growl.

Ciara smiled at him. "Of course he can. Eirik did not mean to imply otherwise."

The dragon shifter said nothing. Gart was turning a bit red and Artair wasn't looking too happy, either.

She dug her elbow in Eirik's side. "Did you?"

He shifted so he almost faced her, his big body blocking her view of the others. "Did I what?"

"Mean to say that their laird was untrustworthy."

"I allowed my people to join his clan."

"I know, but perhaps they are not aware how much you had to trust the Balmoral to have done so."

"'Twas not their decision."

"No, of course not." She barely refrained from rolling her eyes. "The point is—"

"Not important," Gart interrupted, sounding much happier.

She peeked around Eirik, but both the Balmoral guards looked at peace again. Really. Heaven save her from testy warriors.

She looked up at Eirik and lost her breath. His focus was entirely on her and the message in his eyes was hot enough to singe. "Um . . . you . . . I . . . the soldiers . . ."

"What about them, *faolán*?"

"I can't see them around you."

"Mayhap you should not be looking at other men."

"I wasn't looking," she said in outrage. "That way, I mean."

"But you wanted to see them."

"Not like that."

The tiny twitch in the muscle of his cheek finally gave him away.

"You are teasing me," she accused.

"You smell good when you blush."

"Oh, for goodness' sake." She must have the fragrance of a garden right now, because her face was so hot she would have gladly dunked her head in the bucket of water. "Will you shift your behemoth body so I can see Artair and Gart, *please*?"

208 · Lucy Monroe

He moved but ruined her pleasure at his cooperation by asking, "You find me too large?"

"I did not say that." Too large? How could she when she found him perfect in most every way? And that was not a revelation she needed to make, to herself or him. Life as a seer was much more complicated than when she'd merely been a daughter who could avoid all entanglements behind the wall of her adopted family. "It would not be appropriate for me to comment one way or another."

"You called me giant."

"I've also called you dragon. You did not take offense at that."

"I am a dragon."

"And you are a very big man."

"I think you like big." His tone and the heat in his stare said more than the words, and they said *enough*.

"Stop. Please." Ciara turned her attention to Artair and asked somewhat desperately, "Are your clan accepting of them, the Éan I mean?"

She expected they were, but discovering the Éan were known as bird shifters among the Balmoral might put a different light on it. She hoped not, though.

"Oh, aye," Artair said with a decisive nod. "No one treats new clan members as anything but family since our lady came near ten years ago."

"She'd not settle for it," Gart agreed.

Ciara grinned at this mention of Abigail's acknowledged strong-willed sister. "Aunt Emily did not find such a warm welcome among the Sinclairs, I fear."

Artair returned her grin. "So I hear. Though she gave as good as she got, I reckon."

"I think you are right." Ciara laughed softly. "I'm not sure my father has ever gotten over being likened to a goat."

"It's not something a laird would be used to, is it?" Artair asked with another grin.

Eirik growled, similar but different to a wolf, and she stared at him askance only to turn her head quickly at an almost identical sound from Gart.

Artair twisted his lips in a grimace. "Ignore him. We've

been best mates since before we could walk. So, it stands to reason *to him* I should marry his sister. But I'm not joining my spirit with another until I feel the call of a true mate, am I?"

"The old stories claim that in the days of the ancients," Ciara remembered aloud, "none mated unless they felt the connection of a true bond."

"How are you going to know you feel it, until you are mated?" Gart asked with irritation.

Artair gave him a measured look. "I'll know."

"You're so damn stubborn."

"You've been saying so since your first words and it hasn't changed yet. What makes you think it's going to?"

Gart made a sound of exasperation and slammed his now-empty stew bowl down before storming from the hut.

Ciara got up to gather all the bowls before carrying them to the shelf. She would take them out later to wash with sand and water from the sea.

She patted the other Balmoral guard on his arm as she walked by him. "He'll figure it out eventually."

"You think so?" Artair shook his head. "I'm about despaired of it ever happening."

"He's a Chrechte. He can't ignore the call forever."

"He could. Some do."

She couldn't argue that, particularly when she was doing her best to ignore her feelings for Eirik. But she did not think Gart was like her. He wasn't afraid, merely blinded by dreams he'd clearly cherished since childhood.

"He has to let go of his treasured hopes for his sister first." She took the seat beside Artair on the small bench. He did not fill the space like Eirik did. "Perhaps you should encourage him to find his own mate."

The Balmoral soldier gave her a look of pure horror. "Why would I do that?"

"Why did you sit beside him?" Eirik demanded.

She ignored Eirik and told Artair, "So that he will start thinking in the right direction."

"I'll think on it."

Eirik stood up, his expression feral in the dusky light of

the hut. "Your body is touching his," the Éan prince gritted.

She scooted so the small spot where their hips had connected did not touch at all. "There. Are you satisfied? You're being ridiculous. It wasn't anything like when I was sitting beside you."

"Come sit over here." Eirik pointed to the other bench.

"I'm fine right here."

A low rumble sounded and Ciara watched in fascination as Eirik's hands became covered in crimson scales and tipped with lethal-looking claws. Though they remained in proportion to his body.

It was unlike anything she had ever heard of before.

"How did you do that?" she asked with wonder.

"I think, perhaps, I will join Gart outside," Artair said from the doorway.

She hadn't even realized the other man had gotten up. She stood as well and turned to the guard. "That is not necessary."

"I think it is." He gave a significant look toward Eirik.

And she looked back at her dragon. His hands were still amazingly transformed, but he had not moved from his spot. His expression was no longer so ferocious, either.

She turned back to Artair and smiled. "See? He is only feeling protective as he has taken on the role of my guard for this journey. You saw him with our meal, tasting it for me."

Artair was looking at her as if she was spouting gibberish and she sighed. The soldier simply did not appreciate the wonder of Eirik's gifts like she did.

"Lais and Mairi have arrived," Eirik said into the tense quiet.

Ciara spun back to him, all of her suspicions about his abilities confirmed. "Lais told you that, didn't he?"

Eirik didn't reply but left the hut, his shoulders taut, his jaw set. At least his hands had gone back to normal. She did not think it was a gift he needed to go sharing with everyone under the sun.

Artair reached out as if to pat her shoulder but withdrew

his hand before touching her. "The Éan prince will figure it out, too."

She didn't ask what. She was no fool and apparently neither was Artair. "Let's hope not," Ciara said fervently.

"You don't want a mate?" Artair frowned. "Or is that you do not want an Éan for a mate?"

"I want *no* mate, whether he be human, Chrechte or a wild beast for that matter."

"Our *celi di* says that God gifts us what we need, not what we want."

"And sometimes he also takes away what we love most."

"So you would reject the possibility of love to prevent ever losing it again?"

"I want no mate," she repeated doggedly. "There will be no children for me to lose to illness or war."

No mate whose loss would send her into a decline like her mother. Ciara had suffered enough pain when she lost her family, but she had survived. She had learned to live again. Her mother had not.

Because she had lost that which she could not bear, her true bonded mate and her child.

Chapter 17

Human behavior flows from three main sources: desire, emotion and knowledge.

—PLATO

His beast demanding a chance to come out and cast fire at the Balmoral soldier, Eirik waited impatiently for Ciara and Artair to join them on the beach. He could control his dragon, but he did not know if he could control his warrior's instincts to claim the woman so that all would know she belonged to him.

He had not thought to take a mate for several more years, but both his dragon and his raven insisted he make Ciara his. Which was shock enough. He'd thought the fact both his alternate natures were attracted to the little wolf interesting, but the intensity with which his dragon and raven craved Ciara only grew by the day.

He had never had such happen before. While he had not been celibate since coming of age, Eirik had always found putting his duty to his people first easy. No woman had ever invaded his senses like Ciara did, and none caused such an inner disturbance in Eirik.

He'd shown his partial shift to Artair and Ciara without thought. Not only had that never happened before, but it was dangerous for others to know the full extent of Eirik's gifts.

One truth was obvious, he could not serve his people as he needed to if he was in constant conflict with the animals that shared his soul.

There was no choice. He would have to take her for mate.

It would be no hardship, though she was more willful than most. As seer and princess of her people, Ciara would bring more to their mating than simply her person. In truth, there was probably not another woman in the Highlands so well suited to become his wife and bear his children.

Her Chrechte power, though mostly latent until now, was great. And as his mate, that power would serve both the Éan and the Faol once she bonded with him. 'Twas the way it worked between mates.

Eirik had already sworn his allegiance to the Sinclair wolf pack and by doing so dedicating his own Chrechte gifts to their welfare. The mating bond would not change much for him. But it would give his people claim to the gifts of another powerful Chrechte to rely on for *their* well-being.

Yes, even without the insistent cravings of his beasts, Eirik would have had to consider taking Ciara as his mate.

The fact his alternate natures were so enthralled by her only made the probability that their mating would be a true one more tantalizing and real.

Ciara came down to the beach finally, a frown settled on her sweet features, clearly agitated by something. She greeted Mairi and Lais, but was distracted.

He glared at Artair, taking it as his due when the Balmoral soldier flinched and lost his color. "What did you say to Ciara?"

"Me?" Artair asked with a squeak.

Suddenly Gart was there, standing between him and Artair. While Eirik appreciated the loyalty, the other warrior would not stop Eirik from finding out what had upset his mate.

"Stand aside. Artair will answer me."

The slightly smaller soldier pushed his friend to the side

and met Eirik's gaze, his own speculative. "She is not well pleased with God's plans for her future, I think."

"She told you she is a seer?" Eirik demanded, suddenly understanding Ciara's fury when they had first arrived and she'd discovered the Balmoral soldiers knew of his dragon.

"What? No." Artair's expression turned thoughtful. "Mayhap that explains some of her concern about taking a mate though."

Outrage swelled inside Eirik and he felt the partial change taking over his hands again. *You talked to my* faolán *about mating her?"* The dragon was too close to the surface for Eirik's voice to come out with anything but a growl.

"You want to mate the Sinclair femwolf?" Gart demanded, apparently oblivious to the threat of Eirik's dragon, his attention fixed entirely on Artair, and his own tone laced with fury.

"You have both gone mad to even ask me that," Artair said with a growl of his own. He scowled, flinching only slightly at the sight of Eirik's hands, but his gaze quickly locked hostilely with Eirik's. "If you want to know why she's frowning, ask her."

Then Artair turned to his fellow soldier, no diminishment in his anger whatsoever. "As for you, get this through your thick head. I am not going to mate your sister. Ever."

Gart stumbled back a step. "But we were to be brothers."

"I don't want to be your brother." The pain and fury in Artair's voice was difficult to hear.

However, Gart's hurt at the other warrior's words was so great and so obvious, Eirik could not help pitying him as well. And finally, Eirik thought he understood what Artair and Ciara had been talking about in the hut.

The two men were sacred mates, but clearly Gart had blinded himself to this truth, and he could not understand why his best friend would refuse to be his brother.

Eirik had had enough of this ridiculousness and he'd only been witness to it for a short time. No doubt their laird and Artair himself were heartily sick of the Chrechte soldier's willful refusal to see the truth.

Eirik gave Gart a good clout on the back of the head,

knocking the Balmoral guard to his knees. "A Chrechte cannot mate his brother, you idiot."

"Mate?" Gart shook his head, though Eirik doubted his blow had knocked the man's brain loose.

'Twas more likely that single word he was trying to dislodge. Gart looked up at Artair, who was staring at him with an expression Eirik was determined to see on his little femwolf's features in the very near future.

"You want to be my mate?" Gart asked.

"I don't know." Artair did not appear to be teasing; he seemed to have some serious doubts on the topic. "Stupidity is not an attractive feature in a mate, but you seem to have more than your fair share."

Gart surged to his feet and grabbed Artair by his upper arms, shaking him. "Do not get on your high horse right now. Just answer my question."

"Yes." Though Artair wasn't looking all that pleased by the prospect.

"But you're my brother."

This time when Artair flinched, Eirik did not enjoy seeing it quite so much. "I am not."

"You are my best friend."

"Yes."

"And have been for the whole of our lives."

Artair nodded. "What better person to take as a mate?"

"I dreamed of children."

This time there was no flinch, just the scent of sadness. "I cannot give them to you."

"I know." Gart dropped his hands from the other soldier and stepped back, putting more than physical distance between them. "I do not know if I can give up that hope."

"You really are an idiot." Mairi, who had been standing wide-eyed and quiet during this exchange, gave Gart a look of disapproval. "You think love is so common a gift you can just throw it away when it is offered?"

"We are not speaking of love, but of mating," Gart replied with a frown for the small woman.

Mairi looked up at Lais and then back to Gart. "Are they not the same?"

"Nay," Lais answered when Gart did not. "There is no Chrechte law that states mates will love each other."

Mairi's soft features hardened. "I see."

"Besides, a warrior does not live his life by the dictates of his heart," Gart said dismissively.

Eirik could not disagree with him, but it looked like Artair was less than impressed with his friend's sentiments. Mairi didn't look well pleased, either.

Crossing her arms, she gave Lais a look Eirik could not decipher and moved away from him. The eagle looked confused and disgruntled, though he made no move to close the gap between him and the human woman.

"You are right," Artair said, surprising Eirik. "A warrior cannot bow to the dictates of his heart."

The relief on Gart's face was reflected in his scent. "So, you will begin courting my sister?"

"Never." There was enough venom in the word to kill and enough certainty to serve as the foundation of a fortress.

"But—"

"We will feed your companions and then the women can have the hut to sleep in," Artair said to Eirik, cutting his fellow soldier off. "I have first watch on the beach tonight and Gart can sleep outside the hut."

"Ciara will sleep with my dragon in the forest. Lais and Gart can share the hut and watch over Mairi."

"Do not argue about this," he warned the eagle shifter over the Éan royal mind link.

Lais dipped his chin in acknowledgment, but he did not look happy. Eirik did not care. The man was a warrior and he knew better than to gainsay his prince.

Mairi didn't look any happier, but Eirik did not think it had anything to do with the sleeping arrangements. She was glaring at Gart and Artair in turn.

She had a lot of spirit for a woman who could not shift.

Ciara shook her head. "It would be more proper for me to share the hut with Mairi."

"My dragon will protect your dreams," he said in a tone others knew better than to dispute.

Ciara did not look impressed. "I think it would be better the way Artair suggested."

"It will be as I have stated."

"You're truly one of the most stubborn men I have ever known, and I've lived the last seven years with Talorc of the Sinclairs as my father!" The exasperation in her tone made him smile.

Odd.

Mairi reached out and patted Ciara's arm. "Let his dragon protect your dreams this night. This quest will not be easy and you will need your strength."

"Are you speaking as a friend or a seer?" Ciara demanded, sounding annoyed.

"Both."

Eirik placed his hand on the small of Ciara's back and started leading the group toward the forest and the hut concealed there. "Listen to your friend."

"You only say that because she agrees with you. I didn't hear you telling Gart to listen to her."

The soldier in question had left the group already and headed down the beach. "He must make up his own mind about his future."

"But he's hurting both himself and Artair."

"He would cause more pain if he agreed to a mating he resented."

Which did not mean Eirik intended to give *her* much choice in their mating. Her unreasonable determination never to take a mate could not be allowed to stand in the way of the good of both their peoples.

Eventually, she would understand that truth, he was certain.

With nothing but the moonlight to guide them, Eirik led Ciara deeper into the forest. They were headed toward the small clearing protected from view by a dense growth of trees that Artair had suggested would make a good night's resting place for a dragon.

She'd continued to argue about the sleeping arrangements

all through Mairi and Lais eating their stew and making plans for the morrow. However, Ciara came with him when Eirik left the hut. He would count that, at least, a victory.

"I would feel better if we had waited for Gart to return before leaving Mairi and Lais in the hut."

"So you said."

"Well, why didn't you listen?"

"Why does it matter if he has returned to the hut or not? You are worried about him," Eirik guessed.

He had noticed that despite her attempt to keep others at a distance, Ciara showed great concern and compassion for those around her. Abigail had told him that Ciara helped so much with the twins, she was more a second mother than a sister.

In the weeks he had lived among the Sinclairs, Eirik had noted time and again Ciara showing her natural inclination to serve her people. She had not known where that inclination came from, but as keeper of the *Faolchú Chridhe* she would feel the need to take care of the Faol.

No matter how much she told herself she didn't want to care for anyone.

"I'm worried about Mairi," Ciara said, showing again she could not help herself caring for others. "You know the way Lais looks at her."

"You do not trust my warrior to protect her?"

"From himself? No, I do not."

"Lais will not hurt her." She was safer in his presence than she could be anywhere else.

"Define hurt. Will he bed her?" Ciara asked with asperity and genuine worry.

Her time would be better spent in concern for his plans for the night, but he was grateful Ciara showed no concern about spending the night alone with Eirik.

"You are very plainspoken for a clan laird's daughter."

"I am also Faol. I know what happens in the night between men and women."

His sweetly innocent Faol princess? He did not think so. "Oh? What do you know, *faolán*?"

"Never mind," she said, sounding flustered. "I merely

meant to say that there is more than one way for Mairi to be hurt."

"The first time is always uncomfortable." But if Lais compromised the other woman's virtue, he would stand by whatever promise he made her.

Though Eirik doubted very much the healer would claim Mairi this night. She was still recovering from the beating her father had given her. Lais was very protective of his patients and would be doubly so of Mairi.

"How many virgins have you talked into your bed?" Ciara demanded, her scent giving away her anger at the thought even if her tone had not.

"None."

"Then how would you know?"

"Are you jealous of the women I've touched intimately?" he asked, unwilling to pass up the opportunity to goad her.

"Of course not," she said far too quickly and with little conviction. "I have no right to be jealous."

"If you are attempting to mask your deceit, you are doing a poor job of it." The acrid scent of jealousy mixed with the sour smell of a lie in the air around them.

She gasped. "What? You can tell I lied to you?"

She sounded far more worried about her inability to mask her true feelings than the fact she'd been caught in a lie. Contrary *faolán*.

"Aye."

"But that's impossible."

He could not help it. He laughed. She sounded so appalled.

"It happens that way between mates sometimes," Eirik assured her. "Barr can see through the images my sister, Sabrine, projects with her mind."

"I am not your mate," Ciara claimed with no more conviction but a fair amount of horror, and doing no better a job of masking her lie than before.

"My dragon says you are."

"No. Surely your raven—"

"Wants to rub necks with you."

"Oh, no." She backed away from him, her entire body tensed for flight.

Though where she thought she was going, he could not imagine. His dragon could find her across the waters.

I do not want a mate. The trembling sincerity in her voice mixed with the scent of genuine distress made his dragon want to roar.

He would not have her terrified of what she had to know was the natural progression of things. "You have nothing to fear from me."

"You cannot be that naïve."

One thing he had never been accused of was naïveté. It startled a chuckle from him.

"Don't you laugh. This is not funny. I won't do it. I will not take a mate." Her voice rose steadily until she was shouting the last before she turned and ran.

He gave thanks in that moment for the style of clothes Abigail had convinced Ciara to wear because she could not shift into her wolf without destroying them.

Even so, it took him longer to catch her in his human form than he expected. Fear had given her feet wings and her wolf lent her grace and dexterity as she jumped over fallen branches and tree roots without a single stumble.

He could not help admiring her affinity with the forest as another sign of her special Chrechte heritage. Once he caught up with her though, he did not allow that admiration to make him hesitate.

Sweeping her up into his arms even as they ran, he settled her against his chest. He turned direction and slowed to a walk, heading back toward the clearing.

Ciara flailed against him, struggling for release. The fact she did not gain even the hope of it should have told her something about what her instincts were telling her to do. She struggled, but she did not *fight* with her Chrechte skills or strength, and that was telling.

Even if she did not see it.

Eirik simply hugged her tight, preventing her from hurting herself and made dragon noises that had never come from him before meeting her. His own instincts told him the sounds were meant to comfort. The way she settled against him, muttering to herself about arrogant dragons and mates she did not want, implied her wolf recognized the dragon's attempt to calm her.

When they broke through the trees into the open area that was just as Artair had described, Eirik stopped. The near full moon bathed the small clearing with white light that cast shadows at the trees' edge.

Eirik did not release Ciara; he had no desire to spend the night chasing her through the forest. "Are you done running?"

"I will not take a mate." She crossed her arms and glared up at him, the green of her eyes so dark in the moonlight, they looked black.

"You want me."

"I don't."

He shook his head. "I can tell when you're lying, remember."

Her glare went sulfuric, but the evidence of her desire for him remained just as strong. That subtle fragrance that said her body was preparing for him teased at his senses, pushing against his control over both his own desires and his different forms, and nearly taking Eirik to his knees.

Her stubbornness would be both their undoing if he did not take matters into his own hands.

Words were not going to convince his stubborn *faolán* of anything. Their mating was a primal urge and he needed to woo her at the core of her femwolf.

He lowered his head and silenced her continuing arguments, filled as they were with deceit.

Did she even believe herself?

He did not think she could be that deluded, but then Gart had proven just how easily even Chrechte might blind themselves to truth.

Just as he expected, despite all Ciara's claims to the contrary, her lips went soft and parted immediately against his. She wanted him true enough. She might even crave his touch as much as he did touching her.

*T*error pounded in Ciara's heart, but even the fear that had so many years to grow strong could not overwhelm her natural response to her dragon shifter. Her wolf demanded the chance to touch and scent the man holding her so close to his heart.

She broke her mouth from his in a last attempt at defiance. "I am not mating you."

The words sounded like the lie they were, even to her own ears. Her body strained toward the man her wolf had deemed mate, while her heart beat for the chance to join more than their bodies in mating.

'Twas not fair. Nor right, that she should be so at risk for loss, but the most stubborn will in the world could not deny the instincts and emotions roiling through her.

He laughed and shook his head, as if amazed at her audacity, so clearly not deceived by her best attempts. "In the morning, you can tell me that again."

She could try. In the morning, Ciara could fight her wolf's needs and instincts, and she might even win for a time. But she knew deep in her heart that by tomorrow it would be too late to hope to return to the woman with the stone-encased heart.

Tonight, she would give in to the dragon and he would finish the work he began when the first crack happened in the granite around her once-shattered heart.

She acknowledged aloud, "Tomorrow will be too late."

"Aye, it will." His amber gaze challenged her to deny him regardless.

Her wolf growled, not at him, but at Ciara and she knew she was lost. She tilted her head and reconnected their mouths, giving her acquiescence with desperate lips.

He took the kiss like the prince of the Chrechte that he was, with power and possession. His mouth slanted over hers until the last vestiges of her fear drowned under his passion and she could have cried with gratitude. The dread she had lived with since the final loss of her birth family had become a burden almost too heavy to bear.

Continuing the crooning sounds he'd used earlier to calm her, Eirik set Ciara on her feet. Though he kept their mouths fused, his body bowed over hers, his arms encasing her in a way that both excited her and made her feel safe.

She let that feeling of safety wash through her like a cleansing tide. If he could give her this sense of peace, it was almost worth the pain that would inevitably follow.

Finished with thinking, she focused entirely on the sensations he elicited in her with his kiss.

Her hands went to his chest of their own accord, sliding over hard muscles and brushing the tiny nubs they found there. His big body shuddered at the contact and she had to do it again, circling her fingertips around his small male nipples.

Then she traced the lines of the leather straps that held his sword scabbards to his back. They crisscrossed the golden skin of his chest in the most fascinating way. She followed each line, brushing over the brown disks of his nipples again, but moving on as she explored the delicious combination of the leather and his smooth skin.

With a growl he tore his mouth from hers. "Do that again."

"What?" she asked in a husky voice she barely recognized as her own.

"Touch me there." He grabbed one of her hands and guided it to rest over his hardened nub.

She did, no thought to the contrary. Circling and pinching the tender flesh, she exulted in the power she exerted over this giant warrior who shared his nature with both dragon and raven as he shivered with each caress.

"Yes." He threw his head back, pleasure etched in every harsh line of his face. "Excite me as only you can, *faolán*."

She let her hands explore every spot she could reach, but now the leather straps from his sword scabbards were in her way. "Take these off."

"Aye." The look he gave her was hewn from the granite that had used to protect her heart.

Within seconds all of his weapons lay on the ground within easy reaching distance. Not that a dragon who could partially transform needed a sword to defeat his enemy. His boots and kilt followed his weapons in short order and then he stood before her, gloriously naked in the moonlight.

Chapter 18

All that spirits desire, spirits attain.

—Khalil Gibran

ℋo hint of embarrassment or shyness for this prince of the Chrechte. Eirik accepted her intensely fascinated perusal as his due.

A foot taller than her and so broad with muscle only a fool would challenge this man in battle, Eirik's gaze burned through her with promise.

And with a challenge *she* would be a fool not to meet.

He drew her to him without a single gesture or word and she willingly submitted to the siren's call of his body, moving closer. A faint echo of that frightened voice that had lived deep in her heart for so long warned her that like the siren's this man's song of desire would lure her to her doom.

But that voice was not loud enough to stop Ciara reaching out to touch that which held her attention so assiduously— the erection jutting from his body. Her fingertips did not quite touch in their circling of it, but he did not seem to mind, if the bliss crossing his features was anything to go by.

Long and thick, the hard phallus was much too big to fit

inside her, she was sure. Though her wolf argued otherwise, snarling for the chance to be impaled by the Éan prince.

For a moment, Ciara wondered at the sanity of her beast.

That moment was lost as Eirik's hand curled around hers, increasing the tightness of her hold. The dichotomy between his hard, callused fingers over hers and the soft, silky skin covering ungiving hardness beneath took her breath away.

"'Tis amazing," she said on a sigh, looking down at their joint hold on his erection.

"Aye."

He began to guide her in movement, taking their joined hands to the base of his length and pushing his foreskin down so the broad purple head winked up at her. "Like that, sweet little wolf."

"You should be vulnerable here, but you do not feel vulnerable at all." He felt hot, hard and strong beneath her hand.

He gave out a choked sound that could have been a laugh. "Make no mistake, even a dragon shifter's cock is susceptible to pain as much as pleasure."

"There is so much heat," she whispered in wonder. "Are you sure your dragon is not getting ready to cast fire again?"

This time his laugh could be mistaken for nothing but. "It is a kind of fire, but I assure you, it will not burn you, *faolán.*"

"Oh, I think it will." Her heart, if not her body.

He shook his head, his expression turning more feral than she'd yet seen it. "Take your clothes off," he demanded in a guttural voice.

She nodded, once again ignoring that tiny voice that tried to tell her she was swimming in waters too deep. He'd brought the waters with him and they would not recede unless he took them away again.

She undid the pins holding the small shawl over her shoulders first. Why it should feel so very revealing to remove a garment that actually covered cloth, not skin, she did not know, but in that moment she felt truly defenseless.

His look of savage desire did not help. And yet if he looked away from her, she would not be able to continue.

He did not look away and her blouse came next. As she pulled it over her head, for a second, she could not see him and her heart stuttered with atavistic fear.

"Faolán." That was all he said, just calling her his little wolf in a tone that wrapped around her desire and breathed flame into it.

And she was all right, dropping her blouse to the ground. Then she undid the tie on her pleated skirt made to look like a plaid from the Sinclair tartan and let it slide down her hips as well. That left only her shift and her shoes. She knew that even in the moonlight, her shift would do little to maintain her modesty, being of fabric spun very fine and bleached so white it was almost sheer.

His hands fisted and released at his sides, as if he wanted to touch her but dared not.

"Eirik?"

He nodded, as if to himself and strode forward, only to drop to his knees and bend down. He untied her sandals, his fingertips lingering on her ankles, his thumbs brushing the side of her arches. And she felt a curious hitch in her chest looking down at him.

Her wolf whispered, *"Mate,"* and her heart whimpered, *"Dangerous."* All her mouth could say was a *"thank you"* so quiet she wondered if he even heard.

But he inclined his head in welcome. "Step out of them."

She did, the only thing left between her and total nakedness, her sleeveless, almost sheer shift.

Still kneeling before her, he took the hem in his two hands but did not lift. "Now this."

It was not a question, but he still did not move to remove her last garment.

So, she nodded. "Yes."

His smile melted a place in her heart that had been frozen so long, she had not even known it existed anymore.

Pure trust.

He would not hurt her intentionally. He would protect her to the best of his abilities, even from his own lusts.

One moment she wore her shift and the next, she did not. Then she stood naked before him in the moonlight, feeling a strange juxtaposition between the coolness of the night air and the heat of his body so close. Her nipples were already hard, but they tightened into turgid peaks that ached deliciously at the dual sensations.

The flare of his nostrils said he noticed, but how could he not? He was dragon shifter, with senses far superior to human and even other Chrechte.

He leaned forward and kissed the tips of each, before lowering his head so he could give the same homage to her stomach right below her belly button.

It did not feel sexual, though they were both naked and he had just put his lips on her breasts. It felt more like a benediction, like an ancient Chrechte rite she knew nothing about.

And as sacred as the moment felt, she could not stifle the need to go back to touching him. Perhaps because to do so would feel equally blessed.

He seemed to read her mind, because he stood in a fluid movement, his arousal brushing up her body as he rose to his full six and a half feet.

Her wolf's keen senses became aware of a musky scent that he left behind on her skin where his penis had touched and she felt the growl of the wolf's approval in her chest. Without thought, she reached down and fondled the end of his shaft where it glistened with some kind of wetness. The nearly clear fluid was viscous and gave off a mouthwatering aroma.

She brought her fingers to her mouth and tasted, the flavor of her dragon bursting on her tongue. *Mine,* her wolf howled.

"Do you like it?"

"Are you supposed to ask that?" she queried, wanting to avoid an answer and knowing she would not be able to.

Her pleasure in his taste had to be as obvious to him as his lust was to her.

"We are Chrechte," he said quietly, but firmly. "We do not hide from our true natures."

He might not, but she had spent seven years doing her best to tamp down parts of her wolf. Still, she acknowledged his words with a nod.

"I need your touch," he said in a gravelly voice.

The air around them shimmered with Chrechte power and she knew his beasts were close to the surface. As incredible as she found his dragon and as much as she wanted to meet his raven, at this moment, she would scream in frustration if either took over his form. There was only one way to keep the beasts at bay.

Satisfy their hunger.

She took his arousal in both her hands, this time automatically using the grip and movements he taught her. Sliding his foreskin back and forth over that hardened shaft, she found as much pleasure in the doing as he seemed to find in being done to.

"Oh, yes . . . just like that, *faolán*."

"I am not so little." She was not as tall as some of the Chrechte women, but not as short as some of the human females, either.

"You are my little wolf," he said without apology.

And she could not disagree. Not in that moment. Her wolf simply would not let her, nor would that part of her heart he'd managed to unearth.

He made a sound deep in his throat and she could tell his control was slipping, though he was no longer in danger of shifting. Not at all. She increased the pace of her movements, enjoying how slick he'd gotten from the fluid seeping out of the slit in the tip of his penis.

Her wolf loved the scent and wanted another taste, but she could not stop touching him long enough to indulge herself.

And suddenly with a shout, his erection throbbed in her hand and hot ejaculate hit her body. Her head dropped back and she let out a howl in triumph, her human throat emulating her wolf more closely than it had ever done before.

He yanked her into his body and slammed his mouth down on hers in a kiss so hot, she melted under it. Even after his release, his shaft was still hard against her and his hands were busy rubbing his seed into her body.

Her wolf understood what he was doing and approved. Eirik marked her with his scent in a way that unmistakably said she was his.

"Thank you," he whispered against her lips. "Now I can take you without losing control this first time."

His concern for her warmed that place deep in her heart further.

"My wolf liked it."

"I could tell," he said with a smile in his voice.

"She wants to scent you," Ciara admitted.

"After."

Her wolf purred its approval as Ciara's thighs tightened, that place between them throbbing as she agreed with a nod. "After."

He spread her bedding fur on the ground and the blanket on top of it. Then, without warning, he swept her up and laid her on their makeshift bed on the forest floor.

"This is where you belong."

"In your bed?" she asked.

"Aye."

"The plaid and fur are mine though."

"Then 'tis *our* bed."

And why did that sound so good? So perfect to both her wolf and her heart?

He leaned down and nuzzled against her stomach, her breasts, a pleased rumble sounding from his chest. "You smell like me."

"That was the intent, was it not?"

"Aye. My dragon likes it. My raven is cawing in triumph inside me."

His openness and honesty amazed her. "You sound kind of awed. I don't believe you are a virgin."

He was too knowing, and besides he'd implied as much earlier.

"I am not, but my beasts have never craved the same lover."

She realized two things at once. The first, that she had two Chrechte spirits wanting to claim her. Her wolf preened in triumph at the thought.

Ciara's second insight was not so pleasant—*she did not like hearing about his other women.* When her wolf snarled her displeasure at the secondary import of his words, she didn't even try to keep it inside.

"You don't like knowing I have had sex with others." He sounded much too satisfied by that observation for her liking.

But she could not deny it. "No."

It would do no good the way he could scent her deceptions.

"The Éan are not so limiting about acts of sex between Chrechte as your father's pack," Eirik reminded her.

The words did nothing to soothe her. The Donegal pack had not been, either, but Ciara's own views were exactly that. *Her own.* She did not expect others to share them, but nor could he expect the difference between their viewpoints to bring her no pain, either.

"My mother taught me that sex is a sacred act." And Abigail's teachings had supported that belief.

"It can be," Eirik said in surprisingly easy agreement. "It will be between us."

"I . . ." She tried to roll away from him, a hollow pit opening up inside her she wished *she* could ignore. "Maybe we should—"

But he held her fast and nuzzled into her neck. "We should engage in this *sacred act.* It has never been thus for me before. I have never marked another with my scent."

"You marked her when you came inside her." And she still had no idea how many *hers* they were talking about, was not sure she ever *wanted to know.*

"I have never allowed my seed to spill inside another woman." He leaned above her, his eyes demanding she believe him.

She had never heard of such a thing, but then her actual knowledge of sex was rather more limited than she had implied earlier in their conversation. "How did you have sex then?"

"With hands and mouths."

Like they had just done? The thought made her ill. She tried to move away from him again.

But he held fast, forcing their gazes to lock with the sheer force of his will. "Do not reject me as your mate because I cannot come to you as untouched as you come to me. I have never marked any other with my scent. None but you will ever be allowed that part of me."

His words were a vow, but still she ached inside. "You did not let your essence spill on those other women?" Did not rub it into their skin as he had done with hers.

"No. I never wanted to."

"But—"

"To do so would have been to claim them for my dragon, for my raven. That I would not do."

The full import of his words sank in and she shook her head, refuting their meaning, but knowing there was no way to undo what had been done. Had known since their first touch this night.

Nevertheless, she said, "I'm not taking you for a mate." The words came out hollow and even she could not believe them, regardless of how hard she tried to.

"You already have."

"No." He had claimed her, but she had not claimed him back. Had she?

"Your wolf knows."

"No." It was as good as done, but it was not done. Not yet. Was it?

"Tomorrow."

"What?"

"We can argue tomorrow. Right now, let me have you. Please, Ciara?" The pleading in his voice touched her like nothing else could have.

She was certain he'd never begged another woman.

She reached up and touched his lips with wonder. "Do princes say please?"

"For you, this prince will." He thrust his hardness against her hip, making her aware of the desire driving him. "Only for you. My mate."

"Tomorrow." She knew that one word promised far more than she wanted it to, but she was helpless to deny him.

Or herself.

He began kissing her again, his mouth demanding she submit to the claiming. She kissed him back with aggression, telling him with her lips that she was not the only one who would be submitting to a claim this night.

He rumbled against her and she smiled at his dragon making his presence known, but when Eirik broke the kiss to rub neck to neck, she knew that was his raven giving its approval of their joining. And tears of inexplicable joy pricked her eyes.

Allowing her wolf its own desires, Ciara pushed against him with her body, writhing against him, mixing their scents, and reveling in the joy of skin on skin. And the kiss continued, their lips nibbling at each other, his tongue invading her mouth, hers pushing back to taste his.

His hands started moving over her, big warrior's hands that caressed with a gentleness that should not have been possible. He brushed his fingers down her neck, over her collarbone, across her shoulder, down her arm; and everywhere he touched, he left a firestorm of pleasure in his wake.

He cupped her breast, his thumb brushing over her turgid nipple and she keened in delight. She could no more help herself than she could stop breathing. That small caress went clear through her body and landed in her womb with a convulsion of desire.

And Ciara felt an emptiness in her core that she knew only he could fill.

Her hips moved restlessly, her thighs falling apart in an atavistic invitation she could not have prevented if she had tried.

One big hand slid down and accepted the invitation, fondling that place no one had ever touched before.

"You are wet," he whispered into her ear.

She did not know what to say to that. The fragrance of

her desire for him was undeniable and she could feel the moisture between her legs as surely as she could feel the beat of her own heart so fast in her chest.

"Soft, silky . . . so hot." Each word accompanied another soft caress to the oh-so-tender flesh. Then his thumb hit a spot that made her cry out with the sharpness of the pleasure.

"That's right, *faolán*. Sing for me."

She gasped. "Wolves don't sing."

"Don't they?" He brushed that spot again, this time with a swirling motion that prolonged the intense pleasure.

And she keened.

She moved against his hand, wanting something, not sure what. "Please, Eirik . . ."

"What do you want, sweet one?"

"I don't know."

"I do."

She nodded desperately. She was sure he did.

One blunt warrior's finger breached her body, slipping inside and claiming her on another level.

"Yes . . . more . . . I want that . . ." she babbled as he moved that finger, making her body shake with delight.

He pressed deep, hitting something inside her that hurt and she flinched away. He pulled his finger back, but not all the way out. "That is your maidenhead, *faolán*. My cock will breach the barrier and you will be mine."

She did not argue. What would be the point? They would both know the words for the lie they would be.

And she wanted it. Him inside her where no other man would ever be allowed.

He came over her, his straining arousal rubbing between her thighs and pleasuring that spot he'd found so unerringly with his finger. "Do you accept me into your body, Ciara?"

Recognition of the beginning of the Chrechte bonding rite sent alarm spiraling through her with the pleasure. She'd accepted they would join their bodies, but this was more than a physical mating. He was demanding she pledge herself to him until death.

That harsh reality that claimed all too many of those she had loved already.

She wanted to deny him, needed to push him away, stop this before it went further and their actions led to the inevitable terrifying conclusion.

But she could not. That part of her heart he had brought back to life would not let her.

He would not hurt her. Death was a cruel master, but would it be any less a cruelty to lose him without the vows?

And she knew in that instant that it would not.

She loved him with every bit of her heart that had been broken and healed to the best of its ability.

She was no fool. She did not believe that for all Eirik wanted her that he loved her as well, but her heart belonged to him. Vows spoken or not.

He waited above her, his body drawing shivers of bliss from her.

"I'm . . . this is just supposed to be . . . tomorrow . . ." The words came out as disjointed as her thoughts.

He brushed his fingertips down her cheek. "Shh. Do not make this complicated. Your wolf knows what she wants. You know what *you* want." He thrust downward with his hips, making his arousal press tantalizingly against her most sensitive flesh, drawing a moan of desire from her. "Tell me you accept me into your body."

Chapter 19

One should believe in marriage as in the immortality of
the soul.

—Honoré de Balzac

Ciara opened her mouth to deny him, despite her new
inner knowledge, but "Yes, I accept you" came out instead.
And in the ancient language of the Chrechte.

Tears of fear tracked a path down her temples, though a
feeling of exultation filled her as well.

He kissed her temples, sipping at her tears and whispering words of comfort in Chrechte before saying, "I join my
body with yours. I give my dragon to you. You are keeper
of my raven."

"I forsake all others for you." That at least was an easy
promise to make. She would never allow another to touch
her heart or her body the way Eirik had.

"And I give my seed only to you."

She wanted that promise as much as she had never
wanted the risk of having children. And a part of her she
had buried long ago birthed a craving for a babe with
Eirik's amber eyes and regal bearing.

"Now and forever."

"Now and forever," he repeated. And then he shifted so

the blunt, broad tip of his manhood pressed against her opening. "Mine. From this night forward."

"Yours."

He thrust forward, stretching her, filling her, making his words truth in a way she would never again be able to deny.

Her wolf purred in approval despite the dull ache of him pressing against the barrier inside her body. She tilted her hips, allowing him to penetrate farther, and she felt the tearing sensation inside that meant her body was no longer innocent of carnal desires. Though, if the truth be told, it hadn't been since his first kiss.

She had fought it, but this outcome had been inevitable from the initial brush of his lips against hers.

She did not complain about the pain because already pleasure fought for supremacy in her body. He continued to press steadily forward, his face showing the strain of the slow penetration.

She reached up and cupped his cheek. "We are joined."

He turned into the touch and once again her wolf purred.

"We are one," he replied in ancient Chrechte.

She gasped, his words going through her with the power of a winter storm's thunder. He reached beyond her and only when he shifted again could she see why. He'd grabbed her dirk.

The sharp blade shined in the moonlight. "We spill blood to consecrate our union." Again he spoke in the language of their people.

His words the only warning she got before he sliced the palm of his hand and then waited for her to offer her hand. It was a rite so ancient, few Faol even knew about it.

Her mother had told her once though, in her mad ramblings after Ciara's father's death. Her mother had described the bonding of their souls in this rite. She'd been insensible with grief but had claimed it was worth all the pain that came after.

Ciara looked at the blood dripping down Eirik's hand onto his wrist and knew he meant their mating to be as sacred and true as possible for the Chrechte. She did not know if it was an Éan thing, or because he was a prince, but his expectation was clear.

She would shed more than the blood of her maidenhead this night.

He did not rush her but remained still above her, his hardness filling her feminine core, his body covering hers in possession and protection.

The time for trying to hold back had passed. With solemnity she had only experienced when spreading her family's ashes, Ciara lifted her hand, palm up. Eirik did not smile, but his approval glowed in his amber gaze.

He cut a tiny prick on her palm, not even one tenth as long as the cut he had made on his own.

But her blood welled and he pressed their palms together. Their blood mingled, growing unnaturally hot between their palms. The wind swirled around them in a rush of air, leaves and other loose detritus from the forest floor, though nothing but the air touched them. Crimson light flashed and then the white light that accompanied her shift into the wolf.

She felt like she'd been hit by lightning, her entire body burning. But it did not hurt; it was a pleasure so great, she was not sure she could bear it.

Eirik's head was thrown back, his face contorted in ecstasy as she felt his heat spread inside her. Her body convulsed, her womb cramping, her vaginal walls clamping onto his shaft so tightly he could not have moved were he making the effort to do so.

She felt his dragon, the power, the fire, the strength and the need for her. Then the raven, the keen senses, the joy in flight and the abhorrence in killing at odds with the dragon's predatory instincts. The raven agreed with the dragon on its need for her though.

Her wolf reached out to soothe both beasts, sharing her own need to hunt, to run under the moonlight and to mark that which was hers.

"We are true mates." She heard the words in his rich, deep timbre in her head, the only sound around them the still rushing wind.

"I cannot deny it."

Though she wanted to, her fear spiking at the knowledge that Ciara was more lost than her mother had ever been. Because in all her descriptions of the mating rite, her mother had never mentioned anything so profound or magical happening.

The dragon crooned to her, the raven's soft caw joining to comfort her.

She stared up into Eirik's eyes. "Our Chrechte spirits have joined."

"Never to be sundered." Only as he spoke the vow in Chrechte did she realize she'd said the words of confirmation.

And suddenly, the pleasure between them began to increase again, spiraling upward as he started to move, thrusting in her with controlled power.

He claimed her then, in an act as old as time.

When they both reached completion for the second time, she felt a searing heat in her palm. She pulled her hand from his and saw that the small prick had already closed.

She grabbed his hand and looked, only to find a thin scar instead of an open wound on his palm.

He smiled, his entire being suffused with male satisfaction. "Our mating has been blessed."

"Yes." She could only hope that meant it would not be cut short.

"You will sleep now."

So lethargic she couldn't imagine doing anything else, she just sighed some kind of agreement. Let him worry about getting them situated; her body was already relaxing into sleep.

She woke in the arms of her dragon, another night's rest unhindered by dreams of the sacred stone.

Ciara gave her adopted aunt, Emily, news of the family, messages and gifts from Abigail while Eirik and the Balmoral went off to discuss the Éan who had made the island their home. After much cajoling by the boy, they'd agreed to take Feth, Lachlan and Emily's son. Named for an ancient Chrechte king, but a mere seven years, he was far from having his alpha father's stature. Though Feth was near to a match in Lachlan's bearing already.

The men planned to check in on those Éan living nearby as well, so Ciara did not expect their return anytime soon. She understood Eirik's need to check on his people, but she struggled with the urge to move forward in their quest. It was an itch under the skin that she was doing her best to ignore.

Lais had left to call on the Éan healer who had trained him, taking Mairi along under the guise of wanting the other healer to examine her. But Ciara wasn't fooled and she doubted his prince had been, either. The eagle didn't want the non-shifting Chrechte out of his sight, and that was that.

Emily put aside the letter from her sister to read later and took Ciara's hands in her own. "How are you holding up under all this?"

The Balmoral had not shown near the surprise at news of the *Faolchú Chridhe* as Ciara's father had. Emily had been surprisingly accepting as well when Ciara had told them her story. Though her aunt had evinced concern for Ciara's part in the recovery of the stone, she had agreed that the *Faolchú Chridhe* must be found.

Ciara shrugged. "I do not know. I hid my secrets for so long and now they are laid bare."

Just as she was sure her mating the night before was no longer undisclosed. Not after the sulfuric glare the Balmoral laird had given Eirik upon their arrival at the keep.

Ciara had bathed in a stream in the forest, but she had been unable to wash away Eirik's scent completely. And her wolf had refused to let her even try.

Not that it would have done any good. Eirik had given her an incendiary kiss before she'd gotten dressed, rubbing his body against hers in a way that was wholly pleasurable. Afterward, both were marked unmistakably with the other's scent.

Stubborn dragon.

He was probably telling her adopted uncle that they had mated in the way of the Chrechte right this very minute. Short of tying him up and gagging him, Ciara was certain she could not have stopped the prince who considered her his from doing so. But the temptation to do exactly that had been strong not fifteen minutes past.

"It is difficult to hide anything among the Chrechte." Emily squeezed Ciara's hands and released them. "I've had to learn there isn't room for normal boundaries, or embarrassment about things they can't help knowing."

"Like what you've been doing when Lachlan takes you for an unexpected stroll in the forest in the middle of the day?" Ciara asked, remembering a story Abigail had told her.

Emily blushed, but there was no scent of true embarrassment coming off of her. "Exactly like that."

Ciara looked over to where Emily's daughter embroidered cloth with her cousin and Talorc's sister, Caitriona, under the larger than normal window of the solar. The femwolf appeared to be focused on the girls and their project, but Ciara knew her other aunt heard every word she and Emily shared. Moreover, she was no doubt listening with keen interest.

The young girls, on the other hand, would not develop stronger Chrechte senses until their first shift. And from what Niall had said, Lachlan and Emily's daughter would never do so. He and his twin, Barr, had the ability to sense whether a babe in the womb was wolf, human or of the Éan, or so they claimed. And Niall had declared the nine-year-old Abigail Caitriona to be wholly human.

No one would know it from the way the children's father doted on them equally. Laird Lachlan adored his human daughter as much as his Chrechte son and made sure everyone knew it.

"It does not take a wolf's enhanced senses to know something has transpired between you and the Éan prince," Emily said in a gently inquiring tone.

Ciara did not know how to reply. She was still coming to terms with her mating and was definitely not ready to talk about it. Caitriona gave her a look of commiseration, as if she knew exactly what Ciara was thinking and feeling.

Perhaps she did. Ciara hadn't been actively masking her emotions since the men's departure.

"How are the boys?" Emily asked, as if she'd never made the leading comment about Ciara and Eirik.

Ciara forced a grin. It wasn't that hard. Thoughts of the twins always made her happy. "As full of trouble as their father."

Tsking, Emily shook her head, her long, golden brown curls swaying against her back. "Did you know I came to the Highlands to protect my sister from the horror of being married to Talorc?"

Caitriona chuckled, proving she had indeed been listening. "If she doesn't, she's deaf. The warriors of my former clan still gossip like grandmothers about the day you likened him to a goat."

"I eventually conceded he wasn't that bad," Emily offered in her own defense, but the laughter in her voice said the memory amused more than concerned her.

Ciara had heard bits and pieces of the story. Like Caitriona had said, how could she not? "Funny how you came north to become my father's wife but ended up the lady of the Balmoral."

Caitriona took in a sharp breath and Emily looked at Ciara with the sappy expression she usually reserved for her children. "You called Talorc your father."

She shrugged. "He is."

Caitriona laughed with her head thrown back. "You may not share his blood, but you are so like him, no one could doubt you are his daughter."

The words made Ciara warm inside and she didn't hesitate when Emily indicated they should join Caitriona and the girls in the chairs under the window.

"It's a good thing Talorc refused to marry me," Emily said as she adjusted her plaid. "We would have killed each other, I'm thinking. And my sister would never have known the happiness she does now."

Ciara could do nothing but agree. She had met few couples as perfectly suited as her mother and father. Though to hear Abigail tell it, their first year was rockier than the cliffs of Balmoral Island.

Emily handed Ciara a handkerchief to embroider before taking up her own project.

Ciara accepted it gratefully, happy to have something to do with her hands as the need to be in search of the stone made her jittery. "You had another sister, didn't you?"

Any topic was better than dwelling on what the elder Talorc who had sent them to talk might have to say. Laird Lachlan had known exactly who Talorc had meant. Boisin was an old man with a big family, who knew all the old stories and shared them with any Chrechte who would listen.

He was purported to be a master storyteller, so most of the Chrechte, old and young alike, spent time at his cottage in the course of a year.

"We did." Emily frowned, her memories of the other woman clearly not fond. "She wasn't kind to Abigail. Jolenta was our mother's favorite once Abigail lost her hearing from the fever."

Ciara's adopted mother never spoke of her family in England and the femwolf thought she knew why. Abigail refused to speak ill of others, but clearly there was little good to say about the family she had left behind.

"Tell Ciara what became of the vain little dunce," Caitriona suggested with a not-well-concealed smirk.

Emily gave her heart-sister a reproving look. "She married a minor baron. Sybil wrote of the nuptials when they happened. I suppose she thought we'd be jealous."

"Jealous, of being married to an Englishman?" Ciara asked with stunned disbelief.

Both Caitriona and Emily laughed, and Emily said, "I was once English. It is not quite the blight so many in the Highlands believe it to be."

"That is not what I wanted you to tell our dear niece about the vain little Jolenta, and you well know it."

Emily sighed but gave her dear friend another chastising

glance before speaking. "We heard word that Jolenta had been engaged to a lord of much higher standing, but he withdrew from the arrangement."

"She was caught playing the games at court with another gentleman entirely." Caitriona shrugged, looking quite a bit like Talorc herself. "I don't understand these court games and am only glad my brother never sent me to live among the entourage of the Scotland queen."

Ciara could only agree. The last seven years had been difficult enough; to have spent them in the company of people who considered truth naïve and deception an art was unthinkable.

"She fought the mating then?" Lachlan asked Eirik, amusement clear in his tone.

The older man had not been amused when they began their discussion, but after Eirik told Lachlan that he and Ciara had spoken their mating vows despite her earlier protests, the powerful laird relaxed.

"Aye. She did not want a mate." Eirik was fairly certain she still didn't.

"Talorc has said as much."

Eirik was not surprised to find out that the two lairds had discussed Ciara. Both cared for her, one as father, the other as uncle. And the two men were much better friends than appearances might imply.

"Nevertheless, she spoke her vows with conviction." He had no intention of sharing the amazing Chrechte magic that had attended their mating though. "We are well matched."

"Talorc must agree or he would not have allowed her to accompany you on this quest without coming himself, or at the least sending Niall along."

Eirik considered the Balmoral's words and frowned. The sneaky Sinclair alpha wolf had known all along Ciara was his mate. "She could not do better than a dragon for her protector."

"Even the most powerful Chrechte would make a poor mate for a man's daughter, if he was not also a good man."

It was an unlooked-for compliment and Eirik gave it the silent recognition it deserved. "You will send a messenger to inform Talorc of the mating?"

"Aye, that and the wedding."

Eirik didn't ask, "What wedding?" He was no idiot. But he did warn his mate's uncle, "She'll balk."

"I've a way with reluctant brides." Lachlan grinned.

Thinking of what he had heard of the other man's own nuptials and that of his second-in-command, Eirik had to agree. The Balmoral knew how to handle a reluctant bride.

The laird proved himself as adept with a recalcitrant female as Eirik suspected a couple of hours later, when they found the women chatting in the solar after brief visits with the Éan that lived near or at the castle itself.

The Balmoral had announced the wedding was to take place before Ciara and Eirik could leave to find the elder, Boisin.

"What wedding?" Ciara asked, proving she was willing to play dumber than she was.

"The wedding between you and Eirik, lass."

"But, Laird Lachlan—"

"'Tis Uncle Lachlan and well you know it."

"Uncle Lachlan," she said, drawing the name out with more sarcasm than a warrior would dare use on the commanding laird. "There is not going to be any wedding."

"Of course there is, lass. The priest is here now to perform the rite."

And indeed the human man had just entered the solar at a near run. He stopped in front of the Balmoral. "I was told there was an urgent matter for your family that needed my attention."

"Aye." The laird indicated Ciara and Eirik with a sweep of his arm. "These two are to be wed."

"Now?" To his credit, the priest did not sound all that shocked by the demand of his laird, but obviously needing clarification.

There was no give in the Balmoral's expression. "Aye, now."

"No, not now," Ciara inserted.

Her uncle turned to face her. "You would shame your parents, my own sister and brother by marriage by refusing to follow your mating with a proper wedding?"

Instead of answering him, Ciara spun to face Eirik. "You tattletale. Our mating is not a piece of gossip for two warriors to chew on."

"Would you rather he believed I took your innocence without the benefit of our Chrechte vows?"

Ciara's mouth opened and closed and opened again. "You did not have to tell him anything."

"I can respect your obstinacy; 'tis almost charming. But do not play the role of fool. Your uncle was aware of what had transpired between us from the moment we arrived in the keep."

"And whose fault is that?" she demanded with a glare.

"I am not sure, Ciara. I thought we shared equal blame. Are you claiming we do not?"

"You are saying the Éan prince forced his attentions on you?" the Balmoral asked with dangerous quiet.

All color drained from Ciara's face as she gasped. "That is not what I said at all."

"So, it *was* mutual?" the Balmoral pressed.

Blood surged back into Ciara's cheeks and she turned her scowl on her uncle. "Yes," she ground out.

"Then the wedding will commence."

"No, wait. I . . . we can't get married without my father's approval."

"He gave approval to the mating when he sent you on this journey with Eirik alone."

"We are not alone." Ciara's gazed flitted to where Mairi now sat in a chair beside Caitriona and Lais once again stood sentinel behind her. "The eagle shifter and seer accompany us."

She spoke freely in front of the priest, but then the man knew all the secrets of his flock. 'Twas to be expected.

Lachlan did not look impressed with her argument, however. "But if your father objected to Eirik as your mate, *he* would have come as well."

"Or sent Niall," Ciara said with dawning understanding and unwittingly echoing her uncle's earlier words. She frowned. "My father expected this."

"Aye, lass."

"But I don't want to get married."

Chapter 20

Love is often the fruit of marriage.

—Molière

"*I* didn't, either, but it turned out well," Caitriona said with a smile.

"For that matter, I had no intention of marrying Lachlan, but the man has a way with him." Emily's smile belied the spicy stories Eirik had heard about the couple's volatile courtship and beginning of their marriage.

Ciara's breath came out in panicked little gasps. "It's not the same."

"I am sending a messenger to your father." The Balmoral crossed his arms over his massive chest and looked as movable as a rock. "He can carry news of your mating and wedding or your mating alone. 'Tis your choice."

The horror that came over Ciara's countenance would have been amusing if Eirik could not see the genuine fear and pain underneath it as well. She was terrified at the prospect of marriage. To him.

He did not like it. He did not understand it. And he would not allow it.

He moved to stand in front of her so she could see

naught but him. Cupping her nape beneath her brown tresses, he squeezed with reassurance and met her troubled emerald gaze. "You have already spoken the vows that matter most. There is naught to fear in adding the priest's blessing to our union."

"I did not want a mate," she whispered, moisture glazing her eyes.

Aye, she'd made that clear enough. "But you have one."

"Yes."

"I would be your husband as well."

"'Tis the way of things," she agreed with little enthusiasm.

He leaned down so their foreheads touched. "Aye."

"It does not feel right that Abigail and Talorc are not here to witness it." There was too much true sadness in Ciara's words for Eirik to believe she was merely trying to put off the ceremony.

"We will ask my grandmother to come to the Sinclair holding to officiate the public rite of a Chrechte mating upon our return."

"You promise?"

"I do."

"All right."

He lifted his head and kissed the top of hers. "It will be."

She shrugged and it bothered him.

"You are not agreeing simply to avoid your father challenging me." As effective as the Balmoral's methods, Eirik wanted unfettered agreement from the woman who would promise before God and man to share her life with his. "I would not kill him."

Her gaze rose to meet his, her green depths dark with certainty. "I know."

"Good."

"I will not shame him."

Eirik liked that reason even less than her agreeing to the wedding out of fear. "There is no shame in being my mate."

"Do we have to discuss this now?" she asked, jerking her head toward the others in the room as if he had forgotten they were there. "If we are going to stand for the priest's blessing, it is best we get it done."

Eirik had an irrational impulse to call the whole thing off but stifled it. Whatever her reasons, Ciara had agreed to bind her life to his. It was a place of starting.

She would come to understand how well they were matched in time. He would allow no other outcome.

*C*iara's hands were cold as she placed them in Eirik's before the priest spoke his blessing on their marriage. The words in Latin flew over her head without registering as she fought her inner demons over this wedding.

She'd agreed, not out of fear of the challenge or her shame, as Eirik thought. Of course he was right, what kind of shame could there be in mating such a strong and loyal Chrechte? She was proud, if terrified, to claim him for her own.

But she wouldn't have . . . if she'd had the choice. Only she didn't. She'd known that the night before. Her instinct to fight the additional bonds between them that this wedding would create had driven her initial denial, but she was no fool.

Not really. And now that the Chrechte vows had been spoken, there was no going back.

She was mated. If Ciara lost Eirik, she might well lose her mind as her mother had, but the option of living without him was no longer open to Ciara, either.

She could only hope becoming pregnant proved difficult as it did for so many Chrechte. She needed time to conquer one terror before taking on another. And she was far from conquering the dread being mated birthed inside her.

But love was an emotion that would not be denied, no matter how hard she tried. She loved her adopted family every bit as much as the one of her birth. And she loved her mate with everything in her soul.

It was not merely Ciara's wolf that demanded overt connection to him. Her human heart craved it as well.

And always would.

She only hoped that in time, he would learn to love her as well. She suspected that if he did not, the dread inside her would only grow.

Eirik spoke his vows in a strong voice that rang throughout the hall. Ciara said hers with equal conviction. If she was to do this thing, she would do it with the whole of her considerable will.

Emily wanted to host a gathering at the latemeal to celebrate the nuptials, but neither Ciara nor Eirik were willing to put off speaking to the elder, Boisin.

Despite two nights without dreams or visions, Ciara's sense of urgency had continued to grow in regard to finding the *Faolchú Chridhe*. And as her mate, Eirik appeared to share it.

So, after hugs of congratulation and many hearty pats on Eirik's back, their little party of four borrowed horses from the Balmoral and rode out.

Boisin lived in a thatch-roofed cottage nearly an hour's ride from Balmoral Castle. A white-haired old man sat on a bench outside whittling. He ignored, or did not hear, the approach of their horses, his focus entirely on the small wooden figure in his hand.

When Ciara and her companions drew near, Eirik raised his fist to indicate they should stop. Then he swung down from his horse before turning to help Ciara do the same.

The old man stood with the help of a walking stick. "Welcome, clansmen of the Sinclair. You can take the horses around back for a bucket of water and grazing."

"Thank you, elder," Eirik said and then nodded his head toward Lais, who grabbed the reins for two of the horses and led them away.

The others proved their good training by staying where they'd been left.

"You are Boisin?" Eirik asked.

"Aye, and who might you be?" Though the way the elder looked at them, she felt he already knew the answer.

"I am Eirik and this is my mate, Ciara." Eirik laid a proprietary hand on her waist, but Ciara found she did not mind. "Our companions are the healer, Lais, and the seer, Mairi."

Boisin gave Mairi a long look filled with what seemed like joyful relief, but how could that be? "So, that is your name, child. Called after the Virgin Mother then."

"Mairi was my grandmother's name as well," the seer said in a quiet voice.

Boisin nodded and then met Eirik's gaze. "You've come to hear stories, I'm guessing."

"Aye. We came in hopes you would have time to share a conversation and a cup of refreshment with us." Eirik handed the old man a skin of wine. "We would be honored if you would share your stories as well."

"I've a little time, I suppose. My great-granddaughter's birthday is a week off yet; her little figures can wait a bit."

Ciara looked down to the whittling the man had set aside and was surprised to see a set of three exquisitely carved fairies, though the third was not done. No bigger than three inches tall, they were the perfect size for a small fist to hold in play.

"We thank you," Eirik replied.

Boisin cocked his head to one side, giving Eirik a long look before saying, "You're welcome, but we'll be sharing more than stories, Éan prince. You've come for answers and I have them."

Lais came back for the other two horses, giving Mairi a searching look, as if checking for any change in her well-being in the few minutes they had been apart.

She rolled her eyes. "I am fine."

"Aye, she is safe here, with me," Boisin said, his tone as if he was speaking of family, not a total stranger.

And then, leaning heavily on his cane, Boisin led the way into the cottage.

Inside, they found more furniture than most crofters could boast of. A table and four chairs took up one side of the single-room dwelling. A bed and chest took up the other.

The wall by the table had actual cabinets with doors, rather than the open shelves most would have made do with. But the most amazing element to the furniture was the intricate pictures carved into nearly every surface. Chrechte symbols, wolves, and *conriocht* were the most predominant art. The cabinet doors depicted a wolf curled into the body of a dragon though, the dragon's tail curved over her as if in protection.

Chills went up and down Ciara's arms at the sight. It was her and Eirik, she knew it was. Though she could not imagine how that could be.

"Your furniture is lovely," Mairi said into the silence that had fallen over the group inside the cottage.

"I've spent my life carving and working with wood." Boisin grunted. "Most of the furniture you saw at the castle was made by me, or mine."

"You put your visions into your work," Eirik said, his gaze fixed on the cabinet that had so entranced Ciara.

"Sometimes, I do at that. Important visions anyway."

"You are a seer?" Mairi asked with awe.

"Aye, lass. With a few more years' experience than you, but no greater a gift." He shuffled to one of the chairs and sat down. "Join me. I've no mind to get a crick in my neck talking to you all."

Eirik and Ciara sat, but Mairi went to the cabinet and opened it without saying anything. She stood for a moment inspecting the contents before pulling five intricately carved goblets out. She brought them to the table.

Boisin gave her an approving nod, and then poured wine into each goblet before placing it in front of one of them, leaving Lais's near Mairi's.

Ciara's goblet had a wolf carved into one side and a woman holding a stone on the other. The carved lines that radiated out from the stone made it seem like the stone glowed near as bright at the sun.

She looked over to Eirik's goblet and saw that it had a dragon carved all the way around it, but a raven was etched into its base. Mairi's goblet also had a wolf, but the other side had a woman surrounded by the small animals of the forest.

She met Ciara's eyes, her own filled with wonder. Then Mairi cast her glance toward Boisin. "How did you know?"

"About your affinity with the small creatures of the earth? I saw it, just as you saw me in dream after dream.

I've been calling you to come and learn, lass, for years now." He sighed. "But you could not come before this. It has all happened as it must."

"What do you mean?" Ciara asked, feeling like she was in the presence of true wisdom.

"The little one's journey ends here for now. I've much to teach her and not many years left to do it in."

"She said she had to join the quest," Lais said from the doorway. "The *Faolchú Chridhe* has not been found yet."

Boisin took a sip of his wine and gave it an approving nod. "The quest brought her here, where she needs to be. 'Tis all."

"But—"

"You'd best decide if you want a mate, or not, young eagle." Boisin narrowed his eyes at Lais, his expression turning crafty. "I've got a grandson who would find this little girl lovely indeed."

"Want is not the problem," Mairi said softly when Lais looked ready for an apoplectic attack.

Boisin shook his head. "Ah, the boy does not feel worthy."

"I am no boy." Lais had finally found his voice.

Boisin did not appear impressed. "Son, when you've lived the years I have, you can call *boy* those you like."

Lais opened his mouth to argue, but Mairi shoved a goblet of wine into his hands. "You must be thirsty after seeing to the horses. Take a drink."

Looking bewildered, the eagle obeyed, but as he lowered the goblet, his eyes focused on the carving.

Lais's goblet had a wolf with an eagle perched on its back. The other side had the Chrechte symbol for love and mating entwined as it often was in the markings used to signify a mating.

He studied the carving for several seconds in silence and then frowned at Boisin. "What does this mean?"

"It means that if you are man enough, your future can be brighter than you think you deserve."

Lais shook his head, but did not reply. He moved to his usual spot . . . sentinel behind Mairi. Ciara noted that for the first time since she'd met the other woman, the young seer looked unworried by anything.

Boisin pointed a gnarled finger toward Ciara. "I've waited long enough for your arrival as well, child. I was beginning to think I would die before you answered the call of the stone."

"I am sorry." Heat stole into her cheeks as shame at her own cowardice engulfed her.

"You learned to fear your gifts before you learned to use them." The understanding in the old man's still bright gaze soothed the pain in Ciara's heart. "'Tis understandable, but 'tis also reason for rejoicing that you are here now."

"You know of my dreams."

"I have a story to tell you, child. Will you listen?"

"Yes." How could she do anything else?

Boisin cleared his throat, took a sip of wine, and then cleared his throat again. When he began to speak, it was in a voice that could mesmerize an entire clan.

"In the days before our people settled into homes of wood and farming, the Chrechte wandered the earth. We hunted for our food and gathered what the earth provided. Some years were bountiful, some lean, but always we waged war for the right to hunt in bigger territories. Much as the clans fight for bigger borders on their holdings today. In those days, there were three races of the Chrechte. The Faol, a fierce people who shared their natures with the wolves."

"I know what the Faol are," Ciara said with a tinge of exasperation.

"A good story cannot be rushed." Boisin frowned reprovingly. "And it loses its strength when you interrupt, do ye ken?"

Properly chastised, Ciara nodded. "I apologize."

"'Tis understandable. You are impatient to reach the end of your journey, but if you rush, you may miss the signs for which way to go."

"I understand."

"Good. Now, as I was saying." But he went through his sipping his wine and clearing his throat ritual again. At this rate the elder was going to be inebriated before he finished his tale.

Ciara was determined not to interrupt the flow of words again.

"There were the Paindeal, another people fierce in battle and fond of war as well. They shared their natures with the big cats of prey and even a wolf would think twice before engaging them in battle. The final race were the Éan, the people of the Chrechte most likely to remember the true spiritual ways. Though they shared nature with eagles and hawks, birds of prey, they also shared their nature with the ravens, birds with no instinct to kill. 'Twas the ravens who were charged with keeping their sacred stone and designated the rulers of their people."

Ciara had not known that, but it made sense to give those with the greatest power a nature not so warlike. The wolves and cats of prey did not have any species like the ravens in their races.

"Among the Paindeal their keepers of the stone came from the cats as black as night and larger than any wolf in the wild. But the wolves connected to the *Faolchú Chridhe* were white as the snow. The only wolves whose males had the ability to control their shift from their first transformation."

He took a long drought from his goblet. "Each of the races had a protector. The Faol were protected by their *conriocht*, the Éan by the dragon and the Paindeal by the griffin."

Ciara was not the only one to gasp at the confirmation that not only did Paindeal exist but they could become griffins.

"If you would lay your swords on the table," Boisin said to Eirik.

"One is Ciara's."

"Aye."

Ciara nodded her assent when she realized Eirik was waiting for it. Both swords were laid carefully across the table, their hilts in easy reach of Eirik's big warrior's hands.

Boisin pointed to the handle of Ciara's sword with a finger shaky with age. "See for yourself. The *conriocht*, the dragon and the griffin."

Ciara and Eirik had already seen the handles, but Lais and Mairi took a moment to look closely at the decoration on the swords.

"But then where are the Paindeal?" Eirik asked.

"All in good time, Éan prince. All in good time."

Eirik sighed, but nodded.

Boisin cracked a grin. "Ah, the impatience of youth."

"I apologize, elder," Eirik said.

"No matter. Listen well, young prince and you will learn things the Éan have forgotten. Each race had its own particular strengths and weaknesses. The wolves reproduce with the most ease, though not as prolific as their human counterparts. The Paindeal healed from any illness or wound short of a mortal one with a shift. The Éan could shift at a younger age and were gifted with more seers and often had special Chrechte gifts with greater impact than their other brethren."

"So, the Faol can have gifts like the Éan," Ciara mused to herself.

Boisin didn't chide her for interrupting again, but nodded. "They can indeed, though only the Éan have healers like the eagle here, and only those found most worthy by the stone at that."

"Oh." Lais looked dumbstruck as he seemed to realize how very unique and special his gift was.

Mairi merely smiled and nodded at him serenely.

Ciara wondered what the seer had experienced in her dreams of the elder. Whatever it was, Mairi was obviously content to be at the old man's table and listening to his stories.

"In addition to having more children, the wolves' protectors were more numerous. The Paindeal had one, perhaps two griffins who would live for centuries. But when one died, it could be a generation or more before their stone called forth another. The same was true of the Éan's dragons."

"Eirik is going to live hundreds of years?" Ciara asked in shock, forgetting her vow not to interrupt.

"Aye, barring treachery. He will. As will you."

Hope blossomed inside her. "What do you mean?"

"You are the first true *kelle* born in more than a century. All others that have come before you failed to find the *Faolchú Chridhe*, but you will. And you will live to see your loved ones die, though not your mate. *You must live*, for you will save the Faol from utter destruction."

Eirik reached over and took her hand. "All will be well, *faolán.*"

She tried to believe him, but the old seer's words were not comforting, despite his promise of long life for her and Eirik. "Utter destruction?" she asked in a hushed tone.

"Aye." Sadness came over Boisin's features. "A plague is coming. A quickly spreading illness so great, the likes of it have never been seen before. Many will die here and in the lands across the sea. It will attack the Chrechte with even greater a virulence than it does the humans. Without the *Faolchú Chridhe* and its power to heal, the Faol will all die in that time."

Horror sent chills through her. *"No."*

"Aye. A seer is not always pleased by his visions," Boisin said, whether simply in acknowledgment or warning for Ciara and Mairi, she did not know. "You must follow the stone to its hiding place behind the stone wall that is not a wall at all and bring it to the sacred caves on Sinclair land. You will return it to its proper place in the cavern of the Faol. You will know this hidden cavern by the etchings on the wall."

She thought of the cave she had seen in her vision and thought he was right, but that didn't help her in finding the stone or the hidden cavern for that matter. "I don't understand."

"To be sure, I don't, either. If I did, I would tell you. My own family's descendants' lives depend on it."

Chapter 21

Fortune and love favor the brave.

—OVID

"But why is the *Faolchú Chridhe* hidden to begin with?" Ciara asked.

"Because in the time so long ago, when our people wandered the earth, the high *kelle* had a son," Boisin continued in his storyteller's voice. "And this woman of great strength and honor saw a lust for power in her only offspring. He wanted to be king, though his cousin who was but a child was heir to the Faol throne."

"The high *kelle*'s son thought he was superior to other Chrechte, that he deserved to be king. Fearghall believed men were more valuable than women and wolves more valuable than all. He devised a foul plan to ensure his ascendancy to the throne. Already a *conriocht* himself, he would take the *Faolchú Chridhe* and hide it so his young cousin could not be blessed with the spirit of the *conriocht*."

"But the stone would call to the *kelle*. She would find it."

"Not if she were dead," Boisin said in a tone that sent shivers down Ciara's spine.

The others at the table looked equally affected and disgusted by the ancient Chrechte's plan.

"It is within the high *kelle* of the Faol's power to draw forth the *conriocht*. She can determine how many need to exist to protect a generation." Boisin shook his head. "Fearghall knew this, but had convinced himself that he could control the *Faolchú Chridhe* on his own. The keepers of the stone have always been women though. The men of their families can draw on certain powers of the stone, but only the high *kelle* could bring them all forth. Only she can bestow the spirit of the *conriocht* through the laying of hands on the sacred stone."

So, Galen would have failed in his quest even if the stone had been found . . . unless he had convinced Ciara to help him. The thought that he might have easily gotten her innocent still-child self to do so sent dread welling in her.

Apparently not bothered by such disturbing thoughts, Mairi gave a beatific smile to Ciara. "I told you."

"You interpreted the meaning of your dreams correctly." Boisin smiled at his new protégé. "That was well done."

Mairi blushed at the praise.

"But the *kelle* hid the stone herself, didn't she?"

"Aye."

"Why?" Eirik asked.

"Because she knew Fearghall didn't only plan to withhold the *conriocht* from his cousin. The *kelle* hid the stone to stop her son from creating an army of *conriocht* and destroying the other Chrechte, didn't she?" Ciara asked.

"She did."

"But again, I ask, why?" Eirik's face was creased in a frown. "If only the high *kelle* could draw forth the *conriocht*, then Fearghall was bound to fail."

"Not if he could intimidate or seduce the next high *kelle* into doing his bidding." Mairi shivered. "A woman has to be very strong of mind to withstand beating after beating without giving her abuser exactly what he wants."

"But you never gave in to your father," Lais said with

fierce pride. "You never told him what you had seen in your dreams and visions about the *Faolchú Chridhe*."

"He would have only beaten me in certainty I had more to give him."

"You are wise for your young years, little Mairi," Boisin said and then continued his tale. "Fearghall accused the Éan of stealing the stone when it was discovered missing and declared war on them. They were in a generation without a dragon and their people were nearly decimated before the few remaining took to the forests in the north in hiding, making their homes high in the trees away from those who hunted them."

"But what of the Paindeal?" Eirik asked.

"They fought the Faol under Fearghall, but every death was a great loss to their race as not even a true mated couple could be guaranteed to produce shifting offspring."

"You mean their children didn't all shift?"

"Nay. Their griffin fought the *conriocht* bravely, but it was finally decided they would return to the land of their origin."

So the old stories were based in truth, Ciara thought. "They went back across the land bridge that fell into the sea."

"More like they left in boats, but the Paindeal live in the lands of the Norsemen and further south amidst the countries the Romans conquered or sought to do."

"They must be higher in number now," Eirik mused.

"Aye. They live much longer lives and with no wolves hunting them, their numbers have grown."

Eirik's brow creased in a puzzled frown. "You know all this from dreams?"

"And visions. 'Tis a thing I will teach Mairi as your Anya-Gra will train your mate once you have recovered the *Faolchú Chridhe*."

Ciara wasn't sure she wanted the knowledge Boisin spoke of, but her time from hiding from her gifts was past. She would serve their people as Eirik had predicted and just as he promised, she would not do it alone.

For the first time since realizing she had a mate, Ciara felt gratitude instead of fear stir in her heart.

"So, if it needs to be returned to the sacred caves on Sinclair lands, it stands to reason it is not there," Lais observed.

Boisin inclined his head. "I have long believed that to be the case."

"Knowing where it isn't doesn't improve our chances of finding it by much," Ciara said worriedly.

The weight of her people's future now pressed down heavily on her shoulders.

Eirik squeezed her hand again, reminding her he had not let go, that the stubborn man never would let her go. "We will find the *Faolchú Chridhe*; we will save your race. Trust in our Chrechte strength. 'Tis not limited to the increased physical prowess from our animal natures."

She took a deep breath and nodded, trusting in her mate, if nothing else.

"Perhaps we should begin our search in caves on the lands of the clan with the strongest contingent remaining of the Fearghall." Lais caressed Mairi's hair as if he didn't realize he was doing it. "It stands to reason that would be the clan in most direct descent from the high *kelle* and her wicked son."

"'Tis not such a good measure as you might think," Boisin said. "When the Fearghall society was formed, so too were the Cahir."

"The Cahir?" Eirik asked.

"Aye, warriors dedicated to rooting out the Fearghall among the packs and either convincing them the error of their ways or destroying them."

"You are Cahir?" Mairi asked, sounding like she knew the answer.

"I was once. I passed that mantle to my son and he has trained his sons to follow."

"But there are no Fearghall in the Balmoral clan," Ciara said with confusion.

"Why do you think that is, lass?" Boisin shook his head. "The Balmoral clan has Cahir, but some packs did not train the next generation of Cahir and take their vow of protection in belief the cancer no longer existed among them, but without the Cahir, 'twould always return."

"Like in my father's clan," Mairi said, looking up at the eagle with a sad frown.

"Aye, the MacLeod has a like spirit to Fearghall," Boisin said. "Though he does not share such a direct bloodline as our Faol princess."

"I am not a princess," Ciara could not help muttering.

"*Kelle* then."

"I am not *kelle*."

"I will teach you to be a warrior," Eirik promised. "And Anya-Gra will teach you to care for the spiritual welfare of our people. The stone has chosen you as high *kelle*. You have too much courage and honor not to heed the calling."

He was correct that she would not deny her call, but it wasn't because she was courageous. It was because she had no choice.

"*Our* people?" she asked.

"The Chrechte."

"Both Faol and Éan?" she pressed, though she knew the answer.

"Aye."

Boisin nodded. "The races must join to win against the Black Death coming."

Lais got more water for the horses, his thoughts and heart in conflict. He owed his allegiance to Eirik and could not abandon his prince to pursuit of the quest without him, but the thought of leaving Mairi here on Balmoral Island made his eagle claw to get out.

"Boisin has agreed to lead us to the caves the Balmoral use for their sacred Chrechte rites," Eirik said from behind Lais. "Though he is fairly certain the *Faolchú Chridhe* is not there, he wants to show Ciara how to draw on the power of the stone and seek it out."

Lais turned and met his friend and prince's gaze. "Do you think he has truly foreseen the future and this Black Death he mentioned?"

"His gift is true. You have only to look at the goblet he served your wine in to see that."

The images on the goblet had burned inside Lais with hope ever since his first glimpse of them. "Aye."

"The Black Death is coming."

"But not for many years."

"That is what he said."

"So, why find the stone now?"

Eirik frowned and looked off to the distance. "Because the stone needs Ciara to touch and heal the Faol and she needs the stone to prolong her life."

"For centuries . . ." Lais could barely believe such a thing possible.

"That is what the old man said."

"Do you think it is true?"

"I do. Since transforming into my dragon for the first time, I have felt invulnerable."

"Because none could best you in battle."

"I do not get sick. Cuts, wounds . . . they heal far too quickly for even a Chrechte."

"You are going to outlive me."

"Aye." Eirik's grief at the thought lived in his eyes. "My grandmother always warned me my calling would not be an easy one. I thought the hardest thing had already been faced."

"Giving up your right to rule as king."

"Aye."

But worse was yet to come, not that it needed saying. Lais was just as certain that Eirik would learn to take the centuries in stride so long as his mate was by his side.

"I want a mate," Lais blurted out.

Eirik raised a single brow. "I thought you'd already chosen one."

"She deserves better."

"Than my most trusted and closest friend?" Eirik asked with disbelief. "There is no better man."

Lais felt an unmanly prick at his eyes and blinked the sensation away. "You know that is not true."

"Do not be a fool, Lais."

"I am not."

"No." Eirik slapped his shoulder. "You were deceived

once, but you were not a fool then and you are not one now.
Do not act the part."

"I betrayed my alpha and the princess of our people."

"They forgave you. The *Clach Gealach Gra* healed you."

"What if it didn't? What if I cannot give Mairi bairns?"

"What if you can?"

"You make it sound simple."

"'Tis because it is. Would you dismiss the gift to heal
that you have been given because you are unworthy of it?"

"Of course not." He could not believe Eirik had even
asked such a stupid thing. Their people needed Lais's abilities. "I cannot deny the *Clach Gealach Gra* my service in
healing others."

"Then how do you think you have the right to deny this
gift?" Eirik asked in a tone that implied he was not the only
one capable of voicing stupidity.

"You didn't say this to Gart when he chose his dreams
of children over his mate."

"I am not Gart's alpha."

"If it comes to that, you are not actually mine, either."
Though they both knew that prince triumphed over alpha
as a distinction of leadership, no matter what Eirik had sac-
rificed to bring his people to the clans and relative safety.

"I am your friend," Eirik said with certainty. "I would be
remiss if I did not point out when you are being an idiot."

"Boisin said Mairi has to stay here, with him, to train in
her calling as a seer."

"It is no easy thing to leave your mate behind, even if it
is for a short time, but for an indefinite period, it is damn
near impossible."

"Though sometimes it is necessary."

"I trust you as I do no other, but I am dragon. You can
stay here, with your mate, and know naught will befall a
Chrechte of my power."

"Even a dragon needs a friend at his back. I will come
with you." There could be no question of it. Their people,
Éan and Faol alike, relied on the success of this quest.

"Thank you." Eirik clasped his arm, forearm to forearm, in the way of warriors. "You will return to her."

Feeling more at peace than he had since his first whiff of his mate's scent, Lais stepped back. "I will. What do you think the Balmoral would say to requesting his priest perform another wedding this day?"

"He's a man of action. He will understand the need."

*L*ais found Mairi with Ciara, listening to more of Boisin's stories, both women enraptured by the old man's gift.

Smiling, Lais laid his hand on Mairi's shoulder so as not to startle her.

She looked up, her pretty blue eyes filled with question.

"Walk with me a minute?" he asked.

She nodded.

Cackling, Boisin stopped his story. "Is that how you young men do it? Walk with me a minute, he says." Boisin slapped his knee. "My own dear mate led me a merry chase. I'd have not asked her to walk with me for fear she would lay a trap ahead of time."

Lais felt his face heat, but Mairi was standing and she shook her head in amusement at the elder. "Thank you for the stories, Boisin."

"Aye, lass, you're welcome. You'll learn to tell them as well as my own daughter has done and her son after her."

Mairi nodded, looking pleased and Lais's worry at leaving her behind lessened.

He led her out of the cottage and around to the back. "There is a small loch a bit of a walk from here."

His eagle had smelled the water and Lais had gone looking when he'd realized the old man's barrel was half empty. He'd refilled it for Boisin, the least he could do after watering four large horses from the man's reserves.

"You are leaving with the others," Mairi said, resignation in her tone.

"I am coming back."

She looked up at him, but he kept his attention on the path ahead of them. He didn't want to have this conversation until they were well away from the cottage and keen Chrechte ears.

They reached the water and he guided her to a seat in the shade cast by a large oak tree near the bank.

"You are coming back? Why?" she asked, her blue eyes troubled.

"To collect my wife."

Those pretty blue eyes widened now, shock shimmering in their depths. *"Your wife?"*

He smiled. "Aye." He dropped to his knee beside her and took her small hand in his. "Mairi, sweet one, you are my mate."

"That is not what you claimed in the boat." She gave him a very disgruntled frown. "And you ignored me, last night in the guards' hut."

"I did not know when Gart would return; I could not risk him finding us in a compromising circumstance." As it was, the guard had not returned at all, but Artair had come to the hut when his watch was over.

"Now you want to be my mate? Because Boisin threatened you with his randy grandson?"

"Because Eirik told me I was being an idiot and I agreed. You are a gift from God and to deny you is to deny the preciousness of that gift. That I cannot do."

"You said *wife*."

"I did."

"You want to marry me?" she asked on a squeak.

"With everything in me, I do."

"But . . ."

"Say you will accept me, my eagle . . . my past." Perhaps it was not fair to ask it, but 'twould not be fair to consign them both to a lonely future, either.

Mairi was wrong on one count. Lais was not worried about Boisin's grandson, not one bit. Because Mairi was his mate and he was hers. There would be no other, for either of them.

"And will you accept me . . . even if I never gain a wolf?"

That one was easy. "'Tis why I desire the wedding happen now."

"I don't understand." But she was looking at him with such hope.

He would not disappoint her. "If you gain a wolf as you hope to and the wedding came after, you would always wonder if I only claimed you because you shared your soul with the wolf."

"You are right." Her eyes filled with tears that spilled over and she swiped at them. "I *would* have wondered."

"Aye."

"But are you sure? We have known each other such a short time."

"My eagle knew you the moment Eirik laid you on the grass behind the Sinclair keep. I knew I was lost the first moment your eyes opened and caught my own."

"But do you love me?" she asked as if afraid of the answer. "Can you love me?"

"Do you love me?"

"Yes."

"Is love the desire to be with you and no other? To protect you from all harm? The willingness to both kill and die for you? The need to touch whenever we are near? The desire to keep your heart as well as your body for as long as we both draw breath? If this is love, then I love you."

"I will marry you." Then she burst into tears.

He didn't mind. The joy coming off of her was a heady fragrance to Lais's eagle's senses.

He decided that vow needed sealing with a kiss. And so he did.

In the end, *Boisin* sent word to his laird via one of his many grandchildren, and the priest met them in the clearing outside the Balmoral pack's sacred caves. He spoke his blessing over Lais and Mairi before being accompanied by two warriors back to the castle.

The Balmoral then led the way inside the caves to the Chrechte remaining. Lais held Mairi's hand, his heart full and her scent happy after speaking their vows. The others joined in a circle around them. Artair and Gart, who had accompanied their laird from the castle, the Balmoral and his family, Boisin and one of his grandsons, though clearly too young to be the one the elder had used as threat.

The Balmoral performed the Chrechte rite of mating and marriage, prompting Lais and Mairi to speak vows even more binding than those the priest had done.

Afterward, Lais claimed his new mate and wife with yet another kiss that was most satisfying.

Ciara smiled mistily at the couple still kissing.

Boisin chuckled. "Now, that's how we let our mates know of our interest back in my day. *Will you walk with me for a minute?* the boy asked." The old man shook his head, but then turned serious and faced Eirik. "Draw the Faol king's sword, if you please."

Eirik gave Ciara a questioning glance and she nodded.

He pulled the sword from its sheath and laid it across his hands as he'd done in her bedchamber.

Boisin motioned to Ciara. "Take the handle, one hand above the other."

Remembering what had happened the last time she'd touched it, Ciara hesitated.

Boisin patted her shoulder. "Do not fear the visions, lass. They will lead you to the stone."

She nodded, bit her lip and did as the elder had instructed, taking the handle of the sword and moving it so the tip pointed toward the rocky floor of the sacred cave. The handle grew hot against her palms immediately.

"Lend her your strength, dragon," Boisin instructed.

And Eirik's arms came around Ciara, his heat surrounding her like a blanket of safety, his hands curving over hers, promising strength if hers gave out. Peace stole over her and she relaxed against him.

Trusting her mate to keep her safe, her eyes drifted shut.

"Can you feel the presence of the stone in these caves?" Boisin asked her as if from the end of a tunnel.

She thought about it, letting her wolf connect to the spirit of the stone through her grasp on the sword. "I feel the presence of Chrechte magic." Profound magic. "But not the stone."

"Good. For it does not reside here," Boisin said in that strangely distant voice again. "Now allow your spirit to seek it. Do not fear whatever may come. You are safe in the arms of your dragon mate."

She *was* safe, more safe than she had ever been. She could let the visions come and they would not harm her, nor anyone she loved.

She did as Boisin said, letting her senses seek outward as far as they would go in search of the *Faolchú Chridhe*. And between one breath and the next, she was in the cavern again, with the aged *kelle*.

The woman did not look through her this time, but met her gaze with eyes the same shade of deep green. "You are the one."

No time or inclination for false modesty, Ciara dipped her head in acknowledgment.

"I am glad. There is both strength and goodness in your heart."

"Thank you."

"I am sorry for the years the dreams have beset you."

"They are not your fault."

"They are." The old woman frowned, looking guilty but resolute. "I prevented you from finding the stone until you had a worthy protector."

Galen had been her protector when the dreams started. "My brother was not worthy."

"He was deceived by the Fearghall. He wanted to believe himself superior, as your father did."

Chapter 22

Among all the kinds of serpents, there is none comparable to the Dragon.

—EDWARD TOPSELL

*C*iara felt no surprise her father had been a member
of the Fearghall. He certainly had ascribed to the first
Fearghall's belief that men were more valuable than
women.

Yet, she felt compelled to say, "I am sorry."

"Their pride is not your sin." The *kelle* sighed. "No
more than my son's sins are my own. Though I am responsible for calling the *conriocht* spirit to him."

"Did you know of the flaws in his character before you
used the stone to bless him with the *conriocht*?"

The *kelle* shook her head, grief shining in her eyes. "I
knew we did not need more protectors, but he was my son.
His belief in his supremacy came after he learned to shift
into the *conriocht*."

"I am sorry," Ciara said again.

But peace stole over the *kelle*'s features. "It was a long
time ago. What happened when I walked the earth no longer has the power to hurt. Even Fearghall has seen the truth
of love and embraced it."

Ciara couldn't help wondering how many centuries that had taken. "Where did you hide the *Faolchú Chridhe*?"

"Somewhere my son and those who took on his name would never have considered looking." The *kelle*'s sadness had returned and was palpable. "He was too fond of war, respected the power to kill above all others. He had no respect for the power to heal, though his own mate was a gifted raven who had no need of the sacred stone to heal the most grievous injury."

"His mate was raven?" Ciara asked in shock.

"Yes, he killed her the same night he took my life."

"I . . ." To say she was sorry was simply not enough. Not in the face of such treachery.

"His refusal to believe in the power of love over might led to his downfall and eventually the fall of the Faol."

"MacAlpin was his descendant."

"Aye, along with a great many good Chrechte."

Ciara looked around the cavern, taking notice of the carvings and their significance. The story of a mighty warrior and his protection of the Faol was told in picture along one part of the stone wall. "Fearghall was not all bad."

"No, he was not." The *kelle* smiled softly. "Thank you for understanding that. It is yet more proof of your good heart."

Ciara did not comment on that. "Where would he and those who came after not think to look?"

"Deep in the earth. He was convinced his wife stole the *Faolchú Chridhe* and she had an abhorrence for dark, small places. As many of the Éan do to this day. It is not a natural thing for them to go deep in the earth when they crave the sky, particularly not to a place that requires a long journey through a tight, dark tunnel!"

"Was it in the sacred caves of the Donegal or the MacLeod?" Ciara asked, not recalling ever hearing of a cavern that required such a journey to reach.

The *kelle*'s brows drew together in confusion. "I do not know these names. Are they warriors of your pack?"

"No. They are the names associated with territories."

"Like hunting grounds? You name them now, rather than warring over the right to them?"

"There is still plenty of fighting."

The *kelle* gave a twisted smile. "I suppose there is." She frowned in thought and then said, "The caves were ones the *kelle* used only for healing."

"And Fearghall had no interest in healing."

"No. He killed my sister priestesses in his fury at the loss of the stone, never to realize they were the only ones who might have led him to it or who could truly draw on its power."

"Where are these caves?" Ciara asked, a sense of time running short assailing her.

"Do you know the most sacred caves used by the Faol, the Éan and the Paindeal?"

"The Paindeal left the Highlands centuries past."

The *kelle* winced. "Because of Fearghall?"

"Yes. You did not know?"

"I know only what I have learned when called into dreams of the Chrechte since my death. It has not happened often and never before have I been able to converse so freely as I am doing with you."

"Others claim my connection to the stone is very strong."

"As strong as my own." The priestess nodded as if to herself and then smiled reassuringly. "It will lead you to itself."

"I hope so. The seer Boisin says if I do not find it, the Faol will all die from the Black Death."

"It is coming." A different kind of grief shone in the *kelle*'s eyes. "You must learn to connect to the *Faolchú Chridhe* and save our people."

"I want to." And it was the first time Ciara had ever genuinely felt that.

"Then you will. The caves . . . perhaps only the Éan and the Faol use them now?"

"There is a sacred place I know of that is like that. It has been used as long as anyone can remember. Hot springs bubble up into a large pool in the cavern used for the mating ceremony."

"That sounds like the caves of which I speak." The *kelle* sounded both pleased by Ciara's intelligence and relieved.

"Two days' journey south and half a day going west from that place will take you to the healing caves."

"Walking, or running as the wolf?" Ciara asked before trying to determine where the directions the *kelle* had given indicated.

"Running as a wolf. Walking takes so long," the *kelle* said with a puzzled frown. "The wolf can run from dawn to dusk."

Ciara did some quick thinking. That would be on MacLeod land, but not the sacred caves Talorc had spoken of. "Are there landmarks nearby?"

And would they still be there so many hundreds of years later?

"The healing caves are in a dell with a small river running through it. We called it *Kyle Kirksonas*."

Hopefully Mairi would know where the *narrow river of the healing place of worship* was and what dell it ran through. Perhaps it was still called *Kyle Kirksonas* by the MacLeod. Place names did not change so quickly in the Highlands.

The *kelle*'s face twisted in thought. "The entrance to the caves is in the steepest brae, a hillside entirely of stone. It looks like part of the brae, but it is not."

The stone wall that was not. "How will we find it then?" Ciara asked.

"There is a place on the wall carved with our Chrechte symbol for healing. It is this high and about this large," the *kelle* said, making a circle with her hands about as large as a baby's face and near her eye level. "You must press the center with one of the small children from the *Faolchú Chridhe*."

"You mean the stones like the one you wear in your circlet?" Ciara asked.

The *kelle* touched the tiny emerald dangling in the center of her forehead and smiled. "Yes. One of the children, though the key to our healing caves is bigger."

It was a good thing there were "children," as the *kelle* called them, in the handle of Ciara's dirk and hilt of her brother's sword. Hopefully one of them was of the right size to be the key.

An insistent noise buzzed at Ciara's consciousness and the *kelle* looked as if she heard it, too. "It is time for you to leave this place and return to your world."

"You will go back to wherever you were?"

"My spirit is always with God." The *kelle* smiled, this one filled with a beautiful peace. "But when I am called to a dream, the form I had upon death is the one that comes."

"It was an honor to meet you, *kelle*."

"And you as well, princess of the Faol. Never doubt, we will meet again."

Ciara went limp in Eirik's arms and he grabbed her, allowing the sword to fall to the ground.

The Balmoral picked it up and put it back in the sheath on Eirik's back. "Is she well?"

"I do not know." And the possibility that she was not caused feelings inside Eirik that he was far from accustomed to experiencing.

Like terror.

Her breathing had grown increasingly shallow while she was in her vision, her color leaching from her skin until Ciara looked near death. If it were not for the faint but steady beat of her heart, he would be lost. As it was, he wanted to rip someone's head off, preferably any Faol who still followed Fearghall, since the one responsible for the loss of the *Faolchú Chridhe* to the wolves was far beyond Eirik's reach.

"She'll be fine. The lass just needs a bit of rest," Boisin assured them.

"You have seen this before?" Eirik demanded.

"Oh, aye . . . the more powerful and prolonged the vision, the more it will take out of you. But a little sleep and some food and she'll be back to rights again."

Eirik swept his wife into his arms. "Where is the healing chamber?"

He would leave the mating chamber for Lais and Mairi. Eirik wasn't about to attempt consummating their own marriage, until Ciara was fully recovered.

"There is no chamber for healing in these caves," the Balmoral stated. "Without a healer like Lais in our clan, or the sacred stone to draw upon, we are reliant on our Chrechte natures and the healing arts."

Eirik felt sorry for the Faol in that moment. The Éan may have lived in the forest, hunted and in hiding, but they still had the old Chrechte ways.

"So, there is only this cave and your mating chamber?"

"No, there is a cave that branches off to the left there." The Balmoral pointed with his hand. "Many Chrechte have spent the night in there when needing peace and solitude."

It was not a healing chamber, but it sounded better than taking Ciara back to the castle. Eirik remembered to say, "Thank you," before carrying her down the dimly lit tunnel.

Lais led Mairi into the chamber of mating that the Balmoral had directed him to. Like the sacred caves on Sinclair land, it had a pool fed from an underground hot springs. Though the stone bath was smaller than the one in the other caves, it looked perfect for a mating.

Mairi's gaze flitted from place to place in the cave. "There are torches in the walls. Should we light them, do you think?"

"Aye." He wanted to be able to see her lovely body.

"Oh. Are you sure?" she asked, seeming to have had the same thought, but a different reaction to it.

"Very."

She nearly wrung the pleats from her skirt, she was yanking on it so hard. "You have an odd propensity for seeing me without clothing."

"There is nothing strange about it, sweet one." He took his flint and struck it on the wall of the cave to spark each torch.

Tinder dry, they caught fast. There were four torches in all. Enough to cast the small cavern in a soft yellow glow, but not so many all the shadows were dispelled.

He turned back to Mairi to find her staring with some

trepidation at a pile of furs a few feet from the pool casting steam into the air.

"Sweet one, you have naught to fear in our mating bed."

She shook her head. "I know . . . I just . . . do you think others have lain there before?"

"I am sure many Chrechte have consummated their mating vows in that very spot. 'Tis a blessed place." Lais drew closer, scenting the air. "But none have lain on the furs there now."

The Balmoral had told him as much as well.

Mairi let out a breath. "You are certain?"

"Aye. The laird said they are a gift from the pack to each newly mated pair."

"But we are not Balmoral."

"He did not seem to care."

"So, they're replaced after . . ." She cleared her throat. "After each mating?"

"That is what the Balmoral said."

"That is kind, I think, and particularly to us as we are not part of their pack."

"He accepted our vows as Chrechte alpha."

"Still."

"It is good of them," Lais conceded, putting his hands on her shoulders and pulling her back against his body. "You are mine now, Mairi. Only mine."

She turned in his arms, so her face was tilted up toward his, her blue eyes filled with emotion. "And you are mine."

"Aye. From the moment Eirik laid you on the ground at my feet."

Her bow-shaped lips curved. "You make it sound like he gifted me to you."

"Fate did and Eirik was its messenger mayhap."

"You are my gift, Lais. Do you not realize that?"

He opened his mouth to speak, to say he knew not what, but his throat was too tight for words. So, he kissed her. She melted against him, her arms circling his neck, her small hands locking in the hair at his nape.

He undressed her with care, though he knew that after the healing session he had insisted on that morning before leaving the beach hut, she felt no more pain from her beating.

She let him remove her clothing, seemingly oblivious to it even happening. Though she moaned with clear awareness when he cupped her naked breast. 'Twas just the right size to fill his large hand and he kneaded it gently, enjoying both the feel of her silky skin and the tiny noises escaping her mouth against his lips.

He cupped her bottom with his other hand, running his fingertips along where one luscious curve met the back of her thigh. She arched into him, opening her mouth on instinct for him to deepen the kiss.

So innocently sensual, his virginal mate had him ready to explode without ever getting his kilt off.

And that would not do. Her first time must be special; it must show her the care his eagle had for the mate of his heart.

He lifted her and carried her to the furs, laying her down with care.

She smiled up at him. "I believe we have been here before."

Giving the pale beauty of her body a long perusal, he had to disagree. "This is no healing session, little one."

"You think not? But each caress you give me heals my heart a little bit more."

"Then we heal each other." For he had never known such a sense of peace and belonging as he felt when she was in his arms.

"Yes, let us heal each other."

He stripped with hands made clumsy by their urgency, her eyes hot on him with love and desire every second it took. He finally kicked off his boots and joined her on the furs.

She didn't wait for him to renew the kiss but placed her mouth against his. He lowered his body over hers, his aroused and leaking sex trapped between them.

"Heal me," she whispered against his lips.

His heart contracted and then swelled as it overflowed with love for this courageous human woman. He kneed her

legs apart and moved his hand down to fondle her most
intimate flesh. Pleasure surged through him when he realized that she was already wet and slick with need.

Nevertheless, he was not going to rush this.

He took his time stretching tissues that had never known
any sort of invasion. He could feel the proof of her virgin-
ity, but it would not have mattered if he couldn't. This
woman was his in every way and would accept him into
her body with the kind of love he had never even let himself dream about.

They moved together, his hands on her body, her small
ones exploring his until the time came. And they joined.

There was some pain, but he concentrated his Chrechte
gift with more ease than he would ever experience with
another and healed her inner flesh even as his body claimed
hers.

Soon she was begging him to hurry, to go deeper . . .
and he gave her all that she asked for.

Including his heart.

Chrechte power surged through the cavern when they
came and he knew that despite the odds, he had just planted
his seed deep in her womb.

Eirik woke with the change in Ciara's heartbeat that
indicated she was aware of her surroundings once again.
She had slept away the evening and most of the night. With
instincts honed by years of living and hunting in the forest,
he could sense that dawn was not far off.

They had shared their dreams again, his raven taking
her flying in the only landscape they would ever be able to
share the sky together. Then Eirik had lulled her into a
deep sleep within her somnolence that would renew her
strength more completely than normal rest would have.

"Hmmm . . . I suppose I should be used to waking in
the arms of a dragon, but I'm not. It is magical."

And do you like it? This magic? he asked via their mating link, sure he knew the answer.

She rubbed her head along his thick dragon arm she'd used for a pillow. "I do."

Good.

"I think I know where the *Faolchú Chridhe* is."

After all the vision had taken out of her, he would not be happy if it were otherwise. *Where?*

"On MacLeod land, I think." Then Ciara told him about her vision, repeating her dialogue with the *kelle* word for word from the sounds of it.

And Eirik could barely breathe for the shock of his mate conversing with one of the ancient ones. *Anya-Gra has never spoken to an ancestor.*

"Perhaps the Éan have never needed the kind of guidance the Faol do now."

According to Boisin's dreams, both our races need you to find the stone. He brushed along her hip with his tail before curving it around her and tucking Ciara closer to his massive dragon's body.

"You are right. I do not understand why, but I'm not about to question it. Not after everything."

No. She had seen too much in her own visions to question Boisin's. *We return to the mainland immediately after breaking our fast.*

"All right, but can you shift?"

Of course. He did so, allowing his dragon form to shrink back into his man. "You are not yet used to speaking with the mate-link."

"It's not that." The cavern was dark, but he could hear a smile in her voice.

"What then?"

She pulled him into the warmth of the furs, sliding her naked body against his. He'd undressed her, believing she would rest better without all the layers of clothing she usually wore.

She pressed a soft kiss to his lips and then spoke with their mouths only a hairsbreadth apart. "I want my wedding night."

"'Tis almost morning."

"Then you had best get on it, hadn't you?"

Joy unlike anything he'd ever known or expected bubbled from deep inside him as the kiss went incendiary.

This woman was his and she wanted him. Not just the power of his dragon, not only the prince of his people, or the gifts of his raven . . . but him. Eirik Taran Gealach Gra.

And he wanted her, her beauty, her passion, her kind heart she tried so hard to hide. All that made Ciara of the Sinclair who she was. He did not understand the profundity of his emotion any better than she did the prophecy, but like his *faolán*, he would accept.

Gladly.

And he would give her a wedding night never to be forgotten.

Ciara wasn't really surprised to find Niall and two of her father's most trusted warriors waiting with the horses, instead of the eagle shifter they had left there, when she and Eirik landed on the mainland later that morning.

Niall waited for Eirik to transform from his dragon before stepping forward. "The Sinclair has ordered these two Chrechte warriors to accompany you on the remainder of your quest."

He indicated Everett and his younger brother, whose grandmother had been a white wolf. Both men were unmated, but they had controlled the shift from the first glimpse of their wolves.

She cast an anxious glance at Eirik, worried he would take offense at her father's edict.

But her mate merely nodded. "They are welcome. The Balmoral sent one of his wolves and one of the Éan to accompany us as well."

She hadn't known that. "Who?" she demanded.

"Artair and Vegar, one of the strongest and most deadly among Éan guardian warriors."

"Is Vegar a man or woman?" The name was unfamiliar to her.

Eirik smiled. "While all Éan females are trained for

warfare, few become guardian warriors as my sister did. Vegar is a man."

"I see. Why didn't you mention before we left Balmoral Island that two more warriors would be joining us on our journey to the healing caves of our ancestors?"

He frowned as if her question made no sense to him. "Those caves are on MacLeod lands. Of course we will increase our fighting force when venturing among the enemy."

"We aren't going to wage war." Though Ciara wouldn't mind taking her dirk to Mairi's father.

"Your safety is paramount."

Because she was a seer and the keeper of the stone. Ciara shrugged. "You are not going to let anything happen to me."

Eirik was a dragon, for goodness' sake.

"I am but one man and the search will be made easier for the number of eyes on the task."

She was sure he was right about that, but the larger their party, the harder to hide their presence on MacLeod lands. "You are more than a mere man."

"As are the warriors under MacLeod's authority."

"We have learned he is alpha over the largest pack in the Highlands," Niall said grimly.

"But that's not possible. Their clan isn't that large."

Niall's frown was fiercer than usual. "And it is almost entirely Chrechte."

An atavistic thrill of dread went through Ciara. "How can that be?"

"It is not an answer you want," Niall assured her. "Accept only that MacLeod's greatest sin was not beating his daughter."

Then the man's sins must be heinous indeed, for that one was terrible enough.

Everett and his brother both looked a little green and she realized they must have been privy to the MacLeod soldier's interrogation, or at least the results.

"How many Chrechte did he send after Mairi?" Ciara asked her father's second-in-command.

"Six."

"How many live?"

Niall's countenance grew even dourer. "Four."

"Will they submit to our laird?"

"They will, and gladly." It was Everett's turn to speak.

That, more than anything, spoke to the evil that MacLeod perpetrated. Faol were loyal to their pack. "So, it is war?" she asked, fearing she knew the answer.

Niall's jaw ticked. "After the *Faolchú Chridhe* is found."

Chapter 23

Isn't it the sweetest mockery to mock our enemies?

—SOPHOCLES

"Wouldn't a smaller group be better then?" Ciara asked, really wondering now what was driving the warrior's decisions. "We would be less likely to be discovered."

"And protecting you would be more risky," Eirik said, sounding entirely unimpressed by the prospect.

"Surely you jest." She was getting tired of him acting like he wasn't enough to protect her. He was her mate and he was dragon, protector of an entire race. "If we are discovered, no force could stand against your fire. Had my brother and Luag been with a force ten times their size, you would have disintegrated them."

Entire trees had gone up in flame.

Her mate's expression closed and he turned toward the water. "The others will be here shortly."

"That is much faster than he and Mairi made the crossing over."

"There are four able-bodied soldiers to row this time."

"Four?" she asked in confusion and wondered if that was going to be her state from now on.

She'd mated a confusing man who shared only what he thought necessary, which apparently was not a great deal.

"The Balmoral sent his second to get a report on the MacLeod soldiers from Niall."

"Oh." She hadn't known Drustan was making the crossing, but then Ciara hadn't known *any* of the others were coming. "I think I'll go sit over there." She waved vaguely at the fallen log outside the cave where her clan kept supplies. "It's clear my input is not needed here."

Eirik frowned, but he didn't gainsay her.

She crossed the beach with leaden feet. Ciara had always fought the idea of taking a mate because the prospect of losing him and/or any children they might be able to produce terrified her. She'd never once considered the possibility that she might have a mate and yet *not have him* because his heart was not engaged.

You are upset, Eirik said through their mindspeak. Though he was faced away, his focus on the boat pulling closer to shore with every row of the oars.

I am fine.

You are sad.

Stop reading my emotions.

His shoulders tensed, but he didn't turn around. *I cannot help it.*

Well, stop commenting on them at least.

Do you regret our mating?

Did she? *I don't know. It doesn't matter, does it? We're mated and according to the* kelle, *until we were the* Faolchú Chridhe *wasn't going to be found.*

When you are chosen as the protector of your people, your life ceases to be your own. There was a certain amount of bleak acceptance in his tone.

He ought to know. Eirik's life had been all about sacrifice for his people.

Did you mate me for the good of our people? she asked him, not entirely sure she wanted an answer, but unable to stop the question.

The silence in her mind was all the answer she needed.

His, *Not entirely,* came too late and was far too little.

She swallowed back her emotions and forced herself to feel nothing. She'd done it before; she could do it now.

What are you doing? He'd spun to face her, his expression dark with worry.

Nothing, she said in a monotone across their link.

Do not lie to me.

You said I couldn't. You would always be able to tell.

I can.

I am tired.

You were fine on the flight over. Joyful in fact.

I like to fly with your dragon.

I have never enjoyed flight as much as when you ride on my dragon.

That was something, she supposed. *Your raven wants to fly with me.*

You remember our dream.

Yes.

Good.

Why was it good? She'd believed his beasts' desire to share their natures with her meant he would want to share his heart. Clearly, she had been wrong.

Will we always share dreams now? she asked him.

Only when we want to.

So, I can kick you out of my dreams?

You could, yes.

How?

You create a barrier against me with your mind, but why would you want to?

Like this? she asked, drawing on her connection to her Chrechte nature to build a barrier in her mind.

Suddenly he was standing in front of her, amber gaze shooting fire and six feet, five inches of vibrating fury. "Do not ever do that again."

"Why?"

"Our mindspeak is not only a way for us to grow closer in our mating, but it helps me to keep you safe."

Her head started to ache badly and she let the barrier

crumble. Suddenly his voice was in her head again, but it wasn't his human voice. It was his dragon and he was crooning the way he did when trying to comfort her.

Tears filled her eyes, but she refused to let them fall. She'd been weak enough. Her people's future depended on her being strong, on finding the *Faolchú Chridhe*.

She could deal with the pain in her heart later. She wasn't even sure her own thoughts made sense, that her hurt wasn't of her own making. So much had changed too quickly and she had a mate she had always told herself she did not want.

But knew now she would be miserable without.

He'd pulled her into his arms and was caressing her, the soft comforting sounds continuing until she relaxed against him, the headache gone as quickly as it had come. "I am sorry. I won't do that again."

"Thank you."

They traveled by horse, except her father's Faol soldiers. Everett and his brother traveled in their wolf form, scouting ahead of the riders. It took three days to reach the MacLeod border from the sea.

Despite the fact this part of the journey had been on their own, or friendly lands, it had been quiet among their group.

Ciara knew Lais missed Mairi. Leaving his new mate had to have been extremely hard on both of them. But Boisin had encouraged Lais to go, saying Mairi would get further along in the beginning of her training if he was not there.

Vegar was a silent man who could easily be mistaken for a Viking warlord. Artair was not his friendly self, either, having told Ciara that he'd opted to leave Balmoral Island rather than continue pining after a love that would never be.

She'd been shocked to discover her father planned to take Artair into training and was sending one of his own soldiers in exchange to the Balmoral. Less so when she found out that Artair was one of Boisin's grandsons and would be teaching the old stories to the Sinclair Chrechte.

Eirik spoke to her over their mating link, but not often as his keen dragon focus was on potential threats around them. Mairi had told them that her father's soldiers did not limit their patrols to his lands. Knowing how large his force of wolf soldiers was, no one had evinced surprise at that knowledge.

Though the grim attitude prevailing among the warriors made it clear they saw the MacLeod as a serious threat to the other clans in the Highlands. On the border with the Lowlands, he had a closer relationship with Scotland's king as well. Declaring war on him could come with consequences to the country that no one wanted. 'Twas a quandary indeed.

And Ciara chewed on it for hours as they rode. She'd slept in the dragon's arms both nights, but he had not entered her dreams on either occasion.

She was not sure why, but this time was smart enough not to ask since she could not be sure she would like the answer.

They waited to cross the border until night. Niall had told them what he had learned from the former MacLeod soldiers in regard to border guards and patrols. There were far more than even her father indulged in.

Using that knowledge, they rode onto MacLeod lands during the first watch, when the patrols were supposed to be changing.

From the border, Ciara and Eirik had agreed on a route based on the landmarks named by the *kelle* and Mairi's knowledge of her father's holding. The seer had been certain she knew both the dell and the river the *kelle* had spoken of, saying some still called it *Kyle Kirksonas*, though her father had done his best to rename landmarks in homage to himself. Once they reached it, it would simply be a matter of finding the right rock.

Mairi had made her suggestions on where she thought the wall that was not a wall might be, but cautioned against letting down their guard. Mairi had agreed with the soldiers caught in Sinclair forest that the patrols were likely to be heavy, particularly as far into the holding as they would have to go in order to reach the glen.

Nevertheless, they found the glen without incident and as soon as they rode into the narrow valley with high walls, Ciara knew this was indeed the place. She could feel the

Faolchú Chridhe calling to her more strongly than ever, but the sense of Chrechte magic was there as well.

Old and unused, it still resonated off the rocks and from the river as it burbled through the peaceful surround.

They made camp in a *brak*, the hollow in the rocky hillside protecting them from detection on three sides. Eirik assigned each of the warriors to their tasks and then turned to her.

It is time, he said with mindspeak.

She nodded.

Take your dirk into your hand.

To protect myself?

To let the little stones call to the larger and help you determine which direction to search.

I could just take the sword.

He shook his head with a hard jerk in the negative. *It is too risky. You might have another vision.*

And it might lead us straight there.

And it might knock you out again. No.

She didn't argue further. He had a good point, but more importantly, she could sense his worry and she did not want to add to it. Could he be that concerned for her and not care?

Regardless, he took too much on himself and perhaps she could share his burdens if not his heart. She pulled her dirk from the leather sheath under her belt. As her fingers curled round the handle, she felt a faint heat. Though nothing like what holding the sword caused, the sensation was still familiar.

She closed her eyes and concentrated. She could feel the pull of the *Faolchú Chridhe*, but still not what direction it came from. Though she could sense that it was very close and the cavern it rested in flashed behind her eyelids.

Eirik's arms came around her and she let herself relax back against him, concentrating entirely on the call of the sacred stone.

It was as if a veil was lifted and she could feel the pull to her left and forward.

She opened her eyes and pointed. *That way,* she said through their mate connection.

Moss covered the stone side of the steep brae that Ciara led them to. Erik called all but the Sinclair Faol who patrolled the area in their wolf form and Vegar who patrolled the sky to help scrape the moss away in search of the symbol the *kelle* had told Ciara about.

The sun had moved across the sky and they had identified more than forty symbols carved in the stone hillside when Artair raised his fist to indicate he'd found another.

Your kelle could have mentioned the whole bloody ben is covered in ancient symbols, Eirik said to Ciara through their mate-link.

Perhaps she thought I knew. From the way the walls of the cavern in my vision were decorated, I think our ancestors were more artistic with their dwellings and meeting places than we are.

He didn't think the *kelle* had even thought about it. He and Ciara reached Artair at the same time. The symbol he had uncovered was subtly different than the ones they'd seen thus far, all of which had been duplicated at least once.

It looked like the symbol associated by the Chrechte with long life, but with an additional marking that indicated transformation. Perhaps to their ancient forefathers, those symbols together meant healing.

Just like at least half of the other symbols, there was a small indentation in the center. But instead of being circular as the others had been, this one was oval.

Ciara lifted the thumb-sized emerald Eirik had pried from the hilt of the Faol king's sword and placed it in the indentation.

"The fit is perfect," she whispered in awe.

Is it? he asked in her head, not wanting even a whisper to carry to any MacLeod patrols.

She nodded, her teeth worrying at her bottom lip. *But*

it's not doing anything, she said with some despondency, following his lead and using their mindspeak.

He reached around her and added his strength to hers, pressing the emerald into the indentation. Suddenly the sound of stone scraping against stone groaned from inside the hillside. Then the stone wall in front of them slid backward to reveal a narrow opening.

"It's the cave," Ciara whispered excitedly. She grinned at Artair. "You've found it."

He smiled but shook his head, no words issuing forth. He was a well-trained soldier and knew that voices carried in the forest. Though it was unlikely if there *were* any Faol in the area, that they would not have heard the sound the stone had made sliding away from the opening.

Eirik called the others to him with the royal mind link and ordered them to protect the cave's opening along with Artair.

Eirik would accompany Ciara inside.

The passage was narrow and dark, his big body barely fitting at some points, but they pressed forward, their only light a torch he carried. Ciara led the way and though it was against his protective instincts, there was no better alternative. If he led, her back would be unprotected if an enemy made it past the guards at the opening.

Eirik had to hope that the ancient cave held fewer dangers for her than what could well lay behind. Besides, the stubborn and impetuous woman had given him no choice. She had rushed into the cave ahead of him and there was no room in the narrow passage for him to change their positions.

"Do not rush," he cautioned her.

"The *kelle* said nothing about traps in the caves."

"Which means exactly nothing."

"It was the place of healing for the Faol, why would it be trapped?" she asked.

"Why hide the entrance?"

"I do not know. Perhaps it was also considered a refuge. Our ancestors lived very differently than we do."

He had to agree with that. He had no idea how that hidden door could have been managed by cave dwellers when none would know how to create it today.

The passageway began to widen until Eirik could move in front of Ciara.

"What are you doing?"

"Leading the way, as is my responsibility."

She grumbled something that sounded very much like, "Arrogant dragon."

He smiled. Life with her would never be predictable. He was accustomed to those who knew of his status as prince being impressed by it and even more respect garnered by his dragon.

Ciara treated him like . . . well, like her mate. And he found he enjoyed the novelty of her lack of awe.

He had not liked the sadness that had overcome her when they first arrived back on the mainland and he still did not know what caused it. Perhaps she continued to be bothered by the fact her father and mother had been unable to attend their wedding.

Eirik would make sure that all who were important to either of them were in attendance at their Chrechte mating ceremony with Anya-Gra.

His torch flickered and he knew they were near a significant change in the cave; the still air would not have caused the flame to dance otherwise. A few feet later, the passage opened into a huge cavern, bigger than anything he had ever seen underground. Large enough for an entire clan to gather, much less a single pack of the Faol.

This was a meeting place from the days when the Chrechte were as united as any nomadic people who traveled in small family groupings could be.

"The walls do not glow," Ciara said with concern. "And it is too big."

"Your *kelle* said she took the stone to a hidden cavern far beneath the earth. This one is in the hillside."

Ciara nodded, looking around and no doubt seeing what he did. The space was huge, but not altogether empty.

There was a dais in the center with standing torches at its four corners. It was covered in a hide tanned and bleached to near white, the center decorated with a pattern that matched the healing symbol they had found outside.

There were stone benches around the cavern, some grouped together, others alone and even a few tables that held pots and jars similar to the ones he had seen in Lais's room.

"This is where they performed their healing," Eirik said with conviction.

"I think you are right, but it was also a place of meeting, I think."

The idea the cave had been a refuge for the Chrechte seemed more likely now. "It is likely you are right."

"I want to look at everything, but there is no time."

"There isn't. Our enemies could discover our presence at any moment." But he regretted not being able to allow Lais to come inside and examine things.

Then he reconsidered. If Eirik and Ciara were going to go farther into the earth, it would be a good idea to have a guard in the cavern.

He recalled Vegar from his post in the sky to flying closer to the cave entrance so he could help if MacLeod Chrechte showed up. And then, Eirik instructed Lais to come inside to the healing cavern.

The passage is long and narrow, he told his friend in Lais's mind.

I do not like small spaces.

You and half the Éan, but the cavern is huge and you will find it very interesting. Just do not get so interested you forget to pay attention for encroaching soldiers.

Lais agreed and Eirik made his way to the dais in the center of the room. The cavern was too vast for them to see the difference between another passage opening and shadow with the light of only one torch.

The standing torches lit, drawing on some kind of oil . . . he had heard of the Roman's having lamps like this, but the Chrechte's cave-dwelling ancestors? 'Twas amazing.

Ciara was walking along the walls, clearly looking for another opening out of the cavern. They found three.

The first led to a smaller chamber that had obviously been used to store food and other supplies. The second opening led to a series of smaller caves, some of which ended in additional caverns no bigger than most bedchambers that may well have been used by the *kelle* for sleeping and privacy. Other passages simply ended and the lack of any carving on the walls of these led Eirik to believe they were used rarely if ever by the ancient *kelle*.

The third passage was more of the same and by the time they'd finished exploring it, Vegar informed Eirik that dusk had arrived. Ciara and Eirik returned to the cavern and shared roasted meat with Lais for latemeal.

"There must be another passage off of this cavern," Ciara said, her voice strained with fatigue and disappointment.

Eirik tugged her around until she leaned against him. "We will find the *Faolchú Chridhe*, *faolán*. You must trust in yourself and your connection to the stone."

"I can feel it, beneath us here, but I've no idea how to reach it," she said dispiritedly. "I'm tired and I feel this itch between my shoulder blades telling me that MacLeod's soldiers are near."

"I'm feeling the same itch," he admitted.

Lais ate intermittently between examining jars from one of the tables. "More like you are sending your sense of impending trouble to Ciara through your mating bond."

"If that's the case, you can keep your worries to yourself. I've enough of my own," his sweet little mate said rather sourly.

He smiled at her bad temper and reminded her, "Being a mate means sharing your burdens."

"I do not want the burden of dragon senses," she huffed and then sighed, looking lost. "I am sorry. I didn't mean that."

He started rubbing her shoulders and neck, kneading the tension from her. "It will be well, *mo gra*."

"What did you just call me?" she asked in a soft voice, laced with an emotion he wasn't sure of.

It almost sounded like hope, but what had she to hope for? She was his. He was hers. Their mating had been blessed by God himself.

Rather than discuss things that had been set in stone since the moment he caught her in the air after her fall from the tower roof, he mused, "We may have missed something in one of the other passages."

"No." She rubbed her head against his chest. "We were very careful in our search."

"We were just as careful searching out openings in the walls."

Lais said, "Perhaps the way to the hidden cavern is down, not out."

"Of course it is down, I told you I could feel the sacred stone under us . . ." Ciara's voice trailed off. "Oh, I take your meaning, Lais. You think there actually is some kind of opening in the floor."

"The floor of this cavern is smoother than slate prepared by a mason," Eirik observed.

Ciara asked, "But how is that possible?"

Lais shrugged. "I know not, but if our ancestors could fashion an entrance like the one to these caves, and floors so clearly made by man, though seeming of solid stone, they could make a hidden doorway in the floor. I say we move the covering on the dais."

"It's so old . . . it will disintegrate in our hands." Ciara's tone made it clear the idea bothered her.

Lais frowned apologetically. "I've searched the rest of the floor and cannot see any place that could open like the entrance to the cave outside."

Eirik was not surprised the eagle had spent his time searching for the secret passageway, despite his great interest in the cavern itself. The eagle was an honorable Chrechte that knew how to put the good of the many above his own interests and desires.

'Twas one of the reasons Eirik considered him brother more than friend.

Ciara sighed. "I suppose there's no hope for it, but we will be careful. This is a sacred place."

"We will treat the cavern and everything in it with the respect it deserves." Eirik hugged her close, trying to impart his sincerity and matching concern through his touch.

"Thank you."

Chapter 24

Being deeply loved by someone gives you strength,
while loving someone deeply gives you courage.

—Lao-tzu

Her hands trembling, Ciara reached out to touch the
leather covering on the dais. It had been made by warrior
priestesses who had served their people with love and loyalty unto death centuries past.

She tugged experimentally at the corner and found it
surprisingly soft and supple under her fingers. "Let us each
take a side and slide it off onto the floor."

Eirik and Lais followed her direction without comment
and the cover was removed without incident.

A reverent curse slipped from Lais's mouth as both
Ciara and Eirik stood in shocked silence at what had been
revealed.

The dais top was not the gray slab she expected, but a
green stone marbled with amber lines unlike anything she
had ever seen before. It had been polished to such a sheen,
the fire from the torches was reflected on its surface.

The waist-high pedestal it sat on was almost as large as
the dais top. At least six feet long and three feet wide, it did

not look like it was going anywhere to reveal a secret passage.

"The carvings on the pedestal are similar to the ones we found on the hillside," Eirik said thoughtfully.

They were, though the symbols were all connected by knot work similar to the marks worn on the biceps of the Chrechte who led their brethren.

As one, the three dropped to their knees to begin examining the dais for the symbol of healing. Ciara found it in the center of the long side facing north. "I've found it, but there's no indentation like on the larger one outside."

"There is a mark for healing on this side, too," Eirik announced a second later.

Lais said the same as Ciara was already scooting around to the side they had not checked yet. This one did not have the healing symbol on it; instead there was a carving that matched the one on the handle of her brother's sword. Only in this carving, the *conriocht*'s stone was missing, though the dragon and griffin's gems were set in place.

Ciara pressed her emerald to the spot and nearly fell backward as the floor beneath her feet began to move. Eirik was there in a second, his arm protectively around her, his grip on her tight, the message crystal clear. She was going nowhere without him.

The floor stopped moving and Lais swore with great reverence. "Well, will you look at that?"

The floor had opened up to reveal a set of steps in that strange green marbled stone leading below.

"The *kelle* said the *Faolchú Chridhe* was deep in the earth."

"That is deep enough," Eirik said.

Indeed it was. They could not see the bottom of the steps.

"I will guard the entrance," Lais said.

Eirik nodded and turned his attention on her, his focus stern. "I will take the lead."

"The stone is calling to me."

"But your safety is my responsibility."

"It won't do the Chrechte any good if we don't get the sacred stone."

"Make no mistake, our people may need the stone, but your safety is of every use *to me* whether or not we retrieve the *Faolchú Chridhe*."

First he'd called her his love and now this. Had she been wrong? Did her stubborn dragon mate care about her as something more than a means to an end for their people?

"I will follow you."

"You will." He turned and descended the stairs.

Arrogant, wonderful dragon.

The steps ended, but the passageway continued downward until it opened into a cavern that glowed with the strange green light of her dreams. The smell of water warned her before the torch Eirik carried revealed a small stream they would have to cross. The smell of minerals and steam rising from the stream indicated it was fed by the same type of underground spring as the other sacred Chrechte caves.

Without warning, Eirik swung her up with one arm so she dangled above the floor.

She cried out. "What are you doing?"

"Carrying you across. The water may well be too hot to touch."

He was right, but she hadn't even considered it. Concentrating on what her wolf senses were telling her, she realized the water was indeed very hot and could well have burned her badly if she'd tried to walk across the shallow stream.

Eirik made the crossing with a single leap of his long legs. He set her down on the other side. "Your father said there are other caverns like this, but it seems magical to me."

"To me as well," she whispered, her eyes taking in details her mind had difficulty comprehending.

The cavern was about half the size of the one above with dome-shaped walls that glistened with moisture and glowed with that odd green light. The ground was earth pressed flat, the scent stale with minerals she did not recognize.

A tall pedestal made of that foreign green stone stood

alone in the center of the room. And on top sat an emerald the size of Eirik's fist.

"We found it," she said in a voice that barely made it past her tight throat. *"We really did it."*

Her knees went weak and she would have fallen, but Eirik was there, holding her up, kissing her gently while his arms were granite hard around her. Giving safety, security and certainty that she was not alone and never would be again.

She took several deep breaths before taking a step forward, and then another. Her traverse across the cavern was tortuously slow, but her legs were more wobbly than they'd ever been.

They reached the pedestal together, Eirik's strength still supporting her.

"What will happen when I touch it?" she asked, frightened and exhilarated all at once.

The call of the stone was so strong her hands were lifting toward it even now of their own accord.

"I do not know."

Her hands curved around it and the oddest feeling surged through her, her entire body buzzing like a hive of bees. Then the image of wolves slinking through the forest flashed before her eyes. She did not know how she was so certain of it, but she knew these were MacLeod soldiers and they were close.

"We need to go; they're coming."

Eirik didn't ask who or why, he simply dropped the torch and then picked her up securely in his arms. She clutched the *Faolchú Chridhe* to her chest as he rushed back across the underground stream and headed back up the tunnel.

She didn't protest him carrying her; the buzzing under her skin had not diminished and she did not know if she could stand on her own, much less run.

They broke out of the dark into the huge cavern and found Lais already gone and all the standing torches extinguished. A single handheld torch gave off a dim glow from one of the tables.

Eirik ran right past it.

Ciara gasped, "We need the light."

"We do not. You are wolf, I am dragon."

She wanted to argue further, but his sense of urgency was her own. Whatever his Éan warriors had told him via the link he shared with them, and he would be explaining that one sometime very soon, Eirik was determined to get out of the hillside as soon as possible.

Once they reached the narrower part of the passage, he set her on her feet. "Put the sacred stone in your purse."

It barely fit, but it wasn't going anywhere from the snug enclosure, either. "It is done."

"Take hold of the back of my kilt."

She did, gripping tight in the near-suffocating darkness. Then he started to move. "Do not let go."

"I won't."

It took far less time to reach the opening than it had coming in, but the sounds of Chrechte engaged in mortal combat spurred them both to faster movement.

Once they broke out into the moonlit dell, the smell of blood hit Ciara. The air was redolent with it and she could not help the skip in her heart that it might be from their brethren.

Lais and Vegar fought the MacLeod wolves in their human forms, their prowess testament to how well the Éan trained for battle. Even the healers.

The Faol had all shifted for the fight, but even with their three wolves, they were seriously outnumbered by MacLeods.

Eirik spun to face her and then lifted her with strength even beyond a Chrechte so she could sit high on a stone jutting out from the side of the brae. Her perch was precarious, but no wolf was going to reach her, not even a Chrechte.

"Stay."

"Fight," she countered.

He nodded and turned, already drawing both swords. He killed two wolves with a single powerful downward arc.

The fighting grew too close for him to use his swords and he sheathed them, his hands shifting to dragon's claws.

The Sinclair and Balmoral soldiers fought hard, but there were three well-trained Chrechte warriors from the MacLeod clan for every one of theirs. One of the wolves came toward her, taking a running leap at the hillside. His claws clicked as they hit the stone; he almost caught purchase but slid back down the brae.

Not wanting to draw attention from the men fighting for their lives and hers, she did not make a sound. But she drew her dirk and held it as Talorc had taught her. The wolf tried to reach her again, this time making it a little bit closer.

Another joined him, a huge brown cur that was too heavy to get any kind of purchase on the stone with his claws at all. Then he shifted. With a face lined in cruelty, a body honed by war and only a couple of inches shorter than her mate, he sent waves of dread through Ciara.

"Come down, little Sinclair spy, and we might let you live."

She tucked her feet closer to her body and made sure none of her skirt hung over the side for him to grab. "Call your dogs off and you might yet survive this night."

"You're on our land, Sinclair bitch, and I'm sure the MacLeod will be very interested to find out why."

"He won't hear it from me."

The other wolf shifted and approached the ugly-mouthed warrior. "Give me a hand up, Ualraig, and I'll get her down quick enough."

Ualraig didn't have the opportunity to answer because Lais skewered him with his broadsword, pulling it back in a manner that destroyed any chances the other Chrechte had of surviving the wound. "That was for Mairi, you vicious bastard."

"That slut?" Ualraig scowled, the scent of blood and other body fluids so strong Ciara wanted to vomit. "She deserved what she got."

"So did you, it looks like to me," Ciara spat down at the unrepentant Chrechte.

Lais bent over the dying man. "Aye, our princess is right. You'll burn in hell knowing an Éan sent you there, too."

She didn't know what role Ualraig had played in Mairi's

beating, but if Lais found the man a personal affront, it hadn't been minor.

Having shifted back to his animal, the smaller wolf attacked Lais from the side, going straight for his throat. Ciara screamed her warning and Lais spun just in time. The wolf's jaws grazed his shoulder, but Lais punched up with a strong fist and sent the beast flying from him.

It was a Chrechte though, not a normal wolf and it was back in moments, fighting Lais while another tried to scale the brae and get to her.

Eirik raked his opponent's body with his dragon's claws, drawing a spray of blood, before spinning away and rushing to take a position below Ciara.

Can I talk to the wolves the way you talk to your Éan? she asked him across their mate-link.

No surprise at her knowledge came through their connection. *Perhaps. With the stone.*

And perhaps she'd go into a vision if she touched it with her bare hands again, but the flash of the coming trouble the first time had been brief. And while touching the stone had left her body weak with strange sensations, it had not knocked her out like her vision with the sword had done.

She'd have to risk it regardless. Artair was limping from a terrible wound to his thigh, Everett had a gash on his shoulder, Vegar bled down his torso and Lais was in mortal hand-to-hand combat with a wolf. There were several dead already among the MacLeod, but a few more well-connected strikes and her friends were in serious danger of losing one, or more, of their own.

She pulled the *Faolchú Chridhe* from her purse and held on to it, concentrating on her connection to all Chrechte through it. She was prepared for the buzzing sensation below her skin and the heat the stone generated in her hands, but she nearly fell off her perch when her mind connected to Artair, Everett and his brother. She could not read their thoughts any more than she could read Eirik's, but she felt their emotions and knew instinctively their minds were open to hearing her.

Withdraw from combat, she ordered them. *Eirik can't shift to his full dragon and cast fire with you in the way.*

She said the same thing to her mate via their link. She could not read one emotion in the maelstrom coming from him, but his soldiers withdrew and the Sinclair and Balmoral wolves followed.

He must have done as she suggested and ordered them back.

They all looked like they were running, only to double back and herd the MacLeod soldiers into a tighter formation. It wasn't a bad formation for doing battle, but as fodder for dragon fire? It made them twice as vulnerable.

Eirik stripped and shifted with a speed that astonished her and then cast his fire in wave after wave after wave.

When it was over, not even the smell of charred flesh remained because nothing was left but a fine powder of dust.

"This time it will be the Fearghall wondering what has happened to their brethren in the forest," Vegar said, his gravelly voice laced with dour satisfaction.

Put the stone back in your satchel and climb on my back, Eirik ordered inside Ciara's mind.

"But I need to close the cave entrance, so the MacLeod doesn't find it."

Drop the small stone to Artair. He can do it. There was something in Eirik's voice inside her mind that made Ciara want to comply without arguing.

A few moments later, Artair had closed the entrance to the cave and he and the other warriors were doing what was necessary to remove evidence of their presence on MacLeod lands, including speaking the Chrechte words of passing and sweeping the ashes of the fallen Chrechte into the stream.

Ciara realized it was probably the same one that fed the underground cavern and thought it fitting. Enemy, or not, every Chrechte deserved to be given proper send-off of their ashes. Being scattered in waters sacred to their ancestors seemed only right.

When she said so to Eirik through their mate-link, he did not respond but simply waited for Lais to hand her his clothes and weapons before taking to the sky.

They flew much faster than a horse could gallop, or even a Chrechte wolf could run, even faster than they had ever flown together. Ciara had to hide her face against his neck to protect it from the sharp bite of the wind and there was no joy in this flight. Only single-minded purpose.

They reached the sacred caves on Sinclair land as the sun rose over the morning mist.

Tirik was silent as they walked into the caves together. He headed unerringly for the chamber of mating and dropped his weapons and clothing that he had not bothered to don after shifting onto the ground. Without a break in his stride, he walked right into the pool and submerged himself completely in the steaming waters.

Ciara removed her clothing as she waited for her mate to reemerge. He stayed under long enough that she was completely naked and growing worried when he exploded out of the water, sucking in a big lungful of air. Droplets cascaded off of him, getting her and stone surrounding the pool wet.

His head down, he stood there heaving.

She slid into the water and waded over to him. Laying her hand on his bicep, right over the deep blue tattoo that proclaimed him prince of his people, she asked, "Are you all right?"

He didn't reply, just stood there, his breathing an irregular pattern that in any other person would mean they were crying. And then she understood.

"I am sorry," she said softly, not knowing what other words would matter.

"You did not kill them."

"It was my idea."

"It was a good one. Refusing to take my full dragon form put our warriors at risk."

"But fighting other Chrechte in battle is not the same as incinerating them with your fire," she said, voicing her new understanding of the man she'd mated, married and loved with the very depth of her being. "Killing Galen and Luag that way hurt you as much as it hurt me to see it."

"He was your brother."

"He was a Chrechte who had surrendered his honor to the idea of being superior."

"I am the protector of my people."

"And that day, Fidaich and Canaul needed protecting. Just as last night, our soldiers needed your dragon. The MacLeod numbers were too high; we might have won the battle but the cost would have been great."

Finally, Eirik's head lifted and their gazes met. His face was wet, but not all the moisture was from his dip in the pool. "I am dragon, but I am also raven."

"One has the instincts of a predator, the other does not kill." Her heart ached for him and her desire to protect her own emotions disappeared under that pain. "I love your dragon, Eirik. I am grateful, so very grateful for the strength and power he gives you. I love your raven, too. Without instincts from your bird, you could become like Fearghall, but you never will."

"And me? Do you love me?" Eirik asked as if it really mattered to him.

It certainly mattered to her and she would never lie about it. "I do, so very much."

His head dipped again, his voice coming out gravelly. "From the moment of my birth, I have been taught to know my responsibility to my people, to all Chrechte."

"I know." Not releasing her hold on his arm, she laid her other hand over his heart. "This beats with it."

His head came up then, his amber eyes fierce with emotion. "It used to, but now it beats for you. My mate. Last night, you told me to shift and your intent was to save our warriors, but all I could think about was keeping you safe and if annihilating the MacLeod soldiers was necessary to do it, then I would cast fire."

"You have to keep me safe for the future of our people," she tried to soothe him, her own heart stuttering at the thought it could possibly be more than that.

Suddenly, his hands were on either side of her face and their gazes were locked with primal messages arcing between them. "I saved you for me. You are mine. You will always be mine and you will always come first. Before my warriors, before my friends, and God forgive me, even before our people."

"But you˙. . . that's not . . ."

"I love you," he said in ancient Chrechte and the air around them crackled.

Pure white light flashed between them and burning heat seared her breast, right over her heart. Then the air was still, the light gone and she looked down at Eirik's chest, certainty mixed with utter disbelief roiling through her.

But she was right. He now wore a mating mark right over his heart. His hand dropped from her face to trace the spot that had burned so sharply only moments before on her breast. "You are marked as my other half."

"You are marked as mine."

"For eternity." It wasn't just her desire, but the truth. The symbol for it enclosed his mating mark and she was sure her matching one.

"My dragon will have to kill again, in protection of our people."

"And I will be here with you to wash away the pain."

"With your love."

She nodded. "With my love."

And that is exactly what she did.

Abigail, who knew much from her correspondence with a learned abbess, had once told Ciara that the philosopher Aristotle had maintained that love was composed of a single soul inhabiting two bodies.

Ciara thought maybe the ancient philosopher had been part Chrechte, but certainly he'd gotten one thing right. Because her soul was forever entwined with Eirik's and 'twas most definitely love.

For no other power on earth would have been great enough to break through the walls of fear she'd erected around her heart so many years ago and give her hope for a future that might even one day include children.

* * *

*J*t took several days to find the ancient chamber of the Faol, perhaps because Eirik and Ciara were content to spend more time in the sacred caves affirming their love than searching. That, if nothing else, convinced Ciara that Eirik had spoken the truth when he said she was of utmost importance to him.

The cavern was not actually hidden so much as forgotten. Deep in the earth and down another one of those narrow, very long passages, it looked exactly as it had in Ciara's vision.

"I suppose the Faol stopped coming when there was no *Faolchú Chridhe* to lay hands on," she mused.

Eirik frowned and shook his head as he lit the torches on the walls in the stone chamber. "I'm sure Fearghall encouraged any but his chosen few to forget it and the sacred stone's existence."

"Whoever decided we did not need to perform our sacred rites because we no longer had a stone to bless them stole so much from the Faol."

"I am sure the *kelle* will help you remember them," Eirik comforted Ciara.

"She did say I would see her again."

"And you will." Eirik smiled. "I have the feeling the ancient *kelle* will be a lifelong friend and mentor for you."

"You may be right, but as wonderful as that prospect is . . ." Ciara reached up and kissed her mate, her husband with all the love that welled forth from her heart for him in a continuous fount. "It cannot compete with the certainty I will spend that lifetime with you."

Eirik's eyes glinted with moisture she would never comment on as he gave her the brilliant smile she'd seen first the night he admitted his love for her. "Nothing can compete with that truth, *faolán*."

Epilogue

The secret of Happiness is Freedom, and the secret of
Freedom, Courage.

—THUCYDIDES

Their family and dearest friends joined Eirik and
Ciara for the mating ceremony performed by Anya-Gra in
the ancient chamber of the Faol. Both spoke their vows
with such certainty and love that many an eye grew wet
with moisture.

Afterward, they laid hands together on both the *Clach
Gealach Gra* and the *Faolchú Chridhe*. Chrechte magic
swirled in the air around them and each witness of the mating came forward one by one to lay hands on the stone of
their people.

The warriors still wounded from battle with the MacLeod
Chrechte were first and each was healed so that not even
scars remained from wounds so grievous humans would
have died. Sabrine, Eirik's sister, followed with her son.

Then came Mairi. The air around her glowed with green
light, but she did not shift into wolf.

Ciara grinned as she looked at her friend. "You can feel
her spirit in you, can you not?"

Mairi just nodded, tears streaking down her face.

"You'll shift with the first full moon after you give birth. Your bairn will be an eagle shifter," Ciara promised in a voice that was more than her own.

A loud thump revealed Lais's reaction to the news. The healer who fought like a warrior had fainted.

Ciara motioned for her mother to come forth.

"But I am not Chrechte," Abigail said.

"The bairn inside you is," Niall said from beside her.

Abigail nodded and placed her hands on the *Faolchú Chridhe*. Ciara covered her adopted mother's hands with her own and drew forth on the connection between the babe in Abigail's womb and the *Faolchú Chridhe*. Healing light surrounded them and suddenly Abigail cried out.

"What is it?" Talorc demanded.

"I can hear." Abigail began to cry and her sister threw her arms around her, babbling words of love and joy.

Then Ciara spoke, again her voice not quite her own. "The lairds must each lay hands on the *Faolchú Chridhe*."

Each did, green light bathing them for several seconds, before the men stepped back one by one.

"You are worthy protectors of your people," Ciara intoned. "On the next full moon, you will gain the form of the *conriocht*."

And then she turned to her dragon. "The burden is no longer yours alone to bear."

"Soon, the Paindeal will be found and the Chrechte will be one people again," Mairi said, her eyes glowing with blue light.

"But first there is a war to be fought for the hearts of Chrechte turned by the twisted teachings of the Fearghall," Ciara intoned. "The Cahir must rise again and Chrechte of the MacLeod defeat his own."

Love and unity would win, but the war would be long and not every battle without loss.

GLOSSARY OF TERMS

bairn—baby

beguines—self-running nunnery without vows to the church, not supported by the official church as related to Rome (historically accurate term in the British Isles)

ben—hill

Ben Bristecrann—broken tree hill (a sacred spot to Ciara's family)

brae—hillside or slope

Cahir—warriors who fight the Fearghall

celi di—Scottish Highland priest practicing Catholicism with no official ties to the church in Rome (historically accurate term in relation to Scotland and Ireland)

Chrechte—shifters who share their souls with wolves, birds or cats of prey

Clach Gealach Gra—(moon's heart stone) the bird shifters' sacred stone

conriocht—werewolf (protector of the Faol, shifts into giant half-wolf/half-man type creature)

Éan—bird shifters (ravens, eagles and hawks)

Faol—wolf shifters

faolán—little wolf (Gaelic term of endearment)

Faolchú Chridhe—(wolf's heart) the wolf shifters' sacred stone

Fearghall—secret society of wolves intent on wiping out/ subjugating other races of the Chrechte

femwolf—female wolf shifter

keeper of the stone—a Chrechte who has a special link to the sacred stone and can utilize its full potential for healing, gifting and bringing forth the protectors of the races (conriocht, dragon and griffin)

kelle—warrior priestess (mentioned in Celtic mythology)

Kyle Kirksonas—River of the Healing Church

loch—lake

mate—a Chrechte's chosen partner (if it is a mixed mating— Chrechte of different races, or a human mate—children can only result if the bond is a true/sacred one)

mate-link—the special mental bond between true/sacred mates

mindspeak—communicating via a mental link

mo gra—my love

Paindeal—cat shifters (large cats of prey)

Paindeal Neart—(panther's strength) the panther shifters' sacred stone

sacred bond (true bond)—a mating bond that lasts unto death and will not physically allow the Chrechte involved to have intercourse with anyone but the Chrechte's mate

usquebagh—"water of life" (Scotch whiskey)

"Mummy, they're giants!"

It wasn't her son's excited shout that sent a shard of pain spiking through Shona's head, but the sight of soldiers wearing the Sinclair colors approaching at speed—on horses every bit as oversized as they were.

The headache had arrived with the large brown wolf that had paced them for the better part of the morning. Only the pounding in her skull hadn't left when the beast did.

Terrified the animal would attack, she'd ridden tense in her saddle with a dagger at the ready. However, the wolf had maintained its distance, finally running off just before the noon sun cast its shadow.

Her mind and senses already stretched to the point of exhaustion with what had come before this journey, the appearance of the wolf had pushed Shona that much nearer collapse.

But she would not give up. Her children's lives and those of two loyal friends depended on Shona maintaining both sanity and composure.

So she had taken her little daughter, Marjory, back from her companion, Audrey, and ridden on.

Shona had hoped her luck would hold, as it had miraculously for nearly two sennight's of their mad dash north, but it was not to be.

They'd reached Sinclair land late the night before, managing somehow to both evade anyone her stepson may have sent after them and avoid the inhabitants of the clan territories she and her small band had passed through.

Until now.

She had no trouble understanding how her five-year-old son, Eadan, had mistaken the approaching soldiers for giants. These Highlanders would easily stand a head taller, and half again as wide, as any knight who had sworn allegiance to her dead husband.

Considering what was behind her, Shona could wish that these men were of the clan she'd come north to seek refuge with, but she knew she had no friends or family among the Sinclairs. They weren't likely to take kindly to what they would perceive as an Englishwoman trespassing on their land. Perhaps the laird would approve safe passage through, if only to get rid of her and her companions. She could but hope.

She had to make her way to Balmoral Isle.

It was the only chance they had at safety, her one hope to preserve her son's life and her own virtue. Or what was left of it.

At Balmoral, she had family, at least, though the relation was somewhat distant. She had no doubt her arrival would come as something of a shock. She could only hope it was not a wholly unwelcome one.

"They're not giants, sweeting, merely warriors of the clan that makes these lands their home." Shona tried to infuse her tone with confidence while her own mind screamed with warnings and worries.

"Really?" Eadan asked, his eyes, the same indigo blue as his father's, filled with awe.

"These are Highland warriors?" Audrey asked, before Shona had the chance to affirm her assertion to her son. "They're huge."

"'Tis the way of the Highlands, I suppose." And among
some of the clans that bordered the Highlands as well, like
the one in which she'd grown up.

Audrey gave her twin brother a sideways look. "Perhaps
you've got more growing to do, but I don't think you'll
reach their stature, even so."

Thomas looked chagrined. "You don't know that."

Shona couldn't imagine why they were speculating at
all. Thomas was English, just like his sister; children of a
lesser baron whose holding bordered her dead husband's
on the west and was only a few miles from land claimed by
Scotland's king.

Shona's sleeping daughter stirred in her arms and she
looked down to see pretty green eyes so like her own blinking up at her. "Mama, is there giants?"

At three, Marjory was as different from her older brother
as night from day. Petite and quiet-spoken, she adored the
older brother who was and had always been big for his age
and confident to the point of brashness.

So like his father it made Shona's heart ache, though
she'd never let her children see it.

"They're the laird's guard come to greet us," Shona
claimed, her voice maintaining a shocking steadiness
despite the blatant lie she'd just told.

One look from her two adult companions assured her
they weren't fooled by her words. But neither of her children were frightened and that was what mattered.

She just had to believe that the Sinclair was a better man
than some who had been in her life. His reputation as a
fierce but fair leader even as far south as England had led
to her decision to travel on his lands instead of taking a
more circuitous route to her final destination.

They rode for another ten minutes before meeting the
Sinclair warriors.

Shona halted her horse and the rest of her party followed suit.

"Who are you and what are you doing on our land?"
Though the soldier's words were abrupt and his demeanor
nothing less than ferocious, Shona felt no fear. Something

about the man speaking made her think he would not hurt them. Perhaps it was the flash of concern in his eyes when he looked at her children.

The big warrior would have been devastatingly handsome but for the garish scar on his cheek, but Shona felt no draw to him. She had only ever wanted one man in her life, and, despite having been married to another, that had not changed. Nor did she believe it ever would. But she did not lament her lack of interest in the opposite sex. Men could not be trusted and she was better off keeping what was left of her heart for her children and her children alone.

"I am Shona, Lady Heronshire, seeking safe passage through your laird's lands to visit my family on Balmoral Isle." The words were formal, and she spoke them in flawless Gaelic, her native tongue.

"Did you get that scar in a fight?" Eadan asked.

Audrey gasped, but Shona just sighed. Her son had no cork for the things that came out of his mouth.

The warrior's attention moved to Eadan and he studied him closely for several seconds before something that could have been surprise and then speculation flared in his gray gaze. "I did. Do you ride as protector of your mother?"

Shona didn't understand the man's reaction to her son, unless it was to the fact that such a small child spoke Gaelic so well. She'd spoken to both her children in her native tongue since their births and they both communicated equally well in Gaelic and English. Just as she did.

Her son, mayhap, even better than she did.

Eadan puffed up his little boy chest and did his best to frown like the warriors in front of them. "I do."

"You sound like a Scot, lad, but you dress like a Sassenach."

"What's a sassy patch?" Marjory whispered from her perch in Shona's lap.

"An Englishman," the big warrior answered, with a barely there smile for her daughter's interesting pronunciation of the word, proving he'd heard the quietly uttered question.

"Oh." *Pop.* Marjory's thumb went into her mouth. It was

a habit Shona and Audrey had worked hard to break her of, but the little girl still sucked her thumb when she was overly tired or nervous. After two weeks of grueling travel and coming upon men who looked more like giants than soldiers, the tot was no doubt both. Shona sighed again.

This brought the big man's attention back to her. "I am Niall, second-in-command to the Sinclair laird. My men and I will accompany you to the keep."

"Thank you." What Shona really wanted to say was, *Thank you, but no.*

She'd rather head directly for the island. She was tired of traveling and she wasn't going to feel safe until she'd gotten the Balmoral laird's promise of protection for her and her small band.

However, to refuse the hospitality of the other laird would not only be considered rude, but she'd no doubt they would end up traveling to the keep no matter what she might say on the matter.

She'd learned long ago that some things were beyond her control.

The keep was a fortress far superior to that of the MacLeod holding where she'd grown up, and even more formidable than that of her deceased husband's. The high wall surrounding the laird's home and guard towers was stone, though the buildings within were crafted mostly from wood.

The keep itself was on top of a motte, the manmade hill only accessible by a narrow path she just knew Niall was going to tell her they could not take their horses on. Even from this distance the keep looked big enough to easily accommodate fifty or more in the great hall. The imposing nature of the holding made her wish her family was of the Sinclair clan. She could do naught but hope the Balmorals lived equally as secure.

The bailey was busy with warriors and clanspeople alike, many of whom seemed interested in the new arrivals. And slightly suspicious, if the frowns she and her

companions received were anything to go by. But the overt
hostility she might have expected toward those garbed as
the English was surprisingly absent.

Niall stopped his horse and the warriors with him did as
well. Shona guided her tired mare to a halt, so fatigued she
was not absolutely sure she would make it off the horse
without sending both herself and Marjory tumbling.

"Should we dismount then?" Audrey asked, her tone
showing no more enthusiasm for the prospect than Shona
felt.

Shona opened her mouth to answer, only to lose any
hope she had of speaking as her gaze fell upon a warrior
standing near the open area in front of the blacksmith's.
The man, who was easily as tall and as broad as Niall,
wore the MacLeod colors with no shirt beneath the plaid to
give him any hint of civility.

His back to them, his lack of interest in the English
strangers was more than obvious.

But she could not claim the same apathy. Not when
every inch of his arrogant stance was as familiar to her as
the mane on her mare's head.

His black hair was longer than it had been six years ago,
the blue tattoos covering his left shoulder and arm a new
addition, his muscles bulging more, but she had absolutely
no doubt about the identity of the MacLeod soldier standing so confidently among the Sinclairs.

Caelis.

Even the sound of his name in her own thinking made
her heart beat faster and her hands tighten into fists.

Betrayer, screamed that voice in her mind that had never
gone fully silent though she'd been forced to marry another
man. *Mine*, cried the heart that had learned never to trust
again at this man's feet.

She'd given him her love and her innocence.

He had repaid those gifts with repudiation.

She'd thought never to see him again, been certain that
even her return to Scotland would not cause their paths to
cross.

After all, she hadn't gone home to her former clan and

she'd been careful to avoid their lands during the journey northward. She'd no desire to come into contact with her former laird and even less this man. How cruel of fate to dictate differently. To ensure that this man be in this place the one day out of time she would ever spend in the Sinclair keep.

The head of Shona's mare jerked against her tightened hold on the reins and she knew gratitude that they were no longer moving. Marjory slept on, oblivious to the cataclysm happening inside her mother.

As if Caelis could feel the weight of Shona's regard, he turned. Slowly and with no evidence of curiosity, his gaze slid over her, his expression dismissive as he took in her English clothing.

She could tell the moment he recognized her though, the very second he realized she was not just an Englishwoman, but a woman from his past.

He went rigid, his eyes widening with a shock so complete it would have been amusing if she were not so devastated at his appearance in her already turbulent life.

He moved as if to take a step and stumbled.

How odd. He was a surefooted man. Perhaps one of the other warriors had tripped him. Men played games with each other like that.

Even as the nonsensical thoughts floated through her mind, fear screamed through her body. He couldn't see Eadan. Her son could never know the man who had denied his very existence and rejected the woman he had professed to love.

They had to leave. Now. The laird of the Sinclairs would simply have to do without the pleasure of making their acquaintance.

That thought alone gave her the strength to break her gaze from Caelis as she jerked her head around, wildly searching for Eadan.

He was already on the ground, his hand held in Niall's giant paw, a smaller man standing nearby, talking to them both with an engaging smile.

Shona wanted to scream at them to put her son back on

his horse and get out of their way. But no words left her lips because as frantic as her feelings were, she knew her desire to escape was hopeless.

The boy was out of Caelis's line of sight, but that gave Shona little comfort. The warrior was bound to see her child soon, and when he did? He would know the truth, no matter how much he might like to deny it.

"Shona . . ."

She looked down and saw that both Audrey and Thomas were there, standing beside Shona's mare. Audrey's hands were upraised to take Marjory so Shona could dismount.

When had they gotten off their horses?

"Are you all right?" Thomas asked, clearly worried. He and Audrey wore matching expressions of concern. "We've said your name three times."

"I . . . no . . ." she answered with honesty before she thought to control her tongue.

"What is it?" Suddenly Niall was there. "Lady Heronshire, do you need help dismounting?" He reached up as well. "Give me the babe."

Dropping the horse's reins, Shona wrapped her arms around her daughter in an instinctive move of protection.

"Do not touch her." The snarl came from behind Niall, and then Caelis was there, shoving the other warrior away from Shona's horse.

Niall spun on the other man, knocking him back and shouting. "The hell!"

"She's mine," Caelis growled, his voice so animallike the words were barely discernable.

"Calm yourself," Niall snapped, sounding less angry for some reason, though he didn't back away. "The Englishwoman—"

"She is not English."

"Do ye see how she is dressed? She is a lady, Caelis. Stop and think."

But Caelis appeared beyond reason, his aggression not lessening one iota. And Shona did not understand it. In no scenario that she might ever have imagined about this moment would she have considered him laying claim to her . . . or was it her daughter?

None of this made any sense.

Marjory chose that moment to awaken, squirming to sit up. "Mama! Want down."

Caelis jerked as if pierced by an arrow, his gaze landing on the little girl in Shona's arms. Some great emotion twisted his features, and then his blue eyes, so like their son's, locked with hers, the accusation in them unmistakable.

She stared back, defiant, furious like she had not been since the night he told her it was over.

All the fear she'd felt over the past months, the anger she'd experienced at the perfidy of men since his betrayal, followed by others, bolstered her fury so that—if it were possible—she would have burned him to ash with her gaze.

His head snapped back, surprise again showing on his handsome features, this time mixed with confusion. Though what he had to be confused about she didn't know. Did he think that just because he didn't want her that no other man would ever want to wed her?

Arrogant blackguard.

"Mummy?" Eadan's worried voice rose from where he stood beside Niall.

She needed to tell her son all was well, but she could not look away from Caelis's face as he got his first look at the son they had made.

The child he had told her would never happen.

Dear Reader,

I so hope you've enjoyed the excerpt from my next full-length Children of the Moon novel, Warrior's Moon. *One of my more emotional and sexier stories, I'm really hoping readers connect as strongly to the characters as I did.*

Following is an excerpt from the novella, Ecstasy Under the Moon, *which will be released in a summer 2013 anthology with Lora Leigh, Alyssa Day and Meljean Brook. It will open up the world of the Éan living in the forest for my readers and introduce you to two very special characters: Bryant and Una. Una is one of the very rare eagle shifters, haunted by an experience with the Fearghall that has left her nervous of touch, particularly by large men who shift into wolves. Bryant immediately recognizes Una's scent as that of his mate, but convincing the reticent woman to come within five feet of him, much less accept him as a mate? Not a job for the faint of heart or conviction. Luckily for both of these special Chrechte, Bryant is neither.*

Let me know what you think of both excerpts!

Hugs and happy reading,
Lucy
http://lucymonroe.com/contactmail.htm

The Forests of the Éan, Highlands of Scotland
1144 AD, Reign of Dabíd mac Maíl Choluim, King of Scots and
the Reign of Prince Eirik Taran Gra Gealach, Ruler of the Éan

Una stood in shock, terror coursing through her like fire in her veins, burning away reason, destroying the façade of peace she had worked so hard to foster for the past five years.

Her eagle screamed to be released. She wanted to take to the skies and fly as far as her wings could carry her until the sun sank over the waters and the moon rose and set again in the sky.

The high priestess, Anya Gra, smiled on the assembled Éan like she had not just made a pronouncement that could well spell their doom.

Faol were coming here? To the forest of the Éan? To their homeland kept secret for generations? Kept secret for very good reason.

Reason Una had learned to appreciate to the very marrow of her bones five years before.

"No," she whispered into air laden with smoke from the feast's cooking fires. "This cannot be."

Other noises of dissent sounded around her, but her mind could not take them in. It was too busy replaying images she'd tried to bury under years of proper and obedient behavior. Years of not taking chances and staying far away from the human clans that had once intrigued her so.

She'd even avoided Lais, one of the few other eagle shifters among her people. Because he'd come from the outside. From the clan of the Donegal, the clan that spawned devils who called themselves men.

She'd not spoken to him once in the three years he'd lived among their people.

The grumbling around Una grew to such a level, even her own tormented thoughts could not keep it out.

For the first time in her memory, the Éan of their tribe looked on their high priestess with disfavor. Many outright glared at the woman whose face might be lined with age, but maintained a translucent beauty that proclaimed her both princess and spiritual leader.

Others were yelling their displeasure toward the prince of the people, but their monarch let no emotion show on his handsome, though young, features. He merely looked on, his expression stoic, his thoughts hidden behind his amber gaze.

The dissension grew more heated. This was unheard of. In any other circumstance, Una would have been appalled by the behavior of her fellow Chrechte, but not this day.

She hoped beyond hope that the anger and dissent would sway their leaders toward reason.

"Enough!" The prince's bellow was loud and commanding despite the fact he was only a few summers older than Una.

Silence fell like the blacksmith's anvil.

Emotion showed now, his amber eyes glowing like the sacred stone during a ceremony. "We have had the Faol among us on many occasions these past three years."

Those wolves had only come to visit. Una, and many like her—justifiably frightened by the race that had done so much to eradicate their own—had stayed away from the visitors. She'd avoided all contact and had not stolen so much as a peek at any of them.

Not like when she was younger and let her curiosity rule her common sense.

But Anya Gra said these ones, these *emissaries* from the Sinclair, Balmoral and Donegal clans, would live among the Éan for the foreseeable future.

Live. Among. Them. With no end in sight.

Una's breath grew shorter as panic clawed at her insides with the sharpness of her eagle's talons.

"It is time the Chrechte brethren are reunited." Prince Eirik's tone brooked no argument. "It has been foretold this is the only chance for our people to survive as a race. Do you suddenly doubt the visions of your high priestess?"

Many shook their head, but not Una. Because for the first time in her life, she *did* doubt the wisdom of the woman who had led their people spiritually since before Una was born.

"Emissaries are coming to live among us, to learn our ways and teach us the way of the Faol." This time it was another of the royal family who spoke, the head healer. "We will all benefit."

"We know the way of the Faol," one brave soul shouted out. "They kill, maim and destroy the Éan. That is the way of the Faol."

"Not these wolves. The Balmoral, the Sinclair, and the Donegal lairds are as committed to keeping our people safe as I am." The prince's tone rang with sincerity.

The man believed his own words. That was clear.

But Una couldn't bring herself to do so. No wolf would ever care for the Éan as a true brother. It was not in their violent, often sadistic and deceitful natures.

"It is only a few among the Faol today who would harm our people. Far more would see us joined with the clans for our safety and all our advantage."

Join with the clans? Who had conceived of that horrific

notion? First they were talking about having wolves come to live among them and now their leaders were mentioning leaving the forest so the Éan could join the clans?

Una's eagle fought for control, the desperate need to get away growing with each of her rapid heartbeats.

"In the future, we will have no choice," Anya Gra said, as if reading Una's mind. "But for this moment in time, we must only make these few trustworthy wolves welcome among us."

Only? There was no *only* about it. This thing the royal family asked, it was monumental. Beyond terrifying.

It was impossible.

"You ask too much." The sound of Una's father's voice brought a mixture of emotions, as it always did.

Guilt. Grief. Relief. Safety.

Stooped from the grievous wound he had received at the hands of the Faol when rescuing Una from their clutches, he nevertheless made an imposing figure as he pushed his way toward the prince and priestess.

The leather patch covering the eye he'd lost in the same battle gave her father a sinister air she knew to be false. He was the best of men.

And forever marred by wounds that would never allow him to take to the skies again . . . because of her.

"You ask us to make welcome those who did this," he gestured toward himself in a way he would never usually do.

He ignored his disfigurements and expected others to do the same.

"Nay." The prince's arrogant stance was far beyond his years, but entirely fitting his station as the leader of their people. "I *demand* you make welcome wolves who would die to protect you from anything like that happening again."

"Die, for the likes of me?" her father scoffed. "That would be a fine day, indeed, would it not? When a wolf would die to protect a bird."

"Do you doubt *my* desire to protect you and all of my people?" the prince demanded, a flicker of vulnerability quickly gone from his amber eyes.

"Nay. My prince, you love us as your father did before

you. But this? This risk you would take with all our safety, it is foolishness."

Suddenly Anya Gra was standing right in front of Una's father, her expression livid, no desire for conciliation in evidence at all. "Fionn, son of Micael, You dare call *me* foolish?"

Oh, the woman was beyond angry. Even more furious than Una's father had a wont to get.

"Nay, Priestess. Your wisdom has guided our people for many long years."

"Then, it is my visions you doubt," the *celi di* accused with no less fury in her tone.

Una's father shook his head vigorously. "Your visions have always been right and true."

"Then you, and all those who stand before me today," she said, including everyone at the feast with her sharp raven's stare. "All of my people will give these wolves a chance to prove that not every Faol would murder us in our sleep."

"And if you are wrong? If they turn on us?" her father dared to question.

Una's respect for her parent grew. It took great strength to stand up to Anya Gra, spiritual leader and one of the oldest among them.

"Then I will cast my fire and destroy their clans without mercy," the prince promised in a tone no one, even her stalwart father, could deny.

Her father nodded, though he looked no happier at the assurance. "Aye, that's the right of it then."

Prince Eirik let his gaze encompass the whole of their community, his expression one of unequivocal certainty. "I will always protect my people to the best of my ability. Welcoming these honorable men is part of that."

Una noted how he continued to push forth the message that these wolves were good men, *trustworthy* and *honorable*.

He was her prince and she should believe him.

But she couldn't.